# BONDS OF THE WOLF

## THE WILD HUNT LEGACY
BOOK 7

### CHERISE SINCLAIR

VanScoy Publishing Group

*To Mama Bears everywhere.*

**Bonds of the Wolf**
Copyright © 2024 by Cherise Sinclair
ISBN: 978-1-947219-54-0
Published by VanScoy Publishing Group
Cover Art: The Killion Group, Inc
Copy editing by Red Quill Editing, LLC
Content editor: Bianca Sommerland

This book is a work of fiction. Names, characters, places, and incidents are products of the author's imagination or used fictitiously and are not to be construed as real. Any resemblance to persons, living or dead, actual events, locales, business establishments, or organizations is entirely coincidental.

All rights reserved. No part of this eBook may be used, including but not limited to the training or or use by artificial intelligence, or reproduced, scanned, or distributed in any manner whatsoever without prior written permission from the author, except in the case of brief quotations embodied in critical articles and reviews.

This book is licensed for your personal enjoyment only. This book may not be resold or given away to other people. If you would like to share this book with another person, please purchase an additional copy for each recipient. If you're reading this book and did not purchase it, or it was not purchased for your use only, please purchase your own copy.

Thank you for respecting the hard work of this author.

# ACKNOWLEDGMENTS

As y'all probably know, one of the recurring themes in my books is how a community draws together to create a kind of family. Books pull together other types of families. Over the years, somehow this introvert has accumulated a wonderful group of midwives for the book-birthing process. And I wanted to say thank you to you all.

Leagh Christensen is simply wonderful, taking on such diverse tasks, from sending out ARCs to finding T-shirt artists. And Lisa Simo-Kinzer has the most compassionate heart and tactful tongue. What better pair to herd a batch of kittens? You've both had rocky trails for the past years and were still right here when I needed you. Thank you!

JJ Foster and Barb Jack were alpha readers for this book while Bianca Sommerland edited the content. You can thank them for removing my mistakes—like when the hero and heroine didn't disrobe before making love (yeah, oops!). And Bianca talked me into adding the prologue—yes, I blame you, my friend!

Monette Michaels and Fiona Archer—I can't believe how long we've been friends now, and I grow more grateful each year for having you in my life. Thank you for dropping your own writing to answer my *does-this-blurb-work* questions, for brainstorming, handholding, and keeping me out of story hell.

Red Quill Editing with Ekatarina Sayanova, Tracy Damron-Roelle, and Rebecca Cartee: How was I so lucky to find such an amazing team of editors? I adore you three.

Lisa White and Marian Shulman—beta readers extraordinaire—always find where my storytelling logic skips important bits...

and where I manage to totally skip words. You two make the entire world better for being in it.

My adorable Shadowkittens... When you felines discuss my stories, I inevitably end up with more plotlines than I know what to do with—or with a complete turn-about for a character because y'all are simply too soft-hearted. I hope you recognize your handiwork in this book and prance a bit. Because you're just that good.

# PROLOGUE

T*welve years before*

With his brother Fell beside him, Patrin stumbled from the back of the cargo van, landed on his hands and knees...and froze.

Every breath—every single breath—brought him the overwhelming fragrance of evergreens, mosses, and dirt. No harsh cleansers, fear sweat, or death.

He could hear the ugly voices of the humans, the whimpering of cubs younger than him, the pinging of the cooling engine. And his heart lifted because he could also hear wind rustling in the high branches of the fir trees surrounding them.

As a chill breeze from the snow-topped mountains swept over the group of young shifters, Patrin's whole body shivered at the joy of being outside after the long, long months of being held captive in cages underground.

Of seeing the babies and everyone older than thirteen die. Some shot down on the streets of Dogwood. Some from being cut up and...and—his memories flinched away. The babies and anyone past First Shift wasted away from the lack of forest and the metals surrounding them.

He pulled in a hard breath. *Mum growing whiter, thinner. Worrying about him and Fell and Darcy...even as she struggled to breathe. And then...then she hadn't.*

*Gods, Mum. The Scythe didn't bring Darcy with us. How can I keep our sister safe?*

All the male cubs from eight to thirteen years old had been stuffed into the van and brought here, wherever here was. At thirteen, only the littermates, Chester and Graham, and Bryn and Rhys were older than Patrin and Fell.

A big human, the one everyone called "the Colonel", stared down at the group of cubs—and all of them clustered closer as if it'd keep them safe.

Patrin knew better.

"Listen up, mutants." The Colonel's face was all sharp angles, his head shaved. His cruel black eyes were like a bald eagle's looking at a nest of helpless mice. "These are your barracks and training grounds."

Patrin glanced around. The cleared area in the forest held two buildings, one a house, the other looked kinda like a barn. Everything was surrounded by a kind of fence, only this one was made of logs, side by side, with the tops sharpened to a point. Like what some weird primitive barbarians might build. "What's that fence thing called?" he asked in the nearly silent speech all the cubs had learned to use.

His bookworm of a brother said under his breath, "A stockade."

A tiny glow lit Patrin inside. Because Fell had *answered*. His brother blamed himself for being the reason Mum moved them to Dogwood, their village that the Scythe had discovered and destroyed. Fell rarely spoke these days.

Something else to mourn.

"I should just put you abominations to death. Instead, because

I'm merciful, you'll get a chance to be useful." The Colonel's lips twisted into a terrifying smile. "You'll learn to fight, no matter how much it hurts. To kill whoever we tell you to. And you'll obey every damn command you're given."

Although most of the cubs were looking down, Patrin stared at the human. Hating him. *Obey? Never.*

As if he'd heard Patrin's thoughts, the Colonel laughed. "If you disobey, we'll beat you, like any misbehaving mongrel. And then we'll whip the skin from your sister."

Patrin's blood went cold. All their sisters were still imprisoned back at the Seattle compound—including his and Fell's littermate, Darcy.

"Oh, look, the little brains are beginning to get it." The Colonel spoke directly to Patrin. "If one of you stinking mutants act up, your sister will bleed for it. If you run away, we kill *her*."

With that, Patrin understood the trap they were caught in. Because none of them would risk their sisters.

Was this why the shifters without sisters had been killed? The horror of it froze him.

*Gods, what can I do?* Tears burned his eyes, but he held them back as he stared at the Colonel. Even at twelve, he knew an evil person when he saw one.

Humans in black clothing herded them all into the biggest building. The barracks. It held bunk beds around the walls, tables and chairs in the center, and a door leading to a bathroom. After flipping on the light, they closed the door, leaving them there.

The place stank of rancid food, mold, urine, and...humans. They must have used it for humans before the cubs.

The youngest of them began to cry. The others looked at the older ones hopefully. So did Patrin. Someone needed to take charge and tell them all what to do.

But Chester and Graham backed up to a bed, then Graham lay down and curled into a ball, his face toward the wall. Chester sat down beside him.

Patrin's stomach sank. The two had been his and Fell's first friends in Dogwood. Like Patrin, Chester liked to have fun and tell jokes. Graham was just plain nice.

Fell made an unhappy sound, and Patrin nodded. Their friends weren't going to take charge.

The other thirteen-year-old littermates, Bryn and Rhys stared at the floor. Their other brother had been shot and killed in Dogwood. They still hadn't recovered from his littermate bond being broken. They weren't going to take over.

*I can't do this.*

Patrin looked at Fell who jerked his chin toward the littlest cubs, saying without words, *someone must take care of them.*

After clearing his throat—and hoping his voice didn't crack—Patrin pointed at the sink and bathroom. "C'mon, cubs. Let's get this place cleaned up. It stinks."

"B-but, they're gonna make us fight. Hurt us." One of the eight-year-olds clung to his littermate, tears on his cheeks.

"Maybe." Resolve formed in Patrin's chest. "But we're Daonain, and we're strong. We'll stand together, and we'll grow tough. And deadly."

Far, far deadlier than their parents who didn't know how to fight against the murderous humans when they'd attacked Dogwood.

Someday, the Scythe would pay for all the deaths.

His brother's shoulder pressed against his—as always, they stood together.

The other cubs turned toward him and Fell. Their faces filled with hope...and trust.

"We'll make it through this and get free." It was a promise. A vow. And he whispered one more, under his breath. "I'll protect them."

Fell's gaze met his as he said the last thing he would for the days to come. "*We* will."

# CHAPTER ONE

Waxing moon, Cold Creek, North Cascades Territory

Climbing out of the pickup, Patrin took a long stretch, feeling the relief in each aching muscle. They'd started the long drive through the mountains to Cold Creek, Washington, before dawn. "Fuck, my tail end hurts."

"'Cuz it's fat?" Fell's lips twitched as he looked over the roof of the vehicle.

Considering there wasn't an ounce of fat on either one of them, Patrin only laughed. "Why don't you come and kiss my fat, furry ass, brawd."

With a snort, Fell grabbed the sack for Thorson and closed the door.

Together, they crossed the landscaped island dividing Main Street. Spotting a pixie perched in a rose bush, Patrin detoured to leave her a walnut from his pocket. There had been very few OtherFolk around the Scythe compound—and no matter how long he lived, free and with the Daonain, he'd never lose the sense of wonder at seeing them.

After over a decade of being assassins for the Scythe's brutal bloody missions, a year ago, he, Fell, the other shifter-soldiers and their sisters had been freed. And, even better, they'd eliminated any Scythe living in the forest compound as well as those holding their sisters hostage in Seattle.

He pulled in a breath and smiled. *Free.* No more prison compound living. He could go where he wanted. Eat real food. Get a beer and chat with other shifters. Or, like now, stroll through downtown with his brother.

Cold Creek in the North Cascades was a fine little town, even in November. Today, a chilly, silver fog filled the streets and swirled in odd directions as a few young sylphs played air elemental tag.

After this meeting, he and Fell would have a chance to visit Darcy. Patrin could feel the warmth in his chest at the thought. Their sister was doing so fucking well—happy and working at what she loved and even lifemated.

Damn, might she someday have a litter of cublings? Patrin almost stopped walking at the thought. He'd be an *uncle*.

Moving ahead, Fell started perusing the display window for the store named BOOKS.

With a sigh, Patrin opened the door. "Brawd, you don't need more books."

Fell's growl indicated Patrin would get bitten if he kept his brother from indulging.

If they hadn't had an appointment with the boss, Patrin might've pushed a bit more. Been a while since they had a good brawl.

Inside, the gray-haired owner, Thorson, was in his usual spot behind the counter, and Patrin couldn't suppress a smile. Last year, the scarred-up old shifter had taken on the task of teaching

Patrin and Fell about Daonain ways—what they would've learned if raised in the clan.

With minimum appreciation for tradition, they'd been a trial to the tradition-loving shifter. Being fair-minded, Thorson had tried to see their point of view—and had clouted them more than once for disrespecting Daonain ways.

Thorson swept a sharp gaze over them, probably checking for blood. He knew they'd been on an operation for the human spymaster, Wells.

Of course, they *had* been covered in blood by the end, but not being foolish wolves, they'd cleaned up afterward. Showing up in a shifter town while stinking of death was a quick way to start all kinds of rumors.

"Is Wells here yet?" Patrin asked before spotting the lean, gray-haired human by the fireplace, holding a baby. He was talking with the baby's mother, Vicki. Wells might be the only human ever asked to be a *caomhnor*, the Daonain version of a godparent. Then again, Vicki had been a spy for him before a dying Daonain turned her into a shifter.

Unable to look away, Patrin felt an ache in his chest. Somehow, after a life of killing and blood, the spymaster had found a family of sorts. Had a cubling he obviously loved.

The gift of family wasn't one Patrin or his brother would ever receive. There would be no love for a female or a litter of cubs. There was too much death behind them—and their future would hold more. As long as any Scythe who knew of the Daonain was alive, shifters would be in danger.

All of those Scythe had to die.

This was their task.

"Wait for him in the storeroom," Thorson said.

Fell nodded, then set the sack he carried on the counter.

Patrin pushed it toward Thorson. "It's good to see you, old cat."

"Old?" Thorson's growl rasped worse than Fell's—and would've been threatening except for the flash of humor in his eyes. He looked in the sack and a smile...almost...appeared on his leathery face. "Glenfiddich. Good lads."

They smiled back at him. Because they'd both grown more than fond of the grizzled old werecat who was one of the toughest shifters in the entire Western US.

Patrin glanced at Fell and gestured toward the storeroom. "Let's go."

Instead, his flea-bitten, mangy-tailed littermate ignored him to head in a different direction.

Fell saw the annoyance in his brother's expression and smothered a smile. Hey, irritating a littermate was one of the small pleasures in life.

Or maybe he was feeling nippy because the last operation had been long and exhausting, because he had more blood on his paws, more deaths on his soul.

And yeah, maybe he was fucking envious of the spymaster who looked so comfortable holding a cub and chatting with a pretty female.

It'd be nice to be able to talk so easily. Fell sighed once, quietly enough his brother wouldn't hear. Even if he couldn't speak more than a couple of words without choking, he'd like to simply sit by a warm fire, drink coffee, and read an interesting book.

*Sorry, wolf, that's not in your future.*

Although...the coffee was going to happen.

He stalked over to the big machine that Thorson kept for his customers and drew two cups. The aroma of rich brew wafted up. After adding a splash of hazelnut syrup to one cup for his sweet-loving brother, Fell handed it over.

"Thanks, brawd." Patrin's flashing smile appeared, his annoyance gone in seconds.

The Gods couldn't have given Fell a finer brother.

In the storeroom, boxes of books formed a rambling maze. No windows. Feeling penned up again, Fell took up a position against the wall.

"Couldn't he have picked a bar or diner for this meeting?" Patrin used the boxes to build himself a seat.

Fell grunted a response, then automatically started cataloging locations for an ambush.

The door opened, and Wells entered, silent as a werecat, despite being only human. Then again, he'd spent his life doing covert operations. Sweeping the dust off a stack of boxes, he took a seat.

Fell moved a few feet closer but stayed on his feet. Just in case. Maybe, when he was a grizzled old wolf, he'd be able to relax. *Probably won't live that long, though.*

"Gentlemen. Excellent work with your operation," Wells said.

"Thanks." Patrin leaned forward. "Do you have our next target picked out yet?"

Having spent his life in service to the US government, Wells had apparently been infuriated at how the Scythe had manipulated the US and other governments, instigating conflict between them to increase their own riches and power. At this point, the spymaster was as driven to the entire organization's eradication as Patrin and Fell were to eliminating the Pacific Northwest division.

"That's what you're here to talk about." Wells gave them a chilly smile. "Your teams of shifter-soldiers have eliminated every single Scythe operative not directly working with the Colonel or the Director."

"What about the Colonel and the Director then?" Patrin's frustration was obvious.

Matching anger was an itch under Fell's skin. The bastards needed to die.

Twelve years ago, when the Scythe's Pacific Northwest division discovered the Daonain, they'd attacked Dogwood, taking some and killing the rest. In a long-term power play, the division hid the shifter's existence from the larger organization—and thank fuck for that.

Not knowing the fatal effects of confinement and metal, the Scythe imprisoned the kidnapped "research subjects" underground. Far too many of the Daonain died.

*Mum had died.*

Fell took a gulp of coffee, not tasting it at all.

Last year, their sister Darcy escaped, found the Cold Creek shifters, and led a rescue of all the captives. Fell smiled slightly. He was so fucking proud of her.

After being sent to the Daonain Elders for the traditional education, nearly all the shifter-soldiers volunteered to help Wells bury the Scythe. Seemed only fair. The Scythe taught them to kill; the organization was now learning how thoroughly their prisoners had mastered those lessons.

As far as Wells could tell, the Pacific Northwest division hadn't shared information about the Daonain with the rest of the Scythe. Probably because the shifters had quite embarrassingly escaped.

Those Scythe all needed to die before they could tell their leadership about the shifters' existence.

Wells folded his hands on his lap. "Right now, we're at a dead end. The Director's lost most of his operatives; they're easier to find and aren't as trained as the Colonel's. At this point, the Director is scared enough that he wants all of you dead rather than recaptured."

"No surprise. He's a paper pusher who ran the compound for the female hostages. He's no soldier like the Colonel." Patrin frowned, his expression going hard. "Speaking of which—what about the Colonel?"

Fell's gut tightened. The Colonel had been in charge of the

shifter-soldiers and their savage, often lethal, training. The human was at the top of his must-die list.

"He's quite possibly dead. He arrived at a location Bryn and Rhys were watching, and Bryn took a shot." Wells almost smiled. "Nice to see you shifters using tech now and then."

As werecats, Rhys and Bryn had the patience and skill to make excellent snipers.

"What happened?" Patrin rose and started to pace between the boxes.

"Apparently at least one shot hit the Colonel's chest, but Bryn and Rhys had to retreat. Almost got caught. By the time they shook the pursuit and called, the Scythe were long gone. The death hasn't been confirmed."

Fell scowled. Everything inside him demanded to see the Colonel's corpse.

"What about the papers and hard drive we sent you?" Patrin stopped to frown at Wells. After eliminating the Director's operative, they'd taken everything from his office.

And, as always, finished by loading a cloud malware virus into the system to ensure any backups were wiped out.

It'd been one of their fears—that the Scythe might have information about them somewhere. But Wells was a master at eradicating anything that might reveal the Daonain existence.

"Good job there. I went through it, and we possibly have an opportunity." The spymaster's icy blue eyes held a spark. "Did you look at the map you sent?"

Patrin shook his head. "We didn't have a chance to study anything."

"On the map, the town of Ailill Ridge is circled. The notes are scanty, but it appears a Scythe operative might already be there, looking for shifters."

Fell straightened.

Patrin's mouth twisted as if he'd stuck his snout into a mint patch. "Wasn't Ailill Ridge where that idiot Cosantir was from? The one who put up posters about the Solstice Festival?"

Which was why the Scythe had attacked the Solstice Festival —held in neutral territory—last summer. He'd heard the God had called for a new Cosantir.

"That's the town, yes." Wells leaned forward. "Having lost so many operatives over the last few months, the Colonel and Director are growing desperate. My informants in the other divisions say the Director hinted at sharing something exciting. He might have given up on keeping the Daonain secret."

Fell scowled, waiting for Patrin to ask. When he didn't, Fell forced himself to speak up. "Why is he hinting? Why wait?"

"They lost any proof of your existence when we burned their Seattle compound and the training stockade, then hacked their online backups." A corner of Wells' mouth tipped up. "I believe the Director has an operative in Ailill Ridge and hopes to capture shifters for proof."

The idea of another Dogwood made Fell want to vomit. The room felt colder, his skin clammy.

Patrin glanced at him, an eyebrow up.

With a shrug, Fell signaled he was all right.

Yeah, it was a lie. They both knew it.

His brother returned his attention to Wells. "Unlike Dogwood, Ailill Ridge isn't a completely shifter town. Half the population is human."

"Which is why their investigation will take time. They'll have to figure out who in town is a shifter. Although there are a couple of your comrades there. Kennard and Fletcher."

Stiffening, Fell took a step forward. "You think they'll be spotted?" The two were still cubs—no, they might have turned eighteen this year—but young. So fucking young. Wells hadn't allowed any of their under-age shifters to join the hunt for the Scythe.

"Actually, no. The Scythe's photos of you shifters appear to be from a couple of years ago," Wells said. "Those two work on a ranch out of town, and they're not especially distinctive."

Tall, skinny, brown hair and brown eyes. A Scythe beating had damaged Kennard, but most of his scars were on his back and didn't show.

"You're probably right." The pain in Patrin's eyes showed he remembered Kennard's scars. And, like Fell, he couldn't get past the guilt that they hadn't been able to prevent the beating. As if anyone could have.

"Why us?" Fell managed to ask.

Patrin tilted his head. "Maybe...for bait?"

"Exactly." Wells gave him a thin smile. "Of the shifter-soldiers, you two were the most successful. And visible. Unlike Kennard and Fletcher, you don't blend in. If you uncover their spy, we can follow him back to his leader—or lure the leader out."

When Patrin glanced over, Fell nodded, despite the sick feeling in his gut. Time was running out if the Director was going to reveal the Daonain.

And if Kennard and Fletcher were in danger, then Ailill Ridge was where Patrin and Fell needed to be. They'd protected the shifter-soldiers for over a decade. Their job wasn't finished.

Patrin straightened. "Aye, then. We're in. How obvious do you want us to be?"

"I want you working where you can be noticed."

Fell moved closer to Patrin. "The Cosantir?"

Patrin nodded his understanding of the question and turned to Wells, "The Cosantir of Rainier Territory must approve us being in his territory. Do you want him informed as to why we are there?"

"Hell no." Wells scowled. "It's bad enough dealing with Calum, and he's almost reasonable for one of your guardians. I realize the idiot Cosantir in Ailill Ridge was replaced, but let's not ask for trouble."

Patrin looked as if he wanted to argue—Fell certainly did. Pussyfooting around a Cosantir took stupidity to a new level.

After a moment, Patrin shrugged. "In that case, we'll get moving."

Fell finished off his coffee.

Goal accomplished; next mission ready to go. A chance to find and kill the Director.

Sounded good.

## CHAPTER TWO

*Full moon, Ailill Ridge, Rainier Territory*

"Leave. Me. *Alone*." Moya almost vibrated with the need to lash out at the smug-faced, greasy-haired male who just wouldn't back off. Did Brett think his persistence would eventually get her to mate with him?

*I'd rather have sex with pond scum.*

Sure he was big and brawny, so he captured a fair amount of interest from females. He was also a vicious bully. Even worse, when she was near him, she could feel the crawling sensation of him trying to exert control over her through the pack bonds. Thank the gods the hateful male was only a beta and not alpha of the pack.

"You need to listen to me." Moving in far too close, he grabbed her arm.

Knocking his hand away, she spun and hurried outside.

On the wraparound porch, she braced her hands on the railing, drawing in long breaths of the wonderfully crisp, cold November air. Such a relief after the musk-laden stink inside.

*Thank the Mother of All, the Gathering is over.*

One more, way-too-long full moon night.

*Wow, jaded much? At twenty-four?* There were some females far into their child-bearing years who eagerly anticipated the monthly full moon heat and all the matings that went with it.

*Not me.*

Sure, the gatherings were needed to encourage mating and mix up the gene pool, but the actual sex stuff? As far as she was concerned, it was:

1. Find an adequate male.
2. Scratch the "itch."
3. Move on.

She was always polite, of course, because the males were just as influenced by their hormones as she was. Then again, she might react a bit worse than others when being pushed into stuff —even if it was by the gods.

With a sigh, she stretched her arms up and out, looking out at the beginning of a new day. Although the moon had set behind the white-topped mountains, the stars still hung in the slowly brightening sky. Nice and clear. Finally.

Because of the last two days of sleet and strong winds, Roger had rescheduled the wolf pack's monthly run. Not that Moya cared what the boastful, overbearing alpha did. She and Heather and Talitha did their own mini pack runs. None of them could stand Roger or his bullying betas.

Speaking of Talitha... Her fellow co-owner of Espresso Books was down on the lawn, kissing her mate, Eileen, goodbye.

Moya grinned. Such a cute couple. "Hey, Talitha."

"Female." A heavy hand gripped her shoulder.

Startled, panicking, she spun. "Fang off, Brett!"

The male loomed over her, resurrecting nightmarish memories.

*The alpha's hand hitting her face. His roar of—*

Panic flared up so fast her chest hurt. Her left fist shot out, and she punched him with all her might. Her knuckles impacted rock-hard abs.

She sucked in air at the pain. *Oh gods, I must have busted my fingers.*

Her blow rocked the male back on his heels. But that was all.

She swung again—and he caught her right fist in one powerful hand. Holding her hand in the air, he tsked, forced her fingers open, and set her eReader on her palm.

*What?* She looked up into eyes the color of night.

He wasn't Brett. This male had shoulder-length black hair and a short beard, olive skin, and a hard, hard face. In fact, she'd seen him with a black-clad male earlier—and feeling their dominant personalities, she'd kept her distance. Now, she was far too close. And...

*I punched the wrong male.*

When he didn't yell, her fear started to dissipate like fog in bright sunlight. "I'm so sorry. I thought you were someone else when you grabbed me."

"You didn't answer when I called." He eyed her up and down, his expression unimpressed. Then his dark eyes lit with laughter. "Work on your right cross; it lacks strength."

Releasing her hand, he headed down the steps.

Like a lethal shadow, a blue-eyed male standing nearby gave her a short nod and followed him.

"Patrin, Fell, there you are." The sound of Gretchen's haughty voice made Moya's spine go rigid. "Come, my males. I have your rooms all prepared." Taking their arms, the tall blonde female inserted herself between them and led them out of the yard.

Miss Blonde Perfection herself. Moya grimaced. The tall, stunning female always made her feel short and pudgy. Then again, last night, her brothers had once again rejected Gretchen's advances...as more and more of the locals were doing. Eventually, most males figured out beauty only went so far. Her brothers had caught on quicker than most.

She watched as the two males walked away with Gretchen. Hadn't she seen them months before at André's housewarming party? Heather had said they were shifter-soldiers. They'd been admiring Gretchen that day, too, before they disappeared.

Not that she'd been watching for them at the party. *Not me.*

"Moya." The Cosantir was standing farther down the porch. His arms were folded over his chest, and his dark eyes held...disapproval.

Trying not to cringe, she bowed her head respectfully. "Cosantir."

"Fighting is not permitted during Gatherings. Not even for females." The sprinkling of a French-Canadian accent didn't soften the authority in his deep voice.

After taking over the territory around three months ago, the Cosantir made rules about fighting during Gatherings. And she deeply appreciated that brawling had all but stopped.

And now...she'd punched someone. But she had a reason, right? "That male. He...he grabbed me."

"Then you push his hand away and say no. If he persists and one of the bouncers doesn't intervene, *then* you may hit him." Like waves in water, power swirled around the God's appointed guardian of the territory. "You did not even look to see who you were punching. Such behavior is unacceptable."

But... She opened her mouth. *If I explain why I reacted so badly, maybe he'd understand?* Only, she couldn't. She'd never been able to talk about...about what happened in Stanislaus Territory. Not with anyone. Moya forced her voice to stay even. "I'm sorry, Cosantir. I'll..." What could she promise?

His hard face gentled. "You have had this problem for a while now. It's time to work on it, young wolf."

Her throat was so dry her answer stuck in her mouth.

He tilted his head, releasing her, thank the Gods.

With another bow, she backed down the steps and fled across the hedge-enclosed yard to the sidewalk alongside the street.

"Hey, Moya, wait up." Tall and graceful, Talitha caught up and fell into step. "That looked unpleasant."

"I messed up." Moya sighed. "It's cuz Brett was pestering me all night. You know how males get all tail-kinked when a female isn't interested."

Talitha snorted. "Don't we all."

Like a mouse escaping a weasel, Moya still trembled inside. Her hands were shaking. "So I was mad at Brett, and when someone grabbed my shoulder, I thought it was him, and I hit him. Only it was some stranger, trying to give me my eReader."

Guilt was a lump in her belly. The Cosantir was right; she'd overreacted.

"Brett and his brother are revolting weasels. I swear, a lot of males are obnoxious when told no." As one of the rare lesbian shifters, Talitha would know.

However... Moya's eyes narrowed.

Her friend's creamy skin was reddened from beard burn, her lips swollen, her chin-length brown hair tousled.

"Look at you." Moya bumped her shoulder against Talitha's. "Your night must have been better than mine. Did you find a male who knows his way around a female's body?" Since Talitha had no interest in men, pushy ones didn't stand a chance, but she'd occasionally choose one or two respectful ones to scratch her own wolf's itch. Or even to join her and Eileen.

They were hoping for cubs someday.

Talitha snickered. "No male has ever approached the talents of my Eileen, but this one wasn't shabby."

"Huh." A male who could satisfy her gay friend must have talent. "Which one?"

"Won't do you any good, sweetie. He and his brother were just traveling through. They won't be here for the next full moon."

"Figures." Not that she really cared. In all reality, her problems with sex weren't entirely due to a partner's lack of skill. She'd been with some who were pretty talented. She just...wasn't particularly into mating. Although the full moon heat pretty much ensured she'd get off, the earth didn't move or anything. She felt empty afterward.

"André came down on you rather hard," Talitha said softly. "But he was also...right. You need to learn to deal with pushy males and ones in authority."

*Oh fairy farts and demon dung!* Even her friend thought she was out of line? Moya moved away a couple of steps.

Only, she wasn't being fair. She did have a problem. "I know I shouldn't go off and punch people. Not without a better reason." She wasn't a teenager, and the Cosantir who'd caused her so many problems wasn't here. She didn't need to attack to keep from being emotionally assaulted.

Right?

Deep inside, a part of her wasn't convinced. "I need to work on it." Somehow. Because the Cosantir was right. She'd been ignoring the problem.

Farther down the sidewalk, a short, skinny female was yelling at two cubs. "I told you not to go out of the house, but you sneak out to go play with those other cubs? Noisy things. You're my family now, not the stupid pack's."

"Who's Gwendolyn shouting at?" Moya eyed the younglings. About thirteen years old, maybe. "Aren't those the two younglings Heather's cubs run around with?" Their friend Heather had found herself three lifemates—and taken in two orphaned pre-teens.

"Mateo and Alvaro, yes. They're wolf cubs, not long past First Shift. You know how Gwendolyn's wanted to have children for so long..." Talitha's expression was full of understanding.

Because she and Eileen felt the same way. The Daonain had

never figured out why their pregnancy rate was so low or so skewed to male births. Moya bumped her friend's shoulder in sympathy.

"So she hoped for a family, only she's even more of a loner than a lot of felines." Moya frowned. "And being wolves, the pups need affection and physical contact." Some werecats were cuddly; others were the type to hiss and slash if someone tried to hug them.

Gwendolyn was nice enough, but she wasn't a warm 'n' fuzzy sort of shifter.

"Cubs need other cubs—and if they're wolves, they need to belong to the pack. How else will they learn?" Talitha took a step forward and hesitated.

Moya gave her quiet friend a bracing smile. Confrontation wasn't Talitha's way. She might be fifteen years older than Moya, but she was a far more submissive wolf.

Having a volatile Spanish mom and two pushy brothers, Moya had no problem tackling another female. It was only authoritative males who raised the fur on her spine. "C'mon, let's see what we can do."

Quickening her steps, Moya led the way. "Gwendolyn, are you having trouble?"

As the two cubs turned to Moya, all big brown eyes, the female's face scrunched up. "I...I can't do this. They're good younglings, but they are so, so busy. And want to be with other cubs and the pack. So many people. I...can't."

Oh Gods, just last week, a human had been in her bookstore complaining about getting a cute kitten for his kid's birthday, then returning it because it'd never slowed down. He hadn't realized how much work kittens were.

Poor Gwendolyn probably hadn't either. For someone who liked being alone, sociable cubs *were* probably exhausting. The poor werecat hadn't realized what she was getting into. "It's normal for them to want to be with other people, to play with other cubs."

"Gwendolyn, the younglings are wolves." Talitha added softly. "Pack activities are part of a wolf's life."

"I let them go last month, but not again. Some of those wolves were rude to me, and I'm not going to put up with that. Or-or with all this social stuff." Gwendolyn sniffled and shook her head. "I made a mistake. I'm not a family sort of person. I'm sorry, cubs." Grabbing each lad's thin shoulder, she pushed them gently toward Moya and Talitha. "You're wolves. They belong with other wolves."

Moya pulled a cub closer as Talitha did the same.

"I'll bring their stuff over. I...just need a minute. Or an hour." As Gwendolyn slunk away with all the embarrassment a cat shifter could show, the cub leaning against Moya whispered, "We didn't mean to make her mad."

Moya gave him a squeeze. "Pup, she's not mad. She just isn't cut out to be a mum, but she didn't know it until she tried. It's not your fault, and it's not her fault either. It's just how it is."

It was just a sad situation all around. The cubs had probably been timid and quiet when first taken in. Now their true natures were coming out.

Happy pups were usually noisy ones.

Talitha bent her head and spoke to the shorter youngling she held. "You're Alvaro, am I right?"

Face against her shoulder, the cub nodded.

"Then you must be Mateo." Talitha held out her free arm for him.

*Ah, now this might work out well.* Moya nudged Mateo to Talitha and smothered a smile as the lad almost buried himself within a hug.

Open affection was probably something both cubs had missed for a long time, even before undemonstrative Gwendolyn took them in.

Tilting her head to one side, Moya considered. Talitha and Eileen adored younglings, even the teenaged ones.

"You should take them home with you," Moya said.

Talitha jerked her head up, her blue eyes round and startled. "What?"

"You and Eileen have time and energy—and more than enough love—to raise a couple of cubs. These two need you." Heather, the Cosantir's lifemate, would make sure he gave permission. No problem there.

"But..." Despite the protest, Talitha's arms didn't loosen. Mateo and Alvaro burrowed closer.

It broke Moya's heart a little that they weren't pleading the way more secure cublings would.

Talitha noticed, too, and her gaze went soft.

"You know you can't say no. Not to me—and surely not to them." Moya gave her a smug smile. Every now and then, she got accused of arranging peoples' lives. She didn't really; she just helped with a nudge or two, kind of like when she recommended books in her store. She could just see what someone needed or wanted.

"Eileen would love taking them in," Talitha murmured, then she frowned at Moya. "But we both work, and we'll need help. So I'll do it...if you'll help. Like a belated *caomhnor*."

Moya beamed. She'd envied Heather for being the godmother of a baby up in the North Cascades. These two weren't babies, but she would love being their *caomhnor*. "Absolutely."

"Including helping take them to pack runs."

"But..." Oh, cat-scat, she, Heather, and Talitha couldn't take young males on their mini-pack runs. Roger barely tolerated the three of them running together. Adding two males would make the alpha suspect they were setting up a rival pack.

Gods, to have to attend pack runs and deal with Roger, Brett, and Caleb? She rather have her tail bitten off.

But the two younglings were giving her pleading puppy eyes,

and she sure couldn't let the little cubs get picked on. A few of the wolves were meaner than weasels.

"*Fine.* Pack runs too." She blew out a breath. "I guess you meant it when you said I needed to learn to deal with pushy males."

"Perfect. So, Mateo, Alvaro." Talitha ran her hand over their thin cheeks. "If you and the Cosantir agree, you two will be my cubs. Mine and my partner Eileen's—with Moya's help. Yes?"

"Yes!" Seeing the brown eyes light up almost made Moya feel better about her promise.

*Almost.*

---

Fell was still laughing inside as they walked with the tall, blonde bed-and-breakfast manager across the pedestrian bridge to the town square.

He couldn't believe his brother had been punched by a dark-haired mite of a female. Admittedly, Patrin wasn't huge, a lean six feet compared to Fell's bulkier six-three. Still... "You got punched by a feisty fairy."

A curvy one. He'd noticed that, too, along with her huge, dark brown eyes.

Patrin's face lit as it did when Fell managed more than a couple of words. "Yeah, she was a fierce little thing." His smile faded. "But she was scared, even before she saw me." He glanced at the blonde. "Gretchen, that's your name, right?"

She looked at him in disbelief, as if no one had forgotten her name before. "Yes, that's right."

Fell watched with interest. She was a beauty, no denying that. Last night, during the Gathering, when she'd come on to them, they'd taken her upstairs for a mating turn.

And by Herne's hide and hooves, it'd been one of the most boring couplings in the history of all the Daonain. She'd been interested only in her own pleasure yet acted as if she'd done them a favor.

Admittedly, with only a year of attending Gatherings since their escape from the Scythe, he and Patrin weren't exactly experienced in clan traditions. Sex, though, was a different story. During their Scythe-led missions, when their handlers fucked human females, Fell and Patrin had occasionally participated. They'd learned there was more to sex than just—what had one human female called it?—*slam, bam, thank you, ma'am*. There should be give and take, touching and laughter and generosity.

They'd enjoyed none of that with this female.

"So, Gretchen, what's the story with the dark-haired female who punched me?" Patrin asked.

"Moya Moreno?" Gretchen sniffed. "She's nothing special. A wolf—and not too bright. She and her littermates moved to Ailill Ridge a few years ago. A while later, she and another female started Espresso Books."

Uh-huh. How many not-too-bright people ran a business? And a bookstore no less? Moya Moreno was sounding more and more appealing.

Not that it mattered. He and Patrin weren't here for females. The mandatory full moon Gatherings would probably be the most contact they'd have. Which was for the best, really. They didn't fit in with the Daonain—not after growing to adulthood with the Scythe and all the blood on their hands.

"Any reason she'd be afraid of a male?" Patrin asked.

"Who knows? Who cares? She's always getting into fights. Roger complains about her all the time." Catching Patrin's raised brows, she added, "Roger's the pack alpha."

*Damn*. How had they forgotten about the complication of a wolf pack? He exchanged a worried glance with Patrin. As Daonain new to the territory, they were required to check in with the Cosantir as well as the local pack alpha.

Shifters and their fucking traditions were a pain in the tail.

"What are you two going to do today?" Gretchen asked as they entered the three-story Victorian-style B&B.

The décor inside was as annoyingly fussy and fancy as the manager. Floral wallpaper, heavy curtains, uncomfortable antique furniture.

"Eat, sleep in, and meet with the Cosantir tonight." Patrin eyed the female. "Will breakfast be ready soon?"

She stared at him as if disbelieving he'd ask anything of her.

Fell smothered a smile when his brother raised an eyebrow and continued, "This *is* a bed-and-breakfast, is it not? A hot breakfast is part of the description."

"My mother doesn't realize how much work that is." She huffed, then caved under Patrin's stare as most did. "Yes, I'll have coffee and pastries available within a half an hour."

"Very good."

Pastries weren't exactly a hot breakfast. But better than nothing. Fell followed his brother to their two bedrooms on the second floor. There was a sitting area at the end of the hallway, and thankfully, the furniture there was comfortable. "There's no scent of her mother."

"Bet Mum owns the place," Patrin said. "And left it to her cub to run."

"Yeah." No hot breakfast, no access to the kitchen, a female who wasn't likable. "We booked here long?"

Patrin grinned. "We paid for three days. Once we figure out our jobs, we can find somewhere else. It's not like we're hurting for money."

"True." Maybe Fell was cynical, but after his brother had pulled out the wad of bills in his wallet to pay for the B&B, Gretchen's interest zoomed. "Stop flashing money."

"Such a bossy brother." Patrin chuckled. "Still, it's a treat to actually have some to flash."

"Yeah." After a decade of having none, it would take more than a year to get used to having their own money. But none of the shifter-soldiers were broke any longer. Thanks to Wells. With a thinly amused smile, the spymaster said the Scythe owed them years of back pay.

So, before any of them killed a Scythe operative, he'd get the target's financial details and send the information to Fell. Under Wells' tutelage, Fell had learned to suck accounts dry and transfer the money into various offshore accounts. Every month, he divvied the money out to the shifter-soldiers who also shared with their sisters.

"Did you see the mobile toolbox Darcy bought with the last deposit?" Patrin started stripping off his clothes. "It's nice to be able to give her something she wanted."

As his brother disappeared into his bedroom, Fell rubbed his chin. It *had* been nice. Nonetheless, gifts didn't make up for the years they'd lost. Now Darcy had mates, and they'd never regain the closeness shared as cubs. Unlike normal littermates, the Scythe captives hadn't been together for their First Shift. He and Patrin hadn't watched her turn into a little cougar. Hadn't played the games normal cublings enjoyed when learning how to navigate on four legs rather than two.

The Scythe had stolen too fucking much from them.

Breathing out slowly, he forced himself to move on. They had a mission. *Be bait and find the spy.*

First, they needed jobs to ensure the Scythe saw them.

---

The alarm on Moya's desk went off, and she jumped, almost dropping the book she held. Mother's breasts, was it five already? She'd been shelving the new delivery for two hours since her bookstore closed.

Okay, maybe she'd gotten side-tracked a few times, leafing through a few of the more interesting books. Like that one about big cyborg males. Or the historical. Or…

Face it, she liked to read anything and everything—as long as it had a happy ending.

*Isn't it nice that I adore my work?*

A glance through the big bookstore windows showed the lights in the town square had already come on. Time to eat. Her stomach growled in agreement, sounding far too much like an annoyed wolf. She gave her belly a pat. "Be patient just a little longer."

After closing the accordion security grille between her bookstore and the coffee shop area, she headed out, locking the door behind her.

Strolling across the brick-lined town square, she nodded at a couple of humans coming out of the grocery store. At the corner, she saw that the Bullwhacker Bar already had quite a few people inside.

On the northwest corner, a huge building held the Shamrock Restaurant and the Cosantir's local arts-and-crafts gift shop. When André took over the territory, he opened the gift shop as a way for the local shifters to make money. The tourists loved the place.

The Cosantir's littermate Madoc owned the restaurant—and was a wonderful chef. Nearing the Shamrock, Moya took a long happy breath. Did anything smell as incredible as pizza?

It was so nice to have a restaurant in town. Although she occasionally cooked for her brothers, the rest of the time, it wasn't worth fixing meals for only herself. And it made her feel...alone.

Naturally sociable, wolves often did poorly if living alone, which was why unmated, childless females usually lived in a pack house.

Not her. Roger and his betas were always hanging around the pack house, and being near them left her so uneasy she couldn't relax. Or sleep or eat.

Far better to live alone. Besides, at Espresso Books, customers were in and out all day. And book people were the *best* people.

She was *fine*.

Entering the restaurant, Moya realized most of the tables were full. Then again, this was the day after Thanksgiving. The holiday wasn't one the Daonain had much interest in, but the town was half human. And, being a good shifter, Madoc had decorated in a lovely harvest theme with tiny pumpkin and gourd centerpieces.

There was Heather, seated at their favorite window side table. No surprise that Madoc gave his mate the table she liked.

Moya smiled as she crossed the room. Who would have thought one of her best friends would end up lifemated to the Cosantir and his two littermates?

"Hey, you." Moya bent to hug her tall, lanky friend. "Have you been here long?"

"Nope. I rented another one of the clan's houses, and the paperwork kept me late. Heather's russet hair was pulled back in a thick braid. Her soft sweater matched her turquoise eyes—and was form-fitting enough that Moya could check for signs of pregnancy.

Catching the look toward her abdomen, Heather rolled her eyes. "I'm not showing yet. Then again, with a litter rather than just one, my belly will get round soon enough." She snickered. "Niall told me my nipples are bigger."

"He's a male. Of course he noticed before you did." Moya sat and then noticed the wrist splint Heather wore. "What happened?"

"Pure stupidity. We were playing forest tag with Sky and Talam, and I jumped onto a huge stump to escape getting caught."

Moya grinned. Heather and her three mates had taken in Sky and Talam, two orphans who'd had their First Shift the month before. They were the cutest black bear cubs. "You realize they're almost as big as you are already...and they're still growing."

"Oh, don't I know. Two bears versus a wolf? That's why I jumped on the stump." Heather grumbled under her breath. "Then the crow-cursed, termite-riddled wood crumbled under me." She pulled up her sweater sleeves to reveal long red scrapes on both arms. "I'm lucky I only sprained my foreleg rather than something worse."

"It's good it wasn't a hind leg, or you'd be on crutches now." Moya patted Heather's undamaged hand. "Poor wolfy. First, our full moon run gets rained out, and now you can't trot down the trails at all."

"Not for a while. But...André and I talked with Talitha and Eileen about them taking in Mateo and Alvaro—"

"André approved it, didn't he?"

"Of course. Talitha said you suggested it. You did good." Heather's smile turned to a thoughtful frown. "However, she wants to take them on the pack run tomorrow night, and she's..."

Moya could hear the unspoken rest of the sentence. Their friend was the sweetest wolf in the world—and wouldn't dream of biting even when she should. "Don't worry. She conscripted me to go with her and the cubs."

Heather's look was all sympathy. "Poor you, but honestly, I'm glad you'll be there."

"I'll look out for them." Moya glanced at the menu and set it to one side. "Split a pizza with me?"

"You bet. If there's sausage and pepperoni."

"As if I'd say no to more meat."

After they gave their orders and the server dropped off a glass of wine for Moya, Heather pursed her lips. "By the way, Talitha—and André—told me about you punching some male."

Moya scowled. Gossip was fine when it was about other people—not her. "Did you know that humans in cities sometimes don't even know their neighbors. I bet they don't get talked about."

"Instead, they get lonely," Heather said with the authority of a shifter who'd actually gone to a human college. "Now, spill it. Usually the first response to a pushy male is a verbal set-down, but you go straight for the physical. Why is that? How can you fix it?"

*Doesn't she realize I'd have fixed it if I could have?* Moya's temper rose.

Then Heather added, "And how can I help?"

Cat-spit and gnome-guts, so much for getting angry. "I don't think you can." Moya shook her head. "The reason is, well, when someone reminds me of...stuff...that happened when I was younger"—and she sure wasn't going to explain—"it sets me off. Books call the reaction fight or flight."

"Of course, you researched the subject." Heather's lips twitched. "You sure do fall on the fight side. Did you discover something you can do about the reaction? Personally, I think pushy males should get a clout on the snout but..."

"But my reactions are sometimes excessive. I know." *Or I hit the wrong male. Oops.* "There's a bunch of things like meditation and journaling and, I guess, thinking about the cause?"

As the server showed up with cheesy bread sticks and salads, they sat back. "Gods, I'm hungry." Moya picked up a bread stick and breathed in the yeasty aroma.

"The meditation and all that sounds useful although rather tenuous. Was there anything more practical?"

How should she answer Heather's question? Because there were two parts to the practical applications. One was discussing the past trauma with someone. She was supposed to talk about it, live it, and work through it until the memories became more boring than frightening. That...might be difficult. She wasn't exactly someone who confided in others, especially her fears and all the hurt that went with them.

The second practical method though... "I need to let myself in for, I guess it'd be called controlled panics. I need to practice keeping myself in the present to avoid setting off the fight instinct."

Heather paused with her fork in the air. "Huh. Like getting a male to push you around?"

"Exactly, only I'm not sure who to ask." She grinned. "I'm not afraid of your mates anymore, even André. Same with my brothers and yours."

Heather shook her head. "You sure don't want to put this kind of weapon in the hands of our alpha or his betas."

They were the ones who scared her these days. And she'd never trust them not to take advantage of her fears. "No. Definitely not."

"You know, it's strange you have that reaction since the males you always look at twice during a Gathering are the ones on the dominant side."

"I know." Moya stirred her lettuce and croutons around in a circle. "I've always thought dominant males were so, so sexy, only since...the past, now they make me nervous. And I hit them if they come on too strong." It would sure be nice to get past this problem. *Maybe I'd even be able to like mating.*

Doubtful.

"Just let me know if there's anything I can do to help," Heather told her.

As the pizza arrived, they took a minute to move everything out of the way.

"Oh, yum." Putting a slice of pizza on her plate, Moya had to fight down the urge to bite in. Because, the last time, she'd burned the top of her mouth.

Instead, she took a sip of the wonderful cabernet and eyed her friend. "So how are you handling going from living alone to being surrounded by three mates and two bumbling bear cubs?"

"Mother's breasts, let me tell you..."

Grinning, Moya settled in to listen to cub tales. Sky and Talam were blossoming as they slowly began to feel safe and loved. And there was no one in the world who loved as well as Heather.

And Heather's mates were worthy males—André, the Cosantir who protected the clan, and Niall, a cahir and computer-geek, and Madoc who cooked like a dream.

Suppressing a sigh, Moya had to tell herself it was normal to be a bit envious of Heather's life. Since it was something Moya might never have. She could never trust a male enough to give them such power over her. Even worse, males came as a set of two or three brothers, and she had to push herself to mate with just one male at a time, full moon heat or not.

No, mates weren't in her future.

Shoving down the hurtful thought, she smiled at Heather. "Did I tell you how great Sky is doing with his guitar lessons? He's really talented."

Heather totally beamed. "We thought so. I'm hoping my friend Emma—the bard in North Cascades Territory—will make it down here sometime to meet him."

"That would be perfect." Moya picked up her glass for a sip of wine before embarking on the next slice of pizza.

Her glass stopped halfway to her mouth as a tall, muscular male dressed in all black walked into the restaurant.

He was fair skinned with short sandy hair. His stance was predatory as he scanned every person in the restaurant. Did he think someone here would attack him? Or was he always so...vigilant?

When his gaze met hers, she stiffened. The shifter-soldier who'd accompanied the one she'd punched.

As if in confirmation, that dark-haired male followed him in, emanating dominance. Even Roger, the pack alpha, didn't feel so forceful.

*If he grabbed me now, I'd probably end up burying my fist in his gut. Again.* Even if André was watching.

Like the fair-skinned male, he scanned the room before heading straight for the Cosantir.

Moya shivered. *I will totally stay away from those two.*

On the other side of the restaurant, André sipped his cold beer and kept an eye on Heather who was eating with her petite, dark-haired friend. Moya had a problem, but knowing his mate, she'd help the young female work it out. Heather was not only practical, she had the most caring heart in the world.

*And she loves me and my brothers.*

He could only think she was a gift from the Goddess. He and his littermates had never been so happy.

Movement caught his attention. Two males were approaching. The Daonain called them *shifter-soldiers*. Two of the youths from Dogwood who'd been kidnapped by the Scythe and trained to be assassins.

Patrin and Fell had asked to meet him, as was proper for new shifters in a Cosantir's territory. He rose to greet them.

The leaner of the two had black hair and black eyes. Beneath an olive-colored jacket, he wore a white button-up shirt and jeans. He murmured, "Cosantir," and both bowed their heads slightly in the traditional Daonain show of respect.

André almost sighed. It'd only been a little over two months since the god called him to serve as Rainier Territories' guardian. He still wasn't used to being addressed as Cosantir. Might never be.

But he tilted his head in acknowledgement. "Patrin and Fell, as I recall. You were at our housewarming party last month."

"I'm Patrin, yes." The dark-haired male half-grinned. "I must admit the party had some exciting moments."

"*Oui.*" André's jaw tightened. *Ugly moments would be more what he'd call it.* The previous Cosantir had gone feral and attacked the cubs playing on the lawn, including Sky and Talam. "Your assistance was much appreciated." The two wolves had helped the cahirs send the feral male back to the Mother.

The only cure for a feral shifter was death.

He motioned to the other chairs then seated himself. "Are the

Scythe no longer a danger? Has the spymaster released your fellow shifter-soldiers?"

"We've eliminated most of the Scythe who know of our existence, but not all. However, after the last mission, we're on a break. It's a chance to see what normal life might be like."

"Ah, a wise plan." André frowned. "When you arrived, I was worried the Scythe might have targeted my town." Which put the territory at risk.

Shifters under his care and protection might all be in danger because of the previous Cosantir's incompetence. His hands clenched, and his anger rose, feeling like the low rumble of thunder.

When Patrin and Fell edged back warily, he realized his protective fury was rousing the god.

*By the god,* Fell thought as his guts tightened in fear.

Because the male across from him, the Cosantir of Rainier Territory, was visibly in touch with the god. André's eyes had turned black, and damned if it didn't feel like bone-shaking subsonics radiated from him.

The hairs on Fell's nape rose, and he fought the need to flee.

It was even worse since André's guess was right, and it looked as if the Scythe had targeted the town...and Wells had refused to let them warn the Cosantir. They sure weren't on a break.

"Cosantir," Patrin said very quietly. "*André*, we will end the danger from the Scythe. That's our goal. Our job."

André flattened his hands on the table, drew in a breath, and the hum died. "Forgive me, please. I am still learning my way as guardian."

Patrin gave him a sympathetic smile. "Having been dumped back into the Daonain culture, Fell and I understand. Learning curves suck."

André's eyes returned to brown, and he chuckled. "They certainly do."

A male with light brown skin, brown hair, a short beard, and the burly build of a bear shifter stepped up to the table. "Bro, here's your order." He set down a large platter of appetizers, including jalapeno poppers, bruschetta, garlic knots with dip, and spicy onion rings. "What would your guests like to drink?"

Patrin smiled and held out a hand. "Madoc, right? Patrin—we met at your housewarming. And this is my littermate, Fell."

After shaking Patrin's hand, the male took Fell's hand. His grip was firm without being aggressive. "Welcome back to Ailill Ridge."

"Thank you. For drinks, we're happy with just water," Patrin said with a glance at Fell.

Fell nodded. Clear heads were needed for plans and missions. Even one beer could relax a male into an indiscretion.

After Madoc returned to his kitchen, André motioned to the platter. "Please join me. The food here is very good."

As they took some food, the Cosantir tapped his fingers on the table. "You will be looking for jobs? I believe Bron, our police chief, has been wanting more officers."

Patrin smiled. "That'd be good. We could—"

"No." Fell shook his head. What was his brother thinking? A Scythe operative would avoid anyone in law enforcement. "Too much like military."

Patrin narrowed his eyes at Fell before nodding. "Aye, you're right. Something in the service industry would be a nice change. And we'd get to *talk* with *everyone*." He shot Fell an amused glance.

Because Fell didn't talk to anyone given the choice. He shot Patrin a sour look.

*This assignment already sucks.*

Although staying in one location for a while would be a treat. Especially in a town with pretty females.

During their time with the Scythe, when they weren't on a mission, they'd lived in a barracks with the other kidnapped males except for rare visits with their imprisoned sister.

It was only in the last year since they were freed that he'd had a chance to speak with shifter females other than Darcy.

Not that he actually spoke.

Doing an automatic scan of the room, he studied the most interesting female in the room—the tiny female with the meltingly dark eyes who'd punched Patrin. She wasn't a blonde bombshell like their B&B host, Gretchen, but damn, she was fascinating. And her voice had been just as intriguing. Warm with a lilt to it, like a songbird. Did she sing, maybe?

The wild scent of another shifter approaching caught his attention.

The big-bodied male had unkempt yellow hair, like drying corn stalks left in the field, and pallid skin with pale blue eyes. "Cosantir." His bow of the head was slight and brief. "I heard there are visiting wolves talking to you." The male puffed out his chest in an instinctive attempt to dominate them.

Herne's fucking forest, this must be the pack alpha. With a stifled sigh, Fell rose and nudged Patrin to remind him of all those aggravating Daonain formalities the Elders had taught...and taught...and taught.

Face expressionless, Patrin also stood.

The Cosantir didn't rise, which was a slight. But he tilted his head. "Roger, meet the MacCormac brothers who have moved to Ailill Ridge. Patrin, Fell, this is Roger Wendell, the pack alpha. Are you here to welcome them to the territory, Roger?"

The alpha's scowl increased. He'd probably planned to bluster, not welcome. "Of course, Cosantir."

Roger's attention turned to Fell. "The pack normally hunts on the night before a full moon, but due to the storm, ours was postponed. Tomorrow night, starting at moonrise. You can follow the scent trail from behind the pack house, corner of Argonaut and

Mule Train Street. Be there." The alpha's tone was on the verge of antagonistic. Turning, he stalked away.

*Hostility again.*

While traveling on their assignments, he and Patrin suffered the same kind of belligerence from far too many alphas. Shay, the alpha in the North Cascades Territory, said aggression was typical when alphas met another dominant wolf who might challenge them.

Not that Patrin—or Fell—would. They were here on a mission. Besides, neither of them wanted to boss a wolf pack. More the opposite, really. After their losses to the Scythe, Patrin would jump off a cliff before taking on responsibility for anyone else.

*As for me ordering anyone around?* Not interested, especially since he'd have to talk. Protecting them? Now, that was different.

Besides, wolf packs probably were full of even more tradition-laden bullshit. None of which he or Patrin understood.

Face it, they were a mess.

Frustration and sadness made an uncomfortable lump in his gut. *We're never going to manage to find our place with the Daonain.*

# CHAPTER THREE

Hand on the door of Espresso Books, Patrin glanced at his brother. "Before we ask about jobs, I'm getting coffee."

This morning, Gretchen had proudly provided them with a batch of store-bought pastries for breakfast. Not fresh, but as far as Patrin was concerned, the generous amount of frosting improved everything.

Unfortunately, the tasteless, thin liquid she'd brewed bore no resemblance to coffee.

A corner of Fell's mouth tilted up with his agreement, but he didn't speak. He'd been even quieter than usual last night after meeting with the Cosantir and the belligerent alpha.

Something else to worry about.

As they entered Espresso Books, the bell on the door jingled, startling him with the friendly sound.

Sometimes he forgot that not everything and everyone was an enemy.

Wells had warned him about falling into such a mindset. Awareness, yes, he'd said. Paranoia, no. He'd told Patrin to stop now and then and simply enjoy being alive.

*Good point. I'm alive; Fell and Darcy are alive.*

Pausing, he breathed in the heady aroma of coffee and fresh baked goods filling the air. After a moment, he turned his attention to their surroundings. An automatic survey of escape routes and the people showed no threats. The place had been divided in half for the two stores.

On the right, behind a security grill, the bookstore had shelves and displays of books, jigsaw puzzles, board games, and magazines.

The bookstore was obviously still closed. A shame. He'd rather hoped to see the tiny, dark-haired female who'd punched him.

The left side held the coffee bar and pastry counter. Round oak tables and ladderback chairs filled the center of the room.

Foliage plants and vines ran along the tops of the bookcases and windows and filled the corners. Warm-colored rugs covered the hardwood floor. The cozy atmosphere said, *buy a book, grab some coffee, and sit a while*. He slapped Fell's shoulder. "Looks like your kind of place, brawd."

"Yeah." His bookworm of a brother smiled.

*Huh. Maybe I should stop by later and grab a couple of books to cheer Fell up.*

Behind the counter, a slender female, maybe a few years older than him, set up coffee to brew.

The door swung open, admitting four cublings—shifter ones by the scent—and manifesting the usual teenaged stink.

They took seats at a table in the center of the room.

Patrin studied the boys briefly. Two pairs of brothers, he'd guess.

One pair had a freckle-faced cub and a fair-skinned, blue-eyed blond.

The other two boys were stockier and maybe a year older. With brown eyes, hair, and skin, they were probably of Latino ancestry, not Romani like him.

"I don't want to go," one of the browner littermates whined.

He rubbed his shoulder. "It took a whole month for my arm to feel better."

"It'll be okay, Alvaro." His brother had curly hair, cut just below his ears. "Talitha will be there this time."

Alvaro scowled. "Cubs don't take the same trails as the adults, remember? She won't be with us."

The blond, blue-eyed boy looked puzzled. "You don't all run together?"

"Nah. Vigulf said the alpha doesn't like cubs. He makes one of the betas cub-sit. Only after the beta got us started on a trail, he disappeared."

Fell frowned at Patrin and muttered, "Pack run?"

They'd mentioned an alpha and beta, so it must have been a wolf pack event, which meant Alvaro and his brother were wolf shifters. And the other two weren't.

What the cubs described didn't sound safe, even if the youngest were at least twelve, which was when Daonain started to shift. But new shifters were clumsy. And pups needed to be supervised, or things got out of hand.

"How'd you get hurt?" the freckle-faced lad asked Alvaro.

"Vigulf and Torkil knocked me off the trail. It was steep—and Mateo had to pull me out of a bush." Alvaro rubbed his shoulder, then grinned. "At least I had three other legs to use. That's so cool."

*New shifters*. Patrin exchanged smiles with Fell. He still remembered the wonder of having four legs and ears that moved.

"I love having four legs. And a *tail*." Mateo smirked at the other two boys.

The way Blondie and Freckles scowled indicated they lacked tails. Must be bear cubs.

Freckles grinned at Blondie. "Tails are easy to grab during tag —like you did last time, right, Sky?"

Sky's high chortle of victory set all four lads to giggling.

*Too fucking cute.*

"Tonight, we'll do better against the oversize mutts," Mateo assured his brother.

"Why? Because we're a month older?" Alvaro's expression held disbelief. "Stump-head, they'll still be three years older and bigger and outnumber us."

"Can't you, like, tell their parents?" Freckles asked.

"I wish." Mateo sighed. "Their mom's a bear and doesn't care what they do. There are a couple of other sets who have moms who aren't wolves. Two of them give us trouble in town."

"We asked them to leave us alone." Alvaro shook his head. "Mateo got a black eye."

"Yeah, so much for talking." Mateo rubbed his face as if remembering the pain.

Next to Patrin, Fell growled softly. He hated bullies.

Reading his brother's expression, Patrin scowled. *No, bad idea. We have a mission. We don't get involved, especially not with cubs. For fuck's sake.*

Rather than falling into line, his brother nudged him forward with an unspoken *talk to them*.

Patrin sighed. Sure, everyone knew he was the alpha littermate between the two of them. But did the gnome-brains realize how often being in front meant someone was pushing from behind?

Nonetheless, he wanted to help as much as Fell did. The mission could wait a while.

At the table, Patrin went down on his haunches beside Mateo. "Hey. Couldn't help but overhear you."

All four of the boys turned pale...because they'd been careless about what they were discussing.

"Nah, nah, you need to be more careful. But no humans heard you...this time." Patrin jerked his chin toward Fell. "We're wolves too. As it happens, we fought others a lot when we were your age."

Not the same kind of fights. He, Fell, and two other littermate sets were the first to shift in Scythe captivity. The instructors used them as experiments in figuring out what shifters could do. Made them fight each other. Then made them fight sadistic, violent mercenaries. Most of his and Fell's scars had come from those years.

All to make good assassins out of them.

At night in the barracks, the shifter captives would work out how to fight each other and others. How to team up. The cubs who'd seen adult shifters fight taught those techniques.

And year by year, the shifter-soldiers grew so deadly the Scythe came to fear them even as they used them.

Patrin smiled at the two wolf cubs. "Fell and I know ways to fight bigger opponents."

Alvaro's eyes widened. "Really? Could you tell us how?"

"We'll show you." Fell's rough voice had the cubs shrinking back for a second.

Then Mateo bounced back like a bent sapling. "Yes!"

Alvaro shook his head. "The pack run is tonight. We won't get good enough today to win against bigger cubs."

The boy was right. Patrin nodded. "Today, we'll teach dodges to make it more difficult to get shoved around. Later, we can work on winning."

Alvaro's eyes lit. "Really?"

"Can we have a lesson now?" Mateo quivered with excitement.

Hell, this was supposed to be a job-hunting day.

*Eh, fuck it.* Patrin shrugged. "Let us get coffee, and we'll head outside."

The beaming faces made his heart lift.

"Good morning. What can I get you?" The woman behind the counter had the tall, slender build of a dancer. Her chin-length brown hair framed a pretty face and a warm smile.

"Two coffees, please." Patrin gave her his most charming smile in return. "Nothing fancy, just coffee. The biggest size. We're desperate."

She laughed. "Plain coffee it is. And are you two new to town?"

As she turned to the pots, he caught a whiff of her scent. Ah, a Daonain. Perfect. "We are. For the moment, we're at the B&B while we job hunt."

"Ah, yes. I get a lot of Gretchen's guests here."

"I bet," Fell murmured for Patrin's ears.

A minute later, she handed over the large to-go cups. "What kind of work did you have in mind? I know most of the businesses in town."

Friendly, helpful people made covert operations much easier. "We're thinking something in the service industries. Clerk or server." He shared a rueful smile with Fell. "We don't have white-collar skills."

"Most of us don't go off to college. Being surrounded by humans..." Her nose wrinkled.

Patrin blinked. How'd she know they were shifters? The flow of air was away from the counter; she couldn't have caught their scents.

When she glanced at the table of cubs, he realized he could hear them. The shape of the room and ceiling must amplify the sound from the center of the room. She'd obviously caught at least some of what was said at the table.

A chill ran up his spine. He and Fell had been as careless as the younglings. Although, admittedly, it would take shifter ears to distinguish words.

"I'd be very grateful if you could help Mateo and Alvaro." She sighed. "Their mother died last June fighting the Scythe mercenaries, and they've had a rough time of it. They just came to live with me yesterday."

"I'm sorry for their loss." Patrin glanced back at the cubs. He and Fell had been at that nightmarish fight. There had been far too many deaths. Really, any loss was too much, considering the Daonain's tiny population. But it was even worse to lose a female. A mother.

As a child, he'd never noticed the numbers of males to females. But after living in the human world where the ratio was almost even, he'd been shocked to realize Daonain males outnumbered females around five to one. The lack of females influenced many of the shifter traditions.

"So..." The barista leaned her arms on the counter. "As it happens, I could use a part-time person. The hours will vary though. Usually from seven to noon. Sometimes the afternoon shift until three. I have a couple of human part-timers—Corey, my main barista, and Renee."

The job was probably in gratitude for offering to help the cubs. However, this would be a perfect location to meet most of the people in town. He glanced at his brother, who loved coffee—and books.

They'd discussed it last night, knowing they needed very visible jobs where they'd have to interact with customers. At least, a little. For Wells and the Scythe, they'd held down jobs like this, and Fell did fine. Never talked all that much, but he was an excellent listener—and most people loved to hear themselves talk.

Fell nodded at the barista. "I've worked a coffee bar before."

"Excellent. I'm Talitha, by the way."

Patrin tapped his chest. "Patrin—and my brother Fell."

"Welcome to Ailill Ridge. Let me get the paperwork for you to fill out, Fell."

Since their IDs had been destroyed when Wells burned their stockade, the human spymaster had provided the shifter-soldiers with new documents.

As Talitha disappeared into a back room, Patrin glanced at Fell. "One job down. After working with the cubs, we can see if the bar is hiring."

"Won't be open until tonight. Pack run?"

"Fuck." The alpha would expect them to show up. "Then we'll visit the grocery store today and the bar tomorrow." The more places they could be hired—and thus on display for the Scythe operative. All the better.

"The pack run should be...interesting." Fell's jaw was hard.

"Interesting is one word for it." In more ways than one. Last night, the Cosantir had warned them that the alpha was littermate to the feral Cosantir they'd fought during the housewarming party last fall. They'd left right afterward. With luck, Roger might not remember them.

*Anyone who believed in luck was lost to pixie dreams.*

Patrin set his hand on Fell's shoulder. "We'll do our best to keep the cubs safe."

Fell nodded.

Patrin might've officially led the shifter-soldiers, but his brother had been just as involved, trying his damnedest to protect them, even though they were all captives together. Some of Fell's scars were from stepping between the sadistic Scythe guards and the younger shifters.

Patrin sighed. Fighting during a pack run was liable to get them tossed out of the territory.

Why the fuck wasn't the alpha dealing with this kind of scat? Wasn't that his job? It was fucking pitiful not to even know what an alpha was supposed to do.

Just one more glimpse of how poorly he and Fell fit in with their own people.

---

Over at Talitha's house, Moya helped Eileen assemble the cublings' beds Gwendolyn had dropped off late last night. Talitha had left earlier to open the coffee shop.

"I'm gone. I need to grab some groceries." Moya gave Eileen a quick hug and headed toward the town square.

Shortly afterward, grocery sacks in hand, she was in the alley behind Espresso Books. There was a gleam of black eyes behind the dumpster. "Good morning, Gnome."

The eyes blinked.

Smiling, Moya ran up the steps to her second-floor landing. Her door was on the left, with her apartment directly over the book section of the store.

Talitha's door was on the right with her rooms over the coffee shop. Her apartment had been empty ever since she moved out to live with Eileen.

As Moya stored her groceries away, she caught herself sighing over the quiet. During the day, it wasn't bad, but it sure was lonely at night with no one in the other flat. There were no friendly sounds of movement, no music, no voices. No running next door for gossip and to share a drink.

Wolves weren't meant to live alone.

Of course, it hadn't been that bad with Talitha next door. *Now it's just me.* Moya shook her head at the pitiful internal whining.

Really, it was wonderful her best friend had found a partner to love and was so very happy. Unfortunately, since she and Eileen had Mateo and Alvaro to foster, Talitha wouldn't ever move back here.

*I'd better get used to the silence.*

For now, she could run downstairs and get a coffee from Talitha. Give her friend a report on the beds. Using the inside stairs, she exited into the store. Off to one side, lightweight accordion security grills divided the coffee shop area from the closed bookstore. She had to admit, it was nice not having to work on Sundays. Poor Talitha.

Breathing in the lovely fragrance of roasted coffee beans, she wended her way through the center tables to the coffee shop counter.

Only...instead of Talitha, a strange male stood behind the counter. His attention was on the display of the electronic cash register. Moya froze for only a second. "What are you doing back there? Who are you?" She clenched the phone in her pocket with one hand. The other hand curled into a fist.

He was way tall, over six feet, with short blond hair and a hard face. Looking up, he snorted. "Gonna punch me, too, tiny female?"

*Too?* Fairy-farts, it was the shifter-soldier. The littermate of the male she'd punched at the Gathering. He was turning up *everywhere*.

Mother help her, he was big, even taller and more muscular than his friend. And he sure looked a lot meaner. His assessing gaze swept over her before he turned his attention back to the register display.

Ignoring her.

*Good, this is good.* Her breath huffed out, and then she frowned. *No, it isn't good.* "Where. Is. *Talitha?*" She emphasized each word in case he was hard of hearing.

Or a total gnome-brain.

Eyes narrowing, he turned to her again. Guess he didn't like the tone of her voice?

"At. The. Secondhand. Store." His rough voice rasped out each word.

Yeah, he'd disliked her tone. Gods, he was scary. Some blond, blue-eyed males looked like a sunny summer day. Not this one. His face was as harsh as the glacier-scoured ridges of the high Cascade mountains, and his blue eyes were colder than a winter snow.

It didn't matter. "She doesn't shop there." A tremor of worry inched up her spine. Had he killed Talitha?

The door to the store opened, and the big, dark-haired male she'd punched sauntered in, followed by Mateo and Alvaro.

"Yo, Moya!" Mateo ran over with his brother. "Patrin is teaching us to fight!"

"Uhhh, um, really?" She tried to inject enthusiasm in her voice even as she gave the dark-haired male a frown. "Does Talitha know?"

"Yeah. She went with us to the park before going to buy us better shirts." Alvaro stuck his finger through a hole in his T-shirt.

"Oh." Thus the secondhand store. Feeling like a suspicious fool, she turned to the male behind the counter. "Sorry. I thought..." No, she wouldn't tell him what she'd thought.

His lips quirked. Very firm lips.

Patrin eyed her, then his friend at the cash register, and chuckled. "You figured Fell murdered the owner to get into the cash drawer?"

Fell? It was the perfect name for someone who seemed harder than granite. "Of course I didn't think that."

"Yeah, she did." Fell's wintery blue eyes held amusement.

*Yeah, I did.* Moya sighed. "Sorry."

"Watch out, brawd. She's got a good left arm." Patrin gripped her wrist and, once again, pried open her clenched fingers. "Such a ferocious female."

She stared up at him, into eyes that were so dark they were like midnight, and the zing running up her spine held equal parts interest and terror.

Smiling, he gave her fingers a squeeze, released her, and turned. "Cubs, let's go find your foster mom. She might need help carrying shit."

---

This low in the mountain valley, the moist air carried the scent of damp moss and crushed evergreen needles. At the tempting scent of a startled field mouse, Moya's nose quivered.

*No, wolf. No snackies right now.* Talk about setting a bad example for the cubs.

Only a tiny whine of frustration escaped as she loped upward along the forest trail toward the pack's meeting place. She glanced back at the three wolves following her.

Still new-shifter noisy, Mateo and Alvaro clumsily brushed against the bushes as they trotted behind her. Alvaro's fur was a mottled dark brown and gray, Mateo's bluish gray with a lighter gray mask. Both still had a lot of growing to do, and their coats were still lightening from their darker cub coat.

Bringing up the rear, pale gray Talitha was her usual silent self.

Two days past full, the moon's roundness had decreased only slightly, and her silvery light spilled through the tree canopy and glowed off the snow-covered dome of Mt. Rainier.

A few minutes later, as she approached the meeting place, the breeze brought her a multitude of wolf scents. Males and females. Cubs barely past their first shift all the way to wolves with the acrid smell of age and illness.

She also caught the musky stench of Roger, the alpha, and his two betas—three aggressive, boggart-brained males. Her upper lip rose to show her fangs.

*No, behave.* She was here to help Talitha with the cublings. Maybe, this time, the betas wouldn't get up in her muzzle. Right now, she just needed to focus on her goal of getting through the pack run with the cubs being safe and no altercations.

*Keep it smooth, wolf-girl.*

In the clearing, most of the shifters had already trawsfurred to human form to enjoy a few minutes of socializing before the run started.

Several single females clustered around the alpha, and Moya rolled her eyes. Which one was the so-called alpha female these days? Maybe Deidre or Cosette? Roger had dumped Gretchen after she played him against his brother, Pete, one too many times.

Apparently, there'd been no female who was dominant or strong enough to retain the leadership since Roger became alpha.

Considering the way he flitted from one female to another, he probably liked it that way.

Moya's ears flattened with her annoyance. An alpha female should be the nurturing heart of the pack and as protective in her own way as the male alpha. Or that was what Moya remembered from when she was a youngling...before her pack back in Stanislaus Territory turned ugly.

She shook her head hard enough to make her ears flap. The memories dispelled. *Stay in the present. Wasn't that what the books said to do?*

A few feet away, Mateo and Alvaro shifted to their skinny teenaged human forms.

Moya glanced at Talitha, caught her nod, and they also trawsfurred. *Brrr.* The air coming off the snowy mountain peaks was bloody cold against bare skin. Winter was definitely on the way.

"Hey, Moya, Talitha." Petite with a sturdy build, Alana from the construction crew wandered over. "It's so nice to see you two here again. Is Heather coming too?"

Moya half-laughed because Heather hated Roger. Instead, she said diplomatically, "She sprained her wrist badly enough to have it in a brace."

"Oh, that's rough." Alana shook her head. "Well, I'm glad you're here. Come and run with my group when we start."

The welcome made Moya smile.

"Hey, Moya. Welcome back!"

She lifted her hand in answer to Katherine's call, waved at a few more friends, and grinned at her brothers, Zorion and Ramón, who were with the males in their construction crew.

When she noticed Zorion's gaze going past her, she turned.

Stepping out from the tree line was the dangerous-looking male Talitha had hired, the one named Fell. Dark-haired Patrin walked with him.

The big males stopped nearby, and okay, even though nudity

among shifters was scarcely noticed, some bodies were worthy of a second look. These two, despite being way too dominant, were impressive. Patrin was all lean, ripped muscles, and Fell had such powerful musculature, he could probably lift a car without straining.

Then there was the tension in their muscles and the way they stood—balanced and ready for action. Obviously lethal even without moving.

Yanking her gaze away, she noticed a batch of teen wolves had clustered around Caleb. Moya's heart sank. *He* was going to supervise the pups?

The beta was just as violent and mean as his littermate, Brett. During a Gathering, when a female had preferred someone else, Caleb had attacked the young, skinny male. He'd knocked Jens down and deliberately stomped on his leg. Moya shuddered, remembering the sound of the breaking bone and Jens' scream.

"Younglings, meet over here." Caleb's raised voice was harsh.

"Off you go, my sweet cubs," Talitha said lightly, although Moya could hear what an effort it took.

They both knew that if a cub got in the alpha's or beta's way, they wouldn't think twice about backhanding him. And since younglings followed the examples they were given, the pack had more than a few bullies.

Openly reluctant, Mateo and Alvaro trotted over to the youngling group with frequent glances back at Talitha and Moya.

Moya bit her lip. Considering the way Roger felt about her and Talitha, the alpha wouldn't let them join the youngling group. Okay, fine. She'd just follow along with them anyway. Because there was no way she could keep the two safe if she wasn't with them.

Talitha gripped her arm. "Look..."

Patrin sauntered across the clearing, following the younglings. The moonlight shimmered off his long dark hair.

Moya stared. "What is he doing?"

Talitha leaned closer. "In the shop, he and Patrin heard the cubs talking about the last pack run when Alvaro got shoved off the trail. That's why Patrin was showing them defensive moves. Is he going to try to go with them?"

"Caleb won't let him." Or she might be wrong. Moya couldn't hear what they were saying, but the body language was easy to read.

Patrin showed the beta his wrist and grimaced as if it was painful. He motioned toward the adults, then the cubs.

Wait... Had he heard her talking about Heather's wrist and decided the sprain made a good excuse to join the cubs. The youngling group was sent on easier trails.

*Nice.* Caleb could hardly say no.

*Hmm.* Moya studied Patrin. A shifter-soldier, she'd heard. He was obviously strong and deadly, but she hadn't expected him to be *sneaky*. Or that he'd go out of his way to protect two orphan cubs.

Scowling, Caleb motioned for Patrin to join the cubs' group.

Mateo and Alvaro bounced up and down with happiness.

"Thank the Lord and Lady," Talitha whispered. "I was so worried about them."

Moya bumped her shoulder. "Me too. Especially with Caleb leading them. Of course, Brett would be as bad. With Patrin there, the cubs should be all right. Now, all we have to worry about is us."

"Mostly you." Talitha bumped her back. "Roger and his betas will just be rude to me. You're the one who gets harassed. I swear, Brett gets meaner every time you refuse him at full moon."

After hearing his new boss and her adorable dark-haired friend, Fell frowned. Harassed? A female?

That had happened far too fucking often to his sister and the other Dogwood captives, but the aggressors had been human, not

Daonain. With so few female shifters, males were supposed to guard...even cosset...them.

Why the fuck were the leaders of the pack breaking those centuries-long traditions?

There were more than a few overly stuffy Daonain customs he wouldn't mind chewing to pieces; however, the protection of females was admirable. It spoke to every instinct in his body.

Across the clearing, Roger trawsfurred to wolf, barked once, and sprang up the trail. The rest of the pack, minus the cub group, shifted and followed.

Nearby, Talitha and Moya also trawsfurred.

Talitha was a tall, pale gray wolf. Slender and graceful.

Moya, shorter and sturdier, was a dark gray brown with creamy cheek ruffs, neck, and chest. With amber, almond-shaped eyes, she made as pretty a wolf as she did when on two legs.

And her scent... *Mmm, pure female*. He trawsfurred, just to enjoy her fragrance even more thoroughly, and his paws took him right over to her before he regained control.

*No.* He and Patrin were here for a reason, and it didn't include licking the muzzle of a feisty little wolf. Or licking elsewhere.

*Foolish fleabag.* This was not only not the time, there never would be a time for females, no matter how adorable.

Trying not to breathe in more of her scent, he turned his head away.

With a soft yip to her friend, she trotted after the rest of the pack.

Rather than catching up with the males his age, Fell followed. No harm in trailing after the fascinating wolf and his new boss to ensure they stayed safe.

Behind him came the seniors and ones with physical problems. Moya and Talitha had chosen a position in front of the seniors and disabled wolves, far back from the front with the strong runners. Interesting. It only took him a few minutes to see they were perfectly capable of keeping up with the leaders.

Perhaps neither of them wanted to be near the alpha or betas?

What kind of a fucked-up pack was this? Wasn't the alpha supposed to be the ultimate in wolfdom? The strongest and with the best character?

He growled under his breath, then shook his head. Trying to reason things out in animal form was foolish. This was the time to sink deep into the now, to feel the softness of the thick evergreen needles under his paws, to enjoy the brisk wind ruffling his fur, to delight in the way his muscles worked. The scent of the pack surrounded him like a warm fire on a snowy night, and even better, he kept catching fragrant whiffs of the beguiling wolf in front of him.

He and Patrin had been on a few pack runs when on missions in other territories. The forest and the mountains here were magnificent. Especially the massive mountain rising from the southern horizon with the glaciers glowing a silvery white beneath the light of the Mother's moon overhead.

He could run these trails for the rest of his life and never grow tired of them.

---

Loping along behind Mateo and Alvaro, Patrin was looking to the south, marveling at the mountain called Rainier. Simply fucking amazing.

The sounds of the youngsters around him brought his attention back to his self-appointed task. The bumbling pups were humorous. Many of them were still learning how to run down steep slopes, jump downed trees, and maneuver through thick underbrush.

Their bouncy gaits reminded him of his teen years and how wondrous it'd felt to become a wolf. And how bitter it'd been when the Scythe had forced him to kill in wolf form. He'd been all of fourteen.

This here was how it should have been. Just young cubs having fun.

Mostly.

Caleb, the incompetent adult, leading the cubling pack never looked back. He wasn't helping or teaching the cubs. Or going slow enough for the weaker members.

So far, there'd been only a few problems with the bullies. He'd spotted them quickly enough—two sets of older cubs, all males.

The first set had tried to jump Mateo, two on one. Mateo had ducked and dodged sideways, using one of the moves Patrin had taught him. And Alvaro slid in to bite one of them hard enough to get a yip.

Turning to attack, the bullies had noticed Patrin...and sped up to run close to Caleb.

The other two, the ones named Vigulf and Torkil, had tried once to pin Alvaro between them without success due to Mateo's sticking close to his side. They gave up and joined the ones in the front.

Now, they were slowing again, running right in front of Mateo and Alvaro.

Patrin eyed them suspiciously. *Ah-huh.* The ground was getting steeper, and the trail was now running beside a cliff. Even worse, the younger cubs were tiring, stumbling more often.

Seeing how the trail went around a blind corner, Patrin huffed loudly enough that Mateo and Alvaro slowed to look back. *Good cubs.* He darted between the two and took the lead.

Trotting around the corner, he kept his weight centered and his guard up. Damned if Vigulf and Torkil—in human form, no less—jumped out from a blind curve and tried to shove him off the trail.

Unsuccessfully.

He wasn't a thirteen-year-old wolf—and outweighed the two older cubs put together. When their push got nowhere, they yelped, realizing they'd gotten Patrin rather than Alvaro who'd been running a nose in front of Mateo. Not clever, attacking without verifying the target.

Glancing over the side, Patrin saw how badly Alvaro could've been hurt, and yeah, this wasn't going to happen again.

He nipped their arms, calves, then their bare asses, driving them forward until they shifted and fled like a hellhound was on their tail.

Laughing inside, Patrin turned to check on Mateo and Alvaro, and the two were right there, bouncing against him in happiness, giving his muzzle little licks, tails wagging like they were dogs rather than wolf pups.

Felt good though. Yeah, it did.

---

Oh, it'd been a glorious run. They'd brought down a deer, and Moya felt quite proud of herself. As Roger and another of the big males attacked from the front, a few others tried to hamstring the deer's hind legs—and failed.

She'd been fast on her paws, dodged a kick, and successfully found her target. Even as she had taken out that leg, the shifter-soldier, Fell, crippled the other leg.

Once the prey was down and dead, Roger had clawed into the soft belly to eat first. Then, the rest of them moved forward, compelled by the hot scent of blood.

A gray-brown female stepped in front of Moya, and it took her a second to recognize the appearance and scent. Cosette. She'd been running behind Roger and Brett, so probably was the newest alpha female. For what that was worth.

Now, because Moya wasn't popular with the alpha and betas, this lazy female thought she'd block Moya from a deer she'd helped to bring down? As if Moya would roll over at a growl and offer her neck. *In your dreams, fleabag.*

The fur along Moya's spine lifted. Lowering her head to guard her neck, she growled long and low. *Out of my way or my fangs will be in your flesh instead of the deer.*

The female backed up so hastily she bumped into two other pack members before slinking away.

Around Moya came huffs of amusement and muzzles opened in wolfy grins. Alana bumped against her shoulder. On the other side of the deer, Talitha bobbed her head in approval.

*Okay then.* Moya lowered her head to eat, the bloody meat hot and satisfying to her stomach. The companionship filling her heart.

Oh, she'd missed being part of the pack.

A while later, breathing fast and even, Moya and her pack mates loped out into an open area, scoured clean of trees. Moonlight poured over the rocky outcropping.

Roger, with Caleb, Brett, and Cosette, stood on a boulder, waiting for the last of them to arrive.

Off to one side, the cublings entered the clearing from another trail, dispersing to join their family members. The smallest, Mateo and Alvaro, trotted over to touch muzzles with Talitha, then her.

So bouncy and cute. Shifting to human, the pups were whispering in Talitha's furry ears, and Moya had to wonder what had them so excited. It must have been an interesting cub run.

Feeling a presence on her left, she turned her head. Fell stood nearby. He was a damned big wolf, his fur even lighter than Talitha's, a silvery gray with white facial and chest markings. Like a ghost wolf.

Catching her looking, he stepped close enough to bump her shoulder with his before moving back just as quickly. It was a friendly sort of greeting, one she hadn't expected from him... although they had taken down the deer together, in a way.

Patrin stood on Fell's other side, black ears cocked forward. He was almost as big as Fell, his thick fur so dark he almost disappeared into the shadows. Unlike her, he had almost no patterning or facial markings.

Just looking at him made her sidle farther away, trying to get out of range of the dominance he radiated. His littermate wasn't nearly as...as...disconcerting.

As the last of the wolves made it to the clearing, she could feel the warmth of the pack ties inside her. They weren't too strong, not for her. She deliberately avoided the pack activities that strengthened the bonds.

Turning to face the moon, Roger lifted his head and let out a long howl. The betas—and Cosette—joined him.

Around Moya, muzzles tipped up to the moon. Patrin's song was long, and low, and somehow commanding, while Fell's tone was harsher yet harmonized with his brother's. The two lured her in, so she added her own higher howl, shivering in delight at how their voices blended.

The mountain air carried the song of the pack, filled with their gratitude, to the Mother and reaffirming their territory. Their voices would be heard for miles. *We are here, and we are strong.*

Eventually, Roger turned back to them. As silence fell, he shifted to human. "Pack, we have two strangers with us. Patrin and Fell." He pointed, and the wolves turned to look at them.

Patrin bowed his head slightly in a polite acknowledgement. Fell didn't move.

When many of the wolves shifted to human and called out welcomes, the brothers' ears perked up in obvious surprise.

Brett whispered something to Roger, and the alpha cleared his throat. "We also have our straying females back with us. Moya and Talitha."

"I wonder what brought *them* back." Standing off to one side, Gretchen sniffed haughtily.

*Fairy farts and gnome guts.* Moya turned her gaze away from Miss Blonde Perfection and eyed Roger warily. She'd been having such a nice time. Was he going to resume harassing her about moving into the pack house?

Gaze on her, Roger jumped off the ledge and winced as he landed.

Most of the wolves were human now, so Moya followed suit.

Even in human form, the alpha was still bulky with muscles, but his skin was loose, showing he'd lost weight and tone. He had bags under his eyes. Really, he hadn't looked healthy since his littermate Pete went feral and was killed in October.

"Hey, Roger, did you ever get in touch with your sister?" Quintrell, the home-school instructor, asked.

"Yeah. She's still in Wyoming. Doing all right." Roger shrugged. "Her cubs are around five."

Moving next to Moya, Alana whispered, "He sounds kinda off."

"He lost Pete. Losing a littermate must really hurt—and she's the only one left."

Alana tilted her head toward the two shifter-soldiers. "You realize they helped fight at the party when Pete went feral and attacked everyone."

Moya's mouth dropped open. "No. I'd gone out to the car to fetch something and missed all that." Thank the Mother. "Poor Roger."

Alana's blonde eyebrows drew together in a frown. "He has the pack bonds though. Wouldn't those help with feeling alone?"

"I guess they must help, or he'd have left to be with his sister."

After exchanging words with a few more pack members, Roger continued to head for Moya...and, oh cat-spit, Brett and Caleb followed.

"You're buzzard bait, you scrawny fleabag!" Torkil, a big cub, yelled and chased Alvaro across the clearing.

Dodging, Alvaro ran in front of the alpha. Tripping, Roger staggered before catching his balance.

Torkil fled, leaving Alvaro standing before the alpha. Alvaro cringed. "Alpha, I'm sor—"

Snarling, Roger backhanded him to the ground and swung his leg back to kick the cub.

"Hey, stop!" Growling, Moya sprang between them to take the blow on her own leg. The sharp pain made her flinch, teeth gritted.

"For fuck's sake." Fell shoved Roger away from her so hard the alpha landed on his ass.

Patrin pulled Alvaro to his feet and nudged him and Moya toward Talitha. "I thought the Daonain were supposed to protect cubs, not hurt them."

"What do you know, you human-raised coyote-dogs." Face purple with rage, Roger scrambled to his feet and charged the shifter-soldiers.

Fell stepped to one side while Patrin stuck his leg out.

Roger tripped over Patrin's leg and went flying. His head hit a fallen tree trunk with a nasty thud.

Talitha had her arms around the cubs. Moya had positioned herself in front of them, and her heart sank as she watched. Gods, this wasn't good, even though the shifter-soldiers were trying hard not to start an actual fight.

"Time to go," Patrin muttered to Fell. He picked up two packs at the tree line and handed one to his brother.

Pulling on the pack designed to be carried by a wolf, Fell made a guttural sound of agreement before jerking his chin at the cubs —and Moya.

Patrin frowned at Talitha and Moya. "Want to head down with us?"

*Be around this male who feels too much like an alpha?*

She took a step back before she caught herself. *No, Moya. This is what we're supposed to be working on. He's been polite. Protected the cubs. Don't be a gnome-brain.*

Moya eyed Roger who was trying to stand, his legs obviously

wobbly. "Yes, thank you. I think we'd better." The alpha wouldn't be thinking straight. If at all.

After they all shifted to wolf, Patrin led the way. To get farther from him—because battling fears took time—Moya moved back behind Talitha and the cubs.

Talitha perked her ears inquisitively, then fell in behind Patrin.

Fell brought up the rear.

Ears swiveling, Moya listened to the almost soundless way the two males moved through the night, watched how they disappeared in and out of shadows. Especially Patrin, who was almost a shadow himself.

The two were scary deadly. She'd never forget how effortlessly they'd taken Roger out of the fight.

They were halfway down the low mountain when a shout was carried upon the air, coming from where they'd left. "I *challenge*."

---

The end of the night had sucked, Fell thought, as they traveled down the mountain. The alpha might be pissed off enough to ban them from the pack's territory, and fuck knew what'd happened after they left. Wells would be furious if their actions messed up the mission.

Eh, they'd worry about it tomorrow.

Just to be safe, Fell and his littermate escorted the females and cubs to the forest's edge near Talitha's house. A nicely overgrown patch of undergrowth led to a backyard shed with a swinging dog door.

By the time he and Patrin shifted to human and pulled clothes from their packs, the others were already changed.

"Night, everyone." Lifting her hand, Moya disappeared out the side door of the shed.

Before Fell could follow, Talitha turned to him and Patrin. "Come on in for a minute, you two." Talitha led the way across the lawn to the back door of her house and lowered her voice as she entered. "Eileen's probably asleep. Alvaro, Mateo, off to bed with you."

The two cubs hugged her, and after a second, gave Patrin and then Fell swift hugs too.

Speechless, Fell watched the pups dart out of the living room and down the hallway. *A hug. So unexpected.*

Eyes burning, he turned and checked out the room. Nice place. Comfortable furniture. Forest colors. Slightly cluttered. It reminded him of their house in the human-shifter town when he was just a cub.

"Now that you're home, we'll be off," Patrin said.

"No, wait. Mateo and Alvaro told me how you kept them from being hurt. More than once." Talitha lifted a ring full of keys from a door hook, removed two, and handed them to Patrin. "You mentioned you're looking for a place to rent. Before moving in here, I lived above the coffee shop. These are to that apartment. I should have all my stuff out before next Sunday."

Patrin studied the keys in his hand. "An apartment?"

Talitha was probably ten or fifteen years older than them, and her raised eyebrows indicated any argument they offered would be futile. "First month is free. Then, if you want to stay longer, we'll talk about rent."

Patrin shook his head. "We can't just—"

"Give the cubs more self-defense lessons, and we'll call it even." She made shooing motions. "Off with you. I need sleep, and so does Fell since he's working the coffee bar tomorrow."

Patrin glanced over and saw Fell had totally lost his words. The whole evening had been unsettling, and now this. A place to stay. All he could do was nod.

With a smile, Patrin tilted his head. "Thank you, Talitha. We accept."

## CHAPTER FOUR

With a rolling cart beside her, Moya was shelving the new books that'd been delivered this week. The titles were already entered into her inventory system and just had to be put out for sale.

It was already noon, and the task was taking longer than normal—mainly because she was exhausted. After getting home last night, she'd been too wound up to fall asleep. Had felt weirdly uneasy for some reason. So, with a cup of chamomile tea, she opened a new paranormal romance—and hadn't turned off the light until the wee hours.

*Honestly, Moya, you know better.*

This morning, she'd tried to meditate as usual—and fell asleep instead.

*I need more coffee.*

Unfortunately, Talitha had left Fell alone in the coffee shop. And she just couldn't deal with him. He was too... masculine, too potent, too self-assured. Too much for her, that was for sure. She stared across the room, watching him hand over a coffee to Noreen from the wilderness store. Noreen chatted away while Fell offered a rare word here and there.

His black Henley clung to his powerful chest and shoulders. His tanned face looked harsh, not softened in the least by the blond stubble along his jaw.

Then he looked over, his gaze meeting hers, as she stared at him. He'd seen her looking. As her stomach dropped a foot, she flushed head to toes.

Gah, she was an idiot.

Turning away quickly, she picked up a book from the cart.

*Just ignore him and do your job, wolf-girl.*

Determinedly, she found the right place in the line of titles and tucked the book in. Then another and another, breathing the unique fragrance of new books.

Oh, hey, this was one she'd wanted to read, about—

"Yo, sis."

She startled so hard she almost dropped the book.

Her brothers strolled across the room toward her, and she smiled fondly. They were both just a smidge under six feet. They'd been skinny cubs. As adults, construction work had packed muscle onto their broad shoulders.

Zorion had light brown skin with disconcertingly blue eyes. His collar-length hair, dark as hers, was tousled by the wind. A day-old beard shadowed his jaw...and she almost, almost looked over at Fell to compare.

*No, uh-uh, not going to look at the lethal shifter-soldier.*

Instead, she eyed her other brother. After getting his long hair caught in a power tool when he was a teen, now he kept his medium-brown hair ear-length and, despite the late night, his jaw was freshly shaved. Typical of her rule-abiding—and bossy —brother.

Although he and Zorion owned their construction company together, Ramón gave the orders. In contrast, Zorian was rebellious, unconventional, and preferred to follow rather than lead.

She fell somewhere in the middle. Quieter, and not particularly submissive. Back when Heather met a newly changed shifter who'd been in the human military, Moya'd been intrigued and done some research. *So fun.* Heather, with her practical, hands-on nature, would make an excellent gunny. Moya, though, would've ended up being an executive officer, serving under a naval captain, someone like Ramón.

Zorian would undoubtedly spend his time in the brig.

"Hey, you two. Why aren't you at work?" She set her book down on the cart, checking their clothes for fresh blood.

"We're calling this a lunch break." Ramón gave her a one-arm hug, and she saw worry in his dark brown eyes. "We wanted to give you the news since you and those strangers left early last night."

*News?* Her muscles tensed. "What's happened?"

"Remember how Roger hit little Alvaro, and the shifter-soldiers jumped in?"

*And hadn't that been a satisfying sight?* She nodded. "Fell knocked him down; he tried to attack, and Patrin tripped him."

"Roger hit a log and got half-knocked out. He was kind of unfocused when he stood up and looked like he'd hurt his back. He wasn't moving well."

Moya snorted. "He hasn't been in good condition since Pete went feral—not physically, not mentally. Where are you going with this story?"

Ramón could keep a tale going for a long, long time—and was good at it. He was very popular whenever his crew went out for drinks.

Zorion snorted. "The story is that Brett challenged the alpha."

Moya froze, dismay filling her. "No. No, no. Brett didn't win, did he?"

The grim line of Zorion's mouth confirmed vicious Brett was now the alpha.

She touched her chest, realizing there was a missing bond. No wonder she'd felt so uneasy last night—a new alpha had taken over the pack bonds and cut Roger out of them. The wolves tied into the pack more closely had probably been even more unsettled. "I thought Roger was stronger than Brett."

Ramón shook his head. "Roger fought as sloppy as a drunken pixie. He never had a chance."

"Brett didn't k-kill him, did he?"

"No, probably only because a death would've brought the Cosantir down on him. Instead, he ripped Roger out of the pack bonds and kicked him out of our territory."

Moya was appalled. "He hasn't even gotten over losing his brother."

"S'okay, sis." Zorion patted her shoulder. "Quintrell says he'll probably go join his sister in Wyoming. He'll manage."

"If Roger was already hurt, he shouldn't have had to fight." Moya pulled in a breath. "Didn't anyone try to stop the challenge, to say it wasn't fair?"

Zorion snorted. "Quintrell did, and Caleb punched him hard enough to knock him out. Unfortunately, no one felt particularly loyal to Roger. He was a crappy alpha."

"Still...we should have stopped the challenge." Ramón's face was hard. "No one wanted to fight to save Roger's tail. It's a shame; Brett's going to be an even worse alpha."

"Understatement of the year," she muttered. Brett was obsessed with returning to the traditional ways. Back when females' sole purpose was to have babies for the pack.

And he wanted her to have his.

Shaken, she pulled in a long breath. "I feel like I just landed with both paws in an iron-toothed trap."

"I bet." Zorion scratched the dark shadow on his jaw. "It's why we wanted to give you a sniff at what might be coming down the trail."

"Brett's going to harass you about living alone." Ramón squeezed her shoulder. "You can move in with us."

"As if. You know having me in your home would turn into a mess." With the Daonain, male littermates lived together, sharing houses and a mate. But a sister would move out as soon as she reached her first heat at around twenty or so. Because females were territorial, and if brothers brought a lover home, even if just for a night, it could get ugly.

Moya had thought the stories were exaggerated until she tried to share a house with them here in Ailill Ridge. It was after her first heat—and as far as she was concerned it was *her* den. When Zorion had come home with a female, Moya shifted to wolf and almost bit the poor werecat.

"We'll see what happens." She managed a smile. "Thank you for coming to tell me."

"Hey, you're our sister." Ramón kissed her cheek. "Whatever you need, just tell us."

Slinging an arm around her shoulders, Zorion gave her a squeeze. "If you want us to overnight at your place as a deterrent to Brett, you got it. Anytime."

They'd step between her and the new alpha, even if it got them in trouble. She blinked to keep the tears back. "You guys are the best. Thank you."

As they headed back to work, she concentrated on shelving the new books. Trying to find an interest in what she'd bought.

Her fears kept piling up, one after another.

For years, Roger had been trying to make her live in the pack house. It was true that females could live together when they all knew it was temporary. But living somewhere any pushy male wolf could just walk in? Uh-uh.

She sure hadn't wanted to deal with Roger's displeasure when she avoided him. Let alone Brett and Caleb, who thought they were entitled to her time and interest. And got mean when she didn't want them.

Roger eventually backed off.

Brett, being a vindictive brute, wouldn't. *What a mess.* She scrubbed her hands over her face as if that would wash away her problems.

Didn't work.

She glanced over at the coffee bar and saw Fell taking a customer's order. Had he and Patrin heard about the challenge?

It wasn't their fault Roger lost. With his declining health, he wouldn't have stayed alpha much longer. Her mouth tightened. Had Brett been biding his time, waiting for Roger to weaken, before challenging him?

Yes. Yes, he had been. Moya scowled. She'd never realized quite what a cheating coward Brett was. An alpha was supposed to be the strongest and the best. Roger had been horrible enough. Now they had an alpha who was not only cruel and cowardly, he was also...devious.

The pack deserved better.

She picked up another book and tucked it onto the shelf.

Last night, she'd had a wonderful time. Aside from Brett and Caleb and the few weaselly bullies who followed their lead, the wolves were good Daonain. Friends. A healthy pack served as a source of strength to its members. She'd grown up running around with the pack in Stanislaus Territory. Which was why it'd hurt so much when...

Shaking her head dislodged some of the memories.

The cart empty, she pushed it over to the box against the wall and refilled it with puzzles, maps, and mugs.

Even as she worked on setting everything out, she couldn't stop worrying. She put her hand over her increasingly queasy stomach.

*How am I going to handle Brett being the alpha?*

Avoiding him was the first thing to come to mind. But what about her promise to Talitha to support the cubs?

Yet, the more she attended pack activities, the stronger the bonds would get to the pack—and to the alpha. Bile rose into her throat. She knew exactly how it felt to be emotionally assaulted through pack bonds.

"Hey, are you in charge here?" A loud baritone made her jump.

A bulky man in a red sweatshirt and jeans stood at the front of the store. Walking over to her checkout counter, she discreetly sniffed the air. No forest fragrance; he was human. "Can I help you?"

"Yeah, I'm returning this book for a refund."

She glanced at the oversized, coffee-table book about glamorous houses. It probably sold for close to two hundred dollars. "I'm sorry. That's not a book the store carries."

"Bullshit. I bought it here." He stepped closer, raising his voice. "It was probably the last one. That's why you don't have more."

Fear dried her mouth. Her hands fisted. "We've never had that book. You'll have to return the book at the store where you bought it."

"I bought it right here," he shouted, "and I want a refund." Far taller than her, he pushed into her personal space.

Her fists rose. "Show me the receipt."

"I lost it." He scowled. "Doesn't matter. I want a fucking refund. Now."

"She said no." The interruption came from a voice so cold and deadly it cut the very air. "Leave."

The man spun, showing Fell standing right behind him.

Moya felt a tiny flicker of amusement as Fell loomed over the customer the way the man had loomed over her. *How do you like it, you pus-filled maggot?*

"I...I—"

"Fucking crook." Fell's voice dropped to a terrifying growl. "*Run.*"

The human ran as if his tail was on fire.

"Wow. You're very effective." Moya smiled. "Thank you."

"You should've called for me."

"I what?" She shook her head. "I was handling it. If he'd kept being obnoxious, I'd have kicked him out."

He snorted. "Tiny female." His gaze swept over her, then his mouth twitched. "Did you figure to punch him first?"

When he grasped her left hand, her heart rate spiked, and her other hand came up. He didn't move, just waited, his icy gaze trapping hers, until the violence drained out of her.

"Better." His hands were warm and strong as he gently pried open her clenched fingers.

Oh fairy farts, now she felt stupider than a gnome. When she glared at him, his blue eyes filled with laughter.

Gods, he was right. She'd been ready to punch a customer—and Fell too. Feeling totally hopeless, she sagged back against the counter.

"Hey, hey." Fingers under her chin, Fell lifted her head. "What's wrong?"

"Nothing. It's nothing."

There was no softness in the hard angles of his face. "Pisses me off to be lied to."

Mother of all, he was stubborner than a moose in rutting season. "It was a polite means of *trying* to get you to drop the subject."

"Didn't work." He raised his eyebrows.

He was certainly pushy, but her panic was gone. She breathed out, feeling almost as if she'd like to tell him about her problem. And wasn't that just crazy?

Or maybe not. He'd gone out of his way to keep Alvaro from being hurt last night, then had stepped in to help her this morning. "Okay. Maybe later we can talk."

He tipped his chin toward the coffee bar where Renee, a dark-haired human who Talitha had hired last month was brewing coffee. "I'm off duty."

So stubborn.

Then again, maybe she should ask for his help. The meditation and stuff weren't working...or rather, it wasn't meant to cure a person in a couple of days.

She glanced around. As usual on a Monday, the bookstore was quiet. "All right."

"I'll be back." He left her, crossing to the coffee shop side.

Definitely not the chatty sort. Shaking her head, she pushed the cart to behind the checkout desk where it wouldn't be in anyone's way.

Returning, he handed her a coffee and kept one for himself.

She took a sip and blinked. Vanilla latte, one of her go-to drinks. He'd taken the trouble to get her what she liked. "Thank you."

A corner of his mouth pulled up in what seemed to be the Fell version of a smile. He motioned toward the bookstore's comfy couch and chair sitting area near the front window.

*Okay, I can do this.* She sat on the couch.

He took the chair, almost dwarfing it with his size.

How in the world could she ask someone like him for help? Her chest felt tight, and she tried to pull in a breath. When he frowned, she held up her hand and took another breath.

Everything inside Fell tightened. Seeing a female so obviously anxious kicked off all his protective instincts. "Take your time."

"No, no, I'm good." She straightened her spine and met his gaze. Her brown eyes were beautiful, big and lustrous—and vulnerable.

Every protective instinct he had woke up.

"I'd like your help with something, only I'm uncomfortable having it one sided, and I don't know what I could do for you in return."

Interesting kind of dilemma, and one that said a lot about her character. He'd met more than a few humans and shifters who had no problem taking without giving back.

Yeah, he liked this little wolf. "Ask. I'll think." As usual, his voice seized up.

*Dammit.* He'd gotten better. Sometimes, he could manage entire sentences. Other times—none at all.

*Fucking brain.*

"Well..." She rubbed her hands on her jeans. "My problem is if I get scared, I lash out. And sometimes at the wrong person or the wrong time. Like I did with your brother at the Gathering."

Before he could ask what'd caused the problem, she looked away and wrapped her arms around herself. Whatever set her on this trail must have been traumatic.

Through his teens, he'd lived in a barracks filled with grieving, brutalized shifters. He had plenty of experience with trauma of all kinds. And he knew that with them being essentially strangers, she wouldn't open up about her past. Not today.

It would happen. Damned if he wouldn't make sure it did.

He rubbed the back of his neck as he thought. On the way down the mountain last night, he'd seen her scared when a rock gave way over a cliff, almost taking her with it. She'd scrambled for footing, and once balanced, had given them a wolfy grin and pranced down the path.

He'd seen her stare down the alpha female without a quiver.

But... With him, she was anxious. Was it just him?

Hmm, no, she reacted to other males also. With the aggressive customer, her hands had fisted. At the Gathering, she'd punched Patrin, thinking he was Brett—and Brett was an extremely pushy wolf. Even more, she stayed out of arm's reach with Patrin, whose dominance was impossible to conceal.

Yes, he was on the right trail here. "Set off by belligerent males?"

Her mouth dropped open. "How did you know?"

He shrugged. "How can I help?"

Her expression changed from irritation with his nonanswer to relief. "I...I'd like you to jump at me."

*What in the God's green forests?*

"Startle me. Scare me." Her jaw was set tight, her gaze determined. She'd put a lot of thought into this. It wasn't an impulsive request. She knew what she wanted.

*Why me?*

Perhaps because she did know him somewhat, enough to know he wasn't a total weasel, yet he was enough of a stranger she might still be somewhat frightened if he got aggressive. Which was her goal, wasn't it?

Confirming his guess, she added, "Not just once. Lots of times. Off and on." She ran a hand through her hair, pushing it away from her face, as if irritated by...everything. "A bunch of small scares is supposed to eventually diminish my reaction. With enough repetition, I guess I learn to stay in the present and not get tossed into the past and panic."

*The logic wasn't unreasonable.*

Back with the Scythe, the mercs had forced the teens to fight through terror and pain. Over and over.

Moya's plan was a variation of that technique. Although scaring a female went against all his protective Daonain instincts. "You sure?"

"André—the Cosantir—ordered me to work on it."

A Cosantir's orders couldn't be ignored, and Fell could see the determination in her big eyes.

He rose. When she started to stand, he bent to grip her shoulder hard and growled, "Stay put."

Her face paled. Her scent turned acrid with fear. She shoved at his arm, and when he didn't release her, her hands fisted.

Unmoving, he just waited as she started to swing at him.

She managed to pull her punch before it landed. As reason returned to her eyes, she dropped her hand. "Mother of All."

When she shuddered, he wanted to pull her into his arms and hold her. Comfort her.

A little female. Who was scared of him. Yeah, he was brainless as a gnome.

Resuming his seat, he stretched out his legs. The resting

posture should indicate he didn't plan to push around a little wolf. "That what you had in mind?"

Still breathing fast, she scrubbed her hands over her face. "Ah." She swallowed, and he knew how dry her mouth must be. "Yes, I guess so." She hesitated before nodding. "Yes, you did exactly what I had in mind."

He nodded.

"I...I might hit you."

He shrugged. "I'll survive." Somehow. Scaring her would be difficult. She was just so appealing.

When he was a young pup, he had a favorite stuffed toy—a fluffy, soft wolf, perfect for cuddling. After the Scythe, even with the other shifter-soldiers, there'd been no cuddling.

By the Mother, he craved...tenderness. Yeah, everything about her drew him in.

*No, Fell. Mustn't cuddle the little female wolf.* Besides, she'd probably punch him.

"You'll do it?" she asked, obviously holding her breath.

"Yeah."

"Yes! Oh—what can I do for you in return?"

He felt laughter rise, because his first inclination was to ask for a hug after any incident. Unfortunately, the request would probably frighten her even worse. Females—and males—walked wary around him.

*So what could he ask of her?*

He did have something he'd planned to work on. But...with her? He tilted his head and studied her. Adorable, yes. Soft and pretty. And also gutsy. Stubborn. Fear made her fight, not flee. It might work.

She leaned forward. "You've thought of something."

And there, that persistence was what he needed. "Yeah. I don't..." No, this would be impossible. Obviously.

"Don't what?" Her gaze was on his face, then her lips tilted up. "Use your words, Fell."

He'd heard her say that to Alvaro when the teen was sputtering, so angry as to be incoherent. A trickle of humor ran through him at being classed with a cub. "*That's* the problem."

She looked blank for a second, then her mouth formed an "O". "You don't like to talk—or have trouble talking?"

He nodded.

Dimples appeared beside her mouth when she smiled. "This should be fun. After you scare me, I'll get to annoy you by forcing you to hold up your side of a conversation?"

Annoying would be the fucking right word. He nodded again.

Her smile grew. "I can't hear you, Fell. Did you—"

Rising, he loomed over her again, heard her yip of fear, and caught her hand before she punched him. Waited until reason returned to her gaze.

She pulled in another breath, glared at him, then her eyes lit. "So, tell me, how did that make you feel?"

When he scowled, she burst out laughing.

By the God, he was doomed.

## CHAPTER FIVE

Interesting place, this Bullwhacker Bar. Drink orders filled for the moment, Patrin leaned an arm on the glossy, wooden bar top to study the place. The Scythe had taught him to be a bartender since it was an easy way to get close to a target. However, since their targets had been influential people, he'd spent most of his time in cities.

"Fell," he shouted. "Empties in the pool room."

Near the center of the room, his brother lifted a hand in reply.

This small-town bar was quite different from what Patrin was used to. It had a certain rustic charm, being battered and comfortable, much like the owner, Nikolaou Chaconas. Patrin glanced over.

Working the other end of the bar, the owner was slightly under average height and built badger-tough rather than graceful. Graying hair, leathery skin, and a flamboyant gray-white mustache indicated the human had reached his senior years.

Nik had hired Patrin to work behind the bar, and on the busier nights, like this Friday night, Fell would get some hours—picking up empties, washing up, and serving as what Nik called a bouncer. Relieved he wouldn't have to engage in conversation with customers, Fell readily agreed. He just had to occasionally call out Patrin's name.

As Patrin would Fell's. It was good they had unusual names, ones that'd gained a reputation in the PNW Scythe division. Should make any operative take notice if he heard them.

"Hey, Top Dog."

Startled at the unexpected greeting, Patrin spotted two of his shifter-soldiers. At eighteen, the two were still slender, not having put on a male's heavier growth. In worn jeans, flannel shirts, and cowboy hats, they were obviously from one of the outlying ranches. "Kennard, Fletcher." Ah, right, Wells mentioned the brothers were here in Ailill Ridge. *Hmm*. They sure weren't of legal drinking age. "Are you allowed in here?"

Fletcher flashed a smile. "No one asks. No one cares."

Kennard leaned on the bar. "All the ranch hands come in on Friday or Saturday nights." And, of course, even if they were cats and not wolves, these young males wanted to be part of the group.

Patrin couldn't blame them. "All right. No more than two beers or I'll card you."

Kennard fished out his wallet. "Aye, Top Dog. Two light drafts, please."

*Top Dog*. Patrin snorted at hearing the title again from someone besides Fell. As the years went on and he ended up leading the shifter-soldiers, they'd started calling him that. Then again, he'd refused to answer to alpha since the group included panthers and bears as well as wolves.

"What're you doing here anyway?" Fletcher asked. "Is Fell here?"

"Can't say—and yes." Patrin smiled and started filling a couple of mugs.

"Oh." Fletcher's brown eyes darkened with his realization that Patrin and Fell were on assignment. And his face tightened with obvious guilt. Because they weren't with the older shifter-soldiers tracking the Scythe.

"Wipe that expression off your face, cat. We got more than enough of us for the few bad guys that're left." Patrin set the two mugs on the bar. "So how's the job? Ranch work, right?"

A corner of Kennard's mouth tipped up. "It's great."

Fletcher jumped in as usual. "Daniel and Tanner are brothers of the Cosantir's lifemate. They raise horses and cattle—and hay. Kennard and me, we only work livestock. All the ranch hands are"—he glanced right and left and obviously revised his words—"um, pretty much alike, so we get on good."

In other words, the crew was Daonain. "Sounds like you're enjoying yourselves."

"We missed a lot, growing up where we did. They're catching us up," Fletcher said.

Patrin could only nod—and be grateful the young males had help.

"Our sister, Averi, moved to Cold Creek, and we wanted to be near her but not underpaw," Kennard said.

"And Grandsire lives up in the North Cascades Elder Village. So we run up to see him now and then," Fletcher added.

"Hey, F 'n' K, over here." The yell came from a table of males and a few females, all with western hats.

"Go, lads." Patrin smiled at them. "If Fell and I get the chance, we'll try to catch up with you before we leave."

Fletcher grinned.

Despite Kennard's half smile, he also had a glint of tears in his eyes. "Top Dog."

Patrin watched them join their table of ranch hands, and his chest ached. They'd all lost so much to the Scythe—family, friends, and years where they should have been carefree younglings growing to adulthood.

At least the shifter-soldiers were free now. It was reassuring to see Kennard and Fletcher fit in with the other hands.

Feeling lighter, Patrin moved up and down the bar, filling

orders, making conversation with humans and shifters. Really, in a bar, there wasn't much difference in the way they acted.

The noise in the bar increased as a group of men in jeans, work shirts, and boots entered. The one leading the group was waving his hands in the air, obviously finishing a story. Laughing loudly, the men broke apart, some moving toward a table, the rest toward the bar.

"That's the Moreno construction crew." Joining Patrin, Nik pulled two pitchers from under the bar and greeted the group. "Welcome back, boys. What can I get you?"

"It's been a hard day. Let's start with a couple of pitchers, one light, one dark." The storyteller was a muscular male with wavy, medium-brown hair swept straight back. He looked familiar.

He eyed Patrin in turn and nodded cordially.

Catching the male's scent, Patrin realized he'd been at the pack run—and so had many of the rest of the crew.

Across the room, Fell was watching, probably for the same reason. He'd always been more observant than Patrin.

"Finally found some help, Nik?" the male said. "You've been without for a while."

The owner handed over the first pitcher. "Yep. The last of my summer hires headed back to school in September. I figured on handling the place myself over winter, but hell, I'm getting up there in years. I need my sleep."

"Then it's good you have someone to help." The male smiled at Patrin and stuck his hand out. "Welcome to Ailill Ridge. I'm Ramón Moreno."

Moreno. The construction crew must be his. Wait, hadn't Gretchen said that Moya's last name was Moreno? Was this a relative?

Patrin shook his hand, feeling hard calluses. "Thanks." He added, "I'm Patrin," in case the male hadn't heard during the alpha's introduction last night.

Besides, part of the mission was to get the Scythe to move,

and getting his name out there was part of that. No need to add a last name. The Scythe knew it, but he'd just as soon no one associated their sister, Darcy, with them. The North Cascades Territory where she lived wasn't far away.

He jerked his chin toward the front of the bar. "My brother, Fell."

"I remember from..." Ramón halted, undoubtedly recalling he was in a crowded bar with humans around. "Anyway, good to meet you."

"Likewise."

Ramón picked up the pitchers and headed for his crew's table near the right wall. Another male collected a batch of beer mugs and followed.

Patrin watched the group for a minute. Typical pack wolves—slapping each other's arms and backs, shoulder-to-shoulder, rowdy, friendly.

Almost made him homesick for the barracks.

As he filled orders, he tried to pick out the Daonain amongst the humans...and tried to see if any human might be the Scythe spy.

According to Nik, very few tourists remained in town with the weather growing cold. Everyone wore casual clothing—usually jeans and sweaters or sweatshirts.

Two tables of females bracketed the construction crew. At one table were females he'd seen during the pack run. The females at the other table, he figured, were human.

Seated by the front windows near the door were three males. They seemed at ease but without the closeness of the pack wolves, and more watchful as well. Maybe mountain lions.

A group in the narrow pool room caught his attention. Some with a distinctive prowling gait of cougars. Others who talked with big gestures—probably bears.

"There are good people in this town," Nik said, reaching past to grab the jar of cherries. "Although the odd fistfight—even some brawls—do happen. Occasionally."

"Or maybe more often. Probably because alcohol can cause testosterone poisoning." Laughing, Moya slid onto a stool at the bar.

She had a clear, melodic voice, one that made Patrin want to ask her questions, just to hear her speak.

"My dear, you are too cynical." Nik patted her hand. "What would you like to drink?"

"Heather wants a *no* tequila sunrise, and I'd like an Old Fashioned." Her rosy lips were perfectly curved, the top lip tilting up slightly.

And why the fuck was he focused on her lips?

*Keep your paws on the trail, wolf.*

"Coming right up." Nik glanced at Patrin. "Can you make the Old Fashioned? She prefers bourbon."

"Sure." Patrin noticed Moya's small jump when she recognized him. A tiny wrinkle appeared between her delicately arched brows.

He didn't get a smile. Was there a reason she didn't like him?

By the time he'd finished mixing the drink, Nik had handed over the virgin cocktail and taken her money.

Patrin moved closer. "Here you are."

Sliding off the stool and stepping back, she extended her arm for the drink. "Thank you."

"My pleasure."

Her fingers trembled as she took the glass.

Fuck, was she scared of him? After trying to punch him? Twice?

Frowning, he watched her back up several steps, gaze on him, before turning and heading to a table in the middle of the room.

Nik's leathery face held a disapproving expression. "Seems nervous around you—and not in a good way. You hittin' on her?"

"No, actually." Patrin ran his fingers through his hair, scowling.

"Fell and I just got into town and are still trying to get settled. She's adorable, but I'm not ready to add a fe—woman to the mess my life is in."

Nik's laugh was a short bark of sound. "At last, common sense in the younger generation." Chuckling, he moved down the bar toward a man holding up an empty glass.

The old human was a character. Patrin turned away, glancing again at Moya, who was seated across from the Cosantir's mate.

Moving past Moya, Fell stopped and said something. Wait—Fell *talked* to her?

And she laughed, open and easy, not frightened at all. What the fuck? It was Fell who intimidated both males and females, and Patrin who made friends.

By the God, she was sure pretty when she laughed.

Moya watched Fell move away and shook her head. "Whew, he prowls like a cat shifter, only with a little something added."

And that little something added a tingle right up her spine.

Sitting on the other side of the table, Heather considered the big male. "Mmmhmm. I'd call it a helping of *I'll-kill-you-if-you-annoy-me*."

Moya burst out laughing. "Your description isn't funny, only...it really is."

"He reminds me of Zeb. Do you remember him? The cahir who moved to the North Cascades with his partner, Shay? I think you were here a couple of years before they left."

"Of course I remember them. Who could forget a cahir?" The giant-sized protectors of the clan tended to be memorable, although she had always avoided Shay and Zeb.

They had very dominant personalities. It was no surprise Shay was now alpha of the Cold Creek pack. "I think you're right—Zeb and Fell have a killer vibe...and share their proclivity for being chatty."

Heather choked on her drink. "You mean they're both totally uncommunicative."

"Like they believe three words constitutes an entire conversation." At least Fell wanted to change, unlike Zeb. Fell's determination to improve was remarkable—and inspiring.

"I see Fell's brother got hired on here." Heather glanced toward the bar at the back of the room.

Moya turned...and met Patrin's penetrating dark eyes. As he held her gaze, the rest of the room turned to a blur. Gravity lightened until it felt as if her chair was floating.

"Moya?" Heather's voice held enough amusement to break the spell.

Reality returned with an almost palpable thud. "Um." What'd Heather say before? "Right. Fell mentioned they had experience bartending. Patrin is more sociable, I guess, so he took the bartender position, and Fell got bouncer."

"Patrin doesn't appear to have a problem talking." Heather was looking at the bar.

Moya followed her gaze and saw Patrin easily chatting with a couple of her brothers' crew. His white shirt set off his dark beard and olive complexion—and fitted far too well over the finely sculpted musculature. He was seriously good looking.

What was wrong with her? Rather than talking to the sexy wolf, she'd backed away like a kitten spotting a fox.

"There's an annoyed expression." Heather's brows drew together. "Did the male bother you?"

"Oh, no. Uh, yes. It wasn't his fault." When Heather looked blank, Moya explained. "It's the dominance stuff. He simply radiates it."

"Ah. It's good there was a bar between you so you couldn't whack him." Heather grinned at Moya's glare. "Speaking of which, why'd you want to meet here rather than at the Shamrock? Didn't you swear off this place after the last drunk you flattened?"

"I did. But the drunks are why I'm here." Moya took a big

gulp of her Old Fashioned and blinked. Even if Patrin was scary, he made a great drink. "I've worked on all the calming exercises. Now I need practice not answering pushiness with violence."

Over the past four days, Fell had done as she asked, intimidating the spit out of her. Occasionally terrifying her. She'd punched him a few times, especially at first. Only, the more she made him talk to her—as her part of the deal—the less frightened she was. No, *be honest*, her attraction to him was getting stronger than her fear. He was just so...so dangerously masculine.

However, since he couldn't scare her any longer, she'd decided to search out unexpected interactions with strangers.

"Huh." Heather propped her elbows on the table and rested her chin on her laced-together fingers. "I know André ordered you to work on this, but you're putting in more effort than I thought you would."

"Now, see, I would never ignore an order from our magnificent, wonderful, amazing Cosantir," Moya grinned when Heather snickered. "Aside from incurring minor repercussions like being banished if I didn't obey, I really do want to get over my problem with dominant males. You know, *nice* dominant males."

Heather raised her eyebrows. "I feel as if I'm missing something."

"I was thinking over our conversation from the Shamrock about me liking dominant males. And I realized I'm not attracted at all to non-dominant males." Meek males didn't interest her at all. It was only because of a full moon heat that she managed to mate with the shifters who were only mildly dominant or balanced between the two personality types. "The males I *really* desire are also the ones who make me back away." Like Patrin, Gods help her. "Or I punch them."

"Mother's breasts." Heather rolled her eyes. "Talk about a dilemma. I'm not surprised that you prefer powerful guys."

"Huh?"

Heather held up a finger. "One, you like challenges—like

starting a bookstore from scratch." Another finger went up. "Two, you're fairly dominant yourself."

Moya shrugged. No surprise there. In the business, Talitha let her make the decisions. In their mini pack with Heather and Talitha, Moya led the runs. Heather edged toward dominant herself but was enough in the middle to where she'd take command only if the person in charge was weak or incompetent.

Moya liked being out in front. Liked leading.

Heather grinned. "Your ability to direct others is probably why the alpha and betas want to get you for a mate, and they might not even realize why. It's instinct for the alpha to look for a mate who can strengthen the pack. The best alpha females are on the dominant side *and* smart and energetic. Nurturing—and someone who likes dealing with people. That's you...and of course, you're also terminally cute."

*Cute.* Heather knew how Moya felt about that putrid descriptor. "Bite me, bitch."

Heather laughed. "It's so fun seeing you with males who don't know you. None of them expect a pocket-sized wolf to be so dominant."

Pocket-sized? "Girl, I have a fist, and I know how to use it."

Still grinning, Heather glanced around. "All right then. How do you want to go about your *don't-react-to-the-dominants* hunt tonight?"

Pleasure warmed Moya's heart. She wouldn't be all alone as she pushed her limits.

---

Fell wandered through the bar, his nose on alert to pick up any hint of impending fights. Anger, whether human or shifter, held a discernible stink.

After snagging a batch of empties, he deposited them at the end of the bar for the youngling in the back to deal with, then returned to prowling the room. Working as what Nik called a *bouncer* was a comfortable job. Fuck knew, he was used to brawls.

Imprisoned in the Scythe stockade with younger, emotionally volatile male shifters, he and Patrin had spent their time teaching, breaking up fights, talking, breaking up fights, sleeping…and breaking up fights.

So far, this bouncer job at the Bullwhacker felt downright natural.

At the end of the bar where his back would be to the wall, he settled on a stool and did his duty, shouting out his brother's name. "Patrin, a drink!"

Smiling, perfectly content with talking to every fucking person, Patrin brought Fell a lemonade and returned to dispensing drinks to the customers massed around the bar.

Fell would far rather fight them than talk.

His tongue had loosened up some though, what with four days of being harassed by a determined little wolf. Moya had noticed that scaring her bothered the fuck out of him. Taking advantage, she forced him to talk while he tried to calm his instincts.

She now held his hand while doing so. He wasn't sure if it was to reassure him she wasn't hurt or to prevent him from escaping her questions.

Himself? He considered holding hands as his reward. She had a tiny hand, soft and smooth, and even when trembling, her grip was firm.

By the God, she was fun to be with. Turned out they'd read a lot of the same books. And she also liked debating the worth of various stuffy Daonain traditions. Yeah, he enjoyed his time with her, and he was getting better at talking.

At least with her.

Moya saw Fell sitting at the end of the bar, sipping a drink—and had to suppress the urge to join him. It'd be even better to scare him the way he did her, but he was impossible to sneak up on. And she'd tried.

"You want the shelves to match what you have now?"

Emerson Wainwright's question yanked her attention back to the table. He and his brother, Baldwin, had come over to talk about her request for improving the bookstore's children's section. "The same style, yes. The shelves must be short. And colorful—very colorful."

Emerson nodded, taking notes on a paper napkin.

A twinge of guilt ran through her. "You know, I can find a handyman. You two are far too talented to waste your time on making cute children's shelves for the bookstore."

"It won't be a waste of time." Emerson grinned at her. Fair-skinned, tall and lanky, the furniture-makers were around twenty years older than she was—although shifter ages were difficult to guess. With short, dark-brown hair and beard, Baldwin possessed a long face and nose that matched his morose nature. Slightly shorter, Emerson had blue eyes, brown hair, and a reddish beard. His fun-loving, prankster personality had marked his face with a wealth of laugh lines.

Baldwin nodded. "Our nephews are learning to read."

"Your bookstore already appeals to the adults. We can make the cubs' section a lot better." Emerson nudged his brother. "At cost."

Baldwin echoed him. "At cost."

"Me and my budget are grateful." Moya beamed at the cat-shifters. "When can you—"

"Well, well, well, look at who left her den. Haven't seen you in here in a while, Moya."

The nasal tenor made Moya stiffen as irritation vied with dread. She tried to keep her face still as she looked up at the crow-cursed new alpha. "Brett."

His leer made her want to knock his fangs out.

Heather thumped her glass onto the table, diverting his attention. "Brett."

His leer disappeared. He was smart enough to be cautious with the Cosantir's lifemate.

Noticing the Wainwright brothers, he scowled and asked Moya, "Why are you socializing with flea-bitten felines?"

The brothers stiffened.

Fairy farts, did the alphahole want to incite another cat-dog brawl? Before André had arrived, the fighting had grown increasingly vicious—like last summer when a bunch of young wolves attacked some cougars. Afterward, Margery, the banfasa, had spent hours tending the wounded.

*Oh Gods, this is not good. Brett hates cats even more than Roger did.* He'd probably lost some childhood battle with a feline kit, stewed over it ever since, and now Mr. Malicious hated all cats.

How incredibly stupid. A person didn't choose what traits they were born with. Why hate them for that? Their actions, on the other hand... She sure understood despising someone for their behavior. Because she totally loathed *this* gnome-brained bigot.

"I asked you a question, female." Brett nudged her shoulder.

Moya rolled her eyes. "Oh, huh."

He moved in closer, puffing his chest out. "You shouldn't be talking to these mangy-tailed moggies." Calling a werecat a *moggy* was as rude as calling a wolf a mutt or mongrel, implying they were a human pet—and an inferior one to boot.

She had to bite back what would've been a very rude response. He was the alpha in this territory. Openly insulting him might get her kicked out of the territory. Instead, she turned away.

"Don't you ignore me." One hand on the back of her chair, the other on the tabletop, he leaned over her in an aggressively territorial move.

Her hands closed into fists. *Don't hit him; don't hit him.*

Across from her, Baldwin rose to his feet, feline graceful. "Go away, mongrel."

Even if Brett was shorter, his bulky muscles made him wider and heavier. He growled.

"Belligerent roosters," Heather muttered under her breath before raising her voice. "If you want to fight, go elsewhere. A public bar is *not* the place."

So true. In September, when André arrived, he'd been infuriated at the werecats and wolves fighting in the bar. The shifters had been far more discreet ever since.

Would Brett be cautious? He was more cunning than Roger, but far less restrained. Far more of a bully.

"You're right, Heather." Baldwin sneered at Brett. "Let's take it outside, puny alpha. Just you and me. It'll get you away from this sweet wolf who really doesn't like you." He motioned to her to call attention to how she'd moved as far away from Brett's looming body as she could.

*Argh, fang it*. Although defending her, Baldwin was doing it in such a way to escalate the situation.

Straightening, Brett growled. "I'll fight. We *all* will."

Even as he spoke, the weak pack bonds inside Moya prickled with anger, rubbing her nerves raw.

"You fucking moggy, with your chicken-shit name-calling." Brett shouted loud enough to be heard over all the noise in the room. "You cowardly cats can't win against *us*." He called on the pack bonds with an alpha's enhanced strength. *Attack*.

Dismay ripped through Moya. She could feel his manipulation of the ties. Would anyone else?

All around the bar, the wolves shoved back from the tables and stood, faces flushed with anger.

Moya wanted to cry. Roger had pushed the pack into fighting before but never so strongly.

*Oh, Gods, my brothers*. Ramón and Zorion stalked across the room with the wolves from their construction crew behind them.

The Cosantir would banish them all—especially if Heather got hurt in the fracas.

Jumping to her feet, Moya yelled, "Ramón, Zorion, stop."

Startled, they halted, and after a moment, motioned for their crew to stop. Non-crew wolves kept moving forward.

Around the room, the werecats had noticed and were standing. The whole place was going to erupt into a war.

She could spot the humans by their uncomprehending expressions. So far, all they saw was a potential brawl. Mother's breasts, this could get really bad.

A young ranch hand—thankfully, a wolf still in human form—charged toward Emerson.

Hissing, the cat carpenter jumped to his feet, chair toppling.

"No!" Moya jumped between the two and punched the young wolf in his gut, using the strength from her core. She followed with a snappy upper cut to his jaw.

He landed on the floor and sat there, blinking.

"You *dare?*" Brett growled from behind her, then shouted, "Pack!"

Two more wolves headed toward the cats.

Before she could move, Fell grabbed Brett by the collar. "Maggot-brain." He dragged the struggling alpha to the door and flung him out so hard the wolf landed on his back like an upended beetle.

Fell stepped aside just in time for Patrin to toss Baldwin out... right on top of Brett. Then the formidable shifter-soldiers crossed their muscular arms over their chests and stood, deliberately blocking anyone inside from following out the door.

Patrin turned far enough to yell out the door, "If you two want to fight, do it out there, one on one. There'll be no brawling in the Bullwhacker."

"Damn straight," Nik called from behind the bar.

Still seated, Heather snickered and took a sip of her drink.

Pulling in a breath, Moya looked around and blinked. It appeared the war was over.

Laughing, the cats were resuming their seats.

The wolves still stood in place, probably feeling the same thing she was—a chill wash of reality erasing the anger that had simmered through the pack bonds. Tossing Brett outside had dislodged his manipulation and let the wolves come to their senses.

"What in the world was all that about?" a human woman sitting nearby asked her tablemates.

Demon dung, how stupid could everyone be—they'd started this scat in front of *humans*. Time to cover up the scat with a pile of camouflaging dirt. Moya put her hands on her hips and raised her voice. "Honestly, Ramón, if your basketball teams can't behave, you shouldn't go out drinking together."

"Our..." Ramón caught on quickly that there were humans witnessing them. He winced and replied in an equally loud voice, "Yeah, sorry. It was a hard-fought game, and my team lost. Guess we let it get to us more than we should." He motioned to the construction crew to go back to their table.

"I swear, the referee must've been bribed." Zorion patted Moya's shoulder and caught up to his crew.

Thankfully, he hadn't noticed her trembling. The pressure exerted through the pack bonds had been frighteningly similar to the mental compulsion she'd suffered in the past. From Alpha Leonard, the Gods-benighted cur.

At the bar, Nik lifted his hand to someone standing in the restroom hallway.

Moya took a step back at the sight of Bron, the Chief of Police. The tough-looking older female with short dark hair was what a human might call a real hard-ass. And a cahir. If breaking up a brawl, she wouldn't have pulled her punches—and Moya's brothers would've landed in a forest of pain.

Thank the Mother that Patrin and Fell had acted before the Chief got involved.

Noticing everyone's attention was focused on what was happening outside beneath the streetlights, Moya turned to look.

Baldwin had regained his feet. He waited for Brett to stand, then motioned with his hand—*come at me.*

Brett didn't move. After a moment, he sneered and walked away.

"What in the world?" Heather murmured. "After all that, he's just leaving?"

Moya frowned. Was the alpha unwilling to fight unless he had the pack behind him?

Dread crawled up her spine. He hadn't challenged for alpha until after Roger was hurt. Now he walked away from a fair fight. She glanced around, wondering if anyone else realized what she just had—their new alpha was a coward.

Silence fell over the bar as Bron stalked across the room, eyes narrowed. She was obviously in a lousy mood—not that she was ever what one would call jovial.

As the wolves hastily turned back to their conversations, Moya caught Heather's gaze, and they both snickered.

"A brawl in here isn't a laughing matter," Bron snapped.

Heather simply smiled, not engaging the irritable older female who was her lifemates' aunt. Moya smothered a smile. When first arriving here, the cahir had displayed major cattitude. Apparently, Bron had never liked any of her nephews' entanglements. Eventually, the cahir had been won over, probably because very little upset Heather, and even the Chief of Police had to be impressed.

"The fight got stopped before it started," Heather added diplomatically. "Can I buy you a drink?"

Bron's annoyed sigh made Moya burst out laughing and got her an annoyed frown.

The chief turned her attention to Fell and Patrin. She cocked her head. "You're the shifter-soldiers I met at the housewarming party."

When Fell nodded rather than speaking, Moya sighed. Yes, they had more work to do.

Patrin gave her a charming smile. "Chief. Good to see you again."

"And you." Bron glanced around the now-quiet bar. "Not bad work."

Her lips *almost* curved upward before she stalked out the door.

Heather lifted her eyebrows at Patrin. "You know, André was surprised you didn't want a job with her."

"We're staying flexible. In case this territory doesn't suit us," Patrin said easily.

"Oh." Heather shook her head. "I think everyone would be disappointed if you left."

"Really? That's nice to hear." The surprise in Patrin's voice startled Moya.

But it was the flash of longing in Fell's eyes that squeezed her heart.

# CHAPTER SIX

Leaving their pickup parked in a two-car parking space behind Espresso Books, Patrin lugged his duffel bag up the outside steps to the second-floor landing. He unlocked the door and found a hallway with two doors midway down, facing each other. There was a set of stairs at the end.

Patrin hesitated. Which apartment was Talitha's?

Coming up behind him, Fell pointed to the door on the right.

"Ah, Talitha did say she had the right-hand one. I wonder who lives in the other place." Patrin unlocked the door on the right side and stepped into the two-bedroom apartment. The faint fragrance of coffee and pastries drifted up from the coffee shop on the ground floor.

Not a bad place. Feminine, but not too fussy or fancy. Two overstuffed chairs bracketed a comfortable-looking, beige couch and a gleaming wood coffee table. The walls were painted the muted green of a shadowy forest, and an off-white patterned rug covered the dark wood floors. The trim work and fireplace were white. "This'll work. And be a lot better than the B&B."

"Or in Los Angeles?"

Patrin grimaced. The hotel room's garish orange and beige décor had made his paws twitch.

Fell studied the oil paintings of Mt. Rainier, obviously done in different seasons, then squinted at the signature. "Eileen Berger. Talitha's partner?"

"Probably." Patrin started opening doors. There were two adequate-sized bedrooms, both in shades of cream and brown. He tossed his duffel inside one and continued.

The kitchen wasn't large, but it wasn't as if he or Fell would use it much. Neither of them could cook more than the simplest of meals. "Feels different to be in a real apartment and not a hotel or barracks."

Fell glanced at him and nodded. "It does."

Feeling unsettled, Patrin headed downstairs to get the bag with their electronics. Their Scythe handlers and the spymaster Wells had taught them to use the latest human technology. It ended up being just another way they were different from the majority of Daonain.

He passed Fell on the steps and saw his brother had propped open the outside door and the apartment door.

Setting the bag on the coffee table, he started pulling out equipment. Wells would expect a report from them, and Talitha had given them the password to the store's internet.

---

The sound of footsteps in the hallway outside her apartment caught Moya's curiosity. Talitha hadn't mentioned she planned to stop by. Then again, they hadn't had a chance to talk since the pack run. Between her recent move and taking on Mateo and Alvaro, Talitha was swamped. The way her life was blossoming was wonderful.

*I miss her.*

Moya opened her door to say hi and…stared. The door across the hallway stood open, and Patrin was inside, opening a laptop.

To her right, Fell walked in through the outside door, loaded down with grocery bags.

Surely Talitha hadn't rented the place to *them*.

Sure, Moya was getting better. She was pretty much comfortable with Fell, in fact.

But Patrin... Even though he was nice, and he protected cubs from bullies, his power still terrified her.

Her friend wouldn't do this to her...would she?

Moya swallowed hard. Yes, Talitha would—if, by renting to the shifter-soldiers, she could ensure they'd look out for Alvaro and Mateo. The cubs' welfare came first. As it should.

*Mother of All, help me.*

Fell saw her, and she could almost see him force himself to speak. "Moya." He eyed the apartment behind her before asking, "You live there?"

"Yes. It's above my bookstore, just as that one"—she motioned toward the other apartment—"is above the coffee shop. Are you...moving in?"

When he merely nodded, she remembered her part of their bargain. She cleared her throat and lifted her eyebrows.

He shot her an annoyed glance before saying grumpily, "Yes. Talitha rented the place to us." Then a glint of amusement brightened his blue eyes before he set down his bags.

She frowned. What kind of person didn't take groceries into the kitchen?

A second later, he stepped closer, too close, looming over her, one hand on the doorframe just over her head. His rough voice was deep. Threatening. "You got a problem with us living here?"

As her hands fisted, she sucked in air, breathing in the scent of a wolf shifter. And taking a deeper breath because Fell had a uniquely appealing fragrance, like the evening air in a moonlit forest where the trees were huge and old and rooted deep in the land.

Her need to defend herself faded away, leaving only a disconcerting urge to move even closer to the big wolf.

He tilted his head. Rather than try to scare her again, he touched her cheek with his callused fingertips. "Can't frighten you anymore."

She couldn't think past the feeling of his gentle caress, of the heat of his body, of the rough sound of his deep voice. "Um. Right. No. I mean yes."

His laugh was even deeper, and something low in her body tightened in response. Dear Goddess, what was happening to her?

She edged sideways and ducked under his arm. "Um, welcome to the building?"

"Thank you." His cheek creased with his half-smile. Glancing at his groceries, he sighed. "Best I stow those away."

As he picked up the bags, Moya looked past him.

Frowning darkly, Patrin studied her, then his brother, then her again. It was obvious he didn't know—or like—what was going on between her and Fell.

She was pretty sure she didn't either.

Pretty sure.

Patrin bided his time as he and Fell unpacked. They didn't have much. With the Scythe, the shifters had been allowed only enough clothing to fit into human society when on missions. And they'd lost even those few items when they broke free and Wells ordered the stockade burned to the ground.

Since then, the shifter-soldiers stayed on the move, tracking down and eliminating the Scythe before the bastards could disseminate the knowledge of the Daonain's existence. They'd been lucky so far, due to the Director's and Colonel's egos. They didn't want their rivals to learn how the shifters had escaped, let alone how their mercenaries were slaughtered by the Daonain in June. The Scythe didn't tolerate failure.

So... If the Scythe who knew of the Daonain could be eliminated, their threat would come to an end. What would he and Fell do then? Work for Wells, doing more of the same?

Hearing his brother opening and shutting drawers in his bedroom, Patrin rubbed his right arm where an old fracture ached like he'd been savagely bitten. The break had healed, so the ache was probably all in his head.

*Because I'm tired.* It was a difficult admission to make, but true enough. He was tired of moving, of never having a home, of not owning anything more than what would fit into a couple of duffel bags. His envy for people who lived in one place, surrounded by friends and families, kept growing.

Alas, a family and home weren't in his future.

Speaking of which... He leaned on the doorframe to Fell's bedroom. "What's going on between you and that female?"

"I helped with a...project...of hers." Fell put his empty duffel into the bottom drawer of the dresser, then smirked at Patrin. "Your turn now." As a young cub, Fell was what the humans would call a chatterbox and as playful as a pixie high on catnip pollen. After the destruction of their village, he'd grown taciturn, rarely speaking even to Patrin.

How had Fell gotten to know this female thoroughly enough to get roped into her project? And why was he looking amused?

"My turn for what?" Patrin asked warily.

"To dominate her. You'll be good at it." Fell grinned.

Try to dominate the feisty little female? Patrin narrowed his eyes. "You're going to get me punched again, aren't you?"

---

As she turned the heat down on the stovetop, Moya heard footsteps out in the hall. Must be her brothers; the shifter-soldiers hardly made any noise when they moved.

She glanced at the wall clock. They were right on time.

"Hey, sis." Zorion walked into the kitchen. His wavy dark hair was still wet from a recent shower and was dampening his red T-shirt. He handed over the covered dessert carrier she'd gifted him last winter solstice. "One flan, as ordered."

She breathed in the heady aroma of vanilla and caramel escaping from the carrier. The creamy custard was one of her favorite desserts. "Yum. Why don't people start a meal with the dessert?"

"Good plan."

Blatantly sniffing, Ramón strolled in. "Paella? Maybe rabbit?"

"Sorry, I was out of rabbit—you should bring me some. And I had a craving for seafood." She moved past him to set a platter of Croquetas de Jamón on the dining room table.

Not a huge fan of seafood, he heaved a long-suffering sigh. "I'll fetch you some bunnies this week." Following her to the table, he grabbed one of the deep-fried rolls filled with creamy béchamel sauce and ham. "These make up for everything. You are my favorite sister."

She rolled her eyes. "I'm your only sister, gnome-brain."

"That's a lot of food. Are Talitha, Eileen, and the pups coming over?" After grabbing his own tasty croquette bite, Zorion pulled plates from the cupboard to set the table.

"No, they're still working out routines with the cubs. It'll probably be a while." Moya huffed. "I wasn't thinking and made our usual big amount."

A sound had her turning to check the hallway door that Ramón had left open. Had Talitha changed her mind?

No, the noise was her new neighbors. Patrin was bent over the finicky lock to their apartment. Fell saw her looking and nodded.

Ramón spotted them. "Hi there. It's Patrin and Fell, right? Are you—" His brows drew together. "Hold on—are you living in *Talitha's* place?" His tone conveyed displeasure. Undoubtedly, two males living so near Moya troubled her tradition-loving brother.

"Aye, we just moved in today." Patrin abandoned his task and stepped into the doorway with such deadly grace she blinked. Although a wolf, he moved more like a cougar.

Not as cavebound as Ramón, Zorion smiled. "Happy Moving Day." Then the slug-wit went a step too far and added, "Since you're probably not set up for cooking yet, why don't you join us for supper?"

Moya barely managed to smother a protest. By the Mother, she didn't want to be beset by Patrin's dominant aura during a family meal.

*Why me?*

Both males accepted. Gritting her teeth, she escaped to the kitchen.

It was only a few minutes before the food was on the table, and everyone settled down to eat. It warmed her heart to see Patrin and Fell cautiously sample obviously unfamiliar food and then dig in heartily.

"This is amazing," Patrin said, "all of it. It's somewhat like Mexican, but not as spicy—and the spices are different?"

"Our mother was born in Spain." Ramón grabbed another of the rapidly diminishing Croquetas. "When she got homesick, she fixed her favorite foods." He grinned at Moya. "Unlike our sister, who has 'pampering time' with candles and wine when she needs comfort."

Moya backhanded him in the gut. Littermates who teased should expect to get thumped.

Sputtering a little, he cleared his throat. "Anyway, in Mom's Spanish family, everyone helped with the cooking, so she made sure the tradition continued with us. We all learned."

Fell's expression turned unreadable, which she'd learned meant he was unhappy.

Patrin shook his head. "I envy you. We were just learning to cook when the Scythe wiped out our village. Fell and I barely manage to make eggs."

Moya looked across the table at him and directed her question to Fell. "You've been free from them for a year. How can you not have learned to cook?"

When Patrin started to answer, she held up her hand and waited for Fell.

Fell's glare made her grin. Still, this was her job, right? After a moment, he said, "We stay in hotels and B&Bs—and eat out."

Oh, right. They worked for that scary spymaster human.

Moya's heart hurt. Her brothers had been scrawny, all bones and shaggy hair and with perpetually hollow stomachs. They'd loved helping Mamá cook so they could nibble on everything. Her pup memories were happy ones, singing along with the ever-present music while chopping vegetables, dancing while stirring pots, teasing her littermates.

Fell had shared enough that she knew what their teen years had been like. Losing the rest of the family, their whole town, and isolated from the Daonain. Beaten on by humans. Forced to kill.

"I'll teach you to cook." The invitation spilled out before her brain engaged.

*Oh no, did I just say that?*

"Accepted," Patrin said instantly. Encircled by his black beard, his smile flashed white, and his dark, dark eyes were warm, sending a flush through her.

Fell didn't smile, but crinkles appeared at the edges of his eyes. How could such a deadly male be so devastatingly attractive? "Reciprocity?" he asked in his slow, rasping voice.

"Uh, I'll think about it." She glanced at her brothers to see Zorion nod approval. Ramón frowned.

*Eeks, change the subject before Ramón gets all overprotective—and embarrasses me.* "Do you know if the Cosantir came down on Brett for almost starting a public fight?"

"Not just a fight—your idiot alpha wanted to turn it into a bar wide brawl." Patrin's anger was obvious from the growl in his voice. He pointed a fork at Ramón and Zorion. "Why were you jumping in with your crew? Didn't you realize it'd put Moya and André's pregnant mate at risk?"

Ramón flushed. "By Herne's hooves, I don't know. When Brett started yelling, I just wanted to attack something—kill the cats."

Zorion nodded. "It's not like we had much to drink. We don't ever. Too dangerous to do construction the next day if you're hungover. But yeah, I felt the same way."

"Is it a wolf thing?" Patrin asked. "Like through the pack bonds?"

Leaning back in his chair, Fell eyed Moya's brothers, then her. "You weren't affected."

"I noticed it." Of course she had. She knew exactly what coercion felt like. The bitter taste in her mouth made her swallow. "The closer the ties to the pack, the more influence the alpha has over you." There was more than one reason she avoided most pack events.

Ramón reached over to squeeze her shoulder. Her brothers understood the ugly memories this discussion resurrected.

She saw Fell look between Ramón and her.

Following his brother's gaze, Patrin narrowed his eyes. After a moment, he said, "We're new and not really part of the pack. Maybe that's why we felt nothing."

"Makes sense." Zorion cleaned the last bite off his plate. "Gotta say, Brett's already proven he'll be an even worse alpha than Roger was."

Face tight, Ramón pushed his empty plate away. "If we'd brawled in the Bullwhacker, the Cosantir would have flattened all of us, not just Brett. Gods, if André was angry enough, he might cast us out of the Daonain or kick us out of his territory."

Patrin rested his muscular forearm on the table. "Can't you stay away from the pack events like Moya does?"

There was the dilemma of all wolves. Moya shook her head and let her brothers answer.

"Wolves need other wolves to keep them in balance. Moya created a mini pack for runs with Talitha and Heather." Ramón shook his head. "Roger didn't like it, but Heather and Moya were strong enough to stand up to him. And they're female."

Seeing Fell's confusion, Moya explained. "Females aren't a threat. If males joined our mini pack, the alpha would see it as another male setting up a pack in his area. A challenge."

Fell nodded.

"That's why Talitha brought her cubs to the pack run," Patrin said. "Because the cubs are male."

"Exactly." Moya smiled ruefully. "Sometimes, my cat and bear friends envy wolves for having ready-made friends and a support group. But a pack has an ugly side if the leadership is bad."

Fell's expression held disgust. Then he turned to her, and she could see him force himself to speak. "You did good at the bar. Punched an attacking wolf. Didn't punch the alpha."

She blinked in surprise, realizing he was right. She hadn't over-reacted to Brett's assholery and had taken the needed steps with the ranch-hand wolf. Pride swept through her—and pleasure that he'd noticed. "Thank you."

"Huh, I'd have liked seeing you flatten the alpha." Patrin grinned, then cocked a brow at her. "When we gave the Cold Creek Daonain combat lessons, not many females knew anything about fighting. How'd you end up so competent?"

After telling her when they met that her right arm was weak, a compliment on her fighting skills was surprising...and left her speechless.

"Before she started the bookstore, she helped us with construction." Anger darkened Ramón's brown eyes. "Back then, we had humans on the crew. They could be real assholes when it came to a cute, tiny female. She'd had enough trouble bef... Uh, anyway, we taught her to defend herself."

"After she talked us into hiring a couple of her female friends, the problems got worse. We ended up going to an all-shifter crew." Zorion grinned. "It's a relief, not having to be as careful about hiding the shifter part."

"Being stronger, healing faster?" Patrin asked.

"Aye and quitting early on full and dark of the moon nights. How we don't take someone to the hospital if they're badly hurt." Zorion grinned. "Or our sister talking to gnomes and pixies, and the humans unable to see them and thinking she was crazy."

Moya wrinkled her nose at him. "It's rude not to say hi to OtherFolk."

Ramón chuckled. "Considering how she'll talk to anyone and anything, maybe she is a tad crazy."

"Just for that, I'm eating your portion of flan." Moya picked up her empty plate and headed for the kitchen—and escape. Because seeing the two deadly shifter-soldiers grinning made her feel as if the full moon heat had already arrived.

Why couldn't they be ugly?

---

With an unfamiliar feeling of contentment, Patrin leaned back in his chair. His belly was full; the food had been magnificent. The conversation had been engaging. The Moreno brothers were intelligent and, even more important, had good characters.

Then there was Moya. Just as intelligent and honest. Obviously caring. Brave too. His memory provided how she'd stood between the aggressive wolf shifter and the cat she was protecting. Trying to stop a fight.

Right there was the problem. The female brought out every protective instinct in his body.

Fell set his empty plate on top of Patrin's before jerking his head toward the kitchen. "Go be a pushy mongrel."

*What?* Then Patrin remembered the discussion he and Fell had earlier, and he saw that Moya was in the kitchen alone. "By the Gods, I didn't agree to this scat," he muttered. With an annoyed grunt, he picked up the plates and stalked into the kitchen.

Bent over, Moya was filling the dishwasher. And, being a healthy male, he noticed her beautifully heart-shaped ass. One that would fit perfectly against his groin.

Fuck, now his scent was probably filled with interest.

*Okay, get this over with.* He dropped the plates on the counter.

At the loud noise, she jumped up and turned.

He got right into her space and took hold of her shoulder. "You should have asked for help. Why didn't you?" When she looked up at him in shock, he opened the gates to the dominance he normally kept throttled.

She gasped. Her fist hit his gut so hard he took a step back.

He blocked her next punch and gripped her wrists. "Down, little wolf. You're in control, not your reflexes."

She was panting, her eyes too wide.

"Moya, easy now." He kept his voice soft, gentle.

A shudder ran through her as she regained control. "Oh, fairy farts, I did it again."

Her wrists were so tiny in his grip. Hell, she was tiny, the top of her head in line with his mouth. And beneath the scent of fear was an enchanting female fragrance that made him want to wrap her up in his arms so he could sniff and lick her all over.

He sighed. Sometimes the animal nature was a pain in the tail. "You did. Nice punch though." This time, when she tugged at her wrists, he released her.

Her head turned. Fell still sat at the dining room table. She shot him a glare hot enough to singe fur.

Fell held up his hands. And grinned. A rare full-on grin.

"Toothless, mangy-tailed cur." Her glare turned to Patrin like a splash of scalding heat. "He put you up to this."

"He did." Patrin took a step back, imitating Fell and holding up his hands. "It's all his fault."

She snorted at the excuse used by every cub in every age of shifterhood.

## BONDS OF THE WOLF

"What the fuck is going on?" Ramón grabbed Patrin's shoulder and yanked him away from Moya. "Are you bothering our sister?"

The construction contractor had an exceedingly powerful grip, and Patrin concealed a wince. "I was just going along with a request."

"What request?" On Patrin's other side, Zorion stepped in front of Moya.

Despite the awkwardness, Patrin had to appreciate the protectiveness of her brothers. "Ask Moya."

Thrown to the wolves, Moya felt like punching the dominating wolf again. Harder. Much harder.

Even if her hand felt as if she'd hit a stone wall rather than his abdomen.

Gnome guts, now there would be no escaping her brothers. "Let him go, Ramón. Let's have dessert, and I'll explain."

"Dessert?" At the enthusiasm in Patrin's low baritone, she had half a mind to punish him and Fell by kicking them out without any goodies.

Only...being aggressively pushed was what she'd asked of Fell.

And apparently from Patrin. Gods, she'd never forget the sound of his deep, smooth croon as he tried to gentle her down. Her wrist still tingled from the power of his careful grip.

Worse, her nerves hadn't settled from the disconcerting mix of terror and attraction kicked off by the blast of dominance he'd given her.

"Yes, dessert." Ignoring questions, she handed out servings of the flan Zorion had made.

A few minutes later, finished with the explanation, she turned her attention to her own plate to avoid her brothers' scowls.

"That's the stupidest thing I've ever heard of." Ramón crossed his arms over his chest. "This stops here and now. You're not going to—"

Moya stood. Before she could dump her glass of rosé over his head, Patrin and Fell burst out laughing.

"What's so fucking funny?" Ramón demanded, his temper running hot.

"We said something similar to our sister, Darcy." Patrin stroked his short beard with a finger.

"She got pissed off," Fell added.

"Oh yeah. Putting a paw in a metal trap might've hurt less," Patrin said.

"Our sister isn't anything like"—Ramón realized Moya was standing...with a glass in her hand—"Uh...sorry, sis?"

Prudently, Zorion slid his chair away from the table.

"I did the research," Moya said coldly. "This is an accepted technique. Since the Cosantir ordered me to fix my problem, you may argue with him. If you dare."

Ramón eyed her. "André wouldn't—"

Zorion smacked the back of his brother's head. "We're not taking on the Cosantir. I'd prefer to live a few more years if you don't mind."

"That's pretty much how I felt." Moya took a seat and saw the shifter-soldier males still grinning. "You two shut up."

When they saluted her, actually *saluted*, she busted out laughing.

## CHAPTER SEVEN

As Moya climbed the inside stairs to her apartment, a male's deep smooth voice came from down the hall. "Good. Now a double-punch to the gut."

What in the Mother's soft earth..."

A grunt came from—oh, from Patrin and Fell's apartment. The door wasn't shut, and she stopped to look. Snoopy? Why yes, yes, she was.

What a sight. Mateo and Alvaro faced off against Fell. The cubs were maybe an inch shorter than her five-three—so nearly a foot shorter than the powerfully muscular shifter-soldier. Fell's expression was so cold and deadly.

He wouldn't hurt them, would he?

No, she knew better. They'd spent a fair amount of time together now, and she'd learned he had a tender heart for younglings.

He turned his head just far enough to glance at her. And she saw the amusement in his eyes.

Fell was having fun.

"Yah!" Mateo yelled and hit Fell in the belly twice.

Fell didn't seem to even feel the blows. "Better."

Off to one side, Patrin watched, arms crossed over his chest. "Aye, better. Could you feel how much stronger it was?"

Mateo nodded. "Uh-huh. Only I didn't even knock him back or anything."

"Cub, I have trouble knocking him back." As usual, Patrin had a smile on his face, and when he looked at his brother, Moya could practically feel the love there.

And it made her go all soft inside.

Patrin turned, his dark gaze meeting hers. Holding her gaze the way he always did, the way that sent tiny zings through her bloodstream. "Moya."

"Um. Sorry to have interrupted."

"Hey, Moya, I got Fell to grunt when I hit him." Alvaro ran over to give her a hug, enthusiasm making him bounce.

"That's...ah, great." She'd had fighting lessons from her brothers. So why did hearing that Alvaro punched Fell make her want to cringe? She turned and asked, "Fell, are you all right?"

"Aye."

She lifted her chin, giving him her Look.

His sigh was inaudible as he struggled for more words. "They're improving. I'll have some bruises."

Oh, look at the cubs puffing up with pleasure at the compliment. So cute. She gave Fell a smile, not only because he'd talked, but because he'd chosen words that made the younglings feel good about themselves.

And if she wanted to pull up his shirt and see if he really did have bruises on that granite hard, ripped abdomen, she'd keep that thought to herself.

*Girl, back those paws right up.*

"Time for you two to scamper home to Talitha and Eileen." Patrin rocked back as two cubs thumped into him for quick hugs. "Thanks, Top Dog," Mateo said.

The lads turned to Fell, and as he got hugs, too, the smile-crease in his cheek erased his deadly expression. He was so good with the cubs.

Well, okay, so was Patrin...even with dominance streaming off him. Or, partly because of it. Pups felt safer with an authoritative wolf in charge. It was part of being canine.

Probably part of why her inner wolf craved being dominated.

Yes, she was a mess.

As the cubs rocketed out of the apartment, she smiled at Fell. "If you two want another cooking lesson, come on over. Maybe in an hour?"

---

Cleaning up wasn't nearly as fun as cooking, Fell thought as he wiped down the counters. Still, it was rather pleasant. Moya had put on some music—something she called Abba—that was full of energy.

At the sink, Patrin scrubbed pots while she put away the condiments.

There were no leftovers to put away. They'd cooked then devoured the one-pot chicken and rice dish, enjoying the Spanish seasonings.

Satisfaction filled Fell. He'd done most of the actual cooking while Patrin chopped vegetables for the salad. He was pretty sure he could make this dish again—even with the interesting Spanish spice mixture. "Does your mother live in town?"

"No." Moya turned from the fridge. "She fell for a couple of males who were visiting the west, and when they returned to Colorado, she went with them."

Patrin set a pot in the drainer and looked over his shoulder at her. "Do you stay in touch?"

"Oh, we call each other every month and write now and then. It's wonderful to see her in love and having fun." Her smile at the thought of her mother was fond.

With an effort, Fell pushed away the memory of their mother. How she died. For a minute, he scrubbed at a stubborn spot on the counter. *In the past, wolf, it's in the past.*

Finished cleaning, he turned to see what was left to be done.

Singing, "Take a chance on me", Moya was putting away the spices in a cupboard.

Finished washing, Patrin dried his hands, his gaze on how Moya's hips were rocking side-to-side with the beat of the music.

Fell was watching too. She had a gorgeously rounded ass, and when it moved like that? Nice. So were the full breasts beneath her bright pink top. He couldn't help thinking of her pinned between him and Patrin as they did their best to please her. Of how she would feel around him...

With a huff of exasperation, he yanked his gaze away. *No, wolf.* She was a friend. Mating wasn't in the equation, no matter how much he'd enjoy it.

As she hummed, the corners of her mouth tipped upward as if she was smiling to herself. Made him want to kiss each side and see if her smile deepened.

No, what the fuck was he thinking?

By the Gods, his thoughts were out of control.

Patrin saw the flush on his brother's fair skin and almost laughed. Because he knew exactly what Fell had been thinking about.

*Same*.

She was so very tempting, all soft curves and laughter. But no, it was more than that. She was...kind. Yes, that was part of it. She certainly didn't have to be teaching them to cook—or helping them learn some of the subtleties of the Daonain ways.

Part of it was her sense of humor, so much like his own. And her intelligence. And the way she was trying to get over her handicap.

Speaking of which...

He waited until she looked at him, then stalked forward, holding her gaze. Fuck, she had the most beautiful brown eyes, so dark and—

*Dominance, wolf, think dominance.* He leaned into her space, just enough to trigger fear. His voice came out in a growl. "You should come with me and—"

"*No.*" Her hands fisted, but she didn't hit him. Instead, she set her palms on his chest and pushed. He resisted for a second.

Her eyes stayed clear and steady. Even if her fingers trembled slightly, she was in control.

"Very good, little wolf." He bent slightly, testing to see if she stayed firm against panicking. His face was close to hers. Close enough to kiss her. But that would be way out of line. His desire could and would be controlled.

He tugged on her hair, smiled, and backed away. "You're improving."

Although he caught the tiniest hint of interest in her scent, the smell of fear drowned it out.

Would that change during the full moon?

## CHAPTER EIGHT

*Dark of the moon, Rainier Territory*

From behind the coffee counter, Fell spotted his brother strolling around the town square. He'd wanted to walk around Ailill Ridge to see if he could spot the Scythe operative.

Fell shook his head. Having snowed yesterday, it was a cold time to be wandering around.

It was good Patrin was almost done. Ailill Ridge had a Daonain curfew of sunset for the dark of the moon—and according to Moya, the scent of a hellhound had been caught in the area. The Cosantir had sent out warnings to the clan.

Fell glanced outside once again, noting the decrease in light. Sunset was in a little over an hour. He needed to get the coffee shop closed down, and they'd both get their tails up to the apartment before dark. Or to the Shamrock, which was where Moya said she'd hole up for the night.

Yeah, they'd probably go wherever she was. Face it, she brought out every protective instinct in his body. Over the last five days, she'd continued to meet with him—just to talk. It was a relief Patrin now had the job of desensitizing her to being frightened.

He'd been surprised when she followed through on her offer to teach them to cook. For three evenings, she'd given them lessons—and had supper with them.

Except for last night when she had a book club meeting in her store. Such an interesting idea, a group getting together to simply discuss a book. Moya had invited them to join the discussions. Apparently, every Thursday a different club met. And she'd left a book called *Dune* that she said would be discussed at the science fiction-fantasy group.

Patrin had turned her down. His reading tended to be nonfiction and only when he needed to know something.

Fell, though, was enjoying *Dune*. And it sucked that he was interested in the discussion but would undoubtedly fail at trying to speak. Even so, he was working on it. If the little wolf could put up with being terrified over and over, he could damn well get past a simple inability to talk.

This near to closing, the coffee shop was almost empty, except for the table in the center of the room. Looked like a meeting of the heads of the Daonain. The Cosantir sat between his two brothers, Niall, the cahir, and Madoc who owned the Shamrock. Across from André was the cahir Chief of Police shoulder-to-shoulder with one of her officers named Duffy.

Fell had been in town long enough to be able to recognize the four Elders—Schumacher, Ina Donnelly, and the mated grocers, Murtagh and Maeve.

They all looked fucking serious. Probably because of the hellhound.

Come to think of it, this town had only two cahirs. Didn't taking down a hellhound need more than just the two? From what he'd heard, demon dogs were nearly impossible to kill.

Female voices came from the bookstore area where Heather

was keeping Moya company as the little wolf went through her closing checklist. Then Moya's laughter rang out so infectiously Fell's mouth tipped up.

Did she laugh when mating? Or maybe she fell into her cute throaty giggles? He wondered. And hoped, maybe, to find out one day.

The door opened, the bell jingling, as Patrin came in, crossed the room, and leaned on the coffee shop counter. "You nearly done?"

Fell worked on cleaning the espresso machine grates. "About. Got a floor to mop." The cash drawer had been counted out, fridge and rest of the equipment wiped down. "When they're gone."

The group still had a few minutes before the three o'clock closing. Tilting his head, Fell listened to see if they were winding down their meeting.

Eventually, he'd have Patrin inform André about the quirk in the room's acoustics that let any keen-eared shifter behind the counter hear what was discussed at the center table.

Meantime, he got to hear useful gossip.

Resting his forearms on the counter, Fell listened.

"No, my nephew, you can't be bait," Bron said in her rough voice. "You're still limping from spraining your ankle yesterday, Niall. Being bait means *outrunning* a hellhound, not *feeding* it. I'll be bait and lead it to our trap."

The big blond cahir scowled. "And what am I supposed to do? Hibernate while our clan gets slaughtered?"

"Protect the square." Madoc slapped his brother's shoulder. "Like the last one, this hellhound has been sniffing the downtown area. If it attacks here, you're the only one who has a chance of intervening if it goes after someone. I can provide a diversion if needed."

By the Gods. A hellhound loose downtown? Fell's mouth went dry.

## BONDS OF THE WOLF

Patrin walked around the counter to join him.

"Maybe get help to ensure the demon dog finds Bron," Ina added. "We don't want it catching a scent elsewhere and leaving downtown."

"I'm sure we can find volunteers. Especially since we don't want them to fight the hellhound." Murtagh wrinkled up his bulldog face. "I'm concerned about it possibly getting out of the trap—or not falling in."

"Someone could wait on the far side with something heavy to bash the hellhound into the pit if it overjumps or tries to climb out." Madoc frowned. "Maybe I should do that instead."

"As wide as the hole is, it will require two people, one on each of the far corners." André straightened. "I will be one of them."

"No, you will not." Ina's objection was echoed by the other Elders.

André's eyes darkened. "I—"

"Cosantir. There's a reason the God gave us cahirs for enforcers and Cosantirs to lead." Schumacher, the banker, spoke in a diplomatic tone. "The territory is still recovering from Pete Wendell's bad leadership. We cannot afford to lose you."

André looked as pissed off as a winter-starved wolverine.

But the Elders were right. Cosantirs were guarded, not risked.

"I'll take the other side," the other cop at the table said. Duffy was an older male, probably in his eighties. Short and lean.

*By the Gods, what a bad idea.* Fell rubbed his mouth, wanting to speak out. The officer might have the heart, but he lacked the mass to be effective. A hellhound was supposedly heavy as a tank and armored to boot.

Fell turned his head slightly. Yeah, Patrin was already looking at him, one eyebrow raised.

Maybe volunteering was for idiots, but how the fuck could they let this kind of disaster happen? Protecting the clan was in their blood. He nodded.

"Excuse us, please, Cosantir." Patrin smiled as everyone at the table turned. "First, I feel you should know that the acoustics in this room make conversation from that table audible to any shifter behind the counter."

Fell had to smother a laugh as the Elder, especially, realized what Patrin meant.

After a slight narrowing of his eyes, André tilted his head. "Thank you for the information. We will be more discreet in the future." He paused and said, "Did you have a second point?"

"I did." Patrin nudged Fell's shoulder in the way they had from when they were cubs. The bump said they were going to do something risky and stupid, and such was life. "Show us what you have in mind. Fell and I will guard the far corners of the trap. We have the training and the build for it."

There were shocked expressions at the table and then...by the Gods, the relief on their faces sent a wave of warmth through Fell's heart.

*They need us.*

How long had it been since he'd looked past vengeance to... being part of something.

To belonging?

---

Sitting in the middle of a pile of blankets from her apartment, Moya tried not to shiver like a new cubling. Around her in the Shamrock Restaurant, others were forming their own blanket piles or sitting at tables and talking.

Her? She couldn't keep from staring out at the town square and worrying.

Not too much about herself. The iron bars over the windows of the Shamrock Restaurant appeared decorative, but Moya had briefly wrapped her hands around them and knew how sturdy they were. No hellhound would get through them.

The last time there'd been a hellhound in town, soon after

André became Cosantir, she and Talitha had huddled together in this restaurant. Neither of them wanted to hole up at the pack house. But having a view of the square had been terrifying. Seeing the cahirs—and the Cosantir and Madoc—fighting the hellhound... The yells, the blood, then the cubs fleeing.

By the Hunter and the Mother, it had been ghastly to watch and not be able to do *anything* to help.

This time was worse, because Patrin and Fell, along with Ramón and Zorion, were out there. Her gnome-brain brothers had volunteered to ensure the hellhound headed directly to the square where Bron would be waiting. Dammit, they weren't superstrong cahirs or anything. Just normal shifters.

She was so proud of them—and terrified for them.

It was hard to be sitting here alone. Since no one wanted the cubs anywhere close to downtown, Talitha and Eileen were staying in their securely reinforced home with Mateo, Alvaro, and Heather's cubs, Sky and Talam.

"Moya. I was hoping you were here." Looking unsettled, Heather walked over.

"Are you all right?" Where was her lifemate, the Cosantir? Moya glanced around. André was moving through the room, reassuring those who'd taken refuge in the secured restaurant. "Want to join me?"

"Yes, please." Heather joined her on the blanket pile. "I was helping, but..."

But she got tired? That wouldn't stop Heather. "*Aaand* André ordered you to get off your feet?"

Heather huffed. "Yes, that."

"Good for him." Sympathy welling up in her heart, Moya slung an arm around her best friend and pulled her close. Two of Heather's three lifemates were out there with the hellhound. This would be a horribly long night. "Is the trap stuff all set up?"

"Yes." Heather grimaced and added, "At least this time, there shouldn't be any pixie-brained shifters wandering around."

"If nothing else, Portia learned a lesson." The female had ignored the warnings, walked to the grocery store with her two baby cubs, and frozen in fear at the sight of a hellhound. Heather almost died trying to get her to safety.

André had been furious. Now, a few months later, the shifters carefully observed the curfew, and nearly all the shifter-owned houses and businesses were reinforced and barricaded. Those taking refuge in the restaurant and pack house went more for company or, like Moya, to support someone.

As if hearing her thoughts, Heather looked down at her hands. "I'm glad you're here. Thank you."

Moya bumped their shoulders together. "Sure. I'd planned to be here for you. Then I didn't end up with a choice."

"What do you mean?"

"Before they joined the fighters, Patrin and Fell came to my place." Moya rolled her eyes. "And Patrin ordered me to spend the night at the restaurant."

"Ordered?" Heather—perhaps she wasn't such a great friend, after all—had her hand over her mouth. And the snickering came through loud and clear.

"Girl, I almost punched him."

At that, Heather laughed right out loud. "Instead, here you are."

"Yes, here I am." When she tried to close her door on pushy Patrin, Fell had grabbed her collar to drag her here. A second later, he stopped and explained how much they would worry if she was alone.

The effort the harsh hunter made to use his words had wiped out her anger. Then authoritative, dangerous Patrin had carried her stack of blankets to the restaurant just to be sure she was comfortable.

The two males who'd worried about her safety were outside now in the dark and cold. Her eyes burned. They'd barely gotten free from the Scythe, and their whole future lay before them.

And instead, they were risking their lives for a clan they barely knew.

She wanted to run out there, drag them inside for safety, stand in front of them. Protect them like they seemed to think they should protect everyone else.

And she *couldn't*.

---

"This'd be more enjoyable in the summer." Patrin kept his grumble to a bare murmur. To avoid leaving any tracks, he and Fell had circled around the tree groves on each side to reach the pit trap. Now in place, they couldn't move. Icy crust covered the few inches of snow on the ground and crunched audibly with any movement.

The noisy snow did have one benefit—they'd hear anything moving around. Like a hellhound.

The pit trap was cunningly set up in the riverside park that abutted the town square. If the hellhound showed up, Bron would let it see her and then run, inciting its instinct to chase fleeing prey. She'd lead the hellhound to the park and jump the trap.

Hinged covers over the deep pit were just strong enough to hold a light covering of leaves and snow. Under a hellhound's weight, they'd give way.

It'd be good *if* the plan worked.

Most tactical plans for battle didn't.

The downtown lights cast just enough illumination that Patrin could see his brother's dark shape on the other side of the trap, huddled in a mass of evergreen huckleberries. His head lifted, showing the glint of his eyes. His response barely reached Patrin's ears. "Good thing Bron had the warmers."

They were properly bundled up, and Bron had given them hand and foot warmers. Apparently, Canadians were experienced in cold weather.

Overall, Patrin preferred cold to hot, and snow to rain. Wet fur was quite uncomfortable. But long periods of immobility in the cold required more patience than his animal nature enjoyed.

Then again, he could end up stuck patrolling the square with a bum ankle like Niall was.

Moya was probably perched on her pile of blankets. It would've been a treat for him and Fell to join her. Just the thought of being with her warmed him. Aye, she was a far-too-tempting female. And more.

The cooking lessons had been lessons in self-control. Seeing the way her lips would tilt up when she was amused at something they did... Gods, just brushing against her in the kitchen, against those full hips and breasts gave him a half-chubby.

Tonight, she'd noticed him looking at her ass. And simply laughed. Her coconut-scented fragrance had held tantalizing hints of her interest. She wanted him, even if he did scare her. Her fears were disappearing as she got to know him, and damn, that felt good.

He wanted to cup that gorgeous ass in his hands, to pull her against him, to kiss her—and lick her and...

*Yeah, one step too far, slug-wit.* Now he'd be freezing out here with a hard-on.

With a sigh, he settled in.

"Gods help us, it's a hellhound!" Moya's brother, Zorion, had a distinctive voice—and was obviously trying to sound like terrified prey.

---

Perched on top of a house just south of the square, Ramón scowled down at the monster beast below. The streetlights glinted off the pointed armor plates covering the thing. It was huge—and gods, the stench, like week-old carrion, was nauseating.

It was supposed to be moving toward the town square—and

Bron—not sniffing around a house. Especially a place where the door didn't appear nearly sturdy enough. Across the alley, Zorion waited on another roof, a black shadow against the snow-covered shingles. His shout hadn't been enough to capture the hellhound's interest, not with it almost pressed against the front door of the house, focused on the homeowner's scent.

He and Zorion were too high up for the monster to catch their scent.

When the door creaked, his keen ears caught the squeak of fear from inside.

Ramón's protective instincts surged. If it needed a shifter's scent, he'd give it one. He dropped over the side, gloved hands sliding on the downspout to slow his fall. He landed noisily—and not nearly as gracefully as any feline. Wolves weren't meant to be jumping around on roofs, he thought in disgust.

The hellhound turned at the sound.

"Nooo!" Ramón let out a yell of fear—*c'mon, you stupid monster*—and took off running. *Look, easy prey*.

He glanced over his shoulder.

The hellhound's nose was up in the air, and without warning, it charged after Ramón. Gods, it was faster than he'd expected.

Heart pounding, he put his head down and ran, full out—and it was catching up to him. He could almost feel those sharp teeth tearing at him.

*Faster, wolf.*

"Yo, demon dog. Bite *this*!" Zorion's taunting yell came from above, and something crashed from behind. He must have found something to throw at the hellhound to slow it down.

There was the opening to the square. He could see Bron ahead.

With a flash, Zorion appeared, hanging from a balcony railing like a monkey, holding his hand down.

Ramón leaped. Their hands caught, and Zorion swung him up.

Before the hellhound could stop, Bron started to shout.

Panting, drenched in sweat, Ramón leaned against Zorion in their precarious perch. "Thanks, brawd." Fuck, for a few seconds there, he'd been pretty sure he was dead meat.

Down in the alley, the hellhound stopped right below them—and then an axe bounced off its armor.

---

Crouched in the bushes, Patrin listened to the shouts of Moya's brothers, then heard Bron's higher yell.

There was a snarl and a yelp.

He grinned. The Chief had said if the hellhound focused on someone else, she would get its attention—and she'd patted her holstered axe.

A moment later, she screamed, long and loud. More snarling sounded.

Listening hard, Patrin heard the thumps of boots on the brick-lined square. Someone was running. Coming this way.

*Here we go.*

He yanked off his stocking cap, then his gloves. He got a good grip on the lead-cored baseball bat. It was heavy enough to carry a hell of a punch.

Eyes on the path, he performed a few quick squats to ensure his blood was moving and his joints were loose. Across from him, shadows moved as his brother did the same.

Bron let out another scream. Her footsteps were coming closer—and now Patrin could hear the heavy thudding of the hellhound's paws.

*Don't move.*

He watched through the underbrush as the female cahir sprinted faster than he'd have believed possible. And there was the...*demon dog* was the right term.

Fuck, the thing was the size of a grizzly. Light glinted off its

## BONDS OF THE WOLF

skin—no, off something akin to armor plating. Gods, he hadn't really believed Niall's descriptions of the beast.

If it didn't land in the trap, they were screwed. No, not screwed—*dead*.

His hands tightened on the bat; his muscles tensed.

Bron reached the edge of the snow-covered trap, the edge delineated by a branch sticking up through the snow. She leaped and came down halfway across the concealed pit. Her foot landed on the mark indicating where the horizontal bar held the hinged coverings in place, and she sprang to the other side of the trap. She made it—and kept fleeing like prey.

Only a few feet behind, the hellhound bounded after her. Its next leap carried it to the center of the trap, and dammit, one paw landed on the *bar*. As planned, the trap gave way, and the hellhound fell—

*Fuck!* It had gained enough impetus for its front paws to catch the far edge of the pit. Long vicious foreclaws dug into the ground, and it started pulling itself up.

*Move. Now.* Lunging forward, Patrin swung.

Red eyes fixed on him, and the shark-like muzzle opened wide, fangs exposed. *So fucking many teeth.* The demon dog hoisted itself partway out of the pit and snapped at Patrin's leg.

His heavy pants tore like tissue. Shouting, he swung the heavy bat around to hit the hellhound's chest with a solid thunk.

Almost dislodged, hind feet scrambling against the trap wall, it dug its foreclaws into the ground for purchase.

The edge of the pit where Patrin stood crumbled. Unbalanced, he teetered.

"No!" Grabbing Patrin's collar, Fell yanked him back, then slammed his bat at the demon dog's head.

With a snarl, the hellhound fell back into the trap, and then a gut-wrenching shriek split the air as it was impaled on the long iron spikes lining the bottom of the deep pit. The only place the hellhounds lacked armor was a strip on the belly.

*By the Gods.* With a shudder, Patrin took another step back before glancing at his brother. "Thanks." Without him, Patrin might well have been skewered right along with the hellhound.

Fell slapped his shoulder in answer.

"Well done, lads." Bron joined them and drew her pistol. But the hellhound had gone silent.

She shined a flashlight down to illuminate the huge creature and the blood pooling beneath it. The eyes were lifeless, and a few seconds later, it turned human.

"Very well done." She toed the claw marks at the edge of the trap. "Thank Herne, you were here. That was too close."

Patrin pulled in a breath, feeling his heart start to slow . "Glad to help." He smiled as the first glimmer of sunrise showed along the top of the mountain. "Looks like the night is over."

The hellhound was dead. The shifters in the territory were safe.

A little wolf named Moya was safe. Satisfaction filled his soul.

He slapped Fell's shoulder. "Let's go find something to eat."

---

It'd been an unnervingly long night. Moya had spent part of it talking with Heather and other shifters who'd holed up in the Shamrock.

A few of the pack were there. Quintrell and Quenbie. Katherine. Jens. Most of the wolves stayed in their own homes or were at the pack house with the alpha and beta.

Another wolf, Glenys, was here with her two newborns. Holding tiny Gruffudd and Cadfan had been the best part of Moya's night. Baby cublings were so precious.

The rest of the time, she'd curled up on the blanket pile and stared out into the darkness.

Until just a few minutes ago when she'd heard her brothers yelling. At the hellhound. Gods, sure, she knew that was the plan, that they were to lure the demon dog to the square. She still wanted to smack them and ask, *What were you thinking?*

And then the monster had appeared as moving shadows, stalking Niall. In an alley nearby, Madoc watched, prepared to step in.

At the window, André had hissed—and everyone in the Shamrock had gone completely silent.

A minute ago, Moya had barely managed to smother a whimper at the sight of Bron stepping out from between two buildings. Facing the hellhound, the Chief shouted and threw her axe. The monster had yelped and turned away from Niall. Screaming, Bron had run straight toward the riverside park.

The hellhound had chased after her. Heading for where the shifter-soldiers were stationed at the trap.

*Oh Gods, Patrin, Fell, be safe.*

Just then, something gave a hair-raising shriek—and then there was silence.

Her hands clenched so hard her knuckles hurt.

At the front of the Shamrock, André started to open the door.

Beside Moya, Heather gave a squeak but couldn't rise fast enough. Moya scrambled to her feet, sprinted over, and slammed her shoulder against the door before André could get through.

"No, Cosantir," she managed to say and held firm as his eyes darkened.

"I'm sorry, André." Heather joined them and took his arm. "I know. Waiting makes me more irritable than a mother moose. But this is our job tonight."

He murmured a long string of words in French, and Moya had a feeling none of them were suitable for cub ears. Finally, he muttered, "I do not like this job." With a sigh, he put his arms around Heather.

"My poor cat." Heather raised on tiptoes to kiss his jaw, then snuggled into his arms.

As envy sent sharp fangs deep into her chest, Moya turned and went back to her blanket pile. Alone.

The memory of the gruesome shriek sent another shiver up her spine.

Because out there with a hellhound were two shifter-soldiers whom she was coming to care for.

*Mother of All, watch over them.*

---

Fell was ready for a fucking nap. And something warm.

Instead, with help from Zorion and Ramón, he climbed down into the pit to rope the dead hellhound and help lift the carcass off the iron spikes. What a gory mess that was.

To his relief, Officer Duffy was ready at the top with a tarp, and he hauled the bloody body away.

Thank fuck, the police here were shifter and not human.

"Go on back to the Shamrock and warm up," Ramón said to him and Patrin. "We've been moving around and aren't all that cold. You look frozen."

Zorion nodded. "We're going to cover the pit before anyone manages to fall in by accident."

"We can help," Patrin said.

"Nah, we got this." Ramón grinned. "We built the damn thing, after all."

Right, construction contractors.

Zorion returned their bats. "Nice job. In summer, our crew has scrub baseball games with whatever players are around. You'll have to join us."

Fell had to laugh at that. The Moreno brothers were much like their sister, dealing as needed with the dark but moving on to the light.

"Sure," Patrin said with a half-smirk at Fell. Because the last time they'd played had been in Dogwood when they were twelve.

He hoped they would be here long enough to play a game. Doubtful.

Silently, he walked with Patrin and Bron through the park and across the town square. His body was exhausted, yet his nerves still twittered like a pixie in cherry season.

At the door of the Shamrock, Niall waved them in. "Sorry. I know you probably want sleep, but the Cosantir needs a report."

A corner of Patrin's lip tipped up, and he muttered to Fell, "Don't they always?"

Leaning his bat against the wall, Fell nodded cynically. The Scythe higher-ups assigning missions had expected face-to-face reports from their "creatures".

Then he remembered the coffee shop and what they'd heard. Keeping his voice low, he told Patrin, "André would've been out there if they'd let him."

Patrin's step faltered, and the bitter twist to his mouth disappeared. "Yeah, he would've."

"They're not the Scythe." The tightness eased from around Fell's ribs. Killing never felt good, but this time...this time, it'd been to protect their people.

To protect—

"Fell!" He was attacked by a small whirlwind named Moya.

She hugged him hard, arms strong, breasts soft, filling the air with her energy and fragrance. "I was so worried."

"I..." His words dried up, and he glanced over at his brother in hope of help.

Only to see the sadness in Patrin's face. Maybe even envy for a hug freely given.

It hadn't happened often. Gathering matings were pure sex, no affection involved. And Darcy always hugged them whenever they made it to Cold Creek, but she was their sister.

Had he ever had a hug simply because someone worried about him?

Slowly, gently, Fell wrapped his arms around Moya and hugged back, tilting his head so he could press his cheek to the top of her head. Mmm, he could stay like this forever.

Before he managed to force himself to let go, André walked over. "Since many of us were awake all night with watching and worrying, we plan to spend the morning sleeping in a pile, taking comfort from being with the others." He motioned toward large blanket and cushion piles scattered around the room. "After you give your report, we'd like you to join us."

"Ah..." Fell checked Patrin who appeared just as dumbstruck.

Pulling back, Moya studied Fell's expression. Her gaze was soft as she patted his chest and smiled at Patrin. "Come and join a puppy pile. You'll like it."

Fell didn't have the willpower to say no to her. Not after that hug.

To his surprise, Patrin said, his voice almost rusty, "All right."

The confused expressions on the shifter-soldiers' faces almost broke Moya's heart.

Sitting by the other wolves, she watched as André took them away to talk to Niall and Bron for a few minutes.

After the discussion, Patrin and Fell studied the room, the growing heap of furry bodies, glanced at each other—and moved toward the door.

With a sigh of understanding, she rose. It'd been years since she'd come here, a stranger to the town, but she sure remembered the awkward feeling of not belonging.

*No, my darling males, you don't get to escape.*

She cut them off and took Fell's hand. They'd touched enough in the past days that it didn't even seem strange. Although it was best if she didn't think about the zing when his strong fingers closed around hers.

Or the glint in his eyes when he looked at her.

When she looked up at Patrin, his expression was unreadable.

But his eyes... How those dark eyes held something approaching hurt made her ache inside.

Without letting herself panic, she took his hand too.

A second of shock showed in his gaze before he carefully gripped her hand. "Lead on, little wolf. We're at your command."

*As if.* Not with all that dominance still streaming off him. But it was nice he was willing to play along. She smirked at the two. "This is as it should be."

And had to ignore his low chuckle.

She took them to her wide blanket pile where Niall and Madoc had curled around Heather, leaving a space for André and their aunt, Bron.

Moya's brothers had shown up a minute ago and settled in with a few of their construction crew, including Orla, one of their two werecats, and Finnbarr, their bear. Undoubtedly hearing Moya, Zorion lifted his head, ears perking forward. He eyed her, Patrin, and Fell—and simply went back to sleep, using Ramón's flank as a pillow.

Letting go of the shifter-soldiers, she stripped briskly...and flushed at the masculine appreciation in their gazes.

Trawsfurring to wolf, she took a moment to savor the sweep of the Mother's love through her paws, and then picked a spot with room for the three of them.

When the two males didn't move, she whined and pawed the spot beside her.

"Bossy little wolf," Patrin muttered and started stripping.

"She is." Fell's lips tilted up. And he stripped and shifted.

Wow, she'd forgotten what big wolves they were—and how striking. Patrin so dark with lighter fur on his chest. In contrast, Fell's coat was a silvery gray, his facial markings pure white. So pretty.

They stepped onto the blankets as cautiously as traveling over a nest of snakes. *Too funny.* They thought nothing of fighting a hellhound but were anxious about a puppy pile.

She used her nose to nudge Fell over next to her brothers, then tapped her paw beside him for Patrin.

Mr.-Alpha-Without-Being-Alpha padded over and curled into a ball by his brother.

There, all arranged. With a happy sigh...and a shiver of anxiety at being so close to Patrin...she circled her spot and lay down beside the two of them, her muzzle on Fell's foreleg, her rump nestled against Patrin's shoulder.

Fell's breathing had slowed. He was already falling asleep.

Slowly, Patrin was following as he relaxed under the spell of a puppy pile.

Because a puppy pile meant safety and belonging.

---

Oddly enough, Patrin wasn't wakened by a nightmare as usual, but by something heavy pressing on his flank. He blinked and lifted heavy eyelids to see sunlight glinting around the edges of huge black shades. *Where...?*

He was in Madoc's restaurant. Right.

A breath brought him a myriad of scents—all close by. None with any anger or aggression. He lifted his head slightly.

A cougar lay against his feet—André. Another furry body warmed his back.

Facing him, the little wolf was curled in a small space between him and Fell, her head on one of Patrin's paws.

Moya was here; Fell was here. All was right in his world.

The contented fragrance of the animals around him filled the air, sending him back to sleep.

## CHAPTER NINE

Sitting down across from Heather at a window table in Espresso Books, Moya could swear her aching feet sighed with gratitude. *What a long day.*

She took a sip of hot chocolate, closed her eyes, and hummed in happiness,

"Listen to you." Laughing, Talitha flipped the sign on the door to CLOSED and joined them with her own food and drink.

There was nothing like having leftover pastries to snack on. "Hey, it was a long night, and my tail was dragging. I deserve to finish my workday with chocolate and sweets."

"Oh, no, she's using her puppy pout on us." Heather grinned and nibbled on the fruit tart.

"You know, it seems like forever since the three of us were together," Heather said.

"I miss our mini-pack days," Moya admitted.

"Me too." Talitha picked up her cinnamon bun. "Although I can't regret having Mateo and Alvaro as our cubs. Thank you both for bringing us together."

Heather smiled. "I'm glad you have them—and we appreciated

you cub-sitting Sky and Talam last night. They sure didn't need to hear Bron screaming or see the hellhound."

"I wish I hadn't," Moya admitted. *Seeing the monster chase the Chief. Its scream as it died.* "Every time I think of that hellhound, I start shaking." Her drink made waves against the edge of the cup like a surf against a breakwater.

Heather held out her hand, showing her fingers trembling.

"Next time, you two should join us and the cubs at the house," Talitha said.

The thought was awfully tempting. Then again, how could she not be close enough to help if there was need?

"I think watching is almost harder than being out there," Heather grumbled.

"Sure sounded like it." Moya smiled at Talitha. "Madoc fed everyone breakfast and all the shifters who went up against the hellhound were comparing notes on what they'd done—and were laughing their heads off. I swear, those males are as crazy as a passel of pixies—and Bron is just as bad."

"I can't even imagine," Talitha muttered. "I'm so glad Eileen has a non-dangerous job."

Moya snickered. "As long as she doesn't annoy whatever animal she's taking pictures of. Didn't a *real* bear attack her once?"

"She's had a few near disasters. But she doesn't go out expecting to be in a fight." Talitha gave Heather a concerned look. "Are you comfortable with Niall being a cahir?"

Cahirs were the first defense for the Daonain against humans, feral shifters, and hellhounds. It was good the God made them bigger and stronger.

Heather set her hand on her stomach. "I get scared for him, but being protective is who he is right down to his soul and why Herne called him. How could I object?"

"Last night went great though. To success!" Moya held up her cup, and the others tapped theirs against hers.

"Speaking of which," Heather said, "a couple of cahirs from

Cold Creek are visiting tomorrow to see the trap and talk over how the hellhound was funneled to the bait."

It'd worked so much better than the first time when Heather's foster-children, Sky and Talam, almost died. Moya shuddered and turned her thoughts to something happy. "Which cahirs are coming?"

"Ben—a grizzly—and he's bringing his lifemate, Emma, who is a bard. They're spending tomorrow night here." Heather smiled. "We wanted Emma to talk with Sky about being a bard."

"Wonderful. He's learned about everything I can teach him about playing the guitar. I'm sure no bard." Moya smiled, remembering the cub's enthusiasm. "Only Ben, or is there another cahir coming?"

"Owen—a cat—and his lifemate, Darcy."

Darcy. The name was familiar. "Patrin and Fell's sister?" Moya bounced in her chair. "Ooooh, I bet her brothers go all big-over-protective-littermates on her tail." Patrin would be full of bossy advice, and Fell might even speak a few more words.

"Of course they will." Talitha tapped her chin. "Heather, if we have a bard here, do you think we could get her to sing? Maybe we could have a kind of party—a post-hellhound one?"

"Oh, yes." Moya leaned forward. "Perhaps call it *Celebrating Our Heroes*. I know Bron and Niall are cahirs and expect to risk their lives, but they deserve thanks. And so do Madoc, Duffy, Patrin, Fell, and my brothers. They went above and beyond."

Heather tilted her head. "You know, you're right. André loves having reasons to bring the Daonain together for something other than Gatherings. Especially with the colder weather. A thank-you party to celebrate victory—with a bard and dancing? It's perfect.

"Tomorrow is Sunday, so the stores and the Shamrock and Bullwhacker will be closed. More people will be able to come."

"If we have it at *Calon*, we can restrict it to just shifters." Talitha rubbed her hands together. "We can open the entire warehouse up. The portable dividers for the rooms are easy enough to move."

The Cosantir had converted the warehouse behind the Shamrock restaurant into a Daonain community center. One of the Welsh-speaking Elders titled it something long and unpronounceable of which only the one word, *Calon*, meaning heart or center, had stuck.

Moya finished off her hot chocolate. "Among the three of us, we'll be able to get everyone invited. Ask people to bring food and drink, drop off decorations, and/or show up early if they want to help decorate."

After Madoc's giant brunch, Patrin and Fell had disappeared, but she could push a note under their door.

Would they come? What with having been imprisoned by the Scythe, they might never have been to a Daonain dance.

Even as scary as he was to her personally, Patrin was pretty sociable. Not Fell. Yet he'd looked different this morning when he woke up in the puppy pile. Less...watchful?

The shifter-soldiers had been isolated from their people for far too long. Now, she'd just have to grab them by their ruffs and pull them into another activity to show them another way they belonged.

Because they did, even if they didn't realize it yet.

# CHAPTER TEN

Patrin eyed the huge brick building behind the Shamrock Restaurant. Must have been used as a warehouse at one time, considering the location. A sign hung over the door with the word *Calon* in elaborate calligraphy.

Apparently, the place was used as a community center for all sorts of shifter activities. The homeschool, crafting meetings, sports. And events like this.

"I've socialized enough today," Fell muttered beside him.

Patrin grinned. He really had.

There'd been a meeting with the two cahirs from Cold Creek, one of which was Darcy's mate Owen. With Bron, Niall, Madoc, and Moya's brothers, they'd had a good discussion about hellhounds. Owen and Ben had some fucking gory stories.

Then in the afternoon, he and Fell talked with Darcy. She was happy. Involved in her new town, repairing everything in sight—because she was a born tinker. And she was head-over-paws in love with her lifemates, Owen and Gawain.

Her life was everything he and Fell wanted for her. Just seeing the glow on her face made him happy too.

Although she'd brought up something that'd been nagging at

him. *"Once you've killed the Scythe, what will you and Fell do? Will you finally settle into a territory? Maybe the North Cascades Territory so I can see you?"*

He had no answer for her. Wasn't sure he and Fell could quit—or if they'd just go on killing with Wells as their boss. The view of their possible future seemed...gray. Dark.

Shaking his head didn't remove the dismal thoughts.

Patrin stopped in front of the warehouse door. "Okay, brawd, let's get this done."

Fell made a sound of agreement and pulled open the door.

Hearing music and voices, Patrin felt his muscles tighten. Parties were still unfamiliar ground. They'd been to a couple at the Elder Village when they'd first been freed, then Darcy's housewarming, and André's. All had been in houses with people coming and going.

This felt as if it would be a lot bigger.

A guard stood inside a small entry room that blocked access to the rest of the building. He frowned. "I'm sorry, lads, but this is a —" His nostrils flared. "Ah, you're shifters, sorry. I don't think we've met. Would you happen to be the two Moya said might be along?"

"Maybe." Patrin touched his chest. "Patrin, and he's Fell."

"Aye now, you're the ones." With a pleased nod, the guard opened the door. "Your courage with the demon dog is appreciated."

Patrin glanced at Fell. The befuddled expression probably matched Patrin's. Appreciation hadn't been much in their experience. "Ah, our pleasure?"

The guard let out a loud laugh and slapped Patrin's back. "Sure it was. You have a good time tonight."

If Patrin had been in wolf form, his fur would be puffing out. He was comfortable with new experiences if they involved travel or blood and death. Social events?

*Terrifying.*

Fell glanced at him and muttered, "Can we go home now?"

"Hmm..." Patrin stopped to seriously consider it.

With a snort of laughter, Fell shoved him through the door, staying behind, the cowardly mutt.

A few steps into the room, Patrin had to stop to get oriented.

The place was fucking huge—and glittered like a colorful blizzard had swept through. Tiny lights were strung around the doors and windows. Blue and silver tinsel garlands adorned the walls. Giant paper snowflakes dangled from the ceiling beams.

At the far end, tables were loaded down with food. A huge punch bowl was probably the origin of the orange, cinnamon, and cloves perfuming the air.

Whiffs of pine came from tall floor vases filled with evergreen branches.

In the center of the room, a small, two-foot-high, circular stage was decorated with more garlands. A fiddle and guitar leaned against chairs. A flute lay on another chair. Next to it was a mid-size Celtic harp and a bodhrán drum.

"Do you suppose Darcy is here yet?" Patrin looked for their sister. She wouldn't be easy to find.

People filled the room, some seated at chairs and tables near the walls, the rest standing in the center. Rather than the *let's-fuck*, sexy attire for full moon gatherings, everyone wore what he thought of as festival clothing, a lively fusion of medieval and modern clothing.

Thankfully, he and Fell were attired appropriately in full-sleeved, belted tunics over dark jeans and suede boots. Women either wore the same or were in calf-length, floaty dresses that made him think of what the Fae might have worn.

"Patrin, Fell, you made it."

Patrin turned at the compelling sound of Moya's lilting voice. And his body froze.

She was so fucking beautiful. Her dark red dress had a full skirt and was not...quite...sheer, as if it was made of tissue paper.

Thin straps exposed most of her shoulders, but her thin sleeves were attached somehow, looking almost like she had butterfly wings. The top of the dress resembled a corset and pushed her full breasts up.

So much warm, glowing skin. So very touchable.

"Fuck me," he said under his breath, then smiled. "Good evening, Moya. Interesting party."

Her laugh lit her face. "You two look splendid. I'm impressed."

"The first festival we attended was at an Elder Village, and they insisted we needed festival clothing. They gifted us with the tunics and boots." Patrin glanced down at the dark blue fabric. When Maude handed it to him, he'd just...halted, unable to speak. The clothing fit perfectly and was hand-embroidered with dark green vines edging the sleeves and hem. That someone would take so much time for him had left him speechless.

"Elders. Of course they knew exactly what would suit you." Smiling, she took Fell's hand, pulling him behind her. "Come, Patrin. Let me show you where the food is."

Patrin blinked...because his taciturn brother had a half-smile on his face, obviously pleased with the affectionate way Moya had latched on to him.

*But not me. She didn't touch me.*

As the fiddler began to tune his instrument, Patrin frowned. What would it take to earn her trust?

Fell let Moya lead him around the room. Her hand felt so tiny in his. As her shoulder brushed against his arm, he had to resist the urge to pull her closer.

Hell, what was he thinking? No female wanted a male like him. Honestly, it was a wonder he was even still alive—and his future sure wasn't likely to be long.

"You spent time in the human world. Did you ever go to human parties?" Moya asked him and Patrin. "Are they like ours?"

"We attended a few." Patrin shot Fell a look that showed he was trying to figure out how to edit his words.

Fell understood. Talking about their missions wasn't a good subject for a party. They were usually sent on assassinations that could be done out in nature, so the deaths were attributed to wild animals. But not always. Sometimes they had to do research on the target beforehand, so their handlers occasionally took them to human events the target was attending.

Moya didn't need to know the history. Fell offered, "Human festivities are noisier, music and talk."

Especially the music. His ears would feel as if they were bleeding.

Patrin grabbed the conversational bone and ran with it. "The scents..." He wrinkled his nose. "The chemical stink of hair spray, the smelly perfumes and colognes they coat themselves in. And the strong deodorants. It was difficult to even breathe."

Fell grinned. "Gods, the stench." Shifters, with more sensitive noses, avoided anything with a harsh scent. Here, at a shifter party, the room smelled of the cinnamon punch, the evergreen boughs, the personal scent of shifters with the overlay of wildness, and the honey-like fragrance of the beeswax candles.

Nice. So much friendlier.

As they walked around the perimeter of the room, two shifters stepped up onto the stage, picked up a fiddle and a flute, and began to play. According to legend, Celtic tunes had been favorites of their Fae ancestors.

Shifters of all ages moved to the center of the room and formed dance circles. At the Elder village, he and Patrin had watched dancing without participating.

What would it be like to be part of it?

At the food-covered tables, Moya handed Fell and Patrin plates. "Take what looks good—or if you don't know what it is, I probably can tell you."

Fell held the plate for a moment, unsettled—and even more so when the white-haired female on the other side of the table smiled. Ina, one of the Elders who'd been in the coffee shop with André before the hellhound attack.

"Welcome. I'm Ina Donnelly. Are you Patrin or Fell?"

He bowed slightly. "Elder. I'm Fell."

Patrin smiled at her. "I'm Patrin."

"Thank you for your courage." Smiling, she handed them each a serving of what looked like a pastry but smelled like venison. "My grandcubs are your ages, and they adore these. See what you think."

Fell popped one in his mouth. The buttery, flaky pastry dough was stuffed with a savory mix of bacon, onion, and chopped venison. "Gods, yes," Fell muttered.

Beside him, Moya laughed infectiously. "Ina, give them more." Her smile faded slightly. "The crow-cursed Scythe didn't feed them anything except mush and stew, so they're still exploring the world of homemade food."

For a second, Ina looked both furious and sad, and then she dished up a bunch of easy to pick up foods—mushrooms filled with something seafoody, fried chicken in bite-sized portions, something that looked like pizza, but only three inches wide. More pastries followed by various small desserts like tiny frosting-covered cupcakes and cookies. The fruit tarts with whipped cream set Fell's mouth to watering. She glanced at Moya. "Meat and sweets—a guaranteed way to keep males happy."

Fell devoured a couple of chicken bites.

After nibbling the stuffed mushroom, Patrin almost inhaled them, then laughed. "I can't say you're wrong, Elder."

"Thank you, Ina." Rather than filling a plate, Moya picked up a couple of cookies. She'd never been able to resist Madoc's molasses cookies. Taking a bite, she had to stifle a moan.

*Yummy, chewy sweetness.*

"C'mon, you two." As they all moved away from the buffet, the brothers traded desserts until Patrin had anything with frosting, and Fell had anything containing fruit.

They'd never reminded her more strongly of little cubs. Smothering a laugh, she looked around. "Now where should we sit?"

"Hey, Moya, over here." A female sitting with several others beckoned. Her companions turned from watching the dancing.

When Fell tensed slightly, Moya patted his arm and pulled him along with her. "You already know my brothers and some of the others from the pack run. Brett's not here, thank the Mother."

Getting up, Ramón pulled three chairs over from a different table. "Here, sis."

To a chorus of greetings, Moya took a seat next to Alana. "For those of you who weren't at the pack run, this is Fell"—Moya pointed—"and Patrin. They're the two who bashed the hellhound back into the trap before it could climb out."

Damned if Fell knew what to do when people said thank you. After managing a bit of a smile in acknowledgement of the greetings, he busied himself taking a seat next to the Moreno brothers.

"Killing the hellhound was a group effort." Patrin sat down, a lot less uncomfortable than Fell, the boggart. "Like Ramón and Zorion leading the hellhound to the square so Bron could be bait."

Fell gave the Moreno littermates a nod of respect.

Zorion grinned. "You know, I've seen cahirs fight. Never realized just how fast they could run. The Chief was practically flying."

Moya laughed and started introducing the rest. Quite a few were in the Moreno construction crew. Names flew by—blonde

Alana and Jalen, one of her mates. More middle-aged Ena, Lucius, and Kane from the ranch and farm supply store.

Fell nodded at them, trying to fix names with faces.

"How nice, Moya decided to join her people for a change." Brett's nasally tenor had a snide edge that made every muscle in Fell's body tense.

Together, he and Patrin turned to face the new alpha.

Dressed in an eye-wateringly bright red tunic and leather pants, Brett moved to stand right next to Moya where she sat beside Alana. His beta, Caleb, took up a position on Moya's other side.

At the aggressive, territorial positioning, Patrin felt his muscles tense. Next to him, Ramón, Zorion, and Fell were growling, the sound drowned out by the music.

Patrin glanced at Moya's brothers and could see the conflict in their expressions. The alpha had control of the pack, which meant that, although they wanted to protect their sister, both the tradition of obedience to the alpha and the pack bonds themselves made it almost impossible. And if a shifter went against his alpha, he'd probably get kicked out of the territory.

Brett smirked at Moya. "I hear Talitha isn't living in the apartment across from you. Since you're all alone there, it's time for you to move into the pack house."

She shook her head.

"Not your choice, female." Bigger, beefier than Brett, Caleb slapped his hand on her shoulder, reminding Patrin of human movies and how cops treated a criminal.

"Wolves don't live alone, especially females." Brett crossed his arms over his chest, standing up taller. "Either you move in with lovers, or you move into the pack house."

"I have no problem with living alone. Thank you for your

concern." When Moya tried to push Caleb's hand away, he gripped her shoulder so tightly she winced.

*Enough of this scat.* As Patrin rose, he bumped into Caleb's torso.

The male staggered back a step.

"Oops, sorry." Patrin used his most charming smile and heard Fell's almost inaudible snort.

Free of Caleb's hand, Moya stood. Her hands weren't fisted, but she was so ready to fight, he could almost feel her vibrating.

Still sitting, Fell had drawn his feet back so he could spring into an attack if needed. He glanced at Caleb to show who his target would be.

Warmed at knowing his brother always had his back, Patrin nodded slightly. "I'm not sure I understand the problem here."

"Wolves get sick if they're alone too much." The way Brett puffed up his chest was like a rooster trying to look bigger.

*Great, the pack alpha is a fucking chicken.*

His argument was almost logical…if it hadn't been so obvious the alpha and beta wanted the little wolf under their paws. He frowned, thinking of how she said she avoided pack events to keep from being affected by the pack bonds. Considering the firm set of her jaw, she wasn't going to give in.

How could he get her out of this without starting a fight none of them would win? If he and Fell got banished from the territory, it would end their mission to find the Scythe spy—and destroy any chance of protecting Moya and the cubs.

"The alpha makes sense," Fell said.

*What the fuck?* His brother agreed with the cowardly cockroach? "Brawd?"

"A wolf needs pack nearby. Moya stayed healthy because Talitha lived next door," Fell told him.

Brett and Caleb nodded, smiling at Fell's agreement.

Patrin smothered a laugh. His brother was sneakier than a

coyote trying to steal a kill. "I see your point. It's good, then, that you and I are now living in Talitha's apartment."

He turned to Brett, his smile as virtuous as he could manage. "You needn't worry, alpha. Moya has wolves close."

"You're not close. She hardly knows you..." Brett's voice trailed off when Fell pulled Moya onto his lap.

Her eyes widened, then she leaned back against Fell's chest and snuggled closer. "I'm glad that's settled." She smiled sweetly at Brett, then looked up at Patrin. "Now that you finished eating, did you think Ina's stuffed pastries are as tasty as my ham croquettes?"

*Very nice, little wolf.* She was playing along. "Your croquettes are better, but I did like Ina's venison more than ham. Can you make the next ones with venison?"

"For you, of course." Moya beamed at him.

"You are my favorite wolf," Patrin bent and kissed her lightly... and stepped back out of the range of her fists. Just in case.

But she didn't try to hit him...although Fell had wrapped an arm around her waist to prevent just that.

She sat motionless, staring up at him with wide brown eyes.

Had he broken the feisty little wolf?

Or was it himself he'd broken...because he wanted to kiss her again. And again and again.

Patrin had kissed her.

She couldn't move, couldn't stop staring at him.

His eyes were black as the forest during dark of the moon.

Fell tightened his arm around her. His cheek brushed against hers. With his lips next to her ear, he whispered, "Breathe, *blodyn*."

Her lungs filled. Yanking her gaze away from Patrin, she saw Ramón's eyes were narrowed.

Everyone else was watching—including Brett and Caleb.

Oh, that was why Patrin had kissed her.

*Right. Of course. I knew that.*

Brett's face had darkened with anger. "Listen, you can't—"

"Is there a problem here?" With Heather beside him and Niall on his left, the Cosantir strolled up to their group. A dark blue festival tunic set off eyes almost as dark as Patrin's. He studied Moya, then his gaze moved to Brett.

From dark red, Brett's face turned the gray-white color of weathered bone. His mouth opened. Closed. "No problem, Cosantir. Just minor pack business."

"Perhaps conduct such business during pack events, not a party?" André smiled at Moya. "My lifemate is missing the company of her best friend. Might we steal you away?"

Brett and Caleb tensed slightly. The Cosantir would have hard questions for anyone who tried to banish his lifemate's friend.

"Of course, Cosantir." Moya kissed Fell's cheek with a whispered, "Thank you," jumped to her feet and joined Heather.

One hand on her belly as if to emphasize her pregnancy, Heather slung an arm around Moya. "I just don't know what I'd do without you to talk about female things."

As Moya let herself be herded away, she glanced behind her.

Patrin was grinning, and Fell winked at her.

Relieved at her escape from Brett's aggression, Moya let Heather pull her away.

Wasn't it wonderful—and sneaky—how Fell and Patrin had come to her rescue. She touched her lips, still feeling the kiss. And Fell had called her *blodyn*, an affectionate Welsh word for flower, usually used with someone they found lovely—and cute.

Gods, she *liked* them, why was it so difficult to think they might like her in return?

"Moya, you all right?" Heather asked.

"Oh, sorry, I am. Really. Thank you so much for the rescue." Moya turned to smile at André. "And thank you too."

André was still frowning. "By tradition, a Cosantir only becomes involved in pack business if laws are broken. But..."

"No need to get involved." His stepping in would cause problems, especially since he was still a new Cosantir—and worse, new to the territory. New to the country even, since he was Canadian. "I'm sure things will work out."

He eyed her, undoubtedly knowing exactly why she was worried. "We'll see..."

*Fairy farts.* Hopefully, Brett would be smart enough to back off. Moya felt as if she'd swallowed a lead weight. She'd already lost one pack because of the appalling behavior of its alpha. Losing another—losing this town and all her friends. It might break her.

She pushed the worry away as Heather pulled her to a group of four. "Moya, here are my friends from North Cascades Territory. Emma is the bard I wanted you to hear. She's amazing."

Curvy with a big, bear build, the bard was a good half foot taller than Moya with long honey-colored hair and a sweet smile. "It's nice to meet you, Moya."

Moya couldn't help but smile back. "You even sound like a bard. I can't wait to hear you sing."

"Right?" Heather laughed and gestured to the male beside Emma. "This is Ben, one of Emma's lifemates."

Goddess' breasts, the cahir was massive. Rather than a tunic, he wore a shirt the color of blue violets that matched his eyes. Full sleeves with embroidery made it into something festive. "I'm delighted to meet you, Moya." His booming voice held a decided twang, almost like Heather's brother Daniel.

"Oh, are you from Texas? How fun." Moya beamed at him.

"Grew up there." He grinned, totally a sociable sort of person. "I like the mountains here far better."

"Oh, me too. I grew up in Stanislaus Territory. I love how much greener it is here."

Heather gestured to the male next to Ben. "Owen is the other cahir who came to visit."

As usual for cahirs, he was way too tall. His thick brown hair reached his shoulders. He had long sideburns, a cruel scar from his cheek to his neck, and no smile. In fact, he looked displeased to be at a party and not at all happy to meet her.

"Um, hi?" Moya offered.

The female next to him jammed her elbow into his side. "Behave, grumpy cat."

"By the God, little female." Huffing, he rubbed his ribs, but amusement lit his dark green eyes, and he almost smiled at Moya. "Good to meet you."

Heather was laughing. "You so deserved that, cahir. Moya, meet Darcy."

Moya's eyes widened. This was Darcy? Oh, she *was*. "You look so much like Patrin—a smaller, female Patrin." Although Patrin's eyes were a darker brown.

Darcy studied her in turn. "I saw Fell pull you onto his lap. *Fell*. And Patrin *kissed* you."

Oh Goddess, was Darcy upset? Sisters could be possessive of their littermates. "Um, they were just, kind of, helping me to fend off an obnoxious wolf."

"Of course. I'm sure that's all they were doing." Darcy didn't... quite...laugh in Moya's face. Then she grinned at Heather. "You'll have to keep me informed. My brothers don't tell me *anything*."

"Absolutely," Heather said.

Moya turned and gave her friend a look—*traitor*—then drew herself up with dignity, which wasn't easy being as she was only five three and surrounded by giants. "There is nothing to inform anyone about."

Eyes shining, Emma murmured to Ben, "I need to visit Rainier Territory more often. There are obviously stories here to collect and make into songs."

*Oh no, no, no.*

*Wait, though.* A song about the town's courage—and teamwork—in taking on the hellhound would be amazing. "Do you have questions about what happened on the dark of the moon?"

To Moya's relief, Emma did have questions, and the conversation turned to that night, the fight, and what the people in the restaurant had heard, seen, and felt. She could almost see the bard weaving little pieces of a tune together.

"Moya!" Talam appeared from nowhere. Heather's adopted cub was a sturdy lad with brown hair and brown eyes—and his hug was as energetic as he was.

His littermate, Sky, was as fair as his brother was brown, with blond hair and blue eyes. He wrapped his arms around Moya's waist and stared up at her. "I'm 'sposed to play guitar for Emma," he told her, half in joy and half terrified.

"Ooooh," Emma said. "You're *Moya*! You've been teaching him guitar."

"I have." Uh, oh, did she trip over her paws in the instructions?

"Great job. He has the basics down solid." Emma leaned closer to say in a low voice, "He'd feel comfier if you were on-stage playing guitar with him."

"I..." Moya pulled in a breath, saw Sky's pleading eyes, and went belly-up in surrender. "Of course. Music is meant to be shared." Then she added from the heart, "It would be an honor, bard."

Leaning against a wall to listen to the music, Patrin realized he was enjoying himself. It wasn't totally a surprise, since he did like people, but the all-Daonain events usually left him and Fell feeling like outsiders.

Tonight, the atmosphere was so welcoming even Fell was smiling. A little.

Patrin nodded to an older couple with familiar faces. Right,

right, Maeve and Murtagh, who owned the grocery. Murtagh's littermate had died in an avalanche—something common in these mountains—the male and his mate were very close.

The old guy looked as if he'd be fun to work for, but he hadn't needed help, having hired someone a short time before.

Yes, the townspeople here were kind—and the music at this party was fucking amazing. The human world with their singers, bands, and orchestras could be impressive. But nothing—nothing —compared to a bard who could take a shifter's heartstrings and play them like a harp.

The ballad about the first Gathering had him wiping his eyes... and he'd seen Fell doing the same.

Wasn't it a surprise to see Moya and the Cosantir's fosterling, Sky, accompanying the bard with their guitars?

Bending, the bard spoke to Moya and Sky, probably giving them the chords for the next song.

After Moya strummed a quick intro, the bard lifted her voice. "In the dark of the night with starlight shining on the high mountains, a creature stalked its prey.

*In sleepy Ailill Ridge, the demon dog moved through the town. Hideous claws longer than a hand clacked on the bricks, a signal of death approaching.*

*There were only two of the God's warriors to call upon—and one was already injured. They wouldn't survive a hellhound.*

*Everyone knew...and a canny trap had been prepared, filled with iron spikes, like teeth in the bottom. But...how to lead the creature to the trap?*

*Courageous shifters in the town stepped forward. Males to find the hellhound, to lead him to the town center. The injured cahir would draw its attention—and the other cahir would serve as bait.*

*In the hellhound came, each male taking a turn at leading it forward. The injured cahir, already in place, drew its attention, luring it fully into the square. And then the other cahir stepped forward. After giving a hair-raising shriek, she fled. The demon dog's predatory instincts roused, it chased after her.*

*Fleet as a stag, she led it to the tree-lined park. To the trap.*

*But they all knew the massive demon dog might well reach one side or the other. Two more brave shifters had spent hours lying in wait for this moment..."*

*She is singing about...me and Fell?* Patrin stared at the stage, his brain frozen solid in shock.

Beside him, Fell pulled in a breath and muttered, "Oh fuck."

Okay, was it evil that Moya had been waiting for Patrin and Fell to realize where Emma's song was going? Smothering a smile, Moya kept playing. Thank goodness, she was so experienced, she didn't have to look at her fingers, or she would've missed their expressions.

Her brothers had simply grinned as they were mentioned. They had healthy egos—and had never lacked for praise.

Unlike Patrin and Fell. Oh, she'd seen exactly when they caught on. The shock. Fell said something—probably swearing.

Two lethal shifter-soldiers felled by one bard.

The urge to laugh mingled right along with the ache in her heart...because their expressions held disbelief. For a decade, no one had shown any gratitude for their courage and strength.

Tonight, they would get a heap load.

The song turned darker and brutally honest, relating the companionship, the courage shown by the cahirs and volunteers, the terror, the screaming.

It was all there, laid out. The victory over the hellhound. Then the warmth of the puppy pile afterward as if to show what underlay everything—that they had each other in the end.

Patrin's eyes met hers as the song came to an end. The softness in them lured her in, and she barely managed to look away before Fell did the same. His eyes were damp.

Seeing them... Her heart melted like a snowball in the sun.

The whole room was silent for long moments before applause filled the air.

"Thank you." Emma was all smiles. "From all the Daonain, especially here in Rainier Territory, thank you, Bron, Niall, and Madoc. Patrin, Fell, Ramón, Zorion, and Duffy. Thank you for keeping your people safe."

Cheers broke out through the whole room, and her two shifter-soldiers looked as if they'd love to flee into the forest.

Awww, how could two deadly males look just so adorable?

A minute later, Emma motioned to Cronan, the postmaster, who played the flute, and Morcant, a Shamrock chef, who played the fiddle. "I think some dancing is in order."

The two older bears bowed, grinned, and started tuning up.

Emma turned to Sky and Moya. "Thank you for helping. New songs are difficult for me. If I had to play my own accompaniment, I'd probably have forgotten the words."

Moya pulled in a breath. "The ballad was wonderful. I'm so glad you let us be a part of it."

"We'll have to play again." Emma had a wonderful smile. She looked at Sky. "Now, lad, I want you to keep working with Moya on your guitar lessons. André says they'll bring you up to Cold Creek once a month to spend the weekend with me so we can start you on the path to being a bard."

Sky's eyes shone brighter than the sun. "Really?"

"Really." Emma ruffled his hair. "When you're feeling more settled, you'll come and be my apprentice, but that time is in the future."

Smiling, Moya jumped off the stage, pleased to hear Emma would be patient with young Sky. Last summer, he and his brother had been orphaned, made homeless, and then badly used by the former Cosantir. The cubs needed a stable environment. Heather and her lifemates were seeing they got it.

Behind her, Morcant did a quick tuning of his fiddle, then

played a few introductory notes for a dance tune with Cronan's flute joining in.

As Moya reached the chairs, shifters formed a circle around the stage, then two more. Hands joined as the three circles began to move.

Her foot tapped in time with the infectious beat.

"This is different," Patrin said from her left.

"Almost like that Greek bar," Fell said from her right.

Moya grinned. "Only this is more Celtic." The first and third circles moved *deosil*, clockwise, with the second going *widdershins*. Three steps, one foot behind, then a sidestep, and beginning again. The patterned movement turned the dance into an almost communal trance.

And the shifter-soldiers shouldn't be watching but participating instead.

Spotting Talitha in the outer circle, Moya took Patrin's hand then Fell's and pulled them forward. "Talitha."

Glancing over her shoulder, Talitha released the female's hand on her right and took Patrin's—and her group of three was absorbed into the line.

Although Patrin's expression was surprised, and Fell's unreadable, they didn't pull away. Instead, after a moment, they easily followed the steps. A minute later, there was a tiny smile on Fell's lips and an open grin on Patrin's face.

When the dance concluded, everyone was laughing and hugging. Any task undertaken together—even dancing—brought shifters closer. Without even thinking about it, she hugged Fell, and with no hesitation, he hugged her back, all hard body and muscles.

Rather than releasing her, he turned her and pushed her toward... She stiffened as Patrin's arms closed around her.

His dominance was pushed down somehow. "Little wolf," he murmured, and his embrace was loose enough she could escape.

She didn't want to. Instead, she hugged him back and heard his pleased rumble, almost sounding like a cat.

He drew her tighter against him. His muscles were just as hard, but leaner than Fell's. His masculine scent of smoky leather with a hint of cedar reminded her of winter evenings in front of a fire.

And along with that was an unfamiliar sensation—a tingling awareness of being female. Of being held by a male—one she...wanted?

When she pushed back, Patrin let her go. She could feel the hot blush in her face. And the melting warmth lower down.

The next tune started up, one with a soft drumbeat. Zorion must have joined the musicians.

"We should get off the floor," Moya said.

Rather than moving, Patrin took her hand. "We saw this one done at Elder Village. It would be fun to actually dance it."

Smaller circles with four triads in each were forming all over the dance floor...and before Moya could object, she and the shifter-soldiers were included in one.

*Fairy farts.* This dance was for more...involved...shifters. But the music had started, and it was bad form to bow out, since the rest of the circle couldn't continue without all four.

How did she get into these messes?

The music played, sweetly seductive with a pulsing drumbeat that let her body take over. Let her mind quiet as she was spun around, as the males made arches of their joined hands for her to dance under. She was lifted into the air and held there with her hair spilling onto Patrin's face. Somehow, she was on her feet, her back against Fell's chest, his arms around her waist, and they turned. Spinning, he handed her to Patrin. Their hands were big and powerful on her body, and she could feel how careful they were with their strength.

Every breath brought her the tantalizing scent of their interest. And the rise of her own desire.

The music came to an end, and with a final spin and a low chuckle, Fell pulled her against him and took her lips...so disconcertingly gently. A zing of arousal shot through her, warming her from head to toes.

Then, as before, he handed her over to his brother. "Brawd, her lips are soft."

Patrin put one hand behind her waist and pulled her closer. His other hand slipped under her hair, gripping to tilt her head. When she tensed, he paused.

His dark eyes held her as he waited. He must know from her scent she was interested, yet he was giving her mind time to refuse—or agree.

With a tiny exhalation, she offered her mouth.

He kissed her, his lips firm and warm, and she could feel how he was holding back. His control over himself made him even more attractive.

"Thank you for the dancing lessons," he murmured. Then his lips tilted up. "I'll return to working on your no-punching lessons tomorrow."

Just for that, she punched him right in the gut.

And grinned when he broke out laughing.

# CHAPTER ELEVEN

"Speak."

"Baton reporting in." Baton gripped the burner phone hard, anxiety making it difficult to think. The leadership in the Scythe didn't tolerate fuckups.

"Go on."

"I found the two you indicated you had an interest in. Here in Ailill Ridge."

"Acting openly?"

"Very. Jobs in a bar and a coffee shop."

He made a noise, perhaps satisfied, and maybe angry. His anger would be understandable, considering how much damage had been done to the organization. The two named Patrin and Fell had been leaders of the creatures. "How about their sister?"

"I haven't seen her in town." At the disapproving sound, Baton tensed.

What might placate him? Ah. "The two appear interested in a woman. They don't appear to be lovers...yet. If we can't find the sister, this one might give us a hold over them."

"You're right. A lover has potential." There was a pause. "Keep looking for the sister and watch how the interaction with the female goes. If she can serve us in the sister's stead, then it'll be a go."

"Yes, sir."

"Hmm. Also, observe the two—and the female. There will undoubtedly be interactions with humans; however, if they have friends—the friends will most likely be mutants. Take good notes."

Baton nodded, seeing the next step up the ladder within reach. "Yes, sir. It will be as you wish."

"Yes, it will."

Baton swallowed hard at the unspoken threat. *Don't screw this up or else.*

---

Small town grocery stores were different from the ones in cities, Fell decided. The aisles were narrower, the lighting not quite as bright, the smells of food more mingled. But...

A female shifter, one from the pack, smiled brightly at him. "Hi, Fell."

He managed a smile and a *good evening* and considered he'd done enough. Not being basically invisible left him unbalanced, much like when he'd first tried to walk with four legs rather than two.

He shouldn't get used to being greeted or smiled at. When they left Ailill Ridge, they'd go back to being unknown. The thought wasn't as soothing as it should have been.

Setting a bag of potatoes in the basket, he checked the list for the next item. Moya's handwriting was a pleasure to read. So different from his brother's scrawl.

Hopefully, Patrin would have a quiet night at the bar. Mondays weren't busy, according to Nik. Even better, Fell wasn't needed.

He wasn't about to complain, not when he was going to spend time with an engaging, little wolf.

A few minutes ago, he'd heard Moya in the apartment hallway and poked his head out to ask her what the CONV on the oven setting meant. Her explanation of *convection* led to her offering to help him cook a meal. She said it wouldn't be anything involved like what she'd made them a week ago at her place. No, this was to be "a basic roast, potatoes, and veggies. Solid and filling."

He agreed so quickly she'd been startled.

His enthusiasm was, of course, for a home-cooked meal—but also for getting to spend the evening with her.

The longer he knew her, the more time they spent together, the more he wanted to know her. She was so fucking easy to be around, never at a loss for words, yet demanding that he hold up his side of a conversation.

She laughed, easily and often, but never at people getting hurt or embarrassed. If anything, she poked fun at herself. She was smart and, no surprise, well-read, considering her occupation.

He grinned, remembering how there was always music playing in Espresso Books. It was easy to tell who'd chosen the—what had Renee called it?—the *playlist*. Talitha liked soft mystical music, especially harps. Renee liked something called heavy metal. Corey enjoyed country western. Moya always picked bouncy music, from Celtic rock to human pop tunes—and she'd usually be moving in time with the beat, even when she was sitting.

And when she was standing? Those hips of hers were perfection, especially when rocking. Gods, face it—*she* was perfection.

Having reached the end of the list, he joined the checkout line with two customers in front of him.

Murtagh, the short, white-bearded owner, had perfected the art of ringing up sales even as he chatted. He did love to talk.

Bagging groceries at the end of the counter, a bull-necked twenty-something tossed in a few laughing comments.

It really was a friendly town.

"You picked yourself out a fine-looking roast." Smiling,

Murtagh scanned the price. "Looks like you're going to have a nice meal."

Fell nodded, then sighed, almost hearing the soft voice: *Use your words, Fell*. "Aye, Moya is teaching me how to cook it."

"Whoa, dude. Isn't she the sexy chick who works in the bookstore?" The grocery bagger waggled his eyebrows. His scent indicated he was human—and that he lusted after Moya.

Fell barely stifled a growl. "Yes. She's a kind person."

"That she is." Murtagh shot a frown at his bagger. "Gregory."

Gregory's ruddy face darkened. "Sorry."

Murtagh pushed the last of the groceries to the bagger. "That'll be eighty-nine dollars and twenty cents."

Fell tapped his card against the reader. Wells had given them new credit cards, ones they didn't care if someone tracked.

Murtagh handed over the receipt. "All done. Have a good day, Fell."

The bagger blinked and eyed him. "Fell? Sounds like something ominous. What kind of name is that?"

Humans and their curiosity. But saying *fuck off* wasn't considered good manners in small towns. *Use your words*. "Old family surname. A *fell* is a hill or moor."

"Oh, cool." Gregory bagged up the last sack. "Your car in back?"

"No. I live across the square." Stepping around the human, Fell slung the bags over his arms and headed out.

Once through the door, he glanced back.

The bagger was watching him with narrowed eyes.

*Interesting*. Just how long had Gregory been in town?

---

Standing at the end of the kitchen counter, Moya watched Fell put the roasting pan full of potatoes, carrots, onions, and a pork roast into the oven.

The way his broad shoulders strained at the royal blue Henley dried her mouth. Because, well, damn. He really was so very, very male.

Would he still be here for the full moon Gathering in twelve days? Would he be interested in mating? He'd kissed her at the dance. So, maybe?

But would she end up backing away if he asked? He might not be as over-the-top forceful as Patrin, but he was a long way from submissive. It really wasn't fair that her libido wanted dominance and her mind...didn't.

"You're staring at me." Fell's rough voice shattered her thoughts. Leaning an elbow on the counter, he touched her cheek with his fingertips. "What's got you worried, *cariad*."

He'd called her sweetheart.

"I..." She shook her head. "Nothing."

"Bullshit." He studied her, eyes far too discerning. "Is this tied into your thing about pushy males? Am I being pushy?"

"No, no, you aren't."

When she tried to take a step back, he gripped her wrist with his free hand and sniffed. "You're interested."

"No, I'm..." Scat! Lying was wrong. She forced herself to say the words. "I'm interested, only...I'm scared too."

He frowned, and his hand dropped from her face. "I did something?"

Of course he was confused. He hadn't released her wrist, and his thumb traced back and forth as if to gentle her.

"No, I was thinking about Gatherings. How people—males—change on that night. The scent of females in heat increases their testosterone. And aggression."

"Huh." Fell turned, resting his back against the counter, then pulled her between his spread legs. "I don't change."

His blunt statement held assurance, and to her surprise, she believed him. The shifter-soldiers were incredibly controlled. "Oh. Um, okay."

He drew her closer until she was pressed against his groin. Lips curving slightly, he kissed the inside of her wrist with soft lips.

A spike of heat ran up her arm. "Fell." She tried to interject a warning in her tone and instead sounded breathless.

"Moya." He nibbled on her fingers and sent tingles through her. "I've never been with a Daonain outside of a Gathering."

"Me neither, actually."

Laughter lit his eyes. "Want to practice now—when there isn't any full moon?"

Practice...mating? The idea was ridiculous, only every single cell in her body urged her to agree, as if she really was in heat. She'd never felt this way except at Gatherings, and on those nights, any male who fit her criteria would do.

Here and now, the only male she wanted was Fell.

And she wanted him badly.

"Practice." Her voice sounded husky. "Yes."

His gaze never leaving hers, he molded her against him, and Mother's breasts, but he was pure muscle from his wide chest to his washboard stomach to the iron-hard thighs trapping her. His mouth came down on hers, so very gently, but with an assurance that didn't seem inexperienced at all. Yet he'd only been free of the Scythe for a year.

She pulled back. "You said you'd never been with a *Daonain* outside of a Gathering. Does that mean you..."

"Had sex with human women? Aye, when we were on missions with the Scythe." His jaw tightened. "It's different in a way. They don't smell right. But sometimes we were ordered and"—he shrugged—"sometimes it was a way to establish comradery with our human handlers."

"Oh." No wonder he seemed so comfortable with kissing.

"I doubt I could tolerate a human now. Not after learning what mating can be."

What had it been like for him? The thought of mating with a

human was just icky, but what if she was a teen and humans were all there was? Young Daonain males were all testosterone and urges. Yes, she'd probably have done the same.

And...she had to honor how honest Fell had been, despite the awkwardness.

Watching her carefully, he pulled her closer again, lifting her chin and brushing his lips over hers.

Oh, *nice*. Because of the heat during full moon Gatherings, most shifters went straight for the shove it in and climax. She was the same, really—and had almost no experience with this *foreplay* stuff talked about in the human books she enjoyed.

Fell nibbled on her lips and grazed down her jaw to her neck.

She sucked in a breath. *Foreplay is amazing.*

He took her lips again, his tongue probing, stroking hers, demanding a response. Heat rising fast, she teased him in return, successfully enough the kiss turned ravenous.

His hands cupped her ass, bringing her up onto her tiptoes until her tender bits rubbed against a very hard shaft. The friction on her clit made her moan.

He chuckled, then moved her back one step, and swept her up in his arms in a bridal carry.

"*Fell.*" Her head spun, and she clutched his shirt, unsure if she was thrilled or terrified.

A minute later, they were in a bedroom, cool and dark.

Silently, he laid her on top of the bed quilt. When she lifted her arms to him, he joined her, slowly moving his body on top of hers. Oh, he was heavy, and suddenly, she felt...trapped.

---

Fell saw anxiety cross Moya's face, smelled the change in her scent. Propping himself up on one elbow, he cupped her cheek with the other hand. "*Blodyn,* we can stop."

Her eyes cleared, and she set her hand over his, turning her head to kiss his palm. "Uh-uh, I was just...surprised."

Because she hadn't been with a male except at Gatherings. As it happened, he could think of nothing he'd like better than to show her the joy of a slower pace.

It was a shame Patrin wasn't here with them, but...no, she needed more time to trust his brother. She would get there.

Tonight, Fell would go slow, so very slow. He reclaimed her mouth, tasting and stroking, and felt her go boneless beneath him.

Her arms wrapped around his neck, and she answered him with a passion that left him voracious with the need to taste her...everywhere.

He slid his hand under her shirt. Rather than the harness-like contraption females called a bra, she wore a stretchy thing with no zipper or hooks. No way to release it.

As he pushed the thing upward, it squeezed down on the curvy mounds, firming them for his enjoyment. *Nice.* He cupped one warm, soft breast.

Her gasp made him halt, but her back arched, pushing her breast against his hand.

*All right then.* Gently, he kneaded and stroked her soft breasts. Her breathing changed, deepened.

She stroked his shoulders and ran her fingers through his hair, even as she kissed him hungrily.

He nipped her lower lip, bit her chin lightly—and felt a nipple under his fingers harden. If a bite on her chin did that, then...

Kneeling between her legs, he divested himself of his shirt, then pulled hers off along with the stretchy thing. And simply enjoyed the sight laid out on his bed.

Her lips were swollen from his kisses, eyes slumbrous, golden skin flushed. Her creamy-brown breasts were topped with dusky, pebbled nipples. "Fuck, you're beautiful."

Her gaze lingered on his bare chest. "So are you."

That wasn't true, yet the admiration and desire in her gaze made him feel as if he could conquer the world.

He curved his hands on her bare breasts and squeezed gently, before bending to kiss the undersides. When he licked over a nipple, then sucked on it, her fingernails bit into his shoulders.

Concerned, he paused, but her throaty moan made him smile—and he continued. Sucking, licking. Nibbling. A careful nip to the tender underside heightened the fragrance of her arousal. So he used his teeth more, alternating with gentle kisses and licks, working his way around and inward, back to one nipple.

Sucking, circling, then... He captured the peak between his teeth. When he increased the pressure, her eyes went blank, and her hips pushed up.

*This... So damned beautiful.*


There had been a moment when everything fell away, and she saw Fell stop and simply look at her. And through the sexual haze, she thought he was going to quit.

Instead, he moved upward, kissed her blind again, before returning to her breasts, continuing his attentions until they were swollen, the nipples tight and aching.

"Fell...please."

As if he'd been waiting for just that, he moved off the bed to smoothly unfasten and remove her jeans—then his own.

By the Mother, he was more than virile with a strong, corded neck and powerful, wide shoulders. Curly blond chest hair couldn't conceal the solid wall of muscle beneath it. His abdomen was hard-packed, and a line of hair trailed down to a straining thick erection.

Getting up on her knees, she ran her hands over his shoulders, his chest, feeling the way his muscles tensed under her touch, how his breathing sped up. His eyes were a burning blue, his color flushed. Leaning forward, she closed her hands around his erection.

Oh, his sharp inhalation was satisfying. Sliding her hands over him, she explored. So thick and straight with prominent veins below a velvety helmet. She stroked up and down, and when he opened his legs to brace himself, she cupped his heavy testicles.

Males were awfully different. He was fascinating, and just touching him pushed her lust for him higher and higher.

Unable to resist, she ran her tongue over the horizontal ridges on his abdominal muscles. As her wolf instincts surged, she nipped his belly.

And suddenly found herself flat on her back on the bed.

"My turn, little biter." Moving back between her knees, he ran his warm hands up and down her thighs. The slight abrasion of his callused palms was tantalizing. Each stroke brought him closer to her aching pussy.

Spreading his fingers over her pelvis, he used his thumbs to open her before bending down and licking over her in one devastating pass.

She gasped at the ferocious pleasure.

"Mmm." Settling down between her legs, he...feasted, licking and sucking, kneading her labia, tonguing her until ravenous need boiled through her blood. Until she was...right there—every muscle, every nerve right on the precipice.

Her body tight with tension, she shook. "Fell, you toothless mutt." Damn the male, his thick hair was too short to yank.

His head lifted. His gaze met hers, the corners of his eyes crinkling. "You should be happy I'm not using my teeth, little wolf." With a huffed laugh, he closed his lips over her clit and sucked, his tongue tapping on the very top.

The hot pressure pushed her right over. Crying out, hips bucking, she fell into a lake of pure sensation, of singing pleasure.

Goddess, this was so different from full moons.

Rumbling a pleased sound deep in his throat, Fell moved up her body and propped himself up on his elbows. "Beautiful Moya. Stop now or continue?" The hardness at her entrance showed what he meant.

"Continue. Oh, please, yes." She pulled his head down to kiss him. "I want you to enjoy this as much as I did."

His teeth flashed with his smile. "I will." After another long, wet kiss, he balanced on one elbow and reached down to position himself. He met her eyes, watching carefully, as he entered her slowly, hot and thick. Inch after inch pressed in, until he was seated deeply inside her, stretching her impossibly full.

She could feel the aftershocks of her climax pulsing around him with tiny electric zings.

His gaze still trapped hers as he withdrew slightly and pressed back in, then paused, obviously to see if he'd hurt her.

Because the deadly shifter-soldier was disconcertingly protective of her.

She put her hands on each side of his face and felt the harsh stubble on his jaw. "Fell. Take what you need from me."

His lips twitched. Pulling out, he pressed in, faster. Harder.

Oh yes. "Yes." She lifted her hips, meeting him, showing him she could take more.

"Fuck, you're sweet," he muttered. "Put your legs around me."

Oh, really? She'd never done that before. Lifting her knees, she wrapped her legs around him until her heels hit his buttocks.

His cock went deeper.

*So deep. Oh. Ohhh.*

His guttural growl showed how much he liked it too. And that added a zing of delight to all the heat.

Balancing on one hand, he put a hand under her butt and lifted her while angling himself so his pelvis rubbed her clit with every thrust.

Pleasure ripped through her with each dizzying touch against those sensitive nerves. Her legs jerked, tightening around him.

"Yeah, just like that." Smiling slightly, he started pounding into her, thrust after thrust, hard and fast and deep. Pressing over her clit with each stroke.

Inside and outside were being stimulated, the sensations

vibrating through her, until her whole being was in flames. Her climax blazed through her, wave after wave, so intensely the room, the *world* dissolved into white sparkles.

Then his fingers dug into her buttocks, and the warmth of his release filled her. A low growl reached her ears.

Heart still hammering, blood still singing in her veins, she smiled at the realization the sound he made was a happy one.

He brushed his lips over hers. So, so sweetly.

---

Patrin entered the apartment, feet aching from standing behind the bar for hours, ears ringing from people talking and talking. Especially the humans, who didn't have the sensitive ears of the Daonain. Did they have to chatter so fucking loudly?

The apartment was blessedly quiet, and even better, the aroma of meat and potatoes filled the air. His stomach growled in instant hunger.

In one of the armchairs, Fell looked up from the book he was reading. "Brawd, there's a plate of food for you."

It smelled fantastic. "Your cooking...or did Moya help?"

"Moya. She taught me to cook pork roast and potatoes."

"Goddess bless her."

"Clean up. I'll warm the food for you." Fell set the book down.

A quick shower erased the scent of the bar, and Patrin pulled on a pair of sweatpants. Padding barefoot out of his bedroom, he caught another scent. Coming from Fell's room.

It was Moya's light fragrance and...sex?

Another sniff confirmed it.

What in Herne's horn and hooves?

Fell had set a plateful of food on the oval table. A thick slab of pork, potatoes, carrots, with gravy covering it all. The delectable sight was almost enough to distract him. *Almost.* "You and Moya...mated?"

His brother had retaken his armchair. "Aye."

Patrin eyed the faint smile. Not smug, simply...pleased. Happy. Something he hadn't seen nearly often enough on Fell's face. Fuck, did he need to be reminded they were on a mission?

Fell obviously read Patrin's expression. "Don't worry, brawd. We have a job to do. I know."

The tightness in Patrin's gut relaxed. "Okay. I didn't want..." Didn't want his brother hurt—or the little wolf either.

"She said the humans call it *friends with benefits*."

"Interesting." The *benefits* would be the mating outside of a full moon?

The touch of envy was natural—Moya was a desirable female—but, seeing the satisfied contentment in Fell's posture and scent, Patrin could only be happy for him. And pleased, too, because his brother was talking more. Fell would never return to the open-hearted, gregarious boy he'd been before the Scythe, but his time with the gutsy wolf had done him a world of good.

For his brother, Patrin would do everything he could to stay here longer.

Setting his worry to one side, he took a bite of food. The pork was melt-in-the-mouth tender with a savory seasoning. He took another bite.

And saw his brother grin.

## CHAPTER TWELVE

No one had shoveled the sidewalk leading to the pack house, and Moya's boots crunched noisily on the two inches of snow that had fallen last night. The night sky was clear, the air cold enough to sting her face.

Beside her, Talitha snickered as her two fosterlings tried a shortcut through the snowy drifts—and broke through the crust up to their knees.

Moya laughed, eyeing the snow-covered pups. "Mom mentioned a few times how happy she was to raise us in California with far fewer snowy days. Now I know why."

"Ah, well, they'll dry out eventually." Reaching the steps, Talitha raised her voice. "Cubs."

Mateo and Alvaro trotted over and stomped to remove the snow before entering.

In the entry, Moya removed her boots. In stocking feet, she entered the oversized living room and took a place against a wall with Talitha. The couches and chairs were already taken, and she sure wasn't going to sit on the floor beside the cubs.

Her nerves wouldn't let her take such a defenseless position.

When she and her brothers first arrived in Ailill Ridge around four years ago, they'd lived here for a month, then found a house to share. But living with brothers? *So annoying.*

Moving to a place by herself had been wonderful despite how often someone had trotted out the old saying: *Female wolves can't live by themselves.*

*As if.*

She glanced around. The place looked better than when they'd lived here. Probably because Roger had moved out of the house he shared with Pete, the previous Cosantir. *Naturally*, the alpha should have better stuff than anyone else, so he'd used pack funds to buy all new furniture.

With a sigh, she leaned the back of her head against the wall. Roger was gone now.

Brett and Caleb shared a big house on the other side of town. A trickle of amusement ran through her. Several of Pete and Roger's buddies had lived in the territory's clan houses for free until André took over and hired Heather to do the accounting. Now *everyone* living in the clan houses paid rent.

The room was almost full—and no one had food or drink. Apparently, this wasn't going to be a social event.

More wolves entered, then Patrin strolled in, every step a display of coiled power and intimidating self-possession. Her heart skipped a beat and a few more as Fell joined him. The brothers were terrifyingly tempting—and she wasn't the only female who noticed.

Her flash of possessiveness was dismaying. Yes, she'd been with Fell last night, had felt all of him surrounding her, in her, touching her with those big hard hands. Kissing him...But *no, gnome-brain, he's not yours—they're not yours—and never will be yours.*

And she didn't want them to be either. Absolutely not.

*Liar.*

Oh, it was pitiful when she was reduced to calling herself a liar. Her snort of exasperation made Talitha raise her eyebrows.

*Mother of All.* Moya bent and fussily adjusted her socks. *Having unwrinkled socks is very important.* She surely wasn't avoiding Talitha's gaze, let alone those of the MacCormac brothers.

By the Gods, she was a mess. But really, how was a female to deal with having mated a male outside of a Gathering? Being with Fell had been *amazing*.

He hadn't worked in the coffee shop today, or maybe she would've had a chance to work through this...this reaction. Or maybe it would have been even worse.

She patted her chest where her heart was bouncing around like a flower fairy high on rose petals.

Straightening, she looked over at him—and met his piercing blue gaze. Her stomach quivered, and the floor beneath her socks felt funny. Maybe she hadn't smoothed the wrinkles out. Or something.

A corner of his mouth tilted up in his almost-invisible smile.

And, Mother help her, she could feel her face heat with a flush.

Patrin glanced at Fell, saw where he was looking...and grinned.

Her face got hotter.

"Wolves."

*Oh, thank you, Lord and Lady.* She turned all her attention to the alpha, grateful for his nasally interruption.

Brett stood on the wide staircase with his brother two steps down. He raised his voice, silencing the conversations. "As your alpha, I need to tell you how things will be going forward."

He'd obviously prepared for the occasion. His normally greasy, black hair was clean for a change, his scruffy beard trimmed. He crossed his arms over his beefy chest.

Trying to look like a real leader.

Moya exchanged unimpressed glances with Talitha. Heather would've undoubtedly had something trenchant to say, but she'd told Brett she couldn't make it, using her pregnancy as an excuse.

She hadn't lied...because there was no way her lifemates

would've let their pregnant mate attend without them present. Brett and Caleb were hot-tempered, aggressive males, and they disliked Heather.

Really, it was good Heather wasn't here. *I wish I weren't either.*

"As alpha, I intend to return our pack to the traditional ways, back to when wolves were stronger. When we outnumbered the cats. When our females took mates only from our kind, so they'd birth wolf cubs."

*What?* Moya stared at the sprite-snared simpleton in shock. There'd never been a time like that.

Unless lifemated, every fertile shifter had to attend Gatherings, and there, a female mated with whomever she desired, not solely with "their kind." In the grips of a full moon heat, no female gave thought to whether the male was a wolf or something else.

Brett continued, "The pack will also require our single, cubless females to live in the pack house where they will be around potential mates—wolf mates."

Some of the males voiced their approval, the mangy-tailed mutts. Moya eyed them, realizing most were wolves no female wanted.

Most shifters treated females with courtesy and protectiveness. A few, though, took a female's disinterest as an insult—and, worse, felt as if they were entitled to have whoever they wanted for a mate.

"In the future, I'll address the issue of those already in mixed matings."

Beside Moya, Talitha stiffened. Because Eileen was not only female, but a feline. Gods, would Brett try to break them up—or take Mateo and Alvaro away?

"My wolves, there is a danger in associating with felines. They're not our kind, and the vile, devious creatures will try to lure you away from your own sort." Brett's mouth twisted as he pointed to Mateo and Alvaro, then three other cubs. "You've been playing with young moggies. From now on, you play only with our kind...or you'll be disciplined by our beta."

Caleb's face lit at the chance to let his bullying nature loose.

Snarling under her breath, Moya gripped her hands together to keep from making fists. The body language of the wolves around her showed alarm. Dismay. Especially the females and older wolves.

Too many of the wolves her age nodded their smiling approval.

Gods help them all.

Wolves were stronger in a pack. But the need to belong left them easier to manipulate, especially by an alpha. Younger wolves —and males—were especially vulnerable.

Females grew up knowing they might have to raise cubs on their own. Most could be independent if needed.

She glanced at Patrin and Fell. They appeared disgusted...as did her brothers.

Brett smiled at two of the bigger pups—Vigulf and Torkil. "You have been doing just great. I heard about the young werecats you sent yowling home to their mangy mother. Keep up the good work."

The two cubs puffed up their chests...and Moya bit her lip against speaking. Those were the cubs who picked on the younger ones, including Mateo and Alvaro. Brett and Caleb were turning them into bullies.

"I expect everyone to show up to pack runs and any other pack events. If you don't, I'll cast you out, and the pack will drive you out of the territory." Brett smirked. "I'm not Roger. I won't put up with disobedience."

The entire room went silent. Casting out was a fearful threat. Not as bad as a Cosantir's banishment, which resulted in scarring and being shunned by all Daonain anywhere. But if thrown out of the pack, a wolf would be attacked by all the territory pack members.

Fear made a cold lump in Moya's stomach. Even with the Cosantir's warning, Brett was going to proceed. And really, unless Brett broke the Daonain Law, the Cosantir couldn't act.

Gods, she had a business, a home, friends. *I can't afford to be cast out.*

"That's it. Meeting's over." Brett swept his gaze over the roomful of shifters, his gaze settling on Gretchen.

The beautiful blonde preened. "You don't have an alpha female yet. Do you have someone in mind?"

Moya tilted her head. Would the alpha fall for Gretchen's wiles again? The female had a habit of causing problems, like dumping Roger for Pete, and later, playing Roger off against Brett and Caleb...and any other male who looked interested.

Eyes cold and cruel, he lifted his upper lip in a sneer. He probably hadn't forgotten the way Gretchen had made a play for Patrin and Fell at the Gathering. "Not yet. It will take a special female to be mine." He smiled down at the two younger females close to the stairs where he stood. Deidre and Cosette.

Moya sighed. The females were pretty and young and far too weak to be effective alphas. No wonder Brett liked them. He wouldn't want a partner to help lead the pack; he wanted someone to admire him.

He pursued Moya only because she rejected him and raised his predator's instincts. Such an alphahole.

She nudged Talitha and jerked her head at the door. "Let's leave before I lose my cookies."

"I hear you." Talitha's face was pale. "Mateo, Alvaro, let's go."

They herded the two cubs out between them, keeping them safe.

Only...safe was going to be in short supply in the future.

· · ·

Fell followed his brother out of the pack house. Moya had left shortly before, and his wolf was moping that he hadn't had a chance to talk with her. Touch her.

Because since mating with her last night, it'd been difficult to think of anything else. He'd never felt so...close...to anyone except his brother—and with her, it was close in a whole different way.

Just catching whiffs of her scent in the room made his instincts surge to join her. And watching the adorable way she turned red when she saw him?

By the Gods, he liked her.

Unfortunately, by the time they managed to escape the crowded room where everyone was putting on jackets and boots, she'd disappeared.

Perhaps for the best—he wasn't sure what he'd say. And his tongue would undoubtedly trip over words anyway.

Besides, he needed time to think about the alpha's threats that seemed directed at her and Talitha. And the cubs.

Voices came from nearby. Fell turned far enough to see Moya's brothers and their construction crew walking behind them.

"His speech was a complete pile of scat," Ramón said in a low voice to his crew. "If he tries to get us to fire Orla and Jarlath, I'll bite off his tail and shove it up his ass."

Fell frowned. Why would they fire... *Ah, right*. The construction crew had a couple of werecats. At the supper at Moya's, Zorion mentioned cats were perfect for tasks requiring good balance—like roofing.

"Maybe you should challenge for alpha, boss." Killian, the woodworker, said, "You could win."

"You'd have to win," Terence said in a cautionary tone. "You know Brett would cast out anyone who challenged him, if he didn't kill or cripple them."

Listening to the discussion behind him, Fell scowled and muttered to Patrin, "That's one fucked-up alpha."

"Yeah," Patrin said under his breath.

Behind them, Ramón said, "Losing would suck, but I'd probably win. Only trouble is—running a crew with Zorion is enough leadership for me—and Zorion too. We considered challenging, but he doesn't want to be beta, and I don't want to be alpha. Sorry, lads."

When the construction crew made disappointed noises, Fell wanted to join in. Ramón and Zorion would have led the pack as competently as their construction crew. They were as honest and loyal as their sister—not something he'd say about most people.

If Ramón didn't challenge...

Fell rubbed the back of his neck as he thought. The wolves he'd met who'd make good alphas weren't the ones who could win a fight against Brett. The alpha was a big, aggressive wolf... although the way he'd walked away from a one-on-one fight with the feline outside the Bullwhacker raised some questions.

Now, in a Patrin-Brett fight, Patrin would win. Skill and smarts counted. Even if born to be a leader, Patrin didn't want to be responsible for anyone. Not anymore. As teens, leading the shifter-soldiers had scarred him emotionally. He still felt guilty for every wound and every death, not that there was anything he could've done.

It didn't matter, anyway.

The future was set in stone. They would be leaving Ailill Ridge, leaving the pack, leaving *Moya*... The thought was a stab in the heart.

There was no choice.

By now, the Scythe must know their least-favorite shifter-soldiers were living in Ailill Ridge.

---

"Stinks worse than wolverine's piss in here." Patrin wrinkled his nose as he walked into the Scythe operative's bedroom. Wolverines marked their territory, and the scent could make a skunk gag.

Gregory's one-bedroom house reeked of sweat, dirty socks, an inability to hit the toilet—let alone clean it—and rotting food on plates beside the bed. "Want to trade?"

In the living room, hacking the computer, Fell just laughed in answer. Because Patrin had only the most basic skills when it came to tech stuff.

*Fine. I'm a shifter, not a human.*

Trying not to breathe, Patrin searched the usual places: inside, beneath, and behind drawers, electrical outlets, above doors, in vents, picture frames, under or in the mattress. He couldn't go too quickly since everything had to remain in exactly the same place as before the search. And experienced spies often left telltales to know if someone entered the premises while they were gone. Paper in the door, hair across a keyboard... It didn't help that Gregory was a slob.

Then again, the young man appeared to be lazier than a well-fed gnome and probably counted on his security camera to let him know if someone broke in.

Heh, that'd been his first mistake. That technology was easy enough to circumvent.

It was a shame they'd had to wait until the weekend to get into the house. But this was the first time the operative left the house after dark.

"Got everything downloaded." Fell stuck his head in the doorway. "I'll—"

"Here's his spy log." The nightstand drawer had a false bottom. Sloppy work, really. The pseudo-bottom's wood was different from the rest of the nightstand. After photographing each page, Patrin put everything back in place, and within minutes, they were gone.

Fell headed for their apartment to put together a report and send it to Wells. Patrin returned to his job at the bar.

Having entered the Bullwhacker from the back door, Patrin joined the owner behind the bar. A quick glance showed Gregory was still playing pool with a few humans. And wasn't exactly sober either.

*Perfect.*

Nik finished building a drink, handed it to the customer, and lifted his bushy eyebrows at Patrin. "Was your friend all right?"

"I think he'll be fine. Thanks for giving me time to call and talk with him." Even better, it was doubtful anyone noticed that Patrin had left for a short time. Just the way he liked it.

After checking the drink well on his side of the bar, Patrin smiled at Nik. "Sometimes, young men think they can handle everything and get in over their heads. Fuck knows I've done it often enough. A bit of common sense usually sorts us out."

Nik had a hearty laugh, a gold tooth showing in the back of his mouth. "Only if you know someone with common sense."

Patrin filled a couple of orders, then turned when he heard, "Hey, Top Dog."

"Kennard, Fletcher." Without waiting for the two young shifter-soldiers to order, he set a couple of beers on the bar top, charging them to his own account. "Thanks for providing backup."

Last year, the brothers had been furious Wells said they were too young to work for him. So when Patrin asked them to watch Gregory and call if he left the bar, they'd agreed immediately. And being Scythe-trained, they knew better than to ask for more information.

"Call anytime you want help." Fletcher glanced over at the pool room and Gregory. "Need us any longer?"

"Nope. All done."

"In that case, we have a couple of sweeties to chat up." Nudging his brother, Fletcher picked up his beer, his gaze already on a table of young females.

"Good luck, and thanks again." Patrin grinned as the two approached and weren't shot down. Made his heart happy to see his shifter-soldiers making lives for themselves.

And this was why he'd do everything in his power to ensure they stayed free of the Scythe.

---

Moya was in her bookstore arranging a new display of books in the display window and spotted Patrin leaving the café on the square. Jacket open over a green sweater, he sauntered toward the park, eating peanuts from a container. She had to smile, thinking of the differences between the brothers. Patrin sauntered; Fell stalked. Knowing them now, she could tell they were both terrifyingly deadly, but with Fell, his lethalness was all out there to be seen. Patrin hid his ferocity under a sociable front.

Of course, she got reminded all too often of his dangerousness—and dominance—since Fell had assigned him to attack her. Gods, he totally tested her control. Just last night, while she was giving them another cooking lesson, he grabbed her shoulders. She hadn't hit him...not until the mutt had gone and released his dominance. The sensation ran through her—and it was like being tossed into a flooding river, tumbled head over tail. And yep, she punched him.

Gods, how the maggotbrain had laughed.

But she was improving. Partly because, compared to Fell and then Patrin, no one else around here was as dominant. Not even the drunks. Not even Brett. And she'd been spending a lot of time with them. Cooking with them, then often watching a movie or just companionable reading in front of her woodstove.

They liked to *read*.

She grinned. After finding out Fell had read *Dune*, she'd dragged him down to the book club meeting on Thursday night.

It'd been wonderful to see him join in the discussion. She'd already known he thought about the books he read—and could talk about them. Patrin could, too, even if he preferred nonfiction.

Books apparently had been one of the few things they were allowed in the Scythe barracks. Patrin told her that the handlers learned that bored teen shifters tended to destroy things—and they'd get a crate of books from a secondhand store and dump them in the barracks. So the shifter-soldier lads got their education—and learned to discuss books. Now the adult shifter-soldiers were incredibly good at it.

She watched Patrin balance a couple of nuts in the fork of an ornamental tree. For the tree fairy that lived there. Hibernating during the coldest weather, the pixies came out on warmer days—and were always hungry.

That was really sweet.

The other members of the SFF book club had been pleased to have Fell there. Heather and Niall were delighted.

Patrin and Fell seemed to fit right into Rainier Territory.

Would they stay in Ailill Ridge? They seemed to be making a home here. What could she do to help them feel part of the community?

She smiled and glanced at her desk and the *Dune* DVD. She'd have them over, and they could all watch it together.

Maybe she'd get to snuggle? *No, just stop.*

She shook her head and placed another book on the display. The window arrangement looked nicely cozy with a simulated fireplace, a cozy chair, a crocheted blanket, and books. She'd added pretty Solstice decorations, although the humans probably thought they were for Christmas or whatever other religions they had.

She saw Patrin walking along the side of the square. He slowed and left something on the ground.

In the gutter, beady eyes appeared, then a small hand.

*By the Mother of all.* "Did he just leave some peanuts for the gutter gnome?" she said to herself.

"What?" In the center of the room, Fell was wiping down the

coffee shop tables. He joined her at the window, following her gaze. "You mean my brother?"

"Uh-huh." She tried not to notice how his broad shoulder brushed hers. Tried not to feel the thrill of being so close.

"Aye, Patrin feeds pixies and gnomes too. Says we shouldn't skip gnomes just because they're ugly and irritable."

*Huh.* A tender-hearted assassin?

And didn't his attitude make her feel like a low-life badger? Gnomes were good for a town and houses. They kept the alleys and gutters free of bugs and rodents...but she'd never given them goodies.

Fell tugged on her hair with a smile. "The Scythe compound was outside of the Gods' territory, so there weren't many OtherFolk. Seeing them is still a treat."

*Look at the warrior, actually talking.* She bumped her shoulder against his, delighted he was no longer begrudging every word. "Since André became Cosantir, we've had more OtherFolk around. I guess a strong Cosantir draws them."

Outside in the square, Mateo and Alvaro ran up to Patrin, bouncing as enthusiastically as if they were toddlers rather than thirteen. He gave them each a handful of peanuts as they talked.

Oh, it was Saturday, wasn't it? Ah, she had an idea of a way to help them fit in... "I'll be back," she said to Fell and stepped outside. "Mateo, Alvaro."

The younglings ran over.

Leaning over, she whispered her instructions and smiled as excitement filled their faces.

As she walked back inside, they had Patrin by the arms and were dragging him away.

"You ordered the cubs to kidnap my brother?" Fell asked as she joined him back in the store.

"I did. They're taking him to Calon to play basketball." When there wasn't a special event, the warehouse community center was sectioned into room-like areas for various hobbies or meetings.

The far end had basketball hoops as well as adjustable nets for volleyball or pickleball or whatever.

"Basketball." Fell lowered his voice. "I've seen it on television. Bouncing balls and running?"

She laughed. "Great description. It's something active to do when everything is covered in snow. Ramón and Zorion really enjoy it."

Fell blinked. "Do shifters play such a human sport?"

"Maybe not everywhere, but after First Shift, our cubs attend middle and high school with humans. André wants them to blend in, and if half the children from one town are clueless about normal sports..."

"They'll stand out." Fell's mouth compressed. "It's another way for organizations like the Scythe to find us."

"That's what the Cosantir worries about, yes." With all the technology and shrinking of the world, someday the Daonain would be revealed. No one was ready for that time yet.

"He's a far-sighted guardian."

"Mmmhmm." Moya studied Fell. Being short, basketball wasn't her sport, but she figured Patrin would love it. Fell might too. "Are you about ready to leave?" Talitha had started leaving the closing to him.

He turned and called to the young woman behind the counter. "Done, Renee?"

The young woman had been watching them, a smile on her face. Now, she lifted a hand. "Done and on my way out." Of average height and weight, the human barista had wavy black hair to mid-back. She was hardworking and punctual, delighting Talitha after a summer with seasonal college students who rarely showed up for work on time.

Fell smiled at Moya. "Let me lock up."

"Perfect. Want to go watch some basketball?"

He touched her cheek with gentle fingers, fingers that had

touched her during mating. His smile transformed his hard face. "Sounds interesting."

Almost to winter solstice, the sun was already touching the tops of the trees on the mountains as Fell crossed the square with Moya beside him. He smiled down at her, so adorably short, and felt fucking content simply being with her.

Mating with her had been...amazing. But this was good too.

He was still trying to get past the funny feeling he experienced when he realized she'd gone out of her way to get the cubs to show Patrin something he might enjoy. That she knew them enough and cared enough to do so. Even when this basketball wasn't something she played.

Far too often, this female left him...speechless. And happy.

And she was growing more comfortable being around Patrin. With luck, the next time they mated, he could share her with his brother. As littermates did.

A bell over the door rang as they entered the warehouse, and they walked into an area filled with shifters, mostly females, all holding two long sticks and yarn in the odd craft called crocheting—or was it knitting?

The Elder he'd met at the dance looked up. "Moya, how are you, dear?"

"I'm good, Ina. And you?"

"Holding up nicely."

Exchanging greetings, Moya moved past and deeper into the warehouse. "André put the yarn crafters at the front. They make sure anyone who enters is Daonain."

Good protection. He wouldn't want to take on a determined older female armed with pointy sticks.

Fell looked around curiously. Rather than the big space as at the dance, the warehouse was sectioned off with a center aisle.

The freestanding room dividers had been covered in hand painted murals.

They went past an area filled with computers, another that appeared to be an empty schoolroom.

The last section opened into a gym space with free weights and machines. A few shifters there were working out.

The very end was open with hoops mounted high on the walls to the right and left. A group of teenage cubs and adults were doing...something.

"Ah, I knew he wouldn't be able to resist." Moya pointed.

"You do it like this," Mateo called to Patrin, who stood off to one side. The cub bounced a big orange ball while running forward, then jumped and tossed the ball in an arc. The ball hit a wedge of plastic and ricocheted into the hoop.

Fell narrowed his eyes. If not angled just right, the ball would go elsewhere...as Alvaro demonstrated a minute later when he got the ball.

After Alvaro's missed shot, they tossed Patrin the ball.

Fell grinned as his brother bounced the ball carefully, moving forward slowly, then aimed for the spot up behind the hoop.

Missed.

The cubs yelled encouragement—and Patrin grinned and tried again.

Fell took a step forward. Gods, the game looked like fun.

At a melodic laugh, he glanced at the little wolf beside him. Yeah, she was laughing...at him.

"Go." She made a shooing motion with her hands. "Go, join them. You know you want to."

He did.

---

By the time the cublings finished with him and Fell, Patrin could hit the hoop most of the time and throw the ball where he wanted it to go. However, the skill of bouncing the ball faster than a walk needed a lot more practice. What had Mateo called it—dribbling?

Humans truly were bizarre, both in creating this game and the names they came up with.

*Fucking fun though.*

He laughed as Mateo stole the ball from Fell, whose *dribbling* was even worse than Patrin's. "They're too fast for you, brawd."

When Mateo grinned unrepentantly, Fell ruffled his hair. "Fucking mountain goats."

He glanced at the clock high on the wall. "Time to go."

"Right. You've got the bar tonight."

In the free weights area, Moya was talking with Bron and Niall. The tall, slim Chief of Police had a narrow face and short black hair, a definite contrast to Niall with his long golden hair and brawny build.

Beside the oversized cahirs, Moya looked even tinier. Yet he'd never seen her appear intimidated, had he?

"We gotta get home too," Alvaro told Mateo. "Eileen's making chicken, and I'm hungry."

Patrin grinned. Cubs were always hungry. "Go on with you—and thanks for the lesson." He held out his fist in an odd human ritual he'd learned from Vicki, the ex-human soldier up in Cold Creek. It was a very shifter sort of gesture.

As he'd taught them, each cub bumped a smaller fist against his and then fist-bumped Fell. Ritual concluded, the two cubs took off running in the way of younglings everywhere.

In the weight-lifting area, he asked Fell, "Remember when we had that much energy?"

Hearing him, the Chief laughed. "Wait another sixty years. It gets worse."

Sixty years? She didn't look that old. Of course, most Daonain didn't show their age until over a hundred or so.

Come to think of it, Herne wouldn't have called her to be a cahir during her child-bearing years.

"Great, something to look forward to. Thanks, Aunt Bron," Niall grumbled, then smiled at Patrin and Fell. "You two picked up basketball skills quickly."

"Hand-eye coordination was beaten into us," Patrin said matter-of-factly, then noticed the way the others reacted. "Sorry."

Fell offered a faint smile in solidarity. They often forgot how Daonain reacted to their abuse as cubs.

"You appear to be settling in." Bron set down her barbell.

"Should we be keeping an eye out for better jobs for you?" Niall asked. "Part-time work doesn't provide much of a living. I freelance in cybersecurity. Are you good with computers?"

*Oh fuck.* Taken off-guard, Patrin took a moment to find the right words. "Ah, no, but thank you. We're just...looking around. Checking out different territories. Might go back to working for the human spymaster. We won't be here for very long."

"Ah, now that's a shame." Niall grinned. "You two deal just fine with anything coming at you, from hellhounds to fairy-brained alpha wolves."

Patrin's smile faded when he noticed the Chief of Police wasn't laughing. She was studying him and Fell in a way that made the hair on his nape raise.

He checked his brother to see if he'd noticed, but no. Fell's gaze was on the basketball court, then on Moya...and his face had gone unreadable.

As it did when he was hurting inside.

Yeah. For one brilliant moment, they'd both glimpsed an entirely different future...and had forgotten they weren't part of this clan.

His sigh wasn't silent enough, and Fell bumped his shoulder in a bittersweet acknowledgment. It was just the two of them and probably always would be.

After leaving an oddly quiet Moya at her apartment, Patrin pulled one of the burner phones from his luggage. Time to get paws on the trail.

Yesterday, they'd sent Wells all the information from Gregory's house along with his picture. And the spymaster had confirmed their suspicions; Gregory was a known, low-level Scythe operative.

With the prey flushed out, the next stage began. Time to coordinate a trap.

Seeing the phone, Fell propped his forearms on the kitchen island and waited.

Unlike his brother, who became motionless when tense, Patrin tended to pace. Crossing the living room, he listened to the phone ring.

"Wells."

"Phillip here." He rolled his eyes at the insipid pseudonym Wells had saddled them with—because he often referred to Fell and Patrin as F and P, which, in his warped human mind twisted somehow into Phillip. "Want to come visit? My brother wants to play football, and we need some players for the offense."

Since their human Scythe handlers watched the game while on missions, he and Fell had learned the basics.

He stopped next to the island so Fell could hear both sides of the conversation.

"Ah. I do love a good game of football," Wells said jovially—which sounded strange from the cold-as-ice spymaster. There was a silence, a tapping of a keyboard. "What with work and all, evening is better for me and my friends. How about Tuesday night?"

"Sounds good." Patrin kept his voice easy, friendly. Because caution was always wise. "Since we'll be playing on someone else's property, we figure we'll get permission beforehand."

It was always wise to let a Cosantir know what was going on.

"No," Wells said flatly. "I'm sure the owner won't care about a quick game. If he does, he can yell at us afterward."

Fell made an unhappy sound. Angering André would be like jumping into a pit filled with rattlesnakes.

"I prefer to keep everything polite." Patrin injected as much warning into his words as he could.

"I prefer to play without busybodies or law enforcement interrupting a good time. It's happened to me too often."

*Fuck.* "Really, this—"

"No." Wells had a hard edge to his voice. "Not everyone enjoys having an audience. Some are shy."

Yes, the Scythe would vanish at any sniff of a trap. Look how often the Director and the Colonel had escaped them.

Wells added, almost as an afterthought, "Besides, aside from you and your buddies, no one else talks a good game of football."

*Ah.* Patrin exchanged understanding glances with Fell. The spymaster was human and military. Daonain had their own culture, traditions, and priorities. If Patrin and Fell often felt out of place, how much more alienated did the spymaster feel? The shifter-soldiers had spent their teen years being fashioned into soldiers by humans. Of course Wells felt like they spoke his language.

Unfortunately, the spy wouldn't have the language—or patience—to explain a critical operation to the Cosantir. And the human couldn't possibly comprehend a guardian's ties to his territory and to Herne.

To him, this was just the way things were done in the world of covert ops.

Patrin sighed. "I'll send you the address and a map." It hadn't been easy finding a house that fit the requirements needed for the perfect trap for little Scythe fishies. "We'll see you Tuesday night, probably with a kickoff after ten."

"Good enough."

Silence signaled Wells had disconnected. The spymaster rarely said goodbye.

Patrin leaned against the wall and gave his head a thump.

*Fuck.* This operation would *infuriate* André and the two cahirs who'd also expect to be notified of Scythe operatives in their territory.

Yeah, if they survived the trap, the Cosantir would probably kill them.

---

Tipping her face up to the hot spray in her shower, Moya heaved a long, depressed sigh.

When Patrin told Bron that he and Fell weren't staying in Ailill Ridge, she felt almost as if she'd been stabbed. Her heart had actually *hurt*.

Because, somehow, she'd allowed herself to think there was... something between her and Fell? And Patrin too?

*By the Mother's breasts, I'm a gnome-brain.*

They were friends...or should she say: friends with benefits? That's what she'd told Fell. And then let herself want more.

Scowling, she rinsed the soap off her body, squeezed the water from her hair, and stepped out of the shower.

*Friends with benefits. I can do that.* Although, Goddess, she needed to be careful. It appeared that mating outside of the time of the full moon engaged emotions.

She closed her eyes for a moment, thinking of the way Fell kissed. The overwhelming sensation of him entering her. Those *benefits* sure were nice.

Two robes hung on her bathroom door hook. One was long and fluffy and old. Her comfort robe. The other was a purple satin shortie with lace dripping from the three-quarter length sleeves. Not warm, but utterly sensuous. Just wearing it made her feel beautiful and oh-so-female.

Feeling beautiful won. Of course it did, since this was her pamper-Moya evening—a surefire way to beat off the doldrums.

Candles flickered in her living room, a fire crackled cheerfully in her small woodstove, and the enchanting music of Clannad filled the air. She'd sit by the fire, slather coconut oil on her winter-dry skin, and sip the Fragolino sparkling wine she'd been saving.

The satin robe whispered cool against her bare skin. Picking up her tub of coconut oil, she walked out of the bathroom in a cloud of steam.

As she set her wine and a glass on the coffee table, she smiled at the blazing fire—and the small salamander dancing in the flame. "Hey there, fire-girl. You're looking lovely tonight."

She laughed as the elemental flicked its tail in acknowledgement and added an extra spin and flourish to show off.

A knock sounded on the door. *Now who could this be?*

The outside door was locked after dark, so it couldn't be the cubs or Heather or any of her female friends. Or Brett. The only ones who could access her door now were her brothers or...Patrin and Fell.

*No, wait.* Fell was doing the bouncer job at the Bullwhacker tonight, so...

"Moya, are you home?" Patrin called through the door.

After the warehouse, she'd told them she wasn't available for a cooking lesson tonight. What was he doing here?

*Males.*

Even as she grumbled, her heartrate picked up. *Stop it, heart.* She was annoyed, dammit, not excited.

*Stupid heart.*

She yanked open the door to see the male standing there, barefoot, in jeans and a T-shirt. "*What?*"

He didn't speak. And his eyes heated.

Oh cat-scat, she'd forgotten what she was wearing.

. . .

Patrin's lungs seized up as if a moose had stepped on his chest. Because...*fuck*.

A shimmery purple wrap ended just past Moya's hips, showing off bite-worthy legs. A silky belt around her waist accentuated her glorious curves, and when she moved, her breasts wobbled.

His mouth had gone dry.

He pulled in a breath and shook his head, hoping it would knock some of the pure lust out of his thoughts. Because he was wondering just what all that skin felt like. Tasted like.

*Bad mutt.*

"Ah, I was at the Shamrock, and Madoc made those dark chocolate truffles you said you liked, so I brought you some." He held up a sack. "In thanks for all the cooking lessons."

"Oh, wow, thank you." She took the sack. "He's only made them once before, and they're sooo good. Thank you, again."

"You're welcome. Sorry—I probably interrupted your shower." He took a step away.

"Wait."

He turned back.

"I'm sorry for snapping at you." She bit her lip. "Um, want some wine?"

Now, here was a surprise. He didn't think she trusted him enough to have him around without Fell. "I'd love some."

To his surprise, the only light in the room was from squat candles flickering on the coffee table, the woodstove fire, and a Solstice tree with blue and silver mini lights.

In front of the raised woodstove hearth was her round, emerald-green floor cushion, and a bottle of wine on the nearby coffee table. He hesitated. Candles, silky robe, wine. Was she expecting company?

The sharp pain ripping through his chest was unexpected. Because what he was feeling was...jealousy. Pure possessive *"this is my female."* No, actually, *our* Moya. Something he'd never felt before.

She waved at the room. "Sit anywhere you like. I'll get another glass."

Only one glass sat beside the wine bottle. Hmm, hadn't Ramón teased her about her pampering time with candles and wine? Was tonight a pampering night?

Where to sit? He eyed the couch, the chairs, then the seven-foot-across cushion. The coffee table had been pulled next to the floor cushion. She'd obviously planned to sit by the fire.

Sounded good to him.

He dropped down on the thick cushion. The fake fur was plush and soft. "This is more comfortable than it looks."

"I love it." She handed him a glass and moved the coffee table close enough to set the plate with the truffles on it. After a moment of hesitation, she joined him on the cushion—and the trust she showed warmed him.

He had to admit, her efforts to keep covered with the mid-thigh-length robe were as unsuccessful as they were tantalizing.

He poured wine for them both, then took a sip. "This is different." Slightly bubbly, light and delicate with a hint of strawberry flavor.

"It was a gift from when I sang at a handfasting celebration." She tasted it. "This will go great with chocolate.

Biting into one of the small truffle balls, she hummed, her pleasure so open and sexy, he hardened. She smiled at him. "Try one. Madoc makes great food."

He was more of a cake or cookie person, but okay. He chose one with drizzles of white on the dark outside. The deep chocolate taste of the shell turned even richer with the smooth ganache center. "Damn, that *is* good."

"Told you." She took another, alternating nibbles with sips of wine.

Muscle by muscle, Patrin relaxed under the soothing of the drink, the heat from the fire, the soft Celtic music.

For a while, they simply sat together, nibbling on the candy and drinking. A comfortable quiet, one he hadn't found with many others besides Fell.

All the same, there was a tension in the air that sure wasn't there with his brother.

A very primal tension heightened by the way the firelight glowed off her rosy skin, the way her dark hair was curling as it dried, the scent of her body.

"Oh, I need to..." She huffed out a breath. "You're going to think me crazy, but I need to oil up."

Were they speaking the same language? "Oil up?"

From the coffee table, she picked up a plastic tub. "Yes. Air in a heated building dries out skin, and I itch if I don't use this stuff after a shower." Scooping some into her palm, she started stroking it over her left leg.

"Well, we wouldn't want you to have dry skin." Unable to resist, he put two fingers in the tub, feeling a semi-solid substance, and caught the light fragrance of coconut.

As it turned liquid from the heat of his hand, he pulled her right foot into his lap and started massaging. Such a tiny foot, almost disappearing into his big hands. Since she'd stopped moving, he went on and did her left foot, then moved up to her calf.

*Mmm.* Her skin was satin-smooth, warm.

Her dark eyes had widened. Yet...she didn't jerk away from his touch.

He watched her face, her eyes...and continued with his task. Slow, up and down, over her leg.

Since she still wasn't moving, he switched to her right leg. "Your brother said you have pampering time when you need comfort."

Her lips tipped up in a rueful smile. "Yes, it's a pity-party of one. I was feeling sorry for myself."

"Did something happen? To make you sad?"

She snorted. "You did. You and Fell."

*What?* His hands still on her leg as he went back over their interactions. "What did we do?" Admittedly, they weren't particularly adept at interactions with Daonain, especially females, but how had they hurt her?

"When you talked with Bron at the warehouse, you made it clear you aren't staying in Ailill Ridge. You'll be moving on." She looked away. Her voice dropped to where he could barely hear her over the crackling fire and the soft music. "And I'll miss you both."

He closed his eyes for a moment, feeling her words pierce his chest like a thrown spear. They'd found the Scythe spy. They wouldn't be here much longer. "Yeah. We'll miss you too. I'll miss you."

After a silent moment, he continued, stroking over her knees. Her thighs. The skin was softer. Way too fucking tempting.

And if he went any farther upward, he'd be in "let's mate" territory. Perhaps not a good decision.

Swallowing, he sat back. How to retreat without being rude? "Want me to get your back?"

"Um." Her cheeks were flushed. "Sure, that'd be great. I can't reach all the places." Setting her wine on the hearth, she flattened out, belly down on the fuzzy cushion.

By the Gods, he hadn't thought this through. She wasn't wearing anything under that robe. Slowly, carefully, he pulled the satiny cloth off her shoulders, down her back. Strong shoulders. A soft waist just begging for his hands. Tantalizing dimples on each side above her hips.

*No, you can't lick the dimples.*

He stroked oil over her back, letting his hands graze the sides of her waist, determinedly stopping before her ass.

Blowing out a breath, he lay down on his side next to her, propping his head up on one hand. "Little wolf, I'm stopping now. Unless you want me to do your front, in which case, I'll touch… everything and everywhere, inside and out."

With his hand on her low back, he could feel her shiver. Could smell the musky, heady scent of her arousal. She obviously wanted to say yes.

But her dark eyebrows puckered together.

Oh, sprite-spit, she didn't know what to do. Her whole body felt as if it was on fire, needing...more, but a part of her was terrified.

His dark eyes grew intense. With a finger, he moved a strand of hair from her face. "Talk to me, Moya. Is your hesitation because you don't like dominant males? I'm not sure I can remove that from my personality."

A laugh broke from her at the thought, as if it could be plucked out like a stray hair. But he'd asked a question. Rolling onto her side to face him, ignoring how her bare breasts wobbled, she met his gaze. "Yes, partly. I worry about...that coercion stuff, through the pack bonds especially. It's left me wary."

"Fair enough." He rubbed his knuckles on her cheek, sending little tingles through her. "I found Brett's use of the bonds to be reprehensible. I'd never do that to anyone."

His scent, his gaze, his voice—all sang of honesty. "Really?"

He gripped her hand, laying it on his face, connecting them. "Really."

His short beard was soft under her palm. Her thumb rubbed over the sharp angle of his hard jaw. And, without thinking, she leaned forward and set her lips against his.

Breathing in his soft exhalation, she kissed him, slowly discovering what his mouth felt like. *This was nice. Yes.*

Then he curved his hand around the back of her head, tilting her, and taking her mouth. The kiss went right from nice into a sizzle. Every hormone in her body ignited.

"Now, little wolf, I won't use the bonds...but I am dominant, especially in mating." His smooth voice had deepened to a husky growl. "I can't turn that off. Nonetheless, if there is any time you're not comfortable with what we're doing, simply say so. I'll stop or change what we're doing. Aye?" He rubbed his bearded cheek against hers, like a cat might.

He was in charge. She could say no. It was like he was handing her all her most hidden fantasies. Her voice came out a whisper. "Aye."

His hand tightened in her hair, tipping her head back, as he took her mouth again. Not roughly, but his lips were slow, coaxing her mouth open for his tongue. His exploration was thorough even as he teased her into responding. Pulling back, he kissed her temple, her cheek, slowly tipping her onto her back. And covering her with his body, his heavy weight pinning her to the cushion.

Under her hands, his shoulders were all ripped muscle. When she buried her face against his neck, his natural woodsy scent was seductively masculine. She ran her fingers through the wavy black hair, enjoying how the silky strands reached his shoulders.

"Have you ever mated outside of a Gathering? Aside from your time with Fell?" With callused fingers under her chin, he tilted her head up, forcing her to meet his gaze.

"No. Just then and full moons. Why?"

His eyes crinkled. "You're used to being laid out and pleasured and hammered. You're a giving sort of person—you might like a change in positions and a chance to take time to see what you're mating."

"I...don't understand."

He pulled off his shirt, then rolled them both over, putting her on top, pushing her up to where she was sitting up and straddling him. "Go ahead and explore, *blodyn*. My body is yours. For a while, at least." His grin within the dark beard was white and wicked. "I want your hands and mouth on me."

Explore? Being with Fell had been amazing when he'd given her time to enjoy everything. And now, she'd get to satisfy her need to touch and lick and see? "*Yes*." Bending, she kissed him and then began.

The long, corded muscles in his neck were perfect to nibble on. His shoulders were all hard muscle beneath her fingers. Straight dark hair dusted his pectorals.

His small, almost flat, dark nipples were very lickable with a velvety texture like his lips, and as she ran her tongue around one, his breathing hitched.

When he gripped her shoulders, she gave him an uncertain look. Should she stop?

His laugh was almost as gravelly as Fell's. "You feel so good that you're hard on my control, little wolf."

Oh, she could almost feel her nonexistent tail wag. Happily, she tugged off his jeans and knelt beside him.

With a light finger, she traced the silky line of hair over his abs downward until reaching his long, slightly curved shaft. Gods, would it even fit inside her? But, oh, she wanted to know.

Slowly, she ran her hands over his thighs, moving inward to fondle his heavy balls. The skin on them was very different. Bending, she licked over one, then the other, breathing in the heavier musky scent.

And felt him grip her thighs, turning her so her butt was angled in his direction.

Whatever. Smiling slightly, she gently curled her fingers around the shaft.

His low chuckle sounded, and he closed his fingers around hers. "Balls are sensitive, dicks not so much. I'd like it if you gripped me like this."

"Oh. Thank you." Something inside her relaxed. Some people jumped into everything and consulted directions if and when they screwed up. Others were like her and read the whole manual before beginning. Not knowing the guidelines often meant she wouldn't even start. "I like knowing what to do."

His warm hand caressed her hip—which, she realized, he'd placed conveniently for him to touch. "Good—because I like telling you."

She stroked his cock until her mouth demanded a turn. His scent was so beguiling. Licking upward, she hummed in pleasure and ran her tongue over the vein-ridged skin.

Another long lick.

His hand tightened on her hip. "Yes, good."

Fun, this was fun. And...why was doing this making her so much hotter? She was growing really, really wet.

Carefully—she figured teeth were bad—she took him in her mouth and heard a throaty groan. Gradually, she found a steady pace, going deeper each time.

Why, when she gave him pleasure, did her own female parts begin to throb?

Up and down. She braved using her tongue over the top, got another squeeze and a husky, "Keep going, little wolf."

All in, she played, licking, bobbing, even sucking. And felt his hand slide between her thighs, over her slick pussy. Stroking over her clit—and the burst of pleasure made her suck harder.

He laughed—and gripped her thighs, easily lifting her up, over his body, and settling her so his face was between her thighs.

She raised her head. "What are you...?"

Pulling her thighs open farther, he dropped her downward—and onto his face. With a hard hand, he held her there, his lips moving over her pussy, and his tongue stroking over her clit.

*Gods, gods, gods*! A high whine broke from her as her need blazed like a forest fire. Her instinctive attempt to lift up met implacable hands that held her in place.

"Mmmph, you taste like dessert." He curled his tongue around her clit, over it, flickering lightly until she was so close. The pressure rose in her, inevitable as a late afternoon thunderstorm.

And then he pushed her upward, just an inch. His mouth gone. And warm breath washed over her burning, needy bits.

"Patrin." The word came out a long wail.

And the flea-bitten mongrel laughed. "I want your mouth around me, my sweet wolf. And then we'll see."

He was...ordering her? Controlling when she could have a climax? Her frustration felt angry—except everything inside her helplessly melted at his low commanding tone.

Her token growl only made him chuckle, maybe because she was obediently taking his shaft into her mouth, concentrating on him, only on him and not on how her own needs were raging.

When she wrapped her hands around him, pumping even as she sucked and licked, he made the best guttural sound. And he pulled her hips down, his tongue going to work in a devastating way, and again the pressure grew, the pleasure rising so intensely... and his tongue withdrew, his lips working her with tiny touches, keeping her right there, shuddering helplessly on the pinnacle of coming.

Her hands tightened on his cock as she wrenched her head up, panting for air in the exquisite torment. "Please, please..."

"Aye, *blodyn*." His lips closed tightly around her, and he licked—sucked—licked, rubbing firmly.

The sensations erupted into explosive waves of release until there was a roar of sound in her ears as the blood sang through her.

Before she recovered, he moved her, twisting up and setting her on her hands and knees. As her arms went limp, she dropped to her shoulders, her ass still up in the air.

Patrin smiled as the adorable little wolf went limp. The way she came apart under his mouth and hands was the finest thing he'd ever experienced. And how she responded when he gave her orders. It satisfied something deep inside him.

And now, they'd both enjoy the next part. He knelt between her legs, his dick so hard it ached. Leaning forward, he rubbed his chest against her back and whispered in her ear, "I'm going to take you now. Tell me yes or no."

The breathless answer was what he wanted to hear. "Yes."

He moved back onto his knees. Setting his dick against her soft warmth, he eased her open and sank into slick heat. *Herne help me.* "You feel"—his words came out more a growl than speech—"magnificent."

Her laugh made her clench around him and almost blew the top of his head off. Gripping her hips, he started to thrust, working into a hard, driving rhythm—and thoroughly enjoyed the way her ass globes wobbled.

Harder, faster.

Her face was flushing again as her arousal rose. She moved up onto her hands, fingers curled into the cushion, and pushed back to meet each of his thrusts.

Fuck, she felt good.

Time to add to things. He moved his right leg forward and under her, so he was kneeling on one leg with his thigh under her pelvis and her knee on the outside of his right hip. The position opened her wide—and eradicated her ability to direct anything.

She groaned as he surged in deeper—and sped up. Thrusting and rotating his hips. Oh, he could do this forever.

Her arms gave out, and she went down to her elbows.

Perfect. Lowering her leg, he went back on both knees, and leaned forward, then reached around her so he could slide his fingers over her clit. Everything spasmed around him so hard, he almost came right then and there.

Fuck. Her slickness was all over his fingers, the most wonderful feeling along with the scent of their mating. He could hear the slight whine in each breath she took as he brought her up and up. She was tightening around him. Balancing on one arm, he circled her clit with the fingers of his free hand and kept up a ruthless thrusting.

Her back muscles went tense, shivers running through her whole body, and then she came. Her neck arched; her head fell forward, and she cried out in a way that made his wolf fucking happy.

He sat back, hands on her hips, yanked her back against him, fast and hard—and released the control over his body. Heat filled his balls, sizzling through his groin and shooting out his dick. The pleasure with each jerk of his cock was incredible.

Dropping forward, he propped himself up with one hand and put the other under her belly, feeling the tremors still running through her body.

Unable to help himself, he kissed the back of her neck, the curve of her shoulder, and bit the muscle there, firmly enough he heard her suck in a breath. And felt her lose herself to another orgasm.

*Yeah, she was all wolf, this one.*

*My wolf.*

*No. This is Moya, and we're not staying.*

*Dammit.*

---

Silently, Fell let himself into his apartment, feeling weariness dragging at him. Being around so many people, especially humans, put his defensive instincts on high. And kept them there for hours.

The light from the kitchen appliances let him see well enough to cross the room. But wait... He sniffed, catching the faint fragrance of sex and traced it to where his littermate lay, sound asleep on the couch—as he often did until Fell got home.

But sex? Moya's scent was all over his brother.

Fell smiled, pleased beyond all measure. Patrin had gotten to see how amazing a mating could be without the overwhelming urges of a full moon. And with Moya...well, there was no one sweeter in the world.

Picking up a blanket, he started to drape it over his brother when Patrin started to growl. To shake.

*Oh fuck.* Fell stepped back to get out of range of fangs and fists. "Patrin. Wake up, brawd." He could feel the shimmer of an impending trawsfur.

Must be a really bad nightmare, then. He hardened his voice to the cold, brutal tone of the worst of their trainers. "Wake up, MacCormac."

Patrin stiffened, bracing for a blow even before he opened his eyes. Silently, of course. Speaking got them beaten. His gaze wasn't yet focused, but he was awake.

"Hey, brawd, you're safe." Fell kept his voice low and easy. "We're in Ailill Ridge, remember? Living across the hall from pretty Moya?"

"Moya?" Patrin sat up slowly and scrubbed his hands over his face. "Right. Sure. You were at the Bullwhacker tonight."

"And you were with Moya." Relaxing, Fell dropped into a chair next to the couch. "Did you enjoy your evening?"

Wearing jeans and a work shirt, Patrin rested his bare feet on the coffee table. Alertness had returned to his expression, although his eyes were still haunted from the nightmare. "I did. I took her some chocolate truffles from the Shamrock and found her indulging in a—what did she call it—a pity-party."

"A what?" Did that mean a bunch of her friends trying to comfort someone for something?

"Pity-party. Apparently, it means staying home and feeling sorry for yourself."

Fell laughed, then had to admit he'd indulged in that a time or two himself. "I like how she was upfront about what she was doing."

"She's...impressively straightforward." Patrin walked into the kitchen, returning with a couple of glasses of water. He handed one to Fell. "She was feeling sad because she realized when we talked to Bron we don't plan to stay in Ailill Ridge."

"Oh, by the Horned God." Fell set the glass on the coffee table with a thump. Guilt and dismay set up a corrosive burn in his blood.

"She's not angry, just sad." Patrin drank half of the water and leaned back with a sigh. "It feels strange to know someone will miss us when we're gone. Nice, but..."

Fell swallowed and admitted, "I'm going to miss her too." More than that. Whenever he thought of leaving, of not seeing her again, it felt as if someone had taken a blade to his chest.

"Yeah." Patrin gave him a perceptive look. "Yeah, I wish we could have been honest about why we're here—and even more, I...like it here. First time I felt like this. It'd be nice to be closer to Darcy. The territory has good people."

But they couldn't. For the safety of the clan, for the safety of innocents like Moya and Mateo and Alvaro, the Scythe threat needed to be eliminated. "No choice." Fell finished off his water and ran his gaze over his brother. "Another nightmare? Chester and Graham?"

"Yeah." Patrin growled under his breath. "That one and then the other. When I couldn't get them to listen."

By the Gods, couldn't a person's mind have mercy? The time with the Scythe had been brutal. Having been isolated, the young male shifters had grown to be like family. So when training started, seeing their brothers-in-spirit being hurt had been almost unendurable.

Chester and Graham had been the oldest of them all, almost a year older. Quiet, fun, and far too kind. Like all of them, their sister was held hostage for their good behavior. When they'd felt Barbara die, nothing could keep them from trying to escape. Patrin and Fell had tried, but, unlike wolves, cougars had no pack bonds for a leader to use. After cutting out the trackers in their arms, Chester and Graham ran, unaware of the second trackers, buried deeper. Locating the brothers, the Colonel and his men burned a forest to drive them out and brought the bullet-riddled bodies back to lay in front of the barracks for days.

Fell closed his eyes for a moment, trying to erase the pain.

For Patrin it'd been worse. In his brother's head, all the

captive males, no matter what animal, were part of his pack, and he blamed himself for not keeping them safe.

Did all alphas share the same belief—that they should be able to save everyone?

But alphas were not gods. Not everything was under their control. Patrin knew it too...in his mind. His emotions and instincts didn't agree.

Fell reached forward and squeezed his brother's shoulder in sympathy. Not much else he could do to help.

Or...

"You might talk to Moya," Fell suggested. "She's working through something similar. Has some techniques that're helping her."

Patrin's expression closed down at the suggestion of talking about his problem, but after a moment, he tilted his head. "Something similar?" His face darkened. "Like what?"

Fell almost laughed. This might work. If Patrin worried enough about Moya, he might be willing to discuss their mutual problems. Because, as Fell had discovered, Moya wouldn't share unless Patrin did the same. "Not my story to tell, brawd. You'll have to ask her."

"You're a fucking, flea-ridden mongrel." Patrin shot him an annoyed stare, then shook his head. "I'm not going to describe the gory deaths of young shifters to a female. Especially a sheltered sweetheart like Moya."

Fell started to object. But he knew exactly what Patrin was talking about.

Young teenaged shifters, full of raging hormones, were easy to provoke, especially if a littermate was being hurt. And Patrin couldn't halt the bears or lions with the bonds. Fell shook his head, thinking of the scrawny younglings, bleeding, broken on the ground while a Scythe trainer laughed. Too many of them haunted his own nightmares. Describing them to Moya?

Yeah, no. "I understand."

But the nightmares weren't going away. Fuck, if anything, they'd grown worse for him and even more so for Patrin. Not enough sleep, too much tension.

"Guess I'll take a hot shower and try again." Patrin slapped his arm and headed to his bedroom.

Frowning, Fell rubbed the stubble on his jaw, worry gnawing a hole in his gut. Patrin needed a chance to heal, and that meant finding a life not centered around violence and the Scythe.

And there was no way in Herne's green forest that would happen.

## CHAPTER THIRTEEN

"Let's get this done, brawd." Patrin pulled on his jacket, jogging down the alley steps outside their apartment. The icy wind bit his face, making him grateful for his short beard and long hair. Poor Fell had nothing blocking the cold.

They circled the building, entered the square, and headed for the grocery store. The Scythe operative should be bagging up groceries at this hour.

Patrin slowed at the sight of Brett, Caleb, and Gretchen talking to Mateo, Alvaro, and the two cubs who were bullies.

"You heard my orders. Drive those scrawny cats away from the square." Brett pointed to two younglings playing on the five-foot-high snow piled in a corner of the square. "Show them this is *our* downtown."

"Sure, Alpha!" The two bullies ran to comply.

Gretchen looked after them, frowning. "Brett, I don't think—"

Brett took a step toward Mateo and Alvaro. "What're you two waiting for. Get going."

*Fuck.* Patrin growled under his breath. "Fell, you take the bully babies." He stalked forward and slapped his hands down on

Mateo's and Alvaro's shoulders. "Murtagh wanted to talk to you two. Have you done that?"

"Ah, no?" Alvaro said slowly.

Mateo caught on quicker. "Rabid ratshit. I forgot. We better do that now. Excuse us, please, Alpha."

So very politely, they bowed their heads slightly and sprinted toward the grocery store.

*Clever cubs.*

Being an Elder, Murtagh should be able to keep them safe, at least this time.

Hand pressed to her chest, Gretchen was watching Fell, who'd grabbed the bullies by their hoods and yanked them off the smaller feline cubs. With no effort at all, he tossed the wolves onto a different snowbank.

Yelling in anger, the half-buried cubs struggled to get out. The feline cubs scampered away.

Gretchen released an audible breath as the feline cubs ran off. "Good, they got away."

"What in the fuck?" Brett turned on her with a furious scowl. "Good? What's your problem?"

"You're criticizing your alpha?" Caleb snapped at her.

Patrin raised an eyebrow, equally surprised.

Her nose went up in the air. "No Daonain hurts cubs."

"Hey, I've seen you throw rocks at those two the Cosantir took in," Caleb said. "Back when they got into your B&B garbage cans."

"Just to scare them—never to hit them." Her voice sounded different. Lower, almost husky. "Never to *hurt* them."

Brett snorted. "I wasn't hurting them. Cubs are always fighting."

"You sicced bigger ones on littler ones. That's wrong." With a whirl of her blonde hair, Gretchen walked away.

*Huh.* Self-centered, vicious to anyone she didn't see as worthy of her attention, but the female apparently had limits.

A shame the alpha didn't.

He tilted his head at Brett. "What she said." Ignoring the alpha's growl, he continued on his way.

With an amused tilt to his lips, Fell veered off to station himself in the alley behind the grocery store.

*Someone* had enjoyed cooling off the bratty pups in the snow.

Entering the store, Patrin spotted Gregory, the Scythe agent, hard at work bagging groceries. Perfect.

Snagging a shopping cart, Patrin filled it quickly and wheeled it up to check-out.

"Evening, Murtagh." He smiled at the old shifter. After handing the recyclable grocery bags to the human Scythe operative, he started unloading the food onto the counter.

"Patrin, good to see you." Murtagh started scanning the prices.

From the corner of his eye, Patrin noted the Scythe's intent look. *Ah, as we thought, you already have me targeted.*

"And you, Murtagh. Oh fuck, did I lose the candles?" Patrin dug through the cart and pulled up the packet. "Here they are. Now I have to remember where we put our sleeping bags."

"Sleeping bags." Murtagh's appalled expression was amusing as hell. "Surely, you're not camping out in the snow."

"Hah, we're not that crazy." Patrin set the candles on the counter. "We plan to rough it in a house we might rent. It's out to the west on Whistlepunk Street."

"I don't remember seeing a rental sign there." Murtagh never slowed with scanning the groceries.

"The house is dark blue, number 503. We heard a rumor it'd be up for rent and talked to the owner." Actually, they'd arranged for a one-month rental period with Heather since the house was owned by the clan, and she handled the business stuff.

Patrin leaned against the counter, as if settling in to talk—and noticed Gregory was bagging the groceries real slow. "The house seems great, nicely isolated at the end of the street with forest on three sides. But Fell's a light sleeper, and the oddest shit keeps him up at night—like one house where some tree branches rubbed and squeaked."

"Ah, my Maeve's a bit like that." Murtagh nodded his understanding. "So camping?"

"Yeah, to check if the house will work for him before signing a lease. We asked the owner if we can spend tonight there, and she agreed."

"Sounds like a good plan." Murtagh smiled, his gaze full of sympathy. Of course, the Elder knew they were shifter-soldiers and why one of them might have trouble sleeping. "I hope it works well for you and Fell."

"Thanks." Since the bagger was moving so slowly, Patrin tore open a package of M&Ms before it was bagged. He popped a few in his mouth, enjoying the burst of chocolate.

Reminded him of being a cub and their mama buying candy to get Fell to stop chattering. Back when Fell was the one who talked the most.

He rubbed his chest, hurting for his brother. *Not the time, wolf.* Glancing at the total, he paid. "I need to get moving. Got stuff to do."

Seeing the groceries still unbagged, Murtagh narrowed his eyes at Gregory. His voice came out a growl. "Let's see some energy, lad. You're moving slower than a fat slug."

Gregory jumped. "Yes, sir. Sorry, sir." The young human quickly filled the last of the bags and handed them over.

"Thank you, Gregory." Patrin gave him a smile and headed out of the store. Out in the alley, Fell should be in position and ready for the spy.

*Up to you, now, brawd.*


After assessing the alley behind the grocery store, Fell found only one place where he'd be concealed yet within hearing distance.

The well-angled roof was high enough he wouldn't be seen by anyone below. He used a garbage can as a stepping stool to climb up and onto the roof.

Lying flat on the snow-covered shingles, he started getting chilled all too fast.

It'd been about half an hour. Patrin should be done shopping by now. Hopefully, Scythe's weasel would report in quickly.

A couple more minutes passed before the back door to the grocery store creaked open and closed with a dull thud.

Fell stilled, barely breathing.

Footsteps in the snow made crunching sounds before stopping. There were rustling noises and a few loud inhalations.

Ah, right. He'd seen Gregory using one of those human pseudo-cigarettes. A vape-thing. Perhaps stalling and trying to get his courage up?

Good luck, lad. Fell had a moment of sympathy. As a cub, he'd been terrified of the Scythe leaders, especially the cold, merciless Colonel.

"Sir, yes, sir, it's Gregory. No, it's not my normal check-in. But there's a chance here to capture them without much exposure."

Unable to hear the other side of the conversation, Fell scowled.

"Yes, sir. They'll be spending tonight in an isolated house that's surrounded by forest."

Fell grinned as the human went on to explain Patrin's tale of how Fell had trouble sleeping. Really, it was a good story, especially since it wasn't a complete lie. They both had trouble with unfamiliar noises.

There was a pause after Gregory finished with the location of the house and time limit. Fell tensed. Who was Gregory's boss? Probably the Director if Wells was right and the Colonel had been killed.

Had he bought the story?

"Yes, sir. Do you want me to assist?" Gregory sounded half-eager, half-terrified. "I can? Yes! Thank you, sir."

More rustling sounds—probably putting away the phone—then the human heaved a big sigh. The back door creaked and thudded shut.

Waiting to be sure he was gone, Fell grinned.

*Tonight will be a fine hunt, brawd.*

## CHAPTER FOURTEEN

After exploring the house with Patrin, Fell located an electrical socket and plugged in a recording of their voices. The timer would shut it off a little after ten.

In a bedroom, he plugged a reading light into a timer set to turn on at ten-twenty and off fifteen minutes later. Together, the devices would present an illusion of them talking in the living room, then going to bed and reading for a while before lights out.

As the minutes ticked by, the sense of anticipation and worry grew. Gregory had reported to someone. Who?

Wells was in town somewhere with some of the shifter-soldiers. There would be a spotter on each of the two paved roads entering Ailill Ridge. Soon enough, they'd know if the Scythe had taken the bait.

*Stay on task*. Waiting was the hardest part of this job.

Opening his sleeping bag, Fell stuffed in enough clothing to resemble a body. Just in case the Scythe operatives made it into the building.

Hearing Patrin's phone ding, Fell went into the other bedroom to check if there was news.

Patrin set a hand over the phone's receiver to report, "It's

Wells. Congratulations, brawd, the Director was spotted in a car entering town."

Fell moved close enough he could hear the spymaster's cold, aristocratic voice. "For our opening move in football, we'll start by forming a loose semi-circle around the ball."

The ball would be the house. So the other shifter-soldiers would take up position in the forest around the house. "When the quarterback puts the ball into play, we'll close the circle and ensure the other team has no chances to throw the ball."

The quarterback would be the Director. So the shifter-soldiers would block the road and attack from behind the Scythe operatives. The ones in the forest would close in.

"Sounds like a fun game plan," Patrin said. "Make sure you avoid brush clumps. There's a big one on the east. Guess there's a downside to playing football near a forest."

In other words, Patrin and Fell would be hiding in a patch of brush, waiting to join the attack. They'd considered hanging out in a tree, but that wasn't a wolf's favorite place, and thermal imaging made it difficult to hide.

"Noted," Wells said and continued, "The other side plays rough, so do the same. However, the quarterback is fragile. Handle him carefully."

So, the plan was to eliminate everyone except the Director. Not surprising. The Director had information they needed. Like what happened to the Colonel. What was going on with the larger Scythe organization.

"Got it." Patrin hesitated and tried one more time to get Wells to see reason. "I still think you should ask the property owner to join the game. Or at least let him know so he doesn't feel left out. I'd hate to have him unhappy with us."

André was a reasonable sort, but no one in their right minds angered a Cosantir.

"Sorry, no. We'll tell him afterward," Wells said. "Any questions?"

"Guess not. Sounds like it'll be a great game."

"Absolutely. See you later."

"Stubborn human," Patrin said. "Let's get moving; it's getting dark."

"I'm ready." Rather than battle dress, they wore camo cargo pants in shades of gray and black, a tactical vest, sheathed knives, and pistols. Fell picked up his duffel containing his night-vision goggles, food, drink—and a cushion. Why be uncomfortable? On the way out, he turned on the recording and heard him and Patrin talking.

Inside the large pantry, Patrin lifted the trap door and took the steps down into an old-fashioned root cellar. Following, Fell closed the trap door behind them.

In the root cellar, the back wall appeared to be solid rock, but had a narrow door into a rough-cut tunnel. The tunnel had excellent bracing, thank fuck. A cave-in wasn't any way to die.

Closing the rock wall behind him, he followed Patrin through the tunnel, which opened in a clump of underbrush east of the house. The one Patrin warned Wells to avoid.

If in a forest, most shifter homes contained hidden exits. This house and tunnel were very well designed. A Daonain could strip, trawsfur, and emerge in the woods with no chance of being spotted by humans.

Even better, tonight, they could wait in the tunnel and not be detected by Scythe with night-vision or infrared goggles. They'd already tied back a couple of bushes so they could exit the clump of brush without sounding like a herd of buffalo.

When the fighting began, they'd join in.

After opening the door near the end of the tunnel, Patrin took a seat, staying far enough in that infrared imagers wouldn't catch their body heat. He said in a voice that couldn't be heard farther than two feet away, "I fucking hate waiting."

Fell snorted his agreement. It was too dark to play cards and talking in whispers got annoying fast. Getting comfortable on the ground, he leaned back against the cold rock and dirt wall. "I'd rather be getting cooking lessons from a little wolf."

Sampling the food. Sampling her.

Patrin half laughed. "Yeah, me too."

Bending his head, Fell tried not to feel the ache in his chest. By the Gods, how could he be missing her even before they left? But he was.

---

Patrin let his mind wander as the long minutes passed. And despite his best intentions, a whole lot of his thoughts were about the evening with Moya. Sharing food and wine, talking, kissing her. Touching... *No, gnome-brain.* Fighting with a hard-on was like asking to be killed.

Instead, he pushed his thoughts to the next possible targets in their war against the Scythe.

"There," Fell said almost soundlessly. His hearing was better than Patrin's.

Tilting his head and wishing for his wolf ears, Patrin caught the faint rustling of someone moving above. The soft crunch of dry snow.

Time to get their tails out of the cave. A glance at the open tunnel door showed a clear sky with the Lady's moon riding high. No need for the night-vision goggles.

He patted his pockets, adjusted his belt and holsters, checking once again that nothing clanked. *All good.*

Fell, equally silent, nodded to show he was ready.

A minute later, from the other end of the tunnel came the sound of the front door being kicked in. The attack on the house had begun. A flash-bang boomed.

*Clever Scythe.* They'd knew exactly what effect flash-bangs had on Daonain's sensitive senses.

Thank fuck he and Fell were in a tunnel rather than in the house. He grinned at Fell.

The yells of the humans above were muffled by the long tunnel.

"*Clear.*"

"*Clear.*"

"*Clear.*"

At least three Scythe were methodically clearing the house. There'd undoubtedly be more stationed outside the doors and windows to prevent Patrin and Fell from escaping.

*Time to join the party.*

Patrin jogged up the steep rise to the tunnel exit and poked his head out. No one in sight. He caught the wild—and familiar—scents of two fellow shifter-soldiers. A cougar and a wolf. No humans.

Easing out of the tunnel, he stepped aside to make room for Fell.

Once out, Fell sniffed and gave a comradely salute in the direction of the other shifters.

Patrin glanced down at his cargo pants and vest. Even if not downwind to catch scents, the shifter-soldiers should be able to identify Wells' custom camo pattern. Then again, with luck, the Scythe would wear combat helmets and goggles—and decrease the chance of Patrin and Fell dying by friendly fire.

Drawing his pistol, he eased out of the brush patch and moved stealthily toward the house.

Fell followed, slightly off to one side.

The snap, snap, snap of silenced weaponry came from near the house as they slipped through the forest.

*Ah, there.* A Scythe lurked behind a tree, stationed far enough from the house to serve as a backup in case of escape. He held a rifle—not a tranq gun—so his orders were obviously to kill rather than capture.

The thought of the bastard killing Fell was...

Anger lit Patrin's blood on fire. He aimed and shot three times, one to the human's lower spine to fragment the pelvis, then mid-thoracic area, and back of the head—his own version of a military double-tap.

Fell's pistol snapped as he eliminated the human's teammate.

Return gunfire came from the house, and Patrin dove down and behind a tree. Bullets struck the tree over his head, splattering him with bark splinters.

His heart was pounding, his mouth dry. Yeah, that'd been a bit too close. He glanced over, and Fell nodded. *All good.*

Easing sideways, Patrin moved forward quickly and silently. They had a Director to capture and interrogate.

Obviously on perimeter duty, the werecats Bryn and Rhys nodded at him and Fell.

Continuing, Patrin stopped at the forest's edge.

Black shapes lay on the small strip of lawn around the house. One was the grocery bagger, Gregory, and Patrin sighed. Damn the Scythe for corrupting their young with hatred and fear.

The firing petered out to a halt. In the darkness beneath the trees, shadows flitted—Daonain in human form.

Sounded like the fight was over.

"There he is," Patrin said under his breath.

Pistol out and pointing toward the forest, the Director was backing toward his car. The human was in his fifties, balding and had grown even fatter.

The last time Patrin had seen him was over a year ago when the male captives were taken to visit their sisters in Seattle where the female hostages were imprisoned. The Scythe bastard had been smoking a cigar and smirking at the male shifters who couldn't...do...*anything*.

Rage ignited in Patrin's blood. His pistol rose. *Don't shoot him.* Gritting his teeth, he kept his finger from the trigger. Barely.

On the street, Wells and a couple of his operatives took up

station behind the parked cars. The Director wouldn't get away this time.

Patrin glanced at Fell and motioned toward a small wellhouse. It'd give them shelter while—

A cougar flashed down the street, leaped on top of the car nearest the Director, and snarled loudly. The human spun around.

Coming from the side, another cougar attacked the Director, took him to the ground—and ripped out his throat. Black in the moonlight, blood sprayed everywhere.

*What the fuck!*

From behind a car, firearm in one hand, Wells ran forward to stand over the Director's body. "What in the fucking hell have you done? I gave you orders to leave the Director alive."

The cougar standing over the body trawsfurred into a lanky female with short black hair. Bron, the Chief of Police.

"Oh, by Herne's horns and hooves," Fell muttered.

"Yeah," Patrin agreed. From the size of the cougar standing next to her, he'd bet it was the other cahir, Niall. "We are fucked."

He had a cowardly wish to fade back into the forest and disappear. But this was their operation. They'd set it up. And even if Wells was human-stupid about Cosantirs, he'd been a damn good leader for the shifter-soldiers. He had their loyalty.

As they crossed the lawn, the Chief took off the mini pack she'd worn tight against her neck and stomach. Taking out clothing, she pulled on black trail pants, a black hiking shirt, and thin shoes. Once dressed, she crossed her arms over her chest and gave Wells a scathing look. "Explain what is going on here."

Wells scowled. "Who are you, and what are you doing in the middle of my operation?"

"*Your* operation. Good to know who to arrest." Bron's tone was colder than the snow underfoot.

The other cougar had shifted. Rather than dressing, he was talking on a cell phone. "Bron, André says to hold."

"Aye, Cosantir," Bron said in a louder voice, obviously to be heard by the person on the phone.

As Patrin and Fell joined Wells, André came down the street with his second brother, Madoc, beside him. Silently, the Cosantir studied the Director's body and the dead Scythe scattered over the lawn.

When his gaze lifted to the forest, pausing on every single shifter there, a chill ran up Patrin's spine. Of course, Herne's guardian would sense an influx of shifters entering his territory—and would know exactly where each of them was.

André finally turned to Wells. He tilted his head slightly. "You are the spymaster?"

"Wells, yes. You're the new Cosantir?" Wells' clipped voice stayed level, but his weapon was still in his hand.

"*Oui*. This is my territory." The shimmer of power around the Cosantir was growing visible. At least to shifter eyes.

Wells nodded. "In that case, I apologize for the mess."

"Do you now?" André considered the body at his feet, not at all unsettled by the blood everywhere. Then again, the Cosantir had been a Canadian Mountie before being called by the God. "This is the one called the Director?"

André and Madoc had undoubtedly heard Wells shouting at Bron. Patrin almost sighed.

Wells' face darkened. "Yes. I needed him alive, not a meatsack with his throat torn out."

"If we had known of your...operation...and intentions, that might not have happened." André's voice had grown as dark as his eyes. "You have trespassed in my territory, spymaster. The usual consequence is death."

The blast of power from an angry Cosantir buckled Patrin's knees. With a grunt, Fell dropped beside him. From behind them came the thuds and groans of all the shifters in the area. Bron, Madoc, and Niall were also on their knees.

Even without being tied to the God and the Mother, Wells

was openly struggling to stay on his feet. He sucked in a breath. "Cosantir. I..." He paused, then holstered his firearm. "I'm accustomed to operating in the black without notifying the higher-ups. I didn't take into account the authority of a Cosantir."

Wells might have been told, but the human wouldn't have believed that the authority of a Cosantir came directly from the God.

"I screwed up." The way he straightforwardly admitted his error was just one reason why the shifter-soldiers took his orders while hunting the Scythe. "What can I do to make this right?"

Patrin's spirits sank. Nothing would make this right. The Director—and their hope for answers—was dead. For all they knew, these were the last of the Scythe who knew anything about the Daonain.

But they didn't *know*. The thought of continuing the hunt... forever...felt like a weight dragging at his soul.

"I believe the Law of Reciprocity would be most appropriate here." André's eyes were black with the God's presence. His gaze turned to Patrin and then Fell. "I require that you gift me with these two shifters. Release them from your service."

"I...what?" Wells stared at the Cosantir. "You can't just demand two people. This is the United States; there is no slavery here. And I need them."

"You've had them. They are done now."

Wells narrowed his eyes. "What if they don't want to stay here? What if they want to keep after the Scythe?"

André studied Patrin, his gaze piercing. After a long moment, he turned to Fell. A hint of a smile appeared. "Answer the spymaster, please, Fell."

Fell swallowed, glanced at Patrin, and his spine straightened. "We'll stay, Cosantir." He pulled in a breath. "I think this is our home now."

"*Oui*, I believe it is."

Patrin's mouth dropped open. *What?* What had Fell just done? Yet the blossoming sense of...of freedom, of relief shook him.

By the Gods, he wanted to stay.

He was still going to kill his littermate.

André was watching him. He nodded and turned to Wells, his expression implacable. "The others may remain with you if they wish, but their time is also coming to an end. A hunt is not meant to last for years."

Mouth in a straight line, Wells stayed silent.

The Cosantir's gaze swept the area again. "Remove the bodies. And notify me before you enter my territory again."

---

Fell watched his brother stomp up the steps to their apartment.

Patrin's anger was so vivid he should have been glowing red. "What the fuck were you thinking? '*We'll stay, Cosantir.*'" He glared down at Fell before stomping down the hallway.

As Patrin fumbled with the recalcitrant lock, Fell caught up. "I was thinking that—" He broke off as the other apartment door opened.

Moya stepped out. Her eyes were sleepy, her cheeks flushed, hair tousled. In a long, fluffy robe, she looked far too cuddly.

Fuck, they'd woken her. "Ahhh, sorry?" He jerked his head at Patrin. "He's louder than a stompy moose when pissed off."

"I see that." Her ever-ready sense of humor showed in the curve of her lips. "If I'm not overstepping, what did you do to upset him so badly?"

Could he tell her about the operation?

*Why the fuck not?* Bron, Niall, and Madoc had been with André. Down the street, there'd been more Daonain, all within hearing. No point in keeping secrets. Still... "Long story. It's late."

She touched his arm. "You don't look calm enough to sleep, and I'm in the mood for a beer. Would you two like to join me?"

He couldn't imagine a time when he wouldn't want to be with her. "Fair exchange." When his brother didn't move, Fell growled and nudged him toward Moya's.

Patrin's upper lip rose, showing a fang.

*As if.* Fell gave him a look. *Try it, brawd.*

If they'd been alone, there would've been a fight, but not in front of Moya. Patrin turned and stalked across the hall to her place.

A fire had left glowing coals in her woodstove. Bending, she tossed on kindling and a bigger log. "There you go, Sally. Enjoy."

Who was she talking to? Oh, there was a salamander buried in the coals, tail twitching as new flames began to rise.

She really did talk to everyone and everything. As Fell smothered a smile, he saw his brother's expression begin to thaw. Slightly.

"Sit, you two." Moya went into the kitchen, returning with three bottles of beer.

Stiffly, Patrin took a chair.

Fell smiled and sat in the middle of the couch. As if he'd object to sharing the seat with an adorable female. When she handed him a beer, he pulled her down next to him. Close enough her softness pressed against his arm and thigh, and he could breathe in her tantalizing female fragrance.

After the shootings, the blood, the deaths, having her beside him was a tangible reminder of...life. Just by being herself, she balanced his world.

"Okay, I'm ready for a story." She glanced at Patrin, flinched slightly, then turned to Fell. "Sorry, wolf, you'll have to use all the words."

Her ability to lighten his mood—even after everything that'd happened—was a blessing. "Words, right." He turned so he could watch her face. "You know the shifter-soldiers are eliminating any Scythe who know the Daonain exist. The two at the top are the Director and the Colonel, although the Colonel is probably dead.

The Director died tonight when he and his operatives tried to kill me and Patrin."

"What?" Her gasp of horror warmed the coldness still lingering in his chest.

He explained about the trap and Wells' reluctance to share their plans with the Cosantir. Bron had said Murtagh had called her, worried about Gregory's interest.

Fell continued telling her—muting the violence—about the fight, André showing up, and his decree.

"Wow. He didn't give your spymaster any choice." Moya shook her head. "André seems kind and gentle until his limits are crossed. Then the claws come out."

And those claws had been sharp.

"When he was talking..." Patrin finally moved, opening his beer. "His eyes went dark."

Fell nodded. "Like Darcy's Cosantir when we broke the Gathering laws. Tonight, *André's* eyes turned black."

"Fairy farts, your spymaster is lucky to be alive." Moya shivered so hard he could feel it. "Could you hear the difference in the Cosantir's voice?"

André's voice had deepened to something primal. "Yeah."

Moya laced her fingers with his, so tiny and warm. "If a Cosantir's voice goes weird, the God is speaking through him. The judgment came from Herne."

Fell rubbed his face. He and Patrin were less familiar with the Daonain rituals than the rest of the shifter-soldiers. *My fault we weren't taught much as children.* He'd been such a chatterbox, Mum hadn't trusted him not to share shifter secrets with everyone, humans included.

"Why make Wells release us?" Patrin asked. "It doesn't make sense."

Fell half-smiled. It made sense if the Gods actually gave a damn about shifters. Even messed-up shifter-soldiers. "Maybe

Herne knows your nightmares won't go away until you're off the battlefield." *After all, if I can figure it out, surely a god can.*

Patrin blinked in surprise before glowering at Fell for sharing his personal problem.

"Considering what you've been through, of course you have nightmares. I have them too." Rising, she hugged Patrin. "I know how the loss of sleep and the emotions afterward can mess a person up."

Oh, the look on Patrin's *face*. Trying to hold back a laugh, Fell choked. His stoic littermate had no idea how to handle sympathy, especially from the little wolf who was so generous with her kindness.

But Patrin was nothing if not adaptable. After a second of shock, he lifted Moya onto his lap, settling her firmly with his arms around her. "I need lots of comforting."

He glanced at the empty spot on the couch and gave Fell a smug look.

Fell straightened. *Huh. Now this sucks.*

---

Moya wasn't sure what to do. How had her hug turned into sitting on Patrin's lap? With his very muscular arms wrapped around her.

Okay, yes, they'd had sex and all that, but in the three days since, he hadn't been all that different. Friendly, but reserved. He hadn't been affectionate or touchy like now.

Why was he acting different?

And why couldn't she stop thinking about the future?

They'd been here in Ailill Ridge as part of their job working for the spymaster. If they'd been released from that job, did that mean they might stay here in Rainier Territory?

Which led to what was messing her up.

If they stayed, would they be interested in…her? As more than a friend and neighbor?

Just the feel of Patrin's arms around her sent her heart rate into a fast sprint.

"Aw, brawd, did I steal your female?" Patrin chuckled, stood with her in his arms, and sat beside Fell. He set her down with her legs on his thighs and her butt on Fell's lap.

"Nice, Top Dog. You're forgiven." Fell put an arm behind her back and his hand on her stomach...just below her breasts.

She bit her lip, wanting to be touched, wanting them both.

Only...two? At once?

His fingers under her chin, Patrin tipped her face up. His dark eyes were warm. "You're not ready to mate with us both, *blodyn tatws*. Don't worry. We're not going there tonight."

Fell made a sound of agreement.

She studied them, could feel the lingering violence. "All right. How about you go shower and then bed down here in front of the fire?"

"With a little wolf between us?" Patrin asked softly.

"Um. Yes. If it's what you'd like."

"Oh, aye, I like," Fell kissed the top of her head.

Patrin smiled slightly and caressed her cheek. "Aye. Together."

---

As Wells unlocked the door to Thorson's house in Cold Creek, something lightweight bounced off his head.

*What the—* The moonlight revealed a pinecone lying on the steps.

Apparently, he'd annoyed more than a Cosantir this evening. Turning, he glanced around, hoping to see...something.

In the cold night, all he saw were trees and darkness.

Because humans couldn't see OtherFolk. Even when something called a tree fairy threw things at them. *Dammit.* There was so much about the world of the Daonain he didn't know. Earlier, his lack of knowledge—*no, be fair*—his lack of belief had nearly gotten him killed.

With a huff of exasperation, he walked inside.

Thorson's gravelly voice came out of the darkness. "'Bout time you got back."

Of course, the old werecat stayed up to hear about the fight.

"Had a bit of clean-up to do." Wells looked across the dim room, feeling his age in his bones, in his soul. How many of his fellows, his friends, had passed on, leaving him behind?

Odd that the closest thing he had to a friend now was this grumpy old mountain lion shifter. Even odder that they understood each other so well, more than he'd experienced in all his years before.

"You gonna tell me how it went?" Thorson asked.

Recently, Wells had taken to staying in Thorson's house when visiting Cold Creek. When Patrin called to set up the trap, Wells had been in the kitchen. With those damned shifter ears, Thorson had heard both sides of the conversation. In fact, the werecat had wanted to join the operation.

Stubborn old cat.

After checking that the drapes were pulled, Wells turned on a light. "Human eyes, remember?"

"It's a wonder you humans don't hide in your houses the minute the sun sets."

Wells smiled slightly, knowing Thorson's eyes, even when in human form, could see in the dark room. Sometimes, he envied the shifters for their added years of age, for the enhanced senses. And the ability to shift.

He was one to enjoy the unknown, but others weren't. If the Daonain were revealed, narrow-minded people would respond as they always did—by trying to kill the source of their fears.

Others would want to take what they didn't possess, and the Daonain would end up on some lab table, being rendered down in search of those answers.

"How'd it go tonight?" As a werecat, Thorson possessed more than a healthy amount of curiosity.

Wells settled into an armchair and gave the bookseller some Dickens: "*It was the best of times; it was the worst of times...*"

Thorson's laugh sounded like rocks rubbing together. "This sure isn't the *age of wisdom*. What *happened*?"

"The Scythe died. A few injuries otherwise." Some shifter-soldiers had been injured from bullets hitting nearby trees or woodwork. One caught a bullet in the leg. But none of his had died.

Wells had long ago become used to seeing blood on the soldiers and operatives he sent into battle, but deaths... Those never got easier. In fact, the cumulative weight had become draining.

"And Vicki calls *me* terse." Thorson headed to the dining room bar and poured two glasses from the Old Forester birthday bourbon Wells had given him. He handed one over before resuming his seat.

"Appreciated." Wells gently swirled the glass, breathing in the mixed scents of vanilla and aged oak. He took a sip, holding it on his tongue. Soft and smooth with hints of fruit and caramel.

He glanced over at Thorson,

Thorson sipped his drink. "Was the Director there? Did you get your answers?"

And there was the worst of times. "Yes and no. The Chief of Police—a cougar—tore out the Director's throat."

"You brought in shifters from the territory?"

"I didn't, no." Although as von Moltke said—no plan survived contact with the enemy, and all possible outcomes needed to be prepared for. *I fucked that up, didn't I?* "I hadn't expected the local Daonain to butt into our well-laid trap."

Brows pulled together, Thorson leaned forward. His sweater sleeves were pushed up, showing the network of fine scars over his forearms. He was one tough old bastard. "How'd that happen? I heard the Rainier Cosantir was unusually reasonable."

"Not when he isn't informed about an operation in his territory." Wells knew his mouth was twisted into a sour smile.

"Ha! Stepped on your own tail, did you? How'd the Cosantir find out?"

Since the Chief of Police stayed until everything was cleaned up, Wells had taken the opportunity to ask her exactly that.

"It seems the grocery store owner was already suspicious of his bagger. When the operative showed too much interest in Patrin, the grocer notified the Chief of Police. And then..." Wells shook his head. "The Chief said the Cosantir noticed the shifter-soldiers I sent in."

Thorson snorted. "No doubt. Most Cosantirs check their territory every evening. He'd know exactly where your males were."

*Bullshit*. The way shifters boasted about their Cosantir's abilities could drive a rational person to drink.

"The Chief brought her own fighters, including the Cosantir's brother who is a cahir. Like she is."

Male Daonain cahirs resembled the huge weightlifter called the Terminator in an old classic movie. Bron, though... She was like an older, larger Sergeant Victoria Morgan. Impressively dangerous, competent—and striking.

He rolled his glass of bourbon between his palms. "When we had the Director cornered, the Chief jumped in."

"And there went your trap. How angry was the Cosantir?"

"Very." Wells could still feel the sinking sensation in his gut—because he'd truly understood that the Daonain possessed the ability to kill him, right then and there. "Then he gave me the terms for something called the Law of Reciprocity."

"This should be good," Thorson muttered.

"He demanded I release Patrin and Fell—my two best shifter-soldiers—and gift them to him."

It'd been an unwelcome surprise when, rather than arguing, Fell had agreed.

Thorson studied Wells and asked slowly, "Was it André or the God who demanded you release them?"

Wells had seen—rarely—when Calum's eyes turned black, and he hadn't been exactly convinced it wasn't some trick or psychosis. Not this time. This time, he'd known right down to his boots—he was in the presence of something...more. "The God."

"Then that's that." Thorson shook his head. "Maybe you need the lads, but if Herne the Hunter stepped in, then they need their clan and territory more."

*Damn.* Guilt slid like a sharp blade through Wells' defenses. He'd recognized the haunted look in Patrin's eyes—the same one he saw in the mirror every morning. It happened to those with too much blood on their hands and too many deaths weighing down their soul.

To those who needed to get out.

"André was right to take them." The last sip of his drink couldn't cut through the bitterness in his throat. "I think the Scythe who know about you are probably eliminated."

Slowly, he set out his thoughts. "The Director would have brought all his people tonight, the few he had left. Patrin and Fell almost succeeded in killing him the last time—probably why he went for a kill here rather than a capture. He was running scared." And couldn't have gone to the Colonel. They'd had a falling out, each blaming the other for the fiasco of losing their Daonain captives.

"You think it's over?" Thorson straightened.

"It's impossible to know definitively." Wells rubbed his face. Damn, he was tired. "But I am starting to think it's time to let the rest of your shifters go."

The shifter-soldiers were close to each other, even now. Earlier, Patrin and Fell had been swarmed and embraced by their comrades, and it'd been touching to see the affection the rest felt for the two who'd been their leaders in the Scythe compound. "I'll keep the shifters for another month to ensure there are no surprises, then send them back to your territories."

Thorson's eyes narrowed. "What will the spymaster do at that point?"

Good question. He'd turned over most of his responsibilities to his staff in order to pursue this division of the Scythe—the ones who could reveal the shifter's existence.

With that goal accomplished, the rest of the Scythe organization had to be eradicated. But his people could handle that without a problem, just as they were managing his tasks now.

He had no real interest in picking up his duties again.

Did spymasters ever retire?

## CHAPTER FIFTEEN

There was nothing like a wave of customers doing their holiday shopping at the last minute. The humans had presents to buy for their various religious celebrations, and Daonain were looking for Solstice gifts.

Good for the bank account, Moya thought, however...

*By the Gods, my legs and back hurt. Thank goodness closing is in another twenty minutes.*

Across the building, Talitha and Fell were beginning the closing down of the coffee bar.

A few minutes ago, Patrin bought a coffee. At a table with his laptop, he was working on something called an after-action report.

Seizing a moment to get off her aching feet, Moya picked up her guitar and sat down near the children's corner. Lightly strumming the strings along with the music from the speakers, she watched Alana's two adorable cubs build block houses. The two-year-olds were all big eyes and giggles, especially when a building fell down.

Over in the book section, Alana was humming along with the music.

Wasn't it nice to hear her friend so happy? A couple of years ago, Moya had pushed Ramón to hire females on his crew. To his surprise, Alana ended up being one of his best woodworkers. Since then, she'd found her mates in his crew, and now they took turns staying home with the cubs.

"Hey, I found a Roman architecture book Jalen will love and one with crochet designs for Jarlath." Alana joined Moya and cast a loving look at her cubs. "Thanks for watching them. They move too fast to be unsupervised for even a minute."

"They're so fun. I think they inherited your building genes."

"Or Jalen's. He loves designing houses." Alana rolled her eyes. "Hopefully, neither inherited Jarlath's need to be up high." Alana's second mate was a cat shifter and did all the high construction and roofing.

"By the Mother." Moya shuddered, remembering the hazardous games she and her littermates had played on the *ground*. "It must be terrifying to raise werecat cubs."

"I know, right? If they turn out to be cats, neither Jalen nor I will be able to follow them into the trees."

"Well, I bet Bron and Niall get a kick out of chasing younglings through the tree canopy."

"Werecat cahirs. Yes, they probably do." Alana's smile faded. "Moya, are we going to end up in a war between our cat-hating alpha and the Chief of Police?"

"Brett would be crazy to take on Bron, let alone Niall."

"He would, but sometimes I think he *is* crazy." Alana fidgeted with the book in her lap. "He wants wolves—even cubs—to attack cat shifters. At the construction site, he pushed Terence and Killian to attack Jarlath. And they almost did."

"What?" An ugly feeling grew in Moya's belly. "They've been friends for years."

"I know. Yet Terence and Killian had their fists up and started for Jarlath. Zorion saw and yelled at them, and they stopped—and then were shocked at themselves. It was like they were hypnotized or something."

"Or something." Bitterness made her words ugly. "Brett is using the pack bonds to push wolves to attack. They don't realize what he's doing."

Alana's face paled. "That's just wrong."

"It is." What could she—or anyone—do about it? No wolf was both willing and strong enough to take over the pack. Brett sure wouldn't leave without a fight.

Just then, a cub knocked over the block house, and his littermate yelled and jumped on him. The two rolled over and over in a good tussle.

So cute...at least when they were two.

"I'd better get them home for quiet time." Alana handed Moya her books and went to separate her boys.

After a quick checkout, Alana and cubs headed out the door to the square.

Moya looked around. Everyone in town knew the coffee and bookstore hours, so the place had emptied out. Only Patrin remained at his table.

When he met her gaze with his mouth set in a grim line, she realized he'd heard her and Alana talking.

Before she could join him, the three dangling bells over the door tinkled merrily. Talitha must have switched the single bell out, wanting something festive for Yuletide.

Two dwarves entered. Just under five feet tall with bushy hair and long curly beards, they wore fur-lined leather jackets, wool pants, and heavy boots. They headed straight for the coffee bar.

Seeing Fell and Patrin staring, Moya grinned. They might have never seen a dwarf before. The reclusive race visited few villages, although they apparently visited the Wild Hunt tavern for the beer.

A couple of years ago, dwarves from the local Rainier hold had discovered Talitha's extra-strong espresso and now visited frequently during the winter.

After getting their drinks, they walked across to her bookstore.

Moya rose and bowed slightly. "Welcome, Brimir and Vakr. Fair Yuletide to you."

"And to you, young Moya." Brimir's name meant *loud one*—and his thunderous voice bore that out. "What diversions have you in your hoard?"

"Oh, so many." When they first started visiting the coffee shop, a few had wandered into her bookstore. Since then, she'd done her best to keep stocked with their favorite entertainments. "Puzzles first?"

Vakr smoothed his beard. "Já."

They'd deemed conventional cardboard puzzles too flimsy. When she acquired some artisan-made, wooden jigsaw puzzles, they were hooked.

Pulling down a variety of the 500 and 1000 piece ones, she set the puzzles on a table for them to peruse.

Vakr immediately set his hand on the box with a colorful mandala of the tree of life.

*Ha, score.* She knew that one would get them.

With a happy grunt, Brimir picked up a wooden puzzle with a picture of what she'd discovered was their secret weakness.

*Kittens.*

Dwarves were fearsome in aspect, terrifying in battle...and adored baby animals.

*Don't laugh, don't laugh.*

After piling their selections on her checkout desk, she took them to the adult toy section...and motioned to the Lego set for a castle.

When Vakr chortled and grabbed the box, she grinned.

*I am brilliant, yes, I am.*

For payment, Vakr handed her a gold cube. The dwarves

carried currency for inexpensive items like coffee, but at her store, they usually spent a couple of hundred dollars or more, so she now accepted gold.

They never underpaid.

Since they appreciated traditional courtesies, she escorted them to the door.

Stopping there, Brimir looked behind her at Patrin, then Fell. His voice boomed across the almost empty room. "Superior steel is indeed forged by the hottest flame. I see you found worthy males to mate, young Moya."

Her cheeks heated. "No, no, they're just my neighbors."

The dwarf huffed. "You Daonain. Gifted with enhanced senses yet so blind."

"No, Brimir. Hastening the quenching yields a brittle blade." Vakr stroked his beard as he eyed Patrin. "Patience, even caution, is required. Be not dismayed, lass. We will observe and advise you as needed."

Her mouth dropped open. Because there wasn't even a speck of humor in their faces. "Um, thank you for your...interest. But I can—"

There were no words. She bowed slightly, hoping they'd just leave now.

Behind the coffee counter, Talitha was laughing like one of those African hyenas.

Entering the shop, Heather stopped and smiled. "Brimir and Vakr, a warm and happy Solstice to you."

After an exchange of bows and greetings for the Cosantir's mate, the dwarves left.

"Hey, girl." Heather gave Moya a big hug, then called, "Talitha, can I borrow Fell?"

"Sure." Talitha smiled at Fell. "It's almost closing. You can be done. Can you set the door sign to closed?"

"Aye, and thank you."

After turning the sign on the door, he raised his eyebrows at Heather.

"Let's talk," Heather said. "May I join you, Patrin?"

"Sure, Heather." Patrin grinned at having been caught listening. Again. But, hey, who could blame him? Watching Moya with the dwarves was incomparable entertainment.

Although hearing him and Fell considered possible mates for Moya? The idea had him tripping over his paws—yet it was now stuck in his mind like pine tree sap.

He rose and pulled out a chair for the Cosantir's mate. "Please…"

She sat and motioned Fell to take the chair beside her.

Back at her bookstore desk, Moya looked as if she was working on her end-of-the-day bookkeeping. No one who knew her would believe it.

He waited until she looked over, then winked at her. It was oddly pleasing she cared enough to stay within hearing distance.

Besides, fair was fair; he *had* been listening to her and the dwarves.

With a rueful but unapologetic smile at being caught, she bent to her work again.

"What's up, Heather?" Patrin asked, closing his laptop.

"André is still angry and doesn't want to take it out on you, so he sent me," she said in her delightfully straightforward way.

Fell winced.

"Because if a Cosantir is too annoyed, the God might step in and squash us like ants?" Patrin asked.

She half-laughed. "Yes, exactly. It seems Herne surprised him last night."

Patrin exchanged glances with Fell. Moya had been right. The demand for reciprocity had been the God sticking his muzzle in.

"I see. In that case, we're happy it's you here today." He smiled at her snort. "What can we do for you?"

"André plans to talk to you in a few days, but meantime, he'd like you to think about what you want to do here."

"We have jobs."

"Oh, *please*." The sarcastic tone highlighted her impatience. "Barista and bartender aren't exactly career choices. My mates and I were surprised at your minimum-wage choices, but after last night, we realized you deliberately chose the most visible jobs."

By the God, the Cosantir and his mates were more perceptive than he and Fell had anticipated.

"Good thing they don't work for the Scythe," Patrin muttered to his brother, and Fell laughed quietly.

Heather grinned. "None of us think your current work will satisfy your souls. What do you *want* to do?"

Patrin had no answer for her.

Fell appeared equally stumped.

"This is a big territory. Think about it." She patted Patrin's hand, smiled at Fell, and waved at Talitha and Moya as she walked out.

"Unexpected," Fell said.

"Just a mite, yeah. It appears André really does expect us to stay." Patrin leaned back in his chair. "She was right. I don't want to be a bartender, not as a full-time job."

"Same." Fell thrummed his fingers on the tabletop. "I'd go fucking crazy stuck in an office."

Patrin grinned. "You're going fucking crazy working inside in a coffee shop."

"We lack skills, brawd."

They hadn't lied to Talitha when applying for a position. They were unprepared for white-collar work. "Yeah, I know."

What could males who were good at fighting do? Being in law enforcement appealed, but after the mess last night, the Chief of Police sure wouldn't hire them.

"There *are* outside jobs, you know." Moya walked over and joined them. "Like with lumber companies, the forest service, or landscaping companies. You could work for my brothers in construction. Brett and Caleb repair trails during the summer. Tanner and Daniel—Heather's brothers—employ ranch-hands. There are also hunting and hiking guide services."

Patrin let out a breath, feeling as if the world was opening up.

A law enforcement job was still his preference. Rather than killing humans, he could protect and give back to the clan. But the others sounded interesting too. "Thanks, Moya. I wasn't coming up with anything."

"Never figured on having a future," Fell murmured.

From the way Moya's face paled, Fell's comment had been audible—and appalling. "Gods, you two." Bending down, she hugged him from behind, and her big eyes were damp.

*She cares. About us.*

Could something that made him feel so good be wrong?

## CHAPTER SIXTEEN

Moya braced her elbows on the table at the Shamrock and looked at the club members who were still going strong.

The bookstore's romance book club met on the second Thursday of every month. Some nights—like this one—could turn into a loud and crazy time. The group read two popular romances from the bodice-ripper days, and then compared them to their recent contemporary selections. Story tropes were flying as they jumped into a discussion of current and past trends.

*So. Much. Fun.*

As often happened, the meeting ran so long they'd relocated to the Shamrock for a ton of appetizers and...yes, more wine.

Eventually, half the group went home, leaving only herself and five others. "Looks as if the Daonain outlasted the humans." Moya kept her voice low since their oversized table was in the center of the restaurant.

The other females—none of whom were completely sober—giggled.

"This is as it should be," Claire, a red-haired wolf ranch-hand, said with a firm nod.

"Daonain rule!" Orla whispered.

"Hey, bookworms, want more of anything?" Their server, Katherine, stopped by the table.

"Mmm, no, I'm way full." Riona patted her belly. The slender, brunette wolf shifter worked with her family at the café and told the funniest stories of arguing with Maura, her werecat mother. "It's nice to hang out with other shifters."

"Mostly wolves though," Orla from Ramón's construction crew glanced around the table. "Moya, Riona, Ena, and Claire, you're all in the pack, right?"

Katherine raised her hand. "Me too. Although I gotta say it's not something I boast about these days. Not with our new carrion-eating alpha."

*Ouch*. But Katherine was in her fifties and known for bluntness. So was Claire, actually.

Ena, from the ranch and farm supply store, was about Katherine's age, but far more tactful. She grimaced. "It's difficult to disagree."

Orla's gaze met Moya's. "Your brothers are *really* unhappy with Brett. First, he tried to get Terence and Killian to attack Jarlath. And last night, at the grocery store, he tried to get Jalen to push me around, which is crazy since Jalen's littermate is a cat."

"Doesn't make sense," Claire murmured.

"Jalen barely backed off in time—since my foot was heading for his 'nads." Orla had fought her way to a position on Ramón's crew. She was tough. "Only...when he stopped, he looked crushed. Like he hadn't wanted to do it. Brett's anti-cat crusade is messing up our construction crew. We felt like a family before this started."

Anger rose inside Moya. Her brothers tried hard to foster a sense of belonging.

*Damn Brett anyway.* "The ratshit alpha is instigating fights all over town."

"I've heard the same thing." Riona took a sip of her wine. "What a mongrel. Remember when he fought Aiden over a female and reduced the poor bear to a shivering, bleeding mess? I hated Brett so much then, and now, he's our alpha."

"The beta isn't any better." Katherine crossed her arms over her chest. "At one Gathering, I saw Caleb smash Jens to the floor and deliberately stomp on his leg to break it. He'd've done worse if Heather and Moya hadn't intervened."

When she and Heather had stepped up to stop him, most of the shifters watching had lined up also. "Caleb is awful—and a liar too."

"What do you mean?" Riona asked.

"Up in the North Cascades Territory, he and Gretchen told the healer and others that Margery was just pretending to be a banfasa and almost let Caleb bleed to death while she tended her friends." Banfasas didn't have Goddess-given powers of healing but were trained in much the same way.

"Seriously? But Margery is incredibly skilled. I know a few people who would've died or lost limbs without her. Everyone at the ranch was upset when we heard she moved to the North Cascades." Claire slapped her hand on the table. "Lying about her is just plain weasel-nasty."

"It is," Ena agreed. "Did someone in the North Cascades figure out the lies?"

Moya smirked. "The healer did. And when Calum, the Cosantir, found out, he barred Caleb and Gretchen from his territory. Permanently."

"Good for him." Claire wrinkled her nose. "I wish the pack could do the same."

Dervla, a sociable bear shifter who'd moved here and taken over the realty after Pete died, was wide-eyed. "The Gatherings I've been to here weren't that bad. Are fights common?"

"Not any longer." Moya reached across the table and gave her hand a squeeze. "When André took over from Pete, he put a stop to the Gathering brawls. He's an amazing Cosantir. And I never thought I'd say that about a male in authority."

Having seen her poorly controlled responses to being bullied, everyone snickered.

She narrowed her eyes at them, and they laughed harder.

"A shifter who uses his power to push his own warped beliefs shouldn't be alpha. Our Cosantir is trying to pull the clan together, and here's Brett trying to divide us up." Claire's expression was sour. "I don't suppose Ramón or Zorion want to challenge and take over?"

Moya already knew the answer. "Uh-uh. Running a construction crew is one thing; leading a pack is a whole different story. Neither one is that kind of dominant."

"Yeah, guess not." Claire sighed. "What about those two new males, the shifter-soldiers?"

"Patrin and Fell?" If Ena had wolf ears, they would have perked right up. "They're certainly brave enough, considering they risked their lives taking down the hellhound."

"But aren't the shifter-soldiers always on the move?" Riona asked.

No one had asked Moya to stay silent about the shifter-soldiers. And Bron's people would have heard everything. "André apparently told the spymaster bossing the shifter-soldiers to release Patrin and Fell to him. They'll be staying here in Ailill Ridge."

"*Reeeally*." Katherine's eyes lit. "Remember how they protected little Alvaro from Roger? They have the traits we need in an alpha."

Dervla nodded. "Those two are *real* leaders. One of the female hostages came to live in my previous village. When her littermates visited, they said Patrin and Fell kept them safe. Led them. Sounded like her brothers were in awe."

"Well, how can we talk Patrin or Fell into taking over the pack?" Claire asked.

There was a good question. Moya bit her lip. Fell would totally refuse. Patrin, though, was a natural leader, dominant to the bone. Scarily so.

"It's up to them, really, but we can maybe push a little?" Katherine waggled her eyebrows, then picked up the empty glasses. Turning to move away, the server froze.

Moya turned to see what had startled her. *Oh, cat-spit.*

Standing at a nearby table, Brett and Caleb—and Gretchen—were within hearing distance for shifter ears. Gretchen's face looked... If Moya hadn't known how self-centered Gretchen was, she'd think the female's feelings were hurt.

Not so for the alpha and beta. Faces dark with anger, they were almost snarling at Moya's table of females.

*Oh...this is bad.*

## CHAPTER SEVENTEEN

Hearing a tap at the door, Patrin yelled, "Coming," and dried off quickly. The habits instilled by the Scythe and then Wells hadn't left him. He'd just finished his morning PT and followed it with a shower.

After pulling on a pair of jeans, he headed for the door. Must be Moya or Talitha. No one else could get into the hallway.

Be nice if it was Moya. Anticipation rose as he opened the door.

*Oh yeah, the day is starting off nicely.*

He smiled down at the adorable female. Her rich dark hair tumbled over her shoulders, reaching all the way to her curvy ass. So very tempting. "Good morning."

"Um." Her gaze hadn't lifted from his bare chest.

The tantalizing scent of her interest caught his attention. She wanted him.

Yes, they'd mated last weekend, and yes, she liked him. But this... In the cold light of day, perfectly sober, knowing who he was, she still *wanted* him.

It was exhilarating.

"Moya?"

Holding a plastic box to her chest, she blinked and shook her head. Her gaze lifted from his chest to meet his eyes. "Um, good morning. Can we talk? I brought breakfast if you haven't eaten yet."

"Perfect timing." He stepped out of the doorway to let her enter. "I'm starving."

Her half-laugh was sweetly husky. "You're always starving." She handed him the container and took a seat at the kitchen island.

"Coffee or tea or juice?"

"I'd love some juice."

He poured two glasses, handed her one, and opened the container. There were two long tubes of...something? A delectable aroma made his mouth water. "What are these?"

"They're called breakfast burritos. Filled with scrambled eggs, sausage, cheese, and avocado. Kind of spicy; you should like them."

Unable to resist, he picked one up and took a healthy bite. Flavors burst over his tongue. "Mmmm." His second bite was even bigger.

She laughed.

He finished the first one completely before slowing down. Taking a seat across from her, he drank some apple juice to counter the spicy heat. "You wanted to talk?"

"Yes." A wrinkle formed between her brows. Even worried, she had the most beautiful eyes he'd ever seen. Big, dark brown, and warmer than summer sunshine in the mountains.

"Okay, so..." She bit her lip. "One of my book clubs met last night—"

"And you didn't invite us?" He said it teasingly yet wasn't sure if he felt hurt.

She chuckled. "It's the romance book club. Now, if you two enjoy romance stories—"

"No, no, it's good," he said hastily. Although maybe he should read a few. He might learn something about female reasoning. Or not. Books were written by humans, after all, and from what he'd seen, their men were clueless.

"Anyway, we were talking about how Caleb is a liar and bully, and Brett is a terrible alpha."

"No, really?" Patrin smothered a grin. She looked so serious. "Tell me how you really feel."

She shot him an exasperated look. "The others wondered if someone would challenge Brett. It won't be my brothers. Ramón and Zorion run the crew because that's part of owning a construction firm, but leading a pack isn't something they want."

"I can understand that." The Moreno brothers were tough, no doubt about it, and would take charge when needed, but lacked the deep-seated compulsion to lead as well as protect. The brothers were much like Fell. "I understand. But...?" Where was she going with this?

"Your name came up too." She drew circles in the condensation on her glass. "Everyone thinks you'd be a wonderful alpha. They wondered how to get you to challenge."

He choked on the juice he'd been drinking. The bright morning seemed to dim.

"Bit of a surprise, huh? Honestly, I agree with them, but I'm not here to push you toward something you don't want." Moya swirled the last of her juice before finishing it off. "The thing is—Brett and Caleb were nearby and heard."

*Overheard they want me to challenge Brett? For fuck's sake.*

He shoved his anger away. This wasn't her fault.

"Moya, I'm not going to challenge. I won't be an alpha or take any leadership position, for that matter. Ever."

*Never again.*

The memories twisted inside his gut until his jaw locked against the bottomless pain. *The Colonel motioning for Chester's and Graham's bloodied bodies to be thrown down in front of their barracks. Grief-stricken rage flaring up in the shifters.*

*Kennard and Fletcher charging the Colonel. Patrin and Fell too far away to stop them. The gut-wrenching sound as the teens were clubbed down, bones breaking. Kennard still had scars.*

*Because I failed them.*

He swallowed hard against the thickness in his throat.

Over and over, he'd failed.

"Oh." The look of sympathy in her eyes almost broke him. "I don't know what happened, but I'm sorry for it, and sorry that I made you remember something bad."

"It's fine." The words came out sounding like a growl. He walked around the island and tried again. "You'd better get going. Your store opens in a few minutes."

"Of course." She hesitated. "Patrin, the pack run is tonight. If Brett's feeling threatened, things could get ugly."

*Fuck.* She was a far-sighted female. "Good point. Unfortunately, he made attendance at pack events mandatory."

Before this, Brett's threats of banishing misbehaving wolves weren't a concern since they hadn't planned to stay. Thinking, Patrin paced across the room and back. A more important reason for going rose. "Besides, Mateo and Alvaro will be there."

She let out a sigh. "True. Just...be careful?"

"Always."

Her brows pinched together. "Are you all right?"

He tried to ease the tightness from his face. "Sure, just fine."

Her worried expression only deepened. But she just squeezed his hand and left.

The apartment felt colder without her. Emptier. Much like when Fell was absent, as if he'd misplaced a part of himself.

Thank fuck she hadn't asked him any questions about the past.

He'd been useless as a leader. Sure, his comrades had tried to tell him different, as had Fell. But there was no denying he hadn't kept them all safe.

Some had scars that would never fade. Some had returned to

the Mother, their lives ended before ever having really been lived. The pain of failure wasn't something he was willing to risk again.

Leading a pack was not in his destiny.

---

The sun was lowering behind white-capped mountain peaks, and the reddish glow reflected off patches of snow that still lingered here and there. Fell enjoyed the contrast beneath his paw—damp fir needles then slushy snow. Up higher, all the ground would be snow covered.

*This world is so fucking beautiful.*

The pack was running early since tonight was winter solstice, and the clan's celebration began at sunset.

So the pack run would conclude with moonrise, and the wolves would arrive late to the solstice party, which apparently wasn't a problem since the celebration lasted all night.

Really, a sweet hunt was a fine way to start any festivity.

Seeing Patrin almost out of sight, Fell increased his pace to catch up. It was just the two of them on this trail, since Moya, the cubs, and Talitha were leaving from Talitha's house. He and Patrin hadn't wanted Brett to see them all together and vent his anger at the females and younglings.

The sound of voices broke the silence. A few minutes later, Fell followed Patrin out of the trees on top of a low mountain. A bonfire blazed in the clearing. Those who'd shifted to human form stood close enough to stay warm while conversing.

First, he looked for Moya. And there she was. Just seeing her made him...happy. Like moonlight on a dark night, or the fragrance of the first green growth in the spring.

The feeling was disconcerting.

*No, you're not going to stand close to her. Bad wolf.*

Instead, he scanned the rest of the area. The reason for avoiding Moya stood by the fire. Brett and Caleb.

Trying not to growl, Fell diverted himself by trawsfurring.

Patrin did the same. They walked over to join Zorion who was warming his hands at the bonfire.

"Happy Solstice, Zorion," Patrin said. "A question... Does Brett have someone checking off wolves, so he knows who's absent?"

Moya's brother snorted. "Of course he does." He gestured to a male holding a clipboard on the other side of the fire. "Ilya is taking attendance."

Fell met Ilya's gaze and saw him make a check mark. "Obsessive alpha."

"Like a cat with mud in its fur," Patrin said.

"Pretty much. Good thing you're here." Zorion tossed a chunk of wood into the fire. "I daresay he's looking for an excuse to drive you from the territory."

Fell snorted. "He can try."

"Wolves," Brett called from the other side of the fire. Caleb stood with the attendance-taker Ilya and two males Fell didn't know. Brett looked around slowly, obviously surveying the members.

He spotted Fell and Patrin. Rather than anger, smug satisfaction appeared. "Tonight, our run will loop around, ending here for the howling. Fast wolves in the lead, then slower ones. Cubs stay in the rear. Ilya's in charge of you."

Ilya, not Caleb? Couldn't help but be an improvement. Or maybe not. The male was around thirty—and appeared to be good buddies with Caleb. Not a recommendation in Fell's opinion. He glanced at Patrin. "We should run with the cubs."

"Agreed."

Joining Zorion, Ramón cleared his throat. "We'll cub watch for the first half if you two would run with Moya."

Patrin narrowed his eyes. "Why?"

"Talitha says you promised to keep Mateo and Alvaro from

being harassed. We planned to run with Moya for the same reason."

Zorion shook his head. "She doesn't want us. Says we're overprotective."

Fell could just imagine how the fiery wolf scolded her littermates. "Our sister says the same."

"You understand, yes." Ramón grinned. "She'll be happier if you two flank her."

Patrin glanced over, and Fell nodded agreement. Truthfully, he'd like nothing better than to run with Moya. And for half the trail they could run fast and then have a leisurely trot back.

Works for us," Patrin said.

As the wolves prepared, Quintrell and Quenbie volunteered to remain and tend the bonfire. Quenbie laughed and said his aging bones didn't like cold trails and running hard.

Brett and Caleb shifted and headed out onto a forest trail with the current alpha female, Deidre, behind them.

Watching, Fell thought about the pack runs they'd done in other territories. Usually, the alpha female ran beside the alpha or between the alpha and beta.

"There's Moya," Patrin said. Shifting, he loped across the clearing and joined her with a canine grin.

Giving Ramón and Zorion a nod, Fell dropped forward onto his paws. His thick fur cut off the chill afternoon wind. Reaching his brother, Fell bumped Moya's shoulder in a wolf greeting.

Her ears perked forward, her furry expression confused. She knew Talitha expected them to guard the cubs.

Fell turned and looked at Ramón and Zorion who had joined the cubs.

Moya wagged her tail, then delighted Fell by licking along his jaw. She did the same for Patrin, barked once, and darted out to join the line of wolves.

Catching her, they split up to bracket her.

She gave a happy yip. And when her tiny paws danced on the

trail in obvious pleasure at having them with her, Fell couldn't remember when he'd been so content.

---

A while later, on the return trip to the bonfire, Patrin was enjoying himself. It had been one glorious run with the hissing-crunch of paws on the snow-packed trail, along with an occasional yip from the cubs in back or a bark of happiness. A cool breeze ruffled his fur, and occasionally a plop of snow from the tree branches dropped onto his back. The mountain air was thin and crisp, and the scent of his pack was warm in his nostrils.

Then there was Moya, her so-very-female scent mingling with his and Fell's in a way that just felt right. As did the way their shoulders brushed together off and on as they ran.

This...this was what pure happiness must feel like.

And his littermate radiated his own pleasure.

Unfortunately, this trail wasn't the best. Ilya had shifted to human long enough to tell the cubs that since it was still daylight, they'd be taking a more difficult trail back so as to improve their skills. And shortly after, he'd led them away from the rest of the pack onto an alternate path.

Patrin was not impressed, although Ilya had stopped the cubs and taught them how to climb a scree slope without dislodging the loose rocks. It'd taken some time, having them move slowly and testing the footing as they crossed.

After leaving the scree field and reaching the crest of the mountain, they headed downward on a narrow trail with an incredibly steep drop-off to the right.

It was a long way down. Patrin looked over. The river was so far away it was only a ribbon of blue at the bottom of the ravine. Ravens cawed from a lightning-struck tree as if in warning.

Admittedly, the panoramic view of the surrounding mountains under a setting sun was gorgeous. Soon enough, they'd be on a better trail that ended on the smaller mountain crest where the bonfire blazed.

Patrin was bringing up the rear behind Fell who was behind Moya. She kept a short distance between her and the last cub in sight. He knew why—crowding a pup made the youngling feel as if he had to run faster. This trail had been stressful enough.

"Wolves, I need help." The call came from behind Patrin. The three of them paused and turned on the narrow trail.

No one was in sight.

"Back here. Help!" Patrin tilted his ears toward the caller. The voice sounded odd, as if a tenor male was trying to sound like a baritone.

The line of cubs disappeared around the curve of the mountain. Patrin had the urge to stop them, but... Not until he knew what was going on. Retracing his steps, he padded back up the trail slowly, careful on the stone-strewn path.

A few more feet—and still no one was in sight. Perhaps the male was in that cluster of trees off to the right? Patrin lifted his nose, scenting the air.

That smell... It was a light stink of ammonia with an overlay of diesel.

*Fuck, I know that smell.*

Spinning, he barked and growled at Fell to drive him and Moya away. They spun and sprang back up the trail.

*Whomp!* The muffled sound of a buried explosion came from behind Patrin. Rocks and dirt hit him hard, and the trail crumbled out from under his hind legs.

He tried to scramble back up on the trail, but his hind paws had no traction. His short, ineffectual front claws left scrape marks as he slid farther toward the drop.

And then Fell in human form grabbed Patrin's furry nape, holding him from the long, deadly drop. With both hands, Moya grabbed Fell's free arm and pulled, digging her bare feet into the stone-covered trail.

An inch, two, a foot. Patrin's belly scraped on the rocks as they pulled him back until he had all four paws under him. He stood, shakily, panting. He could smell blood. All of them were hurt.

*What if there are more explosives?* Growling, he jerked his muzzle.

Obeying, the other two shifted to wolf, and they all retreated away, down the trail to where the next mountain butted up against this one.

In an open area, Patrin lifted his muzzle and sniffed. No one close. No explosives. Shifting, he swept his gaze over Moya. Steady on all four paws with a few specks of blood in her fur.

She shifted and grabbed him, pushing her face into his shoulder.

He could feel her heart pounding. "How badly are you hurt, *cariad*?"

"I'm fine. Scrapes is all."

She was so brave it filled his heart. Thank the Mother, she'd been the farthest from the explosion. He looked at Fell and saw blood in the pale fur. "You're hurt, brawd."

There was a shimmer of magic as Fell shifted to human. He put his hand to his bloody forehead. "Feels like a dwarf hammered in a nail."

"Sure, that's what happened." Patrin scowled. "You caught one in the head. Again."

"Yeah." A corner of Fell's mouth tilted up. "Nothing new."

It was a long-standing joke in the shifter-soldiers. Fell always got thumped in the head. "How do you feel?"

"Little dizzy. Not bad."

*Right.* Fell's idea of bad was dead.

Patrin gave Moya a squeeze, then held her away so he could look her over.

Her skin was dirty. As she'd said, scrapes here and there.

"What about you?" Moya eyed Patrin in return and made an

unhappy sound. "You're all banged up." She walked to his side and hissed. "Gods, you're bleeding."

Moving his left arm, Patrin saw a chunk of flesh over his ribs was battered to a gory mess. *Rock versus wolf—rock won.* The area hurt like a burning fist was pressed to his skin. Blood made warm trickles down his dirt-covered skin.

Wasn't gushing though. He took a deep breath, twisted slightly—and didn't scream—so his ribs weren't busted. "It'll be fine."

He pressed his hand against it to stop the bleeding—and had to grit his teeth.

*Fuck, that hurts.*

"Patrin, what happened back there?" Moya asked.

"Somebody tried to blow us—probably me—off the trail." Anger roared through him.

"Like...like a *bomb*?"

Definitely a bomb. The fiery rage inside him warred with the need to escape. To take his brother and Moya and simply leave everything behind.

*No, I can't.* If someone tried to kill them, what was to stop the bastard from moving on to the rest of the wolves? The entire pack might be in danger.

The wind carried new noises—the sounds of fast-moving paws and bare feet. Males from the pack in human and wolf form came around the bend. They stopped at the sight of Patrin, noses in the air, obviously catching the scent of blood.

"What happened?" one male asked, walking forward. "The cubs said there was a funny sound behind them—and then noticed you three weren't behind them."

"Did the cubs get back all right?" Patrin asked. He'd been worrying.

"Yes, they're fine." Lucius frowned as he looked at them. He and his brother, Kane, were older wolves who ran the ranch and farm supply store. "How badly are *you* hurt?"

"Just banged up." Patrin pulled in a breath. How the fuck should they handle this? His gaze met Fell's, then Moya's. Should he say that someone had tried to kill them? Fur would fly in a pack that was already a mess.

Moya could obviously see his worry, and her jaw set. She turned to the other wolves. "Someone behind us on the trail called out to us, saying they needed help. When we went back toward the voice, the trail blew up. Like, exploded."

"By the God, seriously?" Lucius stared at her in shock, then his brows drew together. "Fell."

Patrin turned even as Fell staggered sideways. Patrin caught his arm.

"Lean on me." Moya tucked herself under Fell's shoulder on the other side.

"It's too cold to stand here talking. Let's get you back to the fire and *then* deal with this." A burly male ran his hand through his rusty-gray hair. He was one of Ramón's construction crew whose name was...was... *Killian.*

"Good plan," Patrin said. "Some of you go look at the explosion site. See if you can pick up who or what did this. But be careful."

"We're on it." Lucius and Kane shifted and loped up the path while one wolf ran back toward the bonfire. Probably to carry the news.

Killian and two more males exchanged glances—and then arranged themselves around Patrin, Fell, and Moya, almost as if providing cover.

If Fell hadn't been hurt, if Moya hadn't been there, Patrin might have felt insulted. Instead, he was damned grateful.

"Let's go, brawd." He wrapped an arm around Fell's waist, taking some of his weight, with Moya doing the same on the other side.

As they trudged down the trail, so very slowly, Patrin's skin itched in anticipation of another explosion. But they reached the clearing safely.

As worried shifters surrounded them, the outpouring of concern over him and Fell as much as Moya was surprising.

He checked, and yes, the cubs were fine, standing near the fire with their mothers close.

Off to one side, Brett stared at them, an expression of shock and horror on his face. Beside him, Caleb had the same expression.

"Whoever set off the explosive should've stayed to make sure we were dead," Patrin murmured as he and Moya helped Fell to the fire.

Moya let out a tiny growl. "Whoever didn't want anyone seeing they were missed."

She had a point. Whichever asshole set off the explosion must have run straight back here on an alternate trail.

"They lack a contingency plan." Fell carefully settled onto a log near the bonfire.

"Good." Moya nodded firmly and brushed a kiss over Fell's cheek. "Stay here and let your head recover."

He sighed. "Aye."

From the pained line between Fell's brows, Patrin knew his brother's head must hurt like hell.

"Moya!" Ramón yelled as he and Zorion charged over.

"Sis, you all right?" Zorion looked her over with a worried expression.

"I'm okay." At her answer, both her brothers relaxed.

Ramón turned to Patrin. "We heard the trail exploded. What the fuck?"

"Nah, I doubt it was an explosion." Standing by the fire, Brett waved a hand toward the forest. "That trail's been eroding for years. It probably just crumbled like everything does around here."

The two old males who'd gone to check the site of the explosion rejoined them in time to hear Brett.

"It was definitely an explosion," Lucius said. "There were no water channels, it wasn't a washout. It's a gaping round hole with debris blown outward in a circle."

Kane shook his head. "Someone wanted you dead, Patrin. It's a wonder you're not."

"Someone we couldn't see calling for us? I was already wary." Patrin felt the anger in his gut. Because the person calling had deliberately drawn them to the right spot and then detonated the explosive. "Then I caught the smell... Ammonium nitrate-fuel oil has a certain stink to it. Nothing on a forest trail should smell like diesel."

"No wolf knows what explosives smell like," Brett scoffed.

"We were trained by the Scythe," Fell said loudly, his face still too pale.

"You smelled it," Ramón said, "and backed away from the trap?"

"Backed?" Moya leaned against Patrin's side. "More like ran like scared bunnies."

"Scared bunnies live longer," Zorion said.

"Some humans must have done it," Brett said, an edge in his voice. Probably because more and more wolves were turning suspicious looks toward him and Caleb.

Looking disgusted, Kane tugged on his bushy beard. "No human set that bomb. The only scents in the area came from pack."

*Pack?*

After a few seconds of shock, the wolves began shouting in anger and disbelief that pack would kill pack.

Brett and Caleb blustered, saying Lucius and Kane must be mistaken.

"We don't know who did it," Brett said finally. "Maybe it was someone in the pack, but no one saw them."

Anger simmered in Patrin's blood, heating rapidly. He had a good idea of who wanted him and Fell dead. "What was going on here when it happened?"

Hopefully, someone noticed one of the two males missing.

"Brett was yelling at Jens for hogging the fire." Zorion's mouth twitched as he motioned to the huge bonfire. "Had everyone's attention with all the drama."

*Dammit.*

"In the pack," Moya said loudly, "only one person knows explosives and how to use them on a trail. I've heard him boasting about blowing things up."

Suddenly, everyone was looking at Caleb. And then Brett. Because they all know Caleb didn't lift a leg unless Brett told him to.

Ramón pointed at Brett. "Gods, you putrid spawn of a goat, you really did try to kill them—and my sister—in the most dishonorable way possible."

"He's afraid Patrin will challenge him and win." Zorion's words carried across the clearing.

"You, shut up. Shut up!" Brett shouted.

Zorion went silent, although his hands fisted as he opened his mouth, trying to speak.

Brett's expression changed. Cunning lit his eyes. "Patrin and Fell are worse than cats," he yelled. "They were sent by the Scythe. Kill them. Kill them both!"

The *kill* order burned along the pack ties, and several wolves moved toward Patrin. Others stood, and their bodies trembled with the effort to refuse the order.

Ilya picked up a heavy branch, swinging it menacingly. In wolf form, his brother Pavel stalked forward, teeth bared.

"No!" Moya yelled, so furious her voice was unrecognizable. "Don't let Brett use our bonds like this!"

Shock blossomed on faces as the wolves realized what was happening.

With a sense of revulsion, Patrin could still feel Brett's order crawling along the pack bonds. *What a sickening violation.* The bonds were there to protect the pack, not to give the alpha a tool to get his own way.

This male shouldn't be their alpha. Using bonds, using explosives.

*If I hadn't smelled the ANFO, I'd be dead. Probably Fell and Moya too.* Anyone who got in Brett's way was in danger. Moya, Talitha, the cubs.

The pack needed a new alpha. Not him. It couldn't be him.

*I don't want to be responsible for others.*

His shifter-soldiers had died under his leadership.

*Who else is there?*

His shoulder burned, reminding him he wasn't fit. Was damaged. And it didn't matter.

*Someone must protect the pack.*

"Hey, alphahole." His voice rose above the noise, and in the silence, he met Brett's gaze. "I challenge."

*No, no, no.* What was the gnome-brain doing, challenging the alpha? Patrin was wounded, bleeding. Moya pressed her hands over her mouth in dread.

Brett's gaze ran over Patrin, undoubtedly seeing they were the same height, but Brett was far heavier with bulkier muscles than the lean shifter-soldier. His gaze lingered on the blood still trickling from the damage to Patrin's side. "Accepted."

Moya barely smothered her moan of distress.

Brett turned to look at Caleb, who stood isolated from the other wolves. Everyone knew if Brett was guilty, so was his littermate. No matter how ugly the act, Caleb always helped or covered up for Brett.

Caleb nodded at his brother.

When Brett shifted, his wolf was just as heavily muscular. Ears laid back, he showed his fangs.

Moya shivered. Brett had already shown he was willing to kill to stay as alpha. *Patrin, be careful.*

"Let's do this then." Unhurriedly, Patrin cracked his neck and then trawsfurred. Far darker a gray than Brett, he stalked forward, hackles raised, gait stiff. With a low growl, he snapped his jaws.

Startled, Brett flinched—and snarling, charged across the space and slammed into Patrin. So much heavier, the alpha knocked him off his paws.

Patrin rolled, rose quickly, and lunged straight for the throat.

Protecting his neck, Brett ducked his head down and spun away.

Slowly, they circled, fangs bared, testing for weaknesses, looking for an advantage. The low growls sent chills up Moya's spine.

The packed snow under their paws was turning a garish red. Patrin's side was bleeding—and she realized Brett had deliberately rammed into the wound.

Then Patrin attacked so fast, her jaw dropped open. First, a slashing bite to Brett's muzzle, then savaging a front paw deeply enough the alpha yelped. Brett tried to dodge away, and Patrin lunged forward, going for the throat again.

Brett skittered away like the yellow dog he was, creating a wide space between them.

Yelling filled the air, most of the Daonain cheering for Patrin, with only a few for Brett. Caleb's rough voice was notably absent.

Moya stiffened. Where was the beta?

There, off to her right. *Oh Gods.* He'd pulled a pistol from a daypack. He aimed at Patrin.

*No!* Shifting to wolf in mid-jump, she charged him, leaping up to bite his wrist, bearing down hard enough to make him drop the gun. His yell of anger turned to a shriek of pain.

Other wolves attacked and pulled Caleb down, flattening him.

Zorion moved in, baring his fangs over the beta's neck in an open threat. Caleb went limp in surrender.

Turning, Moya saw the fight continued.

Brett was badly torn up, one ear almost ripped off, his muzzle with long gashes that would probably scar.

However, Patrin must be seriously hurt. Head hanging, he limped as he backed away.

*Oh no, Mother, please, don't—*

Victory in sight, Brett charged forward, jaws wide.

Dodging, Patrin grabbed a front paw and yanked sideways, spilling Brett onto his side. Biting high on the alpha's neck, Patrin closed his teeth on the windpipe.

When Brett scrabbled uselessly with his paws, Patrin bit down. Hoarse whines came from the alpha before he tipped his head farther back. Giving up.

Patrin released him but stayed in place, fangs an inch from Brett's neck.

Brett didn't move.

A moment later, cheering filled the air, accompanied by happy yelps from those in wolf form...including Moya.

*He did it!*

Patrin backed a few steps.

Zorion, Ramón, and Lucius lined up in support as Brett rolled to his paws.

Shifting, Patrin crossed his arms over his chest, then turned. His gaze landed on Moya, and he frowned as he saw the pile of wolves beside her.

Beneath them, Caleb's naked body was barely visible. Patrin's mouth twitched as sudden humor lit his dark eyes.

By the Mother, the male could find amusement in anything.

"Let Caleb up, please."

The wolves jumped off.

Caleb's wrist was badly mangled.

Satisfaction ran through her, and her tail waved. However...his blood was in her mouth. *Oh, yuck.* Finding an untrampled pile of snow, she took a couple of quick bites.

Holding his gore-covered arm, Caleb slunk over to join his brother.

When Brett shifted to human, he was covered in bite marks and blood. His face and ear were badly damaged.

She shouldn't find that so gratifying. But she did.

"You lost the challenge," Patrin said flatly. "Normally, you'd get time to close your affairs and leave, but attempted murder changes things. If you're still in the territory by dawn, the pack will drive you out."

"With pleasure," Ramón said, and Moya shook her head. Trust her brother to kick in an opinion. But the low murmuring of the pack showed his sentiment was shared.

Brett fingered his ear, his face reddening with anger.

"The scars on your face will hopefully remind you to fight fair," Patrin said. "I'll send word to other territories to ensure you're never an alpha again."

"You can't do that," Brett spat out.

Patrin lifted his chin. "The alternative is to notify the Cosantir of your actions."

Brett went white. The Cosantir might banish him from all Daonain everywhere. Or even send him back to the Mother.

"Leave." Patrin growled long and low. "Both of you. Never return."

Changing to wolves, the previous alpha and beta fled. And even as they did, Patrin ripped them from the pack bonds.

Moya whined at the burning in her chest—and then there was only an ache where the two bonds had once existed.

"Wasn't that fun," Patrin murmured as he pressed a hand against his wounded side. "Brawd, how're you doing?"

"Eh, I only see one of you now instead of two, so better?"

Patrin's grin flashed. "Two of me would be more fun."

"You barely have enough brain for one."

Laughing, Patrin squeezed his brother's shoulder. "Be a good wolf and stay there."

"I got him, Alpha." Ramón sat down beside Fell.

Patrin blinked at the title, then nodded. "Thanks, Ramón."

"I'm surprised you didn't turn them over to the Cosantir." Lucius had his arm around his mate, Ena.

"André seems to be a kind Cosantir. Being forced by the God to kill a clan member would be..." Patrin's mouth tightened for a moment. "No one needs nightmares like that."

Moya had to agree. Heather had mentioned before how difficult it was for Calum up in the North Cascades to render the God's judgment.

"And sometimes a shocking defeat or major physical damage can open a new trail for the soul." Patrin's smile was a bit rueful. "Not often, I admit, but it could happen."

"An optimistic alpha—and one with a caring heart." Ena smiled at him. "We're grateful to have you, Alpha." When she bent her head in respect, the rest of the pack did the same.

As did Moya. Because Ena was right. He was a gift, and the wolves knew it.

When Patrin looked startled at the overwhelming approval, Moya opened her muzzle in a wolfy grin.

His gaze landed on her, and he frowned. "Why are your jaws bloody?"

*Ugh, thanks for reminding me.* She showed her fangs to let him know her opinion of questions when she was in wolf form—and nipped up more snow.

Zorion shifted to human, already laughing his head off, the fleabag. "Caleb was getting ready to shoot you"—he tapped his foot on the pistol—"and Moya almost chewed his wrist off. The rest of us piled on him, but really, we just wanted some elevation to watch the fight."

Snickering, the shifters who'd helped chimed in. "The beta's butt made a nice soft couch."

"Squishy."

"Warm too."

Patrin chuckled. "Thank you all." His gaze met Moya's, dark with appreciation.

As he turned and looked around at everyone, she could see him pull in a long breath. Not an especially happy one, more like resigned to what had happened.

He hadn't wanted to be alpha.

Sympathy swept through her. Would this give him more nightmares?

Then he shook his head, his mouth tilting in a half-smile. "Pack." His voice was clear, the authority undeniable. "Put out the fire and trawsfur to wolf. The moon is risen, so let's sing—and then join the clan for the Solstice celebration."

Yips and shouts of agreement filled the air.

The flames disappeared under an avalanche of snow, and the night grew dark. A minute later, the clearing was full of wolves.

Dark as the shadows, Patrin paced over to stand beside his silvery-furred brother. Above them, the Mother's moon reigned over the black sky.

Lifting his muzzle, Patrin gave the opening solitary howl, long and sweet. A few seconds later, Fell's deeper tones were added, and then the pack joined in, from the lower bass of the older males to the harmonizing warbling of the females. Finally, the cubs came in with high undulating howls.

There, in the soft moonlight, the pack offered up their song to the Mother of All.

## CHAPTER EIGHTEEN

By Herne's horns and hooves, Patrin hurt all over. He eyed the stairs at the back of their building and sighed.

Fell heard him, and a corner of his mouth tilted up in sympathy.

Yeah, they were a mess. Moya was already at the top, waiting for them.

He lifted his foot, went up one, then the next, one by one until he reached the top. Had the number of steps to their apartment doubled?

Moya followed him and Fell into their apartment. She pointed toward the bathroom. "Patrin, go shower and get the grit out of your wounds."

His protest died unspoken. Meeting Fell's gaze, he shared a rueful smile. Because the little wolf snapped out orders when she was worried. Because she cared.

As he collected a pair of sweatpants from his room, he heard her saying, "Fell, let me see how bad your head is."

His brother didn't even try to protest.

Patrin paused to listen.

"The bleeding has stopped—and you have a nice lump there. I think it's okay."

The couch creaked. She must have sat down.

"Thanks." Fell's voice was rough.

"Gods, I've been so worried. About Patrin and you."

"Me?"

Her sigh sounded exasperated. "Fell, a *rock* hit your *head*. Of course, you."

Grinning, Patrin turned on the shower and stripped off his clothes.

Looking down, he winced. Scrapes and gashes dotted one side and part of his front. The big wound on his side—that Brett had deliberately rammed—was swollen and bruised. The boggart.

*Here goes.* Patrin stepped into the shower.

*Ow, ow, ow, fuck, ow.* Yes, he needed the wounds clean, but Gods, the water felt as if it was flaying the skin off. Gritting his teeth, he washed, rinsed, and patted himself dry as gently as if he were a newborn cub.

Still... The pain was better than thinking about what he'd done tonight. About being responsible for an entire pack of wolves.

Barefoot and dressed in only sweatpants, he walked into the living room. "No Moya?"

"Went to get something for my headache." In a chair, Fell pointed to the coffee table. "Got the first aid kit for you."

"Thanks."

Fell looked him over. "Brawd, you look like a bunny that barely escaped a cougar."

Patrin snorted at the oddly accurate description.

"I have your tea." With a teapot and cup in her hands, Moya walked in and came to a sudden halt, her eyes wide. "Ohhh, Patrin, that must hurt."

He shrugged. "It's not bad." The Scythe had given them worse.

"Uh-huh," she said in a dry voice, then poured the tea into a cup. The bright, clean scent of peppermint filled the air. "This is willow bark tea and has mint and honey to cover the taste."

"Mint and honey sound good," Patrin said.

"None for you, Top Dog. It would help the pain—but would make your bleeding and bruising worse. Sorry."

"Doesn't that just figure." Grumbling just to make her laugh, he went into the kitchen and downed a couple of glasses of water instead.

As he returned, Fell took a sip—and grimaced. Apparently, her mint and honey didn't cover up the astringent taste of willow bark.

At her stern look, he obediently drank it down, looking just like a cowed puppy.

Patrin tried to smother his snicker—*he did try*—but Fell heard. Oh, the *frown*.

Patrin lost his battle with laugher.

"You two." She bent and kissed Fell. "You're going to be fine."

"Good to know." He cupped a hand behind her head and kissed her longer.

Smiling, Patrin rubbed a hand over his chest where there was a tender ache from seeing his brother with Moya. They both felt the same about her. What did she feel for them?

Straightening, Moya picked up the first aid kit, then turned her gaze to the kitchen. "I've been wondering—what smells so yummy?"

Patrin pointed to the slow cooker on the island. After Moya taught them about the human invention, he and Fell bought one. Best purchase ever. "We made the cheesy sausage balls recipe you gave us."

In fact, the aroma of the cheesy sausage balls filling the air was making him hungry. If the food wasn't going to the Solstice potluck, it would be gone by now.

"C'mere, Patrin. Sit." Sitting on the couch, Moya patted the spot beside her.

When he joined her, she checked his wound. "Looks clean." Opening the dressings, she bandaged him up with surprising efficiency and a gentle touch.

"You're good at this," Patrin said.

"My grandfather owned a construction company—and now my brothers do. Accidents come with the business." She lightly covered the nastier gashes with antibiotic ointment. "Be careful for a couple of days. I'm sure you know the drill, right?"

"All too well." Patrin leaned down and kissed her. "Thank you, *cariad*."

"You're welcome." Rising, she smiled at them. "I'm going to go shower and have a quick nap before Ramón and Zorion come over. I'll see you later."

As the door shut behind her, Fell rose. "I'm for sleep. We'll be up all night."

"Yeah, me too." Rather than heading for the bedroom, Patrin stretched out on the couch and sighed as every aching bruise and gash made itself felt. He tried to relax as he processed what had happened.

Almost getting blown up. Then his brother saving him from going over the cliff. Moya hadn't hesitated a moment before grabbing Fell. She was pretty amazing.

*I could've died.* How often had he dodged death? Every time, the realization stabbed icy claws into his gut. At the same time, he didn't really fear returning to the Mother. He had more fear of what his death would do to Fell. Because his littermate would probably follow.

That...hurt.

After a moment, he moved on to thinking about Brett and Caleb. If it'd been a normal challenge, he would've been expected to either let them stay or give them time to arrange to move out of the territory. *So, thanks, alphahole, for trying to murder us.* Kicking them out of the area immediately wouldn't be questioned.

But...fuck.

*I'm the alpha.* Would he end up being called an alphahole too? He sure didn't know anything about how to lead a pack.

Had never wanted to lead a pack.

*I swore I'd never be responsible for others again.* Did the Gods laugh when shifters made sweeping statements and included the word "never"? Because here he was, responsible for a whole pack, from cubs the age of Mateo to seniors.

*Wait...*

His breath stalled in his lungs. The pack actually included the littlest pups who hadn't even shifted yet. Babies and toddlers. And seniors too old to run the trails.

*No, no, no.* Bad enough to lead shifters who could fight, but the most vulnerable?

Narrowing his eyes, he growled. At the God.

*For fuck's sake, Herne, just bite my claws off one by one. It'd be less painful.*

Putting an arm over his eyes, he could swear he heard the God laughing.

---

Still slightly groggy from sleep, Fell unplugged the slow cooker and helped himself to a couple of the sausage balls.

*I need to see if they're edible, right?*

The flavor of tangy, cheesy meat exploded in his mouth. *Oh yeah.* These were just fine.

He raised his voice slightly. "Time to go, brawd." In fact, it was later than he'd planned.

Over on the couch, Patrin sat up and rubbed his face. He didn't look as if he'd benefited much by the quiet time.

"How are you doing?" Fell asked, knowing exactly what answer he'd get.

"Sore, but alive. You?"

Yep, that was the answer. "Good. Headache's only a throb." The nap had helped—and probably Moya's tea. "Still can't believe you're the alpha."

"Yeah, fuck." After a second, laughter lit Patrin's eyes. "If I'm alpha, you're the beta."

"What?" Fell took a step back, feeling as if his brother had yanked the fur off his muzzle. But...yes, this was the tradition. He considered it for a moment. "We'll do better than they did."

"There's a low branch to jump." Patrin rubbed his chest, over his heart. "I can feel all the pack bonds, like a tie to each wolf. Can you?"

Fell flattened his palm against his sternum, and the sensation had changed. "Yeah. Almost as strong as our littermate tie, only... different." As with the littermate one, he couldn't feel emotions or direction. Just a tie that pulled at him, creating a protectiveness for the wolves akin to what he felt for their shifter-soldiers.

This time, though, the intense emotion had sprouted immediately rather than from years together.

Patrin twisted and checked the bandage. "I think this'll hold. She did good work." He rose from the couch. "What do we wear to this festival thing?"

"Talitha said nothing fancy. We'll be outside a lot." The Winter Solstice Vigil lasted until dawn—and apparently, many Daonain stayed all night. "Bright sweaters. Heavy jackets."

Patrin eyed Fell's dark blue sweater and lifted an eyebrow.

"Brightest I own." Most of his clothing was black.

Chuckling, Patrin headed for his bedroom to dress. "At least we won't be barefoot in the snow. My feet still feel frost burned."

"No shit."

Returning in a white pull-over, Patrin grinned at Fell's snort. "Hey, white is bright."

Pulling on jackets, they headed out.

Fell stopped. "Fuck. The food."

"Right." Patrin headed back to the kitchen to rope down the slow cooker lid, put it in a blanket, and then in a carry bag.

Waiting in the hall, Fell saw Moya's door was open again. Bad habit, even if the hallway's outside door was locked.

Her brothers were in the living room with festive wrapping paper and ribbons strewn around their feet. Probably presents?

Zorion spotted him. "Hey, Fell. Happy Solstice. Are you heading to the festival?"

"Aye."

Patrin locked the door and joined Fell.

"Alpha." Zorion bowed his head slightly, and Fell heard Patrin's breathing stop for a moment. Had anyone in the pack bowed their head to Brett—or Roger for that matter?

Patrin cleared his throat. "Merry Solstice, Zorion."

"Is that Patrin and Fell?" Moya's voice came from farther inside her apartment. "Tell them to wait."

A corner of Zorion's mouth tipped up. "You heard her. Wait, please."

Fell snorted and glanced at his littermate. "You should have let her challenge."

She came out of the back dressed in her usual jeans and knee-high suede boots. And a sweater.

*By the Gods.* The bright red sweater embraced her full breasts in a way that made his mouth dry.

*No, you can't touch. Bad wolf.*

"I'm so glad you're going to the festival. How do you feel?" At their silence, she narrowed her eyes, looking them over. "Fell, how's your head?"

"Fine." At her disbelieving frown, he added, "Throbbing some."

"Patrin?"

He smiled at her. "You did a good job of bandaging it, *blodyn*. No bleeding."

"Okay then. I suppose a party won't send you back to the Mother." Picking up two gift-wrapped boxes from the kitchen island, she handed them to Fell since Patrin's hands were full.

Her lips were warm as she pressed a kiss to Fell's cheek. And she had the lightest scent of coconut—and cinnamon. Patrin got a quick kiss too. "You can open them tomorrow. Blessed Solstice to you both."

*Presents. She gave us presents?*

Fell stared at her. "We didn't get you anything."

Her brown eyes were meltingly soft. "Of course you didn't. After being apart from the clan so long, how would you know?"

In a forest green sweater, Ramón pulled on a coat. "Family and close friends exchange small gifts, usually handmade." He winked at Moya. "Or books if you own a bookstore."

Zorion waved at the coffee table. "Ramón got a book of Celtic legends, and she got me drumsticks from a woodcarver in Cold Creek."

Pointing to bottles on the coffee table, Ramón said, "Zorion makes mead and gives us our favorites."

"I like spiced mead," Moya explained. "Ramón prefers the boring traditional stuff."

Their closeness, their knowledge of each other sent a pang of envy through Fell. If only he and Patrin could have grown up differently, with their mother and Darcy, living in a territory.

*Ah, well.*

"Sometimes you gift something to show your wish for the person for the coming year," Zorion added, his gaze on the presents in Fell's hands.

"Next year, you'll get to join in." In her cold weather outer gear, Moya packed up a platter of savory hand pies into a carrier. "Ready. C'mon. We can all walk together."

Patrin answered for both of them. "Thanks, we'd like that."

As Fell set the presents inside their apartment, his tight shoulder muscles relaxed. He and Patrin wouldn't have to face a crowd by themselves. In fact, they'd be with the sweetest, smartest, and most intriguing female in the territory.

---

Carrying the bag with their potluck offering, Patrin walked down the sidewalk with Moya beside him and Fell on her other side. The moon had risen high into the night sky, spreading light everywhere.

Behind them, Ramón and Zorion were amiably discussing the pack run. "You know, I bet we could get that pretty bard to make a ballad about tonight," Zorion said.

Patrin stiffened...until Ramón added, "Maybe have her focus on Moya's attack. The bard could call it *Bloodying the Beta*."

"Fairy farts and gnome guts, there will be no end to this," Moya muttered. She looked up at Patrin and Fell and batted her eyelashes. "Nice alphas and betas would wallop those two for harassing their sweet, innocent sister."

As silence fell behind them, Patrin's grin widened.

"I didn't get to bite anyone earlier," Fell said in a growling rasp. "I could make up for it now."

"Fine, fine," Ramón called, laughter in his voice. "No sweet innocent sisters will be teased tonight."

Zorion whispered audibly, "Do we know any sweet, innocent sisters?"

The good-humored bickering was what Patrin had with Fell and Darcy before the Scythe. Over Moya's head, he and Fell exchanged smiles.

At the Gathering House, a hearty older male guarded the gate. After waving the shifters before them through, he frowned at

Patrin and Fell and sniffed discreetly. His gaze fell on Moya. "Ah, lass, I di'na see you there. Are the lads with you?"

"They are. Patrin, Fell, this is Morcant, who is a chef in the Shamrock."

Smiling at the Scottish accent, Patrin recognized the fiddler-player from the dance.

Moya continued. "Morcant, meet Patrin, our new alpha, and his beta, Fell."

The chef's eyes widened. "A new alpha and beta. Excellent, excellent. Your names—I know those names. You two helped with the hellhound." He was smiling so widely his eyes were almost closed. "Welcome indeed."

Fell did his usual nod and miniscule smile, leaving all the words to Patrin.

"Nice to meet you." Patrin shook the male's hand. "Staying on the good side of a chef is always worthwhile."

Morcant had a robust laugh. He started to wave them through, then stopped. "Lass, have you any food for a starving male?"

"For you, always." She stopped to dig into her bag. "I brought chicken empanadas."

A rumble of happiness came from Morcant.

Stopping inside the gate to wait for her, Fell murmured to Patrin, "Bet he's a bear."

Ramón joined them and laughed. "You'd be right. He and Madoc are always taking days off to catch fish. They go with Oran and Bridget from the bait and tackle shop."

Great, now Fell was hungry for fish.

Across the lawn was the Gathering House, a two-story clapboard with fancy-as-shit trim and a wrap-around porch where groups of shifters were hanging out.

"Fuck," Fell said in a low voice. "It's crowded." The open door revealed far more Daonain inside than had been at the full moon last month.

"Most of them are good people." Zorion gave Fell's shoulder a friendly bump. "Admittedly, the territory had problems over the past years, but André's bringing the clan together."

"With you two in charge, the pack will be rallying with him instead of fighting against his goals." Ramón added, "Thank fuck."

Surprised, Patrin stared at the brothers. So much faith in him and Fell. Exchanging glances with Fell, he sighed. "We'll do our best for you."

Because that was who they were.

When Moya joined them, they walked in and hung their jackets on hooks in the entry.

Inside, the clan house was festive with Solstice decorations. Evergreens on the fireplace mantel added a crisp fragrance to the air. In one corner, a golden sun topped an eight-foot tree bedecked with blue-and-silver sparkling lights.

Shifters in their brightest colors were everywhere. Smiles and greetings came their way...along with more than a few wary looks. At first, he thought it was because he and Fell were new to the territory. Then, he noticed how the annoyed shifters had smooth, more-than-graceful movements. The animosity came from werecats.

Brett had done more damage than Patrin had realized. This was going to have to be fixed. Somehow.

Ramón looked around. "It's good to have a territory Solstice festival again."

"Because of André." Moya linked her arms with Patrin and Fell. "Come, let's greet the Cosantir."

She tried to move forward. Neither he nor Fell took a step.

"Odd, for some reason, we don't seem to be moving forward." She looked up at him, lifting her eyebrows in inquiry.

Fuck, she was adorable. "Ahhh, as I recall, the Cosantir isn't happy with me and Fell."

Fell coughed into his hand. "...royally pissed-off?"

"That was three nights ago—long past. I'm sure he's over it by now." When the stubborn little wolf pulled, they gave in.

The Cosantir stood in front of the fireplace with Heather and his two littermates.

Meeting Patrin's gaze, Niall grinned and murmured something to André.

"How fast can you run, brawd?" Fell muttered.

Real, real fast, Patrin thought.

"Cosantir." Moya tipped her head in respect, then her smile beamed out. "I wanted to formally bring you our new alpha and beta."

André didn't appear surprised. None of the four were.

*Hmm.* Patrin glanced at Fell and murmured, "He already knows." Wasn't Heather one of Moya's best friends? And having a sister had taught them females communicated far better than males.

"I do know." André held out his hand, his smile warm. "I am pleased with the change in pack leadership—and that you two will remain in my territory." His handshake was firm, his gaze honest.

Patrin found himself at an unexpected loss for words. He'd half expected to be fried by the Cosantir for daring to challenge the alpha—a *real* member of the clan.

With a short full beard, bear-sized Madoc grinned. "I'm glad you're here, you two."

Niall's hard hand slapped Patrin's shoulder. "Glad you won, especially since you took on the beefy asshole after you were wounded."

"Are you all right?" Heather frowned at his side where the dressing bulged slightly under his sweater.

"I'm good." Patrin glanced at Fell on the other side of Moya. "And Fell's head is harder than a bighorn ram's."

"Good thing," Madoc said, then frowned. "You haven't been back with the Daonain long. Do you remember Solstice festivals from before the Scythe?"

"Not much, if at all." Patrin shook his head. "We went when we were very young. As older cubs, we didn't attend Daonain activities."

At the confused looks, Fell grated out, "My fault. My mouth ran faster than my brain, and I couldn't be trusted with Daonain secrets. It's why Mum moved us to an all-shifter village."

Patrin could hear the pain in his littermate's voice. Fell still blamed himself for being the reason they'd been in Dogwood when the Scythe destroyed the village.

André's gaze held sympathy. "This is your time to relearn our customs and make new memories."

"Cosantir." Patrin bowed his head. "Thank you for your welcome."

*And for not sending us straight back to the Mother.*

As if he could hear the thought, André chuckled. "Enjoy the night and the return of the sun."

---

*The shifters in the Rainier Territory are fucking crazy.* Fell came to that conclusion after they did a quick tour of the house and back yard. Every room and both sides of the outside patio had food on linen-draped tables. There were beverages, hot and cold, with older shifters supervising the alcoholic varieties.

Zorion stopped at a drink table and waved Moya and Patrin on. "Go unload your food, you two. Fell can help me here."

"Catch up with you in a bit then." Moya led Patrin toward a different table to hand over the potluck offerings.

Zorion pulled off his pack and set it down gently.

Going down on one knee, Fell pulled padded bottles out of the big pack, handing them up to Zorion. "Is this your mead?"

"Aye." Zorion was setting the bottles on the table. "This is my festival mead."

"It's fantastic stuff." The brawny, full-bearded shifter managing the spirits table held up one bottle. Fell recognized the male after a moment. Lorcan owned the wilderness tour business on the square. "I always thought mead was bland until I had some of Zorion's."

Instead of being made from grapes like wine, mead was made from honey. And that was the extent of Fell's knowledge. "I've never had any."

It'd been served in Elder Village where they'd gone soon after getting freed from the Scythe, but they hadn't been comfortable enough to imbibe. He'd still been terrified of doing something wrong and getting kicked out of the clan.

He might not have...entirely...lost that worry.

But mostly.

"By the Gods, in that case, give our new beta a taste, Lorcan." Zorion smiled at Fell. "Lorcan's a bear, by the way."

Fell nodded. "Good to meet you."

"And you." Lorcan selected two bottles. "Two tastes, you'll get, Beta. One of a traditional mead I picked up in Sawtooth Territory. The other will be Zorion's spiced mead." He handed over a heavy mug with a small sample.

Fell took a sip. It tasted like a light, frothy white wine with a sweet honey aftertaste. "Nice. Not something I'd drink for long."

"Agreed." Lorcan took the mug back, rinsed it out, and splashed in mead from one of Zorion's bottles. "Next."

Taking it, Fell sampled and smiled. Full-bodied and complex. He could taste cinnamon and cloves and something else. Again, there was a honey—and maybe citrus—aftertaste. "Now that's good."

"There we go." Lorcan took the mug and added more of Zorion's mead. After eyeing Fell's jeans, he held out a metal snap hook. "Keep the mug. Bring it with you next festival."

Surprised, Fell glanced around to see quite a few shifters had mugs clipped to their belts. "This beats drinking from plastic cups. Thank you."

Lorcan's big smile split the bushy beard. "Merry Solstice, Beta."

*Beta.* It felt odd to have a title for continuing what he'd done for years with the Scythe. Patrin was in charge; Fell backed him up. This was nothing new, no matter what the shifters called it. "A blessed Solstice to you."

Off to one side, Zorion was talking to a couple of older shifters.

Fell looked around for Patrin and Moya when raised voices caught his attention.

"You're stupid, smelly moggies. You don't even have a mother."

"Yeah, and we're gonna mess you up."

The youthful jeering came from a room off to one side. The voices were familiar. Pack cubs, maybe?

Toeing the door open, he walked in on four younglings.

Two were from the pack—the sixteen-year-olds whose names he'd recently learned. Vigulf and Torkil, whose mother was a bear. They were picking on two younger lads, orphan werecats from the sound of it.

Most admirably, the younger ones had their fists up and obviously planned to fight the pack bullies. Good for them. And shame on the two from his pack.

Fell's growl filled the small room, and all four cubs froze.

"Gods, it's the beta," Vigulf whispered to his brother, and both retreated a few steps.

Fell looked at the two orphans. "Our pack asks forgiveness for the rudeness of these two."

The leader of the two werecats pulled in a breath. Brave cub. "Sure. S'okay." When an elbow from his brother impacted his ribs, he hastily added, "Thank you, Beta."

Fell almost laughed. How often had he prompted Patrin that way? Moving aside, he watched them scamper out.

Now to deal with the troublesome pair. "Vigulf, Torkil, you have shamed the pack."

They moved closer together. Vigulf was shaking.

"Only cowards pick on the small and weak."

He waited until their faces flushed with humiliation before adding, "You're better than that."

They straightened slightly. Yes, they had pride. With help, they might turn into honorable shifters and good pack members.

Patrin and Fell had years of helping younglings grow.

Next...

Fell's tongue froze for a moment, but he managed to move past the block to say what he needed them to hear. "If the Daonain can't pull together, the humans will kill us all. Don't be the ones to tear us apart."

At their surprised expressions, he knew it was a concept they'd need time to comprehend. And was something he and Patrin would have to work on with the entire pack.

Because neither of them was completely convinced the Scythe were gone. Wells wasn't either, or he'd have released all the shifter-soldiers. The Daonain needed to be ready.

But these were just cubs, so he added a more immediate threat. "Next time you call werecats names, you'll repeat those insults to the Cosantir and cahirs...who are all werecats."

Vigulf's gulp was audible. Torkil swallowed hard.

Fell jerked his head. "Go."

In full panic, the two jammed up in the narrow doorway before bursting out into the bigger room.

Laughing under his breath, Fell followed them out. But his laughter died as he thought about how cubs imitated adults. He and Patrin were going to have to yank some tails over the werecat issue.

Over by the back door, Patrin and Moya waited, and they all

went outside onto the wide patio. The tantalizing aroma of beef wafted from a huge grill at one end.

He studied the grounds for a moment. It was a typical Daonain property—surrounded by extensive forest. A tall wooden fence provided extra privacy for the lawn area, which had been cleared of snow for the party.

A bonfire blazed in a wide fire pit in the center of the yard. Each end of the patio and the open gazebos boasted low fire tables. With the fence cutting the cold wind, the numerous fires warmed the area. No need for heavy coats.

Around the big fire pit, the dancers wore sweaters and hoodies. From the raucous enthusiasm, they were probably nicely heated from alcohol.

"Looks like fun." Patrin rocked on his heels, gaze on the dancing.

"It really is. You can come out here and dance and talk or go inside to sing and listen to stories. And eat everywhere." Moya grinned. "Since it's the longest night, there's time to catch up with everyone and still dance and sing. You'll see."

The longest night. And they'd be here until dawn.

They could dance with Moya again.

And tomorrow was full moon and a Gathering.

Fell slung his arm over the little wolf's shoulders. He knew just who he hoped to take upstairs to share with his brother.

---

As he and his family stopped in the middle of the living room, André smiled at Niall and Madoc and gave Heather a slow kiss. Turning, he ruffled Sky's blond hair and squeezed Talam's shoulder.

He and his brothers had always celebrated the festivals together, but this year, they had their lifemate and two exceptional cubs with them. He hadn't realized that love simply grew sweeter when extended to more.

And he—they—now had a clan to nurture and protect.

A young cubling, who couldn't be more than five years old, ran up and wrapped his little arms around André's knees. "Cos-tore, Happy Solstice!"

"Blessed Solstice to you." Smiling, André lifted the cub high into the air, enjoying the happy squee.

"Sorry, Cosantir. He's very fast." His laughing, scolding mother accepted her giggling youngling and carried him away.

Still chuckling, André stepped up on the coffee table. The open arrangement of the downstairs living, dining, and kitchen areas made it easy for the clan to see him. More shifters stood on the stairs up to where the door to the second floor blocked off access.

"Blessed Solstice to you all. I'll keep this brief since there's dancing and singing to be done."

"And feasting," a cubling called with open enthusiasm.

"And feasting," he agreed gravely. "Tonight, the longest night ends with the return of the sun and the rebirth of Herne, the horned hunter. With our clan around us, we will keep the vigil in the dark, and as the light grows in the east, we'll sing to the gods."

The low approving murmur of his people showed they were running the same trail with him. These shared ceremonies were part of the foundation of the Daonain, and as Cosantir, he could feel the presence of each of his clan. Warmth filled his spirit.

"Since I have you here, let us welcome our newest clan members born since the last moon." He let his instincts search and find his mate. As they'd planned, Heather had moved next to Glenys. He motioned that direction. "Welcome Gruffudd and Cadfan, cubs of Glenys."

"The clan increases," came the response, with happy smiles thrown to the glowing mother.

He introduced a handful of shifters who'd received his permission to move to Rainier Territory and welcomed several who'd moved away and now returned. The increasing population was a gratifying indication the territory was becoming a happier, more rewarding place to live.

He did notice some wolves and cougars casting angry looks at each other. To have animosity at a festival... It was concerning.

But there was hope for the future...

He smiled at the two shifter-soldiers Herne had reclaimed from the human spymaster. "Many of you have met Patrin and Fell, two of our brave shifters who risked their lives to kill a hellhound. Earlier this evening, they became our wolf pack's new alpha and beta."

There was a moment of silence from those who hadn't heard the news. And then such a gale of cheering that the two males froze in surprise.

They were only in their mid-twenties, but their eyes were old. Their youth had been stripped away many years ago. André couldn't give them back their youngling days, but he'd do his best to ensure the rest of their lives would be filled with joy.

"Congratulations, Alpha and Beta." He smiled at them. Courageous, honest, and still somewhat unsure of their welcome. They'd learn.

And they would be good for his clan.

"Blessed Solstice to you all."

The Daonain called blessings back to him as he jumped off the table—and snagged Patrin before he could disappear into the crowd. "Alpha, perhaps a word?"

The young male stiffened. "Of course, Cosantir." He turned to his littermate and Moya. "Have fun. I'll find you in a bit."

Fell's brows drew together, and he didn't move. André could sense his protectiveness rising.

"Fell, I won't hurt your brother," André said gently.

Both Patrin and Moya appeared shocked. No one questioned

a Cosantir, but Fell met André's gaze with a nod of acceptance. And gratitude.

"Shall we step outside where it's quieter?" Without waiting for an answer, André snagged a cup of hot spiced cider on the way out through the living area. Patrin did the same, and they walked out onto the wrap-around porch.

"What's up?" Patrin asked.

André leaned a hip against the railing, using the senses of a guardian as he looked at the dark-haired, dark-eyed male. Patrin hadn't even reached thirty in years, but experience and trauma had aged his spirit. This new alpha had ample compassion, protectiveness, and honesty. Yes, he would do very well.

If he didn't get overwhelmed...

André took a sip of cider. "Last fall, Niall went missing. Madoc and I found him in Ailill Ridge. We were ready to return to Canada, but Herne decided to replace the current Cosantir. With me."

Patrin's eyes widened. "And I thought I felt out of place."

"*Oui.* I was probably as surprised to have the job dumped in my lap as you were earlier today."

"Yeah. That sounds about right." Patrin thumped his head against a porch post. "I'm not prepared for this. Gods, me and Fell barely know how a pack works."

"You will learn." André laid his hand on Patrin's shoulder and could feel the simmering frustration and fear. "Your pack is dancing with joy at getting you and Fell for their leaders."

Patrin looked startled, then happiness lit his eyes.

"I am pleased as well. Brett caused problems between the wolves and cats. I hope we can work to heal the division."

"Agreed. I'll be talking to the wolves"—Patrin sighed—"my wolves and letting them know that going after cat shifters isn't permitted. It'll take some work and time."

"But no hunt can begin without putting a paw to the trail."

André nodded. "Keep me informed, and let me know how I can help."

"Of course, Cosantir." Patrin's frame was no longer tense. "And thanks."

---

Moya had never enjoyed a festival so much. Oh, she'd had fun at previous Daonain events, which she'd attended with her brothers and friends. This time...

Well, she tried to tell herself Fell and Patrin were just friendly neighbors.

But one of them usually had an arm over her shoulders or around her waist or, like now, a hand pressed against the small of her back to guide her into the house. Patrin's palm was warm, just above her ass, keeping her moving forward.

She didn't like being pushed around, didn't like being dominated. But somehow, when he did, her heart tripped a little faster. Although surrounded by noisy people and music, she could hear only his smooth baritone, feel his hand and the brush of his hard body against hers.

Fell had the same effect.

This felt almost like a full moon heat—only the full moon was tomorrow—and Patrin and Fell were the only males impacting her senses like this.

So confusing.

"Back in a minute," Fell said and disappeared into the kitchen.

What was he up to? And where were they going?

As they waited by the back door, Cosette walked over. "Alpha, I'm so glad you're here." Her plump lips in a pout, she looked up at him. "I didn't get a chance to talk to you at the pack run."

Moya started to move away, but Patrin's arm around her tightened. He studied Cosette for a moment as if trying to remember her name. "Is there a problem we need to discuss?"

"There is." Cosette pushed her long brown hair over her shoulder. "I'm the alpha female. There are many, many things to discuss."

*Oh, fairy farts.* None of them had remembered the alpha female. It wasn't as if Cosette or the previous ones made much of an impression on the pack. However, pack bonds usually drew the alpha male and female together, at least with a strong alpha female.

No telling what would happen with an ineffectual alpha female, but Moya could sure see what Cosette *wanted* to happen. Even though Patrin had his arm around Moya, Cosette was flirting for all she was worth.

Patrin cleared his throat. "This isn't the time or place for serious discussions. Perhaps later, when Fell and I have our paws situated, we'll see what's what."

He nodded to Cosette and guided Moya around the startled female. Away from the door, through the kitchen, across the smaller living room.

Moya planted her feet. "Patrin, you're wandering around the house like a squirrel who forgot where he buried his acorns. Why don't we go back outside?"

Laughter lit his eyes. Honestly, the male found almost everything amusing.

"I was escaping the female, not wandering." He tapped her chin with a finger. "And we're inside because you're chilled, *blodyn*. We needed to keep you where it's warm for a while."

Her mouth dropped open. The three of them had been outside, nibbling on meat hot off the grill, sampling various meads, and dancing. So much fun.

And now...they'd come in because of *her*?

As Patrin stopped in the great room, Fell reappeared. "Found you." He handed her a mug. "This should help."

She took a sip. The heat went straight to her stomach and set up a hearth fire there. The hot chocolate had more than a splash of alcohol. "Wow."

Fell grinned, an actual full grin so devastating it blasted more heat through her than the drink.

"Sounds like there's storytelling in the smaller living room." Patrin moved her forward. "Let's go in there."

She shook her head. The males enjoyed dancing, and they weren't cold. "You don't have to stay with me, you know. I can—"

"Did you want to visit with your friends instead?" Patrin asked softly, his gaze intent.

"No, I mean I can, but I don't want to keep you from—"

When he smiled, the dark beard made his teeth look very white. "Little wolf, we're enjoying your company. Aye, brawd?"

"Aye."

When Fell ran a hand through her hair, tucking it behind her ear, her stomach quivered.

*Climbing him like a tree and kissing him would be inappropriate. Tomorrow though...*

Around the living room fireplace, a semicircle of cubs and adults lounged on floor cushions. An empty couch stood to the right of the hearth. Since this was the storyteller room, the only lighting came from the flames and the candles on the mantel.

Talking in a voice pitched just loud enough to reach the edges of the room, Ramón sat in a chair to the left of the fire.

He'd told her once that entertaining at festivals with traditional Daonain tales was his way of giving back to the clan and the gods. Although everyone considered his story-telling talent a gift from the Gods, he laughed at the idea.

She agreed with the clan.

The fireplace seats were always reserved for the storytellers... and their help. Taking their hands, she drew Patrin and Fell forward with her and settled them all on the long couch.

Without interrupting his tale, Ramón smiled, picked up her guitar from where it leaned against the wall, and handed it to her.

Ignoring Patrin's and Fell's puzzled expressions, she cocked her head. What story was her brother telling?

Ah, the early tale of the Death Gift, one of his favorites. And so sad.

Pushing her hair out of the way behind her shoulders, she started softly strumming and finger-picking minor chords. Adding to the atmosphere.

Ramón continued, his voice soft but clear:

*As the sword stabbed into Feradach's side, his back legs gave out. With the last of his strength, he ripped his sharp claws across the soldier's throat. Ending his life.*

Trawsfurring to human, Feradach collapsed.

"Nay!" That was Colbán's voice. He was one of the humans fighting beside the Daonain against the invaders.

He blinked the blurriness from his eye as the young man dropped to his knees beside him.

"No, no, no. None of the doctors are yet alive." Frantically, Colbán ripped the undersleeve from beneath his chainmail tunic and pressed the fabric against Feradach's wound.

As pain swept over him, Feradach bit back a groan. "Did we win?"

"We won, my friend. Your forests and your clan are safe."

For now. The humans called Romans weren't going to stop.

The problem was no longer one Feradach could solve. He could feel his breath coming hard even as coldness crept up his hands and feet.

The Mother was calling him home.

Yet one last duty remained to him—a gift he could leave for his clan.

This human, Colbán, had kept the secret of the Daonain. Had proven himself in battle.

The warrior had courage and a true heart.

It was hard, so very hard to move. Jaw clenched against crying out, he forced his hand to lift. Pain ripped at him like wolf's fangs tearing into his side.

His memory gave him the Elder's voice, whispering the ancient ritual.

His whisper sounded hoarse. "Fire in the blood." Blood—he had that in plenty, spilling from numerous cuts and the jagged hole in his side.

Colbán gripped his hand. "Don't move, Feradach. I'll—"

"Water from tears," he whispered and touched his blood-covered fingers to his tear-dampened cheek.

"And earth is the dirt we walk on." His body lay on the Mother's sweet ground. It only needed a small movement to press his hand into the damp soil.

*Gods, the pain...* Herne help him, but it *hurt*.

Casting off his body and returning to the Mother would be a blessing.

Not yet. The Daonain had lost too many. They couldn't afford the loss of another warrior.

*I will do this for my clan.*

"Take my breath for the living air." The world had grown so very dark. He squinted, trying to see.

There, a long slash ran down Colbán's forehead.

Feradach lifted his hand, seeing it shake. Finally, he touched Colbán's face, pressing his fingers streaked with dirt, tears, and blood into Colbán's wound.

The human warrior flinched at the pain but didn't draw away. "My friend, help is coming. I'll get you to the next village and—"

Feradach tried to smile at how Colbán called him friend.

Daonain didn't befriend humans. Yet this young male had fought beside him over the last bloody days, each saving the other's life more than once. "Aye, it is right. My *friend*. A charge I lay on thee—that you care for my clan."

"No, Feradach. Stay..." The young human protested the

inevitable as his eyes glossed with tears. And then his jaw turned firm as he accepted the charge. "I will. You have my word."

Sweetness swept through Feradach as the Mother accepted his choice...as She awaited the final part of the gift.

He would hold nothing back.

With his last breath, he whispered, "And I seal it with my spirit."

As he let go, and the Goddess' arms closed around him, he felt only joy.

*The clan loses one—and gains another.*

As Ramón fell silent, Moya felt her own eyes burning. As she softly played an accompaniment in a melancholy minor key, she swallowed against the thickness in her throat.

Out in the room, firelight gleamed on tear-dampened faces. Cubs sobbed. Those in animal form huddled closer together. On each side of her, she heard soft huffs as the shifter-soldiers battled their own tears.

She finger-picked the last few notes to end the story in music and softness. Setting a hand on her guitar, she smiled at her brother. As a pup, Ramón had terrified her and Zorion with scary stories, reduced them to helpless laughter, or made them cry with his tragic tales.

The years had only improved his skill.

"Thank you, Ramón, for the story." Heather walked through the audience and took a seat on the raised fireplace hearth. "Blessings be upon Colbán and werecat Feradach who were shining examples of the Death Gift. After his First Shift, Colbán was a fierce warrior in defense of the Daonain. He lived many years—and sired more than one litter of cubs."

What excellent timing Heather had. The younglings could use some lighthearted talk to recover. Moya winked at her friend, then raised her voice. "Hey, cubs. Did anyone tell you that the

Cosantir in the North Cascades has a mate who received the Death Gift?"

"Really?"

"She was human before?"

"I didn't think that was real."

So many murmurs, including from some adults. She turned to Heather. "You're friends with Vicki, right?"

"You are a thistle-thorned troublemaker," Heather said under her breath, but she was one of the finest females ever, so with a big smile, she added loudly, "Yes, Vicki and I are friends."

Little faces lifted, and the younglings in animal form perked up their ears. Patrin chuckled, saying softly, "So cute and filled with curiosity."

Tilting her head, Moya asked Heather, "Since Vicki had never even heard of the Daonain before she was Gifted, did she have a hard time?"

"Oh, did she." Heather laughed, long and hearty. She leaned forward...and her audience did the same. "Humans can't see OtherFolk at all, so when she suddenly started seeing pixies and then dwarves, she thought she was going crazy."

Cubling giggles were the most infectious sounds in the world.

"As it happens, humans usually only have one cub at a time. When we told her she'd have at least two, she had a hissy fit." Heather snickered. "She ended up with a litter of three."

More giggles.

Really, Moya sympathized with the poor Cosantir's mate. Three cublings would be a pawful.

"What about mates?" a teenaged female cub asked. "Don't human women only mate—marry—one male?"

"That's right." Heather rolled her eyes. "You would think a Cosantir and a cahir could handle telling a female half their size about Daonain full moons and mating and lifemating—but *nooo*, they begged me to tell her. She did *not* take it well. So much cursing."

"Didn't I hear the female was a soldier when she was human?" Talitha asked from the side where she sat with Eileen.

"Humans let their females be soldiers?" Quenbie, an older wolf, asked in a scandalized tone.

"They do. Since they have as many females born as males, they're not nearly as protective," Claire retorted. The young female had fought some battles of her own to get Daniel to hire her as a ranch-hand. "Besides, our females can be soldiers after their child-bearing years. Look at Bron."

Quenbie subsided with a few huffs.

Patrin murmured to Fell, "I thought you and I had trouble adapting to Daonain traditions. I wonder how many times an ex-human soldier butted heads with the more hidebound Daonain traditionalists."

Moya frowned. "But humans have traditions, don't they?"

"Theirs are more...diverse," Fell said.

When he didn't continue, Patrin elaborated. "Various human groups have different religions, different languages. Even within one religion, they argue about what their god really said. All Daonain, though, follow the same trails as our ancestors."

"Huh." Moya considered that. "I fight against the customs sometimes, but mostly, I like our well-worn paths."

"Yeah." Patrin's voice lowered as he murmured to Fell. "In spite of being a stranger and ex-human, Vicki managed to find her place with the Daonain."

Moya turned her attention back to the group, her heart aching for the two shifter-soldiers. Because she could hear unspoken dreams in the roughness of his voice.

*Yes, my shifter-soldiers, there is a place for you here. With us.*

Still sitting on the hearth, Heather hadn't stopped answering questions. "From what I've seen, human gods don't speak to their followers, let alone step in and render judgments. Perhaps Vicki's biggest surprise was how active Herne and the Mother are."

"Like the touch of the Mother when we shift?" one cub asked, having recently experienced her own First Shift.

"Exactly like that." Heather nodded.

"That means the Death Gift really works." Sitting beside his littermate, Talam, Sky's blue eyes were wide with wonder.

"It does. A young male was dying, and he didn't want to leave his grandfather without any family—so he gave Vicki the Death Gift to give Thorson someone to love." Heather's eyes went shiny for a moment. "Now she's lifemated, and Thorson is *caomhnor* to one of the three adorable cubs she's given her clan. He's part of a family again."

At the soft murmuring and *awww*s, Moya smiled at her friend who'd taken Ramón's lesson of the Death Gift and shown why the ritual was so very important to the Daonain.

There might come a time these younglings would need to remember it.

---

The night had been long yet...special, Fell thought as he walked beside Moya with his arm around her waist. Patrin walked on her other side as they joined the flow of the shifters out the back door, across the patio, and onto the lawn.

Shifters spread out around the lawn, forming circles around the fire pit, facing outward. A salamander, half-submerged in the still-glowing coals, poked its head up to watch.

With Moya between them, he and Patrin took the hands of the shifters on their other sides, and in silence, waited. Each breath of air brought the lingering scent of smoke, the crispness of snowy mountains, and the tang of evergreens.

In the west, the setting moon outlined the tops of the mountain peaks. The fires had been smothered and lanterns extinguished. Darkness filled the night.

And then…slowly…the skies lightened with the grayness of pre-dawn.

Fell realized he'd been holding his breath in the taut silence.

A line of gold tipped the white peaks to the east, and inch-by-inch, the bright ball of the sun appeared.

On the patio, a drum began to beat. A flute trilled in a welcome, and then Moya's clear, bright voice rose in the traditional "Welcome" song.

*In the east, the sun is rising…*

The circles were moving, the footsteps simple.

With the second repetition of the song, Fell joined along, welcoming and rejoicing in the return of the light. The steady drumbeat, the music, and the rhythmic steps drew him into a different place, opening his soul to the others around him and even to the presence of the gods.

And as the light crested the mountain and spilled over their circles, he felt part of the Daonain, part of everything.

## CHAPTER NINETEEN

F*ull moon*

In his Seattle hotel room, one of the Colonel's burner phones rang. Rising, he grunted as the ache in his chest reminded him of how close he'd come to dying last month.

Goddamned abominations. The injuries had laid him up for too long, requiring he stay completely hidden. In the meantime, everything had gone to hell.

He picked up the phone labeled "Baton." The operative was assigned to a bumfuck town near Mt. Rainier. "Speak."

"Baton reporting in."

"Go on."

"There has been a..." The operative swallowed audibly.

Such poor bodily control indicated a doubtful future in the Scythe. Typical. Women simply weren't as strong as men operatives. However, women spies were the last to be suspected. "Spit it out, Baton."

"Tuesday night, the Director attempted to eliminate Patrin and Fell. The operation failed. Badly."

"How badly?"

"I wasn't on site but observed the aftermath through a telescope. The creatures were disposing of bodies and vehicles. The Director was one of the bodies."

The Colonel shook his head in disgust. The Director had been so worried about losing his reputation and position in the Scythe, he'd undoubtedly barged ahead with little to no planning. There was a reason the man had babysat the compound with the female hostages rather than conducting operations.

Because he was an idiot.

Fucking wonderful. The Pacific Northwest division couldn't afford disasters like this. The loss of the Director and his operatives couldn't be covered up.

The Colonel rubbed his face. If the Committee heard how the shapeshifters broke free, he'd lose everything he'd worked for. He'd lose his future. And his life.

The Scythe didn't condone failure.

He was out of options. It was time to share everything he'd learned about the shapeshifters, including how they could best be used. But, without a sampling of the abominations, the Scythe Committee would laugh at him.

To re-establish himself, he had be able to demonstrate the shapeshifter's skills. Using some of the soldiers they'd groomed over the years in a critical operation. Preferably the best—Patrin and Fell.

But only if he had a way to hold them.

He tapped his fingers on the desktop. "Were Patrin or Fell damaged, or are they still in place?"

"Still available, sir."

"Good. And their possible romantic interest?"

"The relationship seems to be deepening."

Kidnapping the woman might work. Unfortunately, the female

abominations were weak and liable to waste away. "Are there others we could use as leverage? Friends, family?"

"A couple of teens hang around them. They've protected the boys from bullies."

Of course, they would. Patrin and Fell had often been disciplined for trying to protect younger mutants from being killed or even beaten. Seemed to think it was their job.

*Fools.*

"I've identified others who are probably mutants." Baton paused and then asked, "Couldn't we separate brothers and use one as a hostage?"

"A brother isn't as effective. The abominations will obey to prevent a child or sister from being hurt. But they won't protect their brothers. In fact, they're far more dangerous then since they'll do suicidal attacks."

"Oh."

He tapped his fingers on the desk. "The young boys are a good option. We managed to keep them alive and…"

The idea he had right then was momentous. Brilliant. Years ago, the scientists told him all the infants and adult mutants had died from being imprisoned in metal cages underground.

Which meant, they could capture adult mutants and keep them alive.

"Sir?" The operative's voice was tentative.

"Wait one minute, Baton." He glanced at his laptop with the update of current events. The Scythe had invested heavily in some bumfuck country with rare earth exports. Unfortunately, the corrupt, bribable government was in danger of being overthrown by insurgents using guerilla warfare.

No military camp would survive the abominations. If he could lay his hand on a sufficient number of them, he'd have the finest demonstration possible. And a win over his worst rival.

*Yes.*

If he obtained cubs, he'd have a new generation to train, and in the interim, could use them for hostages...and bait.

*Oh, yes. Bait.*

"All right, Baton. Plan to acquire all the young creatures you can, human or mutant. We'll scoop them up along with Patrin and Fell and the bitch they favor—and sort them out afterward."

Once they had a way to get the bait, he'd work out how to obtain the adults.

"Yes, sir. I'll have the information ready."

"Good. Move to the next phone in line. I'll contact you when I have everyone we need for a quick strike."

"You're coming here?" There was a pause. "Um, sir?"

"Yes. I'll supervise this directly so there are no mistakes." Because if he didn't capture the abominations to show off to the Committee, he'd be dead.

*I'll see that town burn first.*

---

Brushing his hands off, feeling the sting of his scraped knuckles, Fell walked back into the Gathering House. "That felt good." A shame they had to return inside. The entire fucking place was filled with shifters in heat.

Beside him, Patrin huffed a laugh. "Yeah. I needed an outlet. Thumping an idiot male works well."

*No fucking lie.* The full moon was driving Fell mad—and all for one female. He and Patrin wanted to spend as much time with her as possible—something frowned upon during Gathering Nights—so they were waiting to be her last choices for the night.

But under the light of the full moon, the need for her became an intolerable compulsion. She was so beautiful, her rich brown hair loose over her shoulder, her dark eyes pulling him in. Her skin...

*Stop, gnome-brain.* He sucked the blood off his fingers, growling under his breath as the scents of females in heat and of far too much testosterone clogged his nostrils. High voices, throaty with need, filled the air.

And he was listening for only one. For a warm, melodic voice.

For Moya. No one else had interested them all evening.

"I wish we could tell her why we haven't approached," Patrin muttered.

"Yeah." But simply seeing her was driving him mad with desire. If he went over there... If her heady scent held interest for him, any chance of waiting would be over. He'd have her over his shoulder and upstairs before the next breath.

*So, stay out of scenting range.* "Over there." Fell pointed to a place at the island, as far away from the little wolf as they could get.

Patrin gave him an understanding glance. "Agreed. My self-control is in shreds."

It had grown intolerable before they'd even been inside a couple of hours. So they'd asked the Cosantir to let them work as his Gathering House bouncers...preferably outside.

Many Daonain enjoyed flirting around the firepits in the gazebos. However, too many males ended up fighting over the females out there, away from the Cosantir's watchful gaze.

He and Patrin got a chance to work off their frustration by breaking up the fights.

But it was close to the time when they could be with Moya. They needed to be in here.

As growing impatience simmered inside Fell, all he could do was wait.

---

The light of the full moon shone through the Gathering House windows in a glowing reminder of why the room was filled with people. With her stocking feet propped on the coffee table, Moya lounged in a chair across from Talitha and Eileen who shared a couch.

None of them particularly wanted to be here, but here they were. For the good of their people, for tradition.

Wasn't it interesting how the stubbornest of Daonain accepted this coercion that'd been issued by the Gods. The humans sure didn't go into heat every moon.

Then again, without the full moon heat, the shifters would probably have died off. The population had declined every generation since the Fae left the world. The Gatherings did help. So, it was a toss-up between being coerced or the Daonain surviving.

*Fine, I consent to the monthly annoyances.*

"It's sure different without Brett or Caleb here," Moya commented. There'd still been male posturing and occasional loud voices, but she'd been able to—almost—relax. "They might not have brawled, but they sure made a lot of females uncomfortable."

"Good riddance to them," Eileen said. She'd dyed her spiky hair purple and blue—to fit the season.

"Why are our wolves sitting with a stinky moggy?"

The sneering voice made Moya stiffen and turn. *Oh, fairy farts.* Pavel and Ilya, a couple of Brett's followers, were glaring at Eileen.

Anger swept away any trace of the full moon heat, and she started to rise.

Until she saw Patrin. He walked up behind the two mangy mutts and smacked the back of each head as if they were cublings.

When they turned on him, the blast of alpha dominance made them actually cringe.

"I can't believe my own wolves would harass a female at a Gathering—or any other time." Patrin gripped their napes and moved them away, lecturing sternly enough that if they'd been in wolf form, their tails would be tucked under their bellies.

Leaning against a wall with his arms folded over his big chest,

Fell watched his brother. If the young males didn't get their paws on the right trail, they'd get nipped.

Her alpha and beta were going to set the pack straight—and she loved it.

She *didn't* love how the commanding sound in Patrin's deep voice had made her heart turn somersaults. Or how she couldn't stop staring at the rounded bulge of Fell's biceps.

*Down, wolf, down.*

"I see the Cosantir put our alpha and beta to work," Talitha said.

"They volunteered," André said, having obviously heard the comment. "They have done an excellent job."

"I'm glad." Talitha smiled at him. "Gatherings feel so much safer with you and your bouncers around."

Moya knew her friend remembered all the past harassments she and Eileen had endured.

"That is why we're here." André smiled at Talitha, before turning to Moya. "Young wolf, have none here tonight appealed to you?"

Over the long hours, the musky scents and low notes of masculine voices had tingled through her. Yet whenever a male approached, she lost any interest in mating whatsoever.

"Um..."

"Huh, you're right, Cosantir." Talitha frowned. She and Eileen had done better than Moya in finding bedding partners tonight. The two had enjoyed their usual mating room visit together and later each found a male to enjoy. "Moya's always picky but has never rejected *everyone* before. Hey, Moya, did you switch your preference to females?"

Startled, Moya blinked, then laughed. "No, I just don't like the choices, I guess."

André's lips quirked. "Perhaps I should ask other Cosantirs to send a sampling of their uninvolved males. To give you a better selection."

"I... No. No, no." Moya shook her head. The idea of meeting new males wasn't appealing at all. *Be polite to the Cosantir.* "But, ah, thank you for the thought, Cosantir."

"You've never turned down Daniel before." Eileen studied her. "I always thought if Tanner had been as into you as Daniel, you'd have them for mates."

"Maybe. When I was younger." Moya shrugged. "I don't know what's wrong tonight. Maybe I'm getting sick."

André's eyes narrowed as if he could tell it was a total bald-faced lie.

Because she felt fine. She just desired two specific males, and in wanting them, she couldn't find an interest in anyone else. The moon was well into the west now. In two or three hours, the night would be over, and they hadn't approached her.

Which made no sense. Yesterday, Patrin had said he'd be asking for her favor. So had Fell.

So many times tonight she'd told herself to stop being a cowardly cur and go ask them to join her upstairs. One or the other—or even both together, although she'd never mated two at the same time. Heather had told her it was fun, but...it sounded a bit frightening.

As it happened, having two wasn't a concern—since she hadn't attracted even one of them. Admittedly, they'd been outside for a big part of the night. Only they were inside now and...still staying away. Maybe it was because they had far more attractive options.

In fact, since they'd come inside a few minutes ago, the females had flocked over to flirt with the sexy, new alpha and beta. Moya had repositioned her chair to keep her back to them and the stairs. She wouldn't be able to stand seeing them take someone up to the mating rooms.

André studied her for a moment longer, looked over her shoulder at something, and smiled. He really did have a simply gorgeous smile. "Then I will simply hope these last hours of the evening will improve for you."

As he walked away, Moya dropped her head into her hands. Getting the attention of the Cosantir for a lack of mating? This night really was a steaming pile of bear droppings.

"Bugger off, Gretch." A female's loud voice stilled the room for a moment.

"Is someone cursing out Gretchen? This should be good." Talitha looked past Moya toward the other side of the room.

Moya turned, spotted Miss Blonde Perfection, and frowned. Gretchen wasn't her usual stunning self. Her eyes were red, lids swollen, face blotchy. What could have caused the normally reserved female to look almost...heartbroken?

"Isn't that Gretchen's sister?" Eileen motioned toward the short, curvy brunette beside Gretchen.

"Yes, that's Sarah," Moya sat back in her chair. "I thought she lived in the North Cascades Territory."

"She does." Eileen shook her head. "But she has to come here to see her sister. The North Cascades Cosantir won't let Gretchen into his territory."

"Right, I forgot." Moya felt her chest tighten. "If Sarah heard we have a new alpha and beta, she might be here for them. She and Gretchen compete worse than males trying to win a female."

Eileen wrinkled her nose. "If that's what sisters do, I'm glad I don't have one. It's surprising though. Male littermates don't battle; they share."

"Mmm, females are wired differently." Talitha shook her head. "And those two aren't exactly normal. Having two females in one litter is so rare, they were completely spoiled. Their mama convinced them they're more special than anyone else."

"They really are spectacularly beautiful though." Moya made a face. "If I'm near Gretchen, I feel like a gnome, all stunted and pudgy."

"As if." Eileen leaned forward and patted Moya's knee. "You're just a pocket-sized beauty rather than being stretched out."

Gaze on the other side of the room, Talitha murmured, "The drama continues."

Who could resist watching the show? Moya turned in her chair.

*Oh no. This isn't fair.*

Her heart sank.

Sarah wore a mini skirt that barely covered her crotch and a low-cut top to make the most of bounteous breasts. Unlike most of the shifters, she hadn't removed her footwear before coming inside. Her shoes looked incredibly uncomfortable with pointed toes and high heels.

And her obvious target was Patrin and Fell, who sat side-by-side at the kitchen island. With a lascivious smile, the curvy brunette wiggled between the two males, rubbing her hips against them.

With a shake of his head, Fell said something to her.

Her mouth dropped open. She shot him a vicious glare before running her hand up Patrin's arm and leaning against him.

Patrin's voice was louder than Fell's. "No, thank you."

"What do you mean, no?" Sarah set her hands on her hips. "You can't tell me no. It's full moon. I know you want me."

With a cynical smile, Patrin sniffed his own wrist. "Nope. No interest here." He stood and stepped around the brunette. "C'mon, brawd. We've waited long enough."

"'Bout time." Fell followed, leaving Sarah staring after them, mouth open in shock.

"Oh, that was oddly satisfying to watch," Eileen said.

But Moya couldn't answer...because Patrin's gaze had met hers. Trapped hers. The two males headed straight for her, covering the space quickly with their long-legged strides.

For the first time that night, heat bloomed inside her.

"Moya." Patrin stood in front of her, and the glorious masculine scent of him made her heart dance like a rose-intoxicated flower fairy.

She swallowed. "Um, hey."

Talitha made a snickering sound.

Patrin's darker-than-dark eyes were piercing. The feeling of his callused hand closing around hers sent a surge of heat through her.

Gods, what was happening to her? She hadn't felt this out of control since her first full moon heat.

Maybe not even then.

"Come upstairs with us, little wolf," Patrin murmured.

"*Us*...?" Her gaze jerked up.

Fell stood beside Patrin, his blue eyes holding hers.

The chair beneath her seemed to dissolve, leaving her floating in air.

A corner of Fell's mouth tipped up, and he touched her cheek with gentle fingers. "Both of us."

Patrin pulled her to her feet and stopped. "Aye?"

Because the decision was hers.

"Both of you. I've never..." She breathed in, and when Fell's compelling forest scent mingled with Patrin's, there was no way she could say no. "Aye."

Fell's smile grew. Taking her free hand, he kissed the palm, sending tingles all the way up her arm.

Hand-in-hand-in-hand, they escorted her up the stairs.

Tucked as she was between them, she breathed in their scents...and stopped.

Patrin looked down at her. "Are you changing your mind, *blodyn*?"

"No. Not at all. It's just..." She sniffed him, then Fell.

She'd learned that despite showering after mating, a faint scent would always linger afterward. On Patrin and Fell, she could smell where the females downstairs had touched them, but nothing else. "Neither of you smell like you...mated. Earlier."

Patrin raised an eyebrow. Oh, oops, her question *was* borderline rude. One didn't ask about previous matings, after all. Then a corner of his mouth tipped up. "Good nose, little wolf. You're the first tonight. The only tonight."

"But..." She closed her eyes for a moment, trying to wrap her head around what he meant. "I've been downstairs all night."

*Waiting. All. Night.*

Her question came out with a growl. "Why *now*?"

Fell tugged on her hair. "It's close enough to moonset."

"Huh?"

Patrin said, "This late, no one will be upset if we keep you to ourselves until moonset."

*Oh.* Shifters weren't supposed to linger together after a mating. There were always others wanting to mate with the participants or needing the room. But this close to dawn, no one would care.

"I'm sorry, Moya. We wanted to explain, only if we got near you, we wouldn't've been able to wait." Patrin leaned down and breathed her in. "Gods, you smell good."

"It's why we had to go outside." Fell bent and kissed the top of her head. His voice came out a low growl. "But now... We plan to take our time with you."

*Mother of All.* The surge of desire made her head spin.

Her heart was pounding as they led her down the long line of mating rooms that ran around the open center of the house. She glanced over the railing down to the first floor, saw Sarah staring up spitefully, and let the animosity bounce right off.

Nothing mattered at this moment other than being with Patrin and Fell. Desire hummed in her blood.

At a door half-open, Fell looked inside and winced.

Moya leaned forward. *Right, the citrus room.* The walls were a bright orange with equally vibrant, colorful cushions on the floor.

"Gods help me, I'm blind. We are not using this room." Patrin moved her past the door so quickly, she started to giggle. "I've been wondering—why are all the rooms different?"

Fell caught up to them, still looking appalled.

"It was one of the Cosantir's ways of getting the clan involved in fixing the Gathering house. He and Heather had groups pick rooms and choose the décor. Everyone had a wonderful time."

Fell eyed her with a small smile. "Which ones did you work on?"

Would she get to mate in a room she'd decorated? Looking down the line of rooms, she bounced on her toes, and heard Patrin chuckle.

The moon room door was closed, but really, they'd like the one farther away even better, and its door was open.

"This is one of them." She stopped in the doorway, surprised at how much she wanted them to like it.

After a moment, Fell muttered, "Oh yeah, this one."

Patrin entered. "I've never seen a mating room like this."

"I've visited a lot of houses—and it's fascinating how shifters decorate to suit their animals. And, right then, the book club was reading historical romances."

"Medieval period?" Fell turned in a circle taking it in.

"Mmmhmm. I wanted it to look like a bear's cozy den...in a castle. Eileen painted the walls." And she'd done such a good job that the dark gray walls really looked like stone. "She did the stained-glass window too."

The full moon glowed brightly through the window, scattering beams of glowing colors across the velvet, damask, and brocade cushions.

Patrin studied the wrought iron chandelier with the myriad of candle-like bulbs and used the rheostat on the wall to dim them slightly. "Your imaginary bear shifter must have been wealthy."

"Totally." Moya smiled at the faux stone walls where she and Talitha had hung tree of life and stag tapestries in colors of burgundy and muted green. "I'd just finished rereading *Lord of the Rings* and might've been unduly influenced by Gondor."

Fell grinned. They'd discussed the books before—and how

much Tolkien's dwarves resembled real ones. The author must have had the Sight.

With a slight smirk, he pulled her into the room. "I can pretend to be rich." Tilting her chin up, he kissed her, long and slow.

The full moon heat, delayed for a moment by their talk, flared to life.

When he released her and stepped to one side, Patrin pressed her against the wall, taking his own kiss.

Fire roared upward in an unstoppable demand. *By the Mother, I need to be mated.* She gripped the bottom of his shirt and pulled it over his head.

He stared at her, surprised at her audacity, then smiled. "Full moon heat. I forgot."

Beside him, Fell caressed her cheek. "So demanding. You up to it, brawd?"

Patrin backhanded his brother in the stomach, and his grin flashed at the pained grunt. Taking his turn, he pulled Moya's shirt right over her head and off, then hummed in happiness. "I *thought* these were unfettered."

When his hands covered her breasts, callused and demanding, it took a moment for her to get past the wave of sensation to realize what he meant. *No bra.*

Right now, she was totally happy to be...unfettered.

It wasn't easy, but Patrin managed to release the little wolf's soft, soft breasts and take a step back. His every breath brought him her scent, filled with desire.

She wanted him and Fell. The knowledge was heady—and made him harder than an oak tree.

*Stop and think, wolf. We need her naked.* Yes, that was the priority. Pulling her forward, he kicked the door shut and nodded at Fell.

As usual, his littermate understood exactly what Patrin

intended. Coming up behind her, Fell pulled her back against his chest—and took advantage of the position to fondle her breasts.

Patrin smiled at the way her face flushed pink. *Simply lovely.* Bending, he undid her jeans. "Lift, brawd."

Hands around her waist, Fell lifted her up.

Patrin stripped off her socks and jeans and, unable to resist, nuzzled her groin. Sweet, silky curls were trimmed short enough to see her pink folds. The fragrance made him want to bury himself there immediately.

*Control, wolf.*

Instead, he exchanged smiles with Fell. On mission for the Scythe, they'd shared a human female a few times. And now, during Gatherings, if a female was amenable, they'd both mate her, even if it usually meant one of them didn't get off.

They'd looked forward to sharing Moya.

After his brother disrobed, Patrin pointed to the cushioned floor beneath the chandelier where the colored moonlight through the stained-glass window would spill over their beautiful female. "There."

"Nice." Fell swept her up in his arms, and Patrin grinned at her startled squeak—and at the second "*Eep,*" when his brother dropped her six inches onto the squashy cushions.

After stripping off his own clothes, Patrin knelt beside her, smiling at how her nipples made hard peaks. When he rubbed his knuckles over one, her eyes went half-lidded. And his restraint went out the window.

"You have the prettiest breasts I've ever seen," he murmured and flattened her on her back. Bending, he licked around one nipple, closed his mouth over it, and sucked.

Her gasp shivered down his spine and straight to his balls.

Was there any nicer sound in the world? "Brawd," he prompted, "she has two breasts."

Fell's low laugh sounded before he knelt on her other side and started kissing her other breast.

Patrin saw her hand curl around Fell's head, pulling him closer before small fingers closed in his own hair, gripping and holding him to her chest.

She was definitely going to be demanding this night—and they would enjoy the fuck out of it.

He smiled against the soft, warm flesh, then started teasing and licking and simply savoring the finest task given to a male.

Eventually, when he could feel how hot and swollen her breast was, he moved to kiss her.

Fell repositioned himself near her hips, and Patrin considered what to do next. His brother was very good at satisfying a female —but not this time.

"Fell, stop." Since it was the twenty-second—an even day—Patrin would mate her first. But it'd be more fun to share, especially since Moya had learned about what the humans called a blowjob. "Kneel up, brawd."

Giving Patrin a puzzled stare, Fell did as ordered.

Smiling, Patrin rolled Moya and set her on her hands and knees with her head pointed toward Fell. "Remember what I taught you, *blodyn*? Can you show Fell what you learned?"

Hair spilling over her naked back, she looked over her shoulder at him, eyes half-glassy with her heat. She was breathing hard and obviously wanted to demand he take her immediately. Fuck knew, most females insisted on a straightforward mating with no delays.

Fell stared at him in surprise.

But this was Moya who was as generously giving as anyone Patrin had ever met.

She pulled in a breath, then her mouth curved. "Of course." Her voice was husky with desire. Balancing on one hand, she wrapped the other around Fell's cock and took him in her mouth.

Fell's low groan of pleasure made Patrin grin.

"While you do that, I'll give you what you want, little wolf." Patrin pushed her knees apart and knelt between them. He ran his hands over her gorgeous ass, massaging the delightfully plump cheeks, and felt her shiver. Moving his hand down, he savored the wet heat between her legs. So slick and ready.

He slid his fingers between the soft lips of her pussy—just to provoke her enticing whine. He could feel her tremble as her need increased.

*She was going. To. Die.* As Patrin's fingers eased her open, she was swamped in pleasure—and it set off an overwhelming urgency.

The arm she was balanced on was shaking, and she blinked. Her hand was wrapped around Fell's cock.

*Right. Concentrate.* She sucked gently on the thick shaft, savored the so-very-masculine musky taste, and swirled her tongue around the tip.

He made a most-gratifying sound, and his hands closed in her hair. His hips tilted forward even as he pushed down. She froze for a second, but he wasn't shoving, just…encouraging. Wanting more.

Much like she'd done in holding his and Patrin's heads against her breasts.

Laughing under her breath, she obediently bobbed her head up and down, and oh, the sound of his raspy growl melted her insides.

Removing his fingers, Patrin bent over her. His long hair swept over her back in a cool caress. She felt the brush of his beard on her cheek as he whispered in her ear. "You are so beautiful." He nipped her shoulder in a wolf's possessive gesture before straightening slightly.

Reaching around her, he rubbed over her clit.

*"Aaaah."* Shocking pleasure swept through her. She gripped the base of Fell's shaft harder and heard his choked laugh. What was she doing again?

"Now, Moya, let's have fun." The head of Patrin's cock

pushed at her entrance and slid in an inch as if to warn her. She managed one breath before his implacable penetration turned her mind blank with the incredible sensation of being filled completely.

Mouth filled with Fell's cock, she couldn't do anything but groan in pleasure.

Fell sucked in a breath. "*Mmm.* That felt great."

She was pinned between them, one in her mouth, one in her pussy, helpless to do anything. Fell guided her head, up and down, as behind her, Patrin thrust in and out. When he leaned forward and started rubbing her clit, the vise of need grew so fast, she was moaning with every breath.

Then...right when she near to climaxing, Patrin moved his slick finger between her buttocks to circle the rim of her ass.

She lifted her head, releasing Fell. "What...?"

With a huffed laugh, Fell slid down to lie beside her. With hard hands, he fondled her dangling breasts, and the unexpected shock of pleasure made her back arch.

But...Patrin's finger. "Patrin?" Her voice shook with the word.

"There may come a time we want to take you here, *cariad*," Patrin murmured. "Would you be interested in that? Do you like this?"

His finger circled without intruding. And the shivery feeling was tempting. Would more be better? "I don't know. Maybe?"

"Want to try, little wolf?" His cock was motionless, deep inside her, even as the light brush of his finger outside her backhole wakened new nerves.

He waited patiently, letting her decide.

"Yes."

Slowly, so slowly, he pushed a finger inside.

The feeling was different, incredibly intimate, and so very hot. More sensations added to the nerves already singing.

Her need rose higher and higher.

Pulling his cock back, he began thrusting again, alternating with his finger, and her whole lower half felt submerged in pleasure.

Fell rolled her nipples, and the sparks zoomed straight to her clit.

*Oh, I'm going to come. Going to—*

Patrin slowed, so damned slow, keeping her there, right on the edge, the pleasure almost too much, and the need to climax was almost painful.

"Not yet," he murmured. Fell had stopped, his hands simply cupping her hanging breasts. She could hear herself panting, whining.

*Needing.*

The slow thrusts were just enough to keep her on the razor's edge. Her muscles tightened, tightened...

Mean as a wolverine, Patrin made a huff of a laugh. "Now, let's get you off, little wolf."

He began to drive into her, hard and fast and merciless. Between her buttocks, he added another finger, stretching her painfully, wonderfully, and the two fingers thrusting rhythmically.

When Fell pinched and tugged on her nipples, she gasped and shook—and everything shoved her right off the cliff. She plummeted into a lake of sensation, rolled over and over, and drowned in pleasure.

*Gods, gods, gods.*


Patrin felt her tighten around his dick and then the infinitely wonderful battering as she spasmed around his shaft and his fingers. Her whining gasps were music to his ears.

And impossible for his control.

He met Fell's gaze—his littermate was grinning—and returned a wry smile of defeat at his inability to hold out longer. He pulled his fingers out, gripped her hips with both hands, and pounded into her.

Heat roared down his spine, into his balls, and he fought it off, savoring the burn before letting it all jet through him and out. Pleasure soared through him as he filled her with his seed.

Minutes passed as he recovered and, finger by finger, released his hold on her hips.

The moonlight streamed over her damp, velvety skin, and he took a moment to simply appreciate her beautiful body. And her generous nature. Leaning forward with his chest to her back, he nipped her shoulder—*mine*—then rubbed his cheek against hers. "Thank you, beautiful Moya."

She made a soft sound, almost a purr. "Mmm."

He knew the feeling. His brain might have melted too." Slowly, he withdrew, already regretting the loss of the soft heat.

Fell handed him a warm washcloth.

"Thanks, brawd." After cleaning her up, then himself, he and Fell gently rolled her onto her back.

Patrin lay down on her right and propped himself up on an elbow. He caressed her cheek, then ran a finger over her pink swollen lips. She'd given his littermate pleasure with that soft mouth. Unable to resist, he took a long, slow kiss.

Dark eyes gazed up at him, and a dimple appeared in her cheek. "You destroyed me, you two. Shame on you." The way her soprano had turned husky was fucking sexy.

Lying on her left, up on one elbow, Fell curved his free hand over her breast. "Can't think of anything I enjoyed more."

"Yeah," Patrin said under his breath in agreement. He circled one breast with a finger. Her nipples, reddened from Fell's teasing, were flat again, soft with satisfaction. Moving his hand down, he smiled. Her belly had a pretty—very bitable—curve.

Next time.

Right now, she was perfect where she was. Between them where she belonged.

He blinked and frowned. *What was that thought? Where she belongs?*

But just as he could feel her body against his, he could feel her in the pack bonds. Because one tie, brighter than the rest hummed joyfully: *This is Moya*.

There was no darkness in that bond, no deceit, no cruelty. She was just who she seemed to be. Warm and open and...precious. He wanted to curl around her and protect her with everything inside him.

Fuck, had he fallen in love with her?

*Looks like I have.*

He looked over at his brother.

Fell bent to kiss the little wolf, his expression gentle. Caring. Tender.

*Yeah, I'm not the only one falling hard.*

Lying on his side next to Moya, Fell had a hard-on that wouldn't quit, but he didn't mind in the least. It'd been worth it to feel her mouth around him. And he'd cherished her little glances upward to check if she was pleasing him, even when Patrin had done his best to distract her.

It'd been wonderful to watch his brother mate with her, hear her soft gasps.

Hearing she wanted to prepare to take both of them someday left him speechless. He and Patrin were always happier when they could share—and to share Moya? Nothing could be better.

Gently stroking up and down her curvy body wasn't helping his dick go down, but she was impossible to resist. Oh, he knew his cock wouldn't be satisfied tonight—she'd already climaxed, and on full moon nights, females needed a while to become aroused again.

Maybe that was the Gods' way to ensure females would move on rather than staying with one male for long periods of the night?

Whatever the reason, he was all right with not getting off.

But he couldn't stop touching.

"Do we need to get up and moving?" she asked, a tiny frown on her forehead. Reaching out, she rested a hand on each of their shoulders. Her fingers stroked over his muscles, the sensation intoxicating.

"No, *blodyn,* unless you object, we'll watch moonset from in here." Patrin kissed her cheek, then deliberately cupped her right breast, started to fondle it, and grinned at Fell.

*All right then.* Fell cupped her left breast, following Patrin's movements, fondling, kneading, tugging at the nipples.

He knew she loved having her breasts touched...as well as something else. He lifted his chin to get Patrin's attention, then sucked on one pink peak before using his teeth in a gentle nibble.

She pulled in an audible breath, and her nipples stood erect. Her scent deepened with arousal.

Being the observant male he was, Patrin caught on immediately. He grinned and began to use his teeth also.

"Ooooh." Her back arched up, offering her breasts for more.

*Fuck, this was fun.*

Even as Fell teased her breast with his tongue, teeth, and mouth, he slid his hand down her abdomen and then lower. When he ran a finger up and down her hot, slick folds, her hips wiggled.

Patrin, never one to be left out of the fun, added his finger on the other side of her pussy. When they each rubbed on different areas of her clit, she moaned, long and low.

"You are both evil mongrels." Her voice was breathy, her face flushed, and her fingernails were digging into his shoulder.

Fell lifted his head, propping himself up on one elbow. Her nipple was nicely wet and pink. He puffed a breath over it, fascinated at how it grew even more rigid. "Not evil. We just like touching you."

Wait...did she maybe feel as if he was trying to—what did the human men call it—*score?* "We can stop, *cariad,* and go back downstairs."

Her eyes were dark and soft as she looked up at him. She laid her hand on his face, running her fingers along his jaw. "A while back, I asked Heather why she'd taken *two* males upstairs at a Gathering. After all, what good was a second male?"

Patrin leaned back and tilted his head. "Even if not wanting seconds, more hands and more mouths are nice, aye, little wolf?"

"Aye, so nice."

Fell released the breath he'd been holding. She wasn't unhappy with them. When she combed her fingers through his hair, he leaned into her touch.

Her lips curved. "Did you know your wolf coat is longer than your human hair?"

He snorted. "No, really?"

Her husky giggle made him want to kiss her again.

"Anyway, Heather said if the mating was wonderful, and she liked the males, she'd go again."

Fell's breathing paused. Had she implied...

Sitting up, she took his face between her hands and gave him a stern look. "You got me all aroused again. And needy."

"Huh. We can't have that," he murmured. Cupping the back of her head, he pulled her down for a long, satisfying kiss.

"How about I play backrest?" Patrin asked. Kneeling, he pulled Moya between his legs with her head propped against his stomach. His hands over her breasts kept her secured.

Her eyes went wide...but the scent of her arousal only increased.

Fell smiled. There was nothing like watching Patrin render a female helpless—if it was what she enjoyed. Her butt was on the floor cushions, her legs splayed. He pushed a pillow under her ass, putting her at the perfect height to be taken.

*So pretty.* He ran his hands up and down her thighs, feeling the slight quiver every time his thumbs neared the junction between her legs. Eventually, he touched her there, using his thumbs to open her folds. Her clit was pink and glistening, engorged with need.

Pinching a velvety inner fold between each thumb and forefinger, he tugged downward, forcing the hood to cover her clit. Pulling up, he watched the nub pop back out. Down and up, over and over, letting the hood do all the teasing.

Her clit grew more swollen, and her breathing quickened. "Ooooh, please." Knees bent, feet on the cushions, she lifted her hips in a very female demand.

Playing with her breasts, Patrin grinned at him. "Sounds like she's ready."

It did, didn't it? "All right, little wolf."

He set his shaft against her opening and teased her, pushing the head in and out, slightly farther each time until she was moaning. Until he was fully embedded.

Fuck, she was swollen and hot and so-wonderfully-tight around him. "Damn, you feel good."

Her eyes were only half-focused, but her mouth tilted up. "So do you. Faster, wolf. I want faster." She raised her hips, trying to pump him to get more speed.

She was just plain fucking adorable. And her attempt to push him wasn't going to work. "Here, bro. Make yourself useful." He took a foot in each hand and lifted.

Patrin's arms were long enough he could grip her ankles and hold her legs straight up. It removed any chance she had at control and let him go even deeper.

Her shivery groan almost made him come, right then and there.

He thrust in a steady rhythm. Deep—and slow. His balls hit her buttocks each time, adding a dancing counterpoint. Every few strokes, he changed the angle until...there. He could feel her shudder and contract hard around him.

*Perfect.*

Her eyes were closed, her breathing fast, her cheeks and lips darkened to a lovely red. Her breasts bounced with every thrust.

Fell's jaw tightened as he strove for control. She felt far too good—he wouldn't last much longer. "A little more open, brawd."

Patrin spread her legs wider apart, exposing her clit.

Gasping, she gripped his forearms...as if she could stop what was going to happen.

Fell slid his finger alongside her clit, rubbing upward as he drove in, downward as he pulled back. He could feel the ball of nerves grow firmer. Her nipples jutted into tight peaks.

Now, he sped up into hard, driving thrusts, keeping up the pressure on her clit.

Her hips began to buck. "Oh, oh, oh."

He could feel her spasming around his dick, hot and wet, as she came with a high cry.

Fuck, he wanted to start all over just to experience it again.

Instead, he curled his hands around her raised thighs, pulling her down hard onto his cock as he pumped short and fast and then held there, deep, deep inside her.

He came with a hard growl, giving her the essence of all he was.

Joining her in the most intimate way on this night of the full moon.

## CHAPTER TWENTY

Sprawled in a living room chair, Fell scowled at the apartment window where the last remnants of the sun had disappeared. Winter sucked. The world turned black just after four fucking o'clock—and didn't that just suit his mood.

"You look like a gnome chewed on your tail," Patrin said. His sleeves were pushed up, showing the scratches Moya had left on his forearms.

Fell was slightly envious, although he had crescent-shaped fingernail marks on his shoulder. Made his cock stir every time he moved and felt them.

Which accounted for his foul frame of mind. "Thinking about her."

Patrin glanced in the direction of Moya's apartment, showing he followed exactly who "her" was. "The thoughts don't make you happy?"

"Last night was great." Their time with the feisty female had been like nothing he'd ever experienced before. The act of mating had been sublime, but it was more than that. The way she touched them and the look in her eyes as if she really cared...or more.

He couldn't refuse to admit he wanted her, cared for her. With everything in him.

*But...*

He ran his hand through his hair in frustration. How to say this? By the Gods, talking with his littermate wasn't usually a problem. "Brawd, how much of her...affection...was due to the full moon heat?"

Brows drawing together, Patrin set down the carton of milk he'd taken from the fridge. "She... I...don't know." His mouth tightened. "Yeah, now I'm sharing your mood. Thanks for that."

Fell nodded at his brother's reaction. "You feel it, too, that we have something special with her."

Because he wanted them to lay their hearts at her feet in the same way they'd bring her a plump rabbit for her dinner.

"Yeah, I did." Patrin shook his head. "I do."

Now they just had to figure out what she felt for them.

---

Leaning over the stove, Moya breathed in. The comforting aroma of the *lentejas* mingled with the fragrance of the *pan de barra* just out of the oven. Bread and a hearty stew were a classic for a reason.

When possible after a Gathering, Moya would take a long decadent bath to soak away any soreness, get a few hours of sleep, and then cook her favorite foods. After a night of feeling more like a body than a person, she usually needed the self-cosseting.

Today, she felt different—not like merely a body.

She'd been the only female Patrin and Fell mated last night. The wonder still shook her. She wasn't just a body to them—they knew her, were her friends, and cared about her. It'd shown in everything they did while mating with her.

Even when ordering her around.

But despite staying in charge, Patrin had used only his voice and his hands. He was totally dominant, just by being himself. He'd said he wouldn't use the pack bonds, and he hadn't.

He was worthy of her trust.

Why did the sweetness of that make her want to cry?

She sniffled—and then laughed, remembering her checklist of bath, sleeping, baking. The first thing had been a long hot bath for aches and pains—and Gods, this time, she'd definitely been sore.

A hot tingle ran through her as she remembered Patrin's length and Fell's girth. They'd filled her so very full...and had taken her over and over.

*Mmmm.*

The sigh she gave was too much like some swooning historical romance heroine. *Don't be a bramble-bitten birdbrain.* The night had been wonderful, but the Gathering was over.

It was time to re-enter the real world.

Shifters were tied to the moon, emotionally, physically, and spiritually, and as everyone knew, passions raised beneath a full moon rarely continued past dawn. Far too many shifters made fools of themselves thinking they'd started the most wonderful of romances only to learn the other shifter had simply been in heat.

The light of day had come and—she glanced at the dark window— was gone again.

*I'm no swooning heroine.*

Perhaps, the MacCormac brothers were tail-over-snout in love with her. If so, they hadn't said anything.

Wasn't it a shame bonds didn't gift a shifter with mind-reading abilities? Aside from permitting disgusting alpha commands that were less telepathy and more a one-word emotion—*stay, come, adore me*—the bonds were worthless for helping communication.

A wolf had to use their words. And there had been no words.

The three of them had enjoyed a sexy Gathering together. Possibly whatever they had together would grow to more. She rubbed the heel of her hand over her chest. The glimpse of a future where they cared about her the way she cared about them made her heart yearn.

If she wanted more, she might have to start the discussion. Patrin and Fell hadn't had a normal growing up time, And face it, very few males enjoyed sharing their feelings. Or maybe they weren't as far along the trail to caring as she was.

*So... Okay, I'll give them time—like a month?—and then tell them how I feel.*

Inside, her anxiety warred with determination. *I can do this.*

For now, they'd be friends, with an occasional benefit, as the humans would say. And she'd enjoy what they had together. Time with them was never wasted. *I can handle this.*

A firm knock on her door made her jump. Who was visiting? Not her brothers or Talitha's family for a Sunday meal, not after a Gathering. To compensate for hours in the noisy, crowded house, most shifters chose to do something quiet and peaceful the following day.

Maybe it was Patrin or Fell? A surge of anticipation made her suck in a breath.

She opened the door, and her heart did a happy somersault.

*Dammit, heart, didn't we have this talk?*

"Um, hi. What's up?"

His expression unreadable, Patrin put two fingers under her chin, then bent and kissed her lightly, yet lingering until the temperature in the room rose five degrees. He nibbled down her jaw, down her neck, then inhaled deeply.

When he stepped back, he was smiling. "Good evening, pretty wolf."

She stared at him. His kiss was much more intense than one from a mere neighbor with benefits.

Huffing a laugh, Fell pulled her against him, and took her lips, not lightly at all. Deep and wet and thorough.

So nice. Warmth blossomed low in her belly.

Lifting his head, he rubbed his cheek against hers, like an

affectionate feline rather than a wolf. "Oh yeah. Fuck the full moon."

Patrin laughed, and then asked her, "Are you hungry?"

"Am I...what?" Their behavior was as scrambled as a tree fairy's after an orchard pruning.

"Hungry. It happens when stomachs get empty," Patrin said.

Fell hadn't released her, and she was far too aware of his hands on her waist. Of his so-very-male woodsy scent.

She swallowed. Why were they acting like this? Like they were her lovers or something. *Breathe, girl.*

She took that breath and then another before looking up.

Fell was watching her like a famished wolf stalking a breakfast bunny.

"You look hungry," she blurted.

Crinkles appeared at the corners of his eyes. "Yeah. Very, very hungry." He rubbed his knuckles along the side of her breast.

The rushing heat almost made her knees buckle.

"Bad beta." Chuckling, Patrin shouldered Fell to one side. "Sorry, Moya. We came over to see if you wanted to eat with us. Guess we got distracted."

*Oh.* Maybe their affection was simply lingering from the full moon. She shouldn't read anything else into it.

She was totally running the trail toward heartbreak. Hadn't she just told herself *no benefits?*

*But...do I want to live my life in fear of being hurt? Is that truly living?*

Sure, there would be pain when they inevitably backed away, but... Losing people was part of life. Older shifters, even when mourning a mate, would say love was a gift from the Mother, and they had no regrets for embracing it.

So, she'd face up to being hurt when the time came—and would celebrate every moment with them until then. "Actually, why don't you join me? The bread just came out of the oven."

"You made bread?" Fell stared at her as if she'd turned into the goddess right before his eyes.

She had to laugh. "I did—it's to go with the *lentejas*." At their confused expressions, she added, "It's a stew with lentils and chorizo. You'll like it."

Patrin wrapped an arm around her waist. "Sounds good. Afterward, we can share dessert, brawd...if our little wolf will invite us to spend the night."

His scent, the nip of teeth on her neck, and the rumble of need told her what—*who*—would be dessert. Even better, the appallingly dominant wolf was waiting for an invite rather than assuming.

And then his words registered. *Our little wolf. Spend the night.*

Happiness bubbled through her. They did want to be... together. Not forever, maybe not. Or maybe someday? For now? She'd celebrate what they had. "Yes. Yes, yes, yes."

# CHAPTER TWENTY-ONE

A tall wooden fence enclosed the pack house and grounds. Patrin walked through the gate with Moya and Fell beside him. Folding his arms over his chest, he studied the building. The noon sun mercilessly revealed the faded paint and worn shingles.

The pack house. Another thing he was supposed to be in charge of.

Another thing he knew nothing about.

Frustration gnawed at him. Sure, he was a better alpha than brutal, incompetent Brett, but that wasn't saying much. He glanced at his littermate. "I have no fucking clue what I'm doing."

"Makes two of us." Fell eyed the house. "Needs work. Any fool can see that."

"The pack has able-bodied members we can recruit for the actual work." *Fuck, what about actual materials?* "How do we pay for the paint and lumber?"

"Oh, I forgot you haven't joined a territory before." Moya patted his arm. "The pack has money. You and Heather need to talk. She's a CPA."

"Talk about what?" Patrin glanced at Fell, who looked equally confused.

"About the pack account and money coming in." Moya smiled wryly. "Just like the US government, the Daonain have taxes. We all pay a percentage to our territory, and the Cosantir oversees those funds. Wolves pay a smaller sum to the pack, and you, Alpha, oversee the money."

"I do?" Frustrated past endurance, he considered punching the fence post, but he'd probably knock it down. "Dealing with money isn't in my skill set. Did Brett make off with the funds?"

That could be a problem.

"No, he didn't get the chance. Before the Solstice ceremony, I called Heather to tell her you were our new alpha. She was worried and asked Friedrich to freeze the accounts until you and Quin can deal with them."

"Thank fuck." He knew Quintrell was an older wolf who was the homeschool teacher but hadn't met anyone named Friedrich. "Who is Friedrich?"

"Friedrich Schumacher. Werecat and Elder." Moya took his and Fell's hand, leading them up the sidewalk to the house. "He also owns and manages the bank. Quin has handled the pack finances for years."

"But he didn't keep up with the maintenance here?" Fell asked.

"The alpha must approve expenditures, and Roger was a pinchpenny. Although he did buy new furniture for the house when he moved in. The weasel." She wrinkled her nose. "I guess we should be glad he didn't steal pack funds the way his brother, Pete, embezzled from the clan. Roger wasn't a thief."

"Taxes. Pack funds and houses... For fuck's sake, this is like entering a dark cave even knowing it to be a bear den." Patrin growled in frustration. "I don't even know what I don't know."

"Sorry, brawd." Fell's eyes darkened. "My fault we didn't grow up in a pack. Because I couldn't be trusted."

"By the Gods, you were trustworthy enough; you just never stopped talking." Patrin backhanded his gnome-brain brother in the gut. "Besides, you're not the only reason we moved to Dogwood. Mum was hoping to find mates."

Rubbing his abdomen, Fell shot Patrin a disgruntled glare. "Toothless fleabag." After a moment, he asked, his voice quiet, "She actually wanted to move?"

"Yeah, I overheard her talking to the neighbor. Apparently, she'd mated with all good local males during Gatherings, and no one suited her, and Dogwood had a better selection." Patrin huffed a laugh. "Now that we've attended Gatherings, I finally understand what she was talking about. At the time, I was clueless."

"Huh." Some of the remorse was gone from Fell's eyes.

Moya burst out laughing. "Gods, you two are just like Ramón and Zorion. If you were female, Fell would've gotten a hug for feeling bad. But *noooo*, instead you hit him."

"Awww, do you want a hug, brawd?" Patrin asked in a sweet, sweet voice—and almost landed on his ass from his brother's shove.

They were both grinning though—because the sound of the little wolf's laughter brightened the entire day.

Pulling her close, Patrin kissed the top of her head.

And fuck, the feeling of her soft body, her feminine scent, reminded him of other activities they could be doing rather than inspecting a pack house.

Tilting her head up, she went up on tiptoes to kiss him...and undoubtedly caught a whiff of his lust. "Concentrate, Alpha. We have work to do."

"I'd rather play," he muttered and heard Fell's echo, "Me too."

"Males." Shaking her head, Moya towed them onto the porch.

Patrin exchanged a grin with his brother over the top of her head. She was decidedly appealing when she got bossy.

No, she was always appealing.

Since the Gathering last Saturday, they'd spent most of their free time with her. The bookstore and bar had closed for a couple of days during the human holiday called Christmas, and they'd had snowball fights and run the trails as wolves.

Other days, he played basketball with various cubs and Talitha, while Fell, Moya, and Eileen lifted weights. The three would occasionally stop to cheer a basket.

Patrin smiled—because Moya's Solstice present for him had been a basketball, a baseball, and a mitt. She knew him well.

When he worked at the Bullwhacker, Moya and Fell sat at the bar, kept him company, and she'd introduce shifters they hadn't met. The female knew everyone.

Aside from a couple of dinners at the Shamrock, they cooked together. Having the patience—something Patrin lacked—to wait for eggs to cook, Fell was growing skilled at breakfast and other meals. Probably why Moya had given him a cookbook for Solstice—one handwritten with traditional Daonain recipes. They'd found some their mother used to make and had called Darcy to share.

Patrin was mastering the slow-cooker device—a wonder of human invention. Dump everything in it in the morning and feast in the evening.

In reciprocity for cooking lessons, he and Fell sparred with Moya in wolf and human forms, improving her already competent fighting skills. It was certainly no chore. If she got dumped on her tail, she'd just laugh and try again. They all had fun—and her sneaky attacks could be quite effective.

Still...being wakened in the morning by a tickle attack was simply *wrong*.

Worth it though to have her in their bed. A few days ago, hoping for the best, he and Fell tied their beds together in Patrin's room. It worked. They all slept together every single night.

Last night, Moya had shooed them away and taken the evening to unwind and read, then appeared at bedtime and joined them for the night. He and Fell had been so fucking pleased. Everything was better with her tucked between them.

As Moya opened the pack house door and called a greeting, Patrin squeezed her hand. He hadn't been this content since he was a cubling running with Darcy and Fell. And he'd never had such peaceful, loving nights or such fulfilling days.

This was what he wanted—for him and Fell to share this brave, brilliant, caring female—and to be granted the gift of loving her all the rest of their days.

"It's Moya and the alpha and beta!" someone inside shouted.

The wolves came running. Moya was hugged by the females and cubs.

To Patrin's surprise, a tiny youngling wrapped her arms around his knees and beamed up at him. "Affa. Hi."

He grinned and picked her up. As he cuddled her, his heart turned to liquid inside his chest. "You must be the bravest wolf in our pack," he told her.

"Am," she agreed.

"Nope." Fell held a small male, ginger-haired cub against his chest, and his rasping chuckle sounded when the pup bounced happily in his arms. "Mine is."

The adults in the house were wide-eyed and silent, staring at the terrifying shifter-soldiers—who'd been reduced to pure goo by cublings.

Then they welcomed Patrin and Fell inside with open enthusiasm.

*Our pack.*

A while later, after they'd figured out what repairs needed to be made and formulated a plan, Patrin raised his voice. "Next week, there's supposed to be a snowstorm, but for now, the snow is almost melted. Would the pack enjoy a fun twilight run?"

The ground was damp under his paws, soft and fragrant from the recent warm days, and the wolf in Fell loved it all. His littermate ran in front or beside him, close enough they'd occasionally bump shoulders. To his disappointment, Moya chose to run with her pregnant friend Heather near the rear of this half of the pack.

Since they were hunting, the wolves ran quietly, creating only faint sounds of paws on the trail.

The other half of the group—the slower ones or those feeling lazy, along with the cubs—were on a different trail, parallel to this one but farther upslope. Not silent, that batch. He could hear occasional growls, blundering paws, and a yip or two from overly enthusiastic pups.

This wouldn't be a long run since he and Patrin wanted to let the cubs participate. When leading the shifter-soldiers, they'd learned that everyone in a group needed to feel involved.

But with some extra safety measures.

With input from the seniors, he and Patrin had designated responsible older cubs to lead small packs of younglings. Adults would monitor each group and leader. Bullying wouldn't be tolerated, and new skills would be taught.

One more thing to do as beta—he needed to scrutinize the cubs' current mentors and remove any who pushed Brett's divisive attitudes.

A couple of hours ago, he and Patrin had scouted out a deer herd. The noisy half of the pack would drive them in this direction.

At the front, Patrin changed direction, angling off to keep the group downwind.

As the scent of the deer blew toward them, the delectable fragrance sharpened every instinct in Fell's body. The change ran through the rest of the group, pulling them together with one purpose. To hunt.

The reddish rays of the setting sun angled through the trees, illuminating a small meadow where most of the snow had melted.

There, a small herd browsed on the exposed grass and short bushes.

A yip sounded from across the meadow, and Fell would have laughed if he'd been human. A cub would be getting a scolding later.

As the other pack closed in, a deer lifted its head, blowing loudly to alert the herd to danger.

Howling loudly, the younglings and senior wolves charged out of the forest. Panicking, the herd fled toward Fell's group.

*Perfect.*

Fell started to move but felt the order to hold through the pack bonds. The alpha's command halted his paws, leaving him quivering in place. Annoyed, he managed to take a step forward as did a few others, but Patrin's directive was clear. *Wait.*

They waited.

Then he released them: *hunt now.*

With the rest of the group, Fell streaked forward.

Faced with the new group of oncoming wolves, the herd veered sharply. The deer were headed toward a creek he and Patrin had located earlier. Still half-covered with snow, the stream wasn't easy to see. Several deer floundered as ice cracked under their hooves. The healthiest, most agile ones escaped into the forest, leaving the slower ones behind.

An older buck had broken its leg and had just managed to gain the top of the bank. Patrin led the attack.

It was a big damn buck—and like most of the herd, hadn't yet shed its antlers.

The pack began to circle as two wolves struck from the rear, biting at the deer's hind end, then darting away. When the buck spun and swung its antlers, others attacked from the sides, slashing at its shoulders and flanks. Again and again.

Moya, a small dark-gray wolf, danced in to attack, here and there. Damn, she was fast.

A yelp came from a slower wolf kicked by a flailing hoof.

As the buck slowed with exhaustion and blood loss, Fell sprang upward and closed his jaws on the animal's nose. His weight pulled its head down as his fellow wolves completed the kill.

Filled with the victory of a successful hunt, all wolves ate well. Fell spotted Moya in the midst of the cubs with her female friends. He might be disappointed she hadn't joined him and Patrin but couldn't begrudge the rest of the pack her fun company.

Eventually, Patrin led them on a leisurely trot back to the clearing to where the pack would disperse and return down the assorted trails to their cars or houses.

Fell moved back under the trees to keep an eye on everything...and to wait for their precious little wolf.

---

Still seething with anger, Moya was one of the very last to reach the clearing. She'd had to stay with the cubs and Heather, or she'd have been long gone before the lying alpha and his beta arrived.

She hurt with the stabbing sense of betrayal. Patrin had used the pack bonds to force them all to obey him. To force *her* to obey.

The sweet memory of their first night together when he promised he'd never use coercion on her, on anyone, was shattered into jagged pieces. It had been replaced with the horror of being paralyzed, unable to move at all, shivering as someone else controlled her body.

*He did that to me.*

She'd trusted him and had been so happy he was the alpha. She'd opened herself to the pack bonds, and it'd felt so sweet to run with the wolves tonight and revel in the sense of belonging.

Until his betrayal turned it all to ash.

*I loved him.*

*I was a fool.*

In the clearing, she nosed Heather to join Talitha and the cubs. Talitha would keep an eye on their pregnant friend. They'd all be safe.

Believing Moya would go home with Patrin and Fell, her friends disappeared down the trail.

The males had already shifted to human and were talking.

Growling low, Moya trawsfurred.

Patrin smiled at her, even as he shook his head. "Moya, you should stay wolf. You're going to get—"

"Oh, are you going to force me to do that too?" The words tangled in her throat, burning like fire. "You...you used the pack bonds on me. On everyone."

Confusion crossed Patrin's face. "But...we were hunting."

"You promised. Y-you—"

"*Cariad.*" Frowning, Fell followed Patrin toward her. "That's what the bonds are for. It's a tactical advantage."

How dare he side with his littermate. How dare he agree to take away everything she was for a "tactical advantage".

"I've heard that before. The bonds are there so the alpha can make the pack do whatever he wants. And you did, didn't you!" Anger roaring in her ears, she punched Patrin with all the strength in her body.

"Umph." He staggered back, only a step, before raising a hand to his jaw. "What in the gods'—"

"Don't talk to me. Don't ever speak to me again." She took two steps away and then turned. "If you ever use the pack bonds on me again, I'll tear your throat out."

Shifting to four paws, she escaped down the trail. Toward town. Toward her apartment that was no longer a refuge. Not with the vile, traitorous alpha and his brother living right there across from her.

In the darkness, she submerged herself further into the wolf, into the present where all that existed was the feeling of the damp, needle-strewn dirt under her paws, the scent of the forest in her nose, the wind ruffling her fur.

Wolves didn't cry.

In the morning she'd have a hard think about closing her store and moving far, far away.

## CHAPTER TWENTY-TWO

*Progress!* Baton cheerfully took coffee orders late Sunday morning and thought about how nicely everything was coming together for her and the Colonel.

Thank goodness the Director's spy, Gregory, was no longer underfoot—and the Director was gone too. It had been embarrassing to watch Gregory's incompetence. She'd spotted him right away, but he'd never even known she was in town.

Scythe operatives were supposed to be better than that. Then again, the Colonel had higher standards than the Director.

In fact, the Colonel was incredible. Last night, he'd finally shared his plan for the mutants, and the scope of it left her breathless.

Today, she was ready to kick off another step in the plan.

Yesterday, she'd managed to find the perfect house to use to capture the abominations. Following the Colonel's guidelines, she'd located a two-story home with forest surrounding it except for a long expanse of lawn in front.

Of course, it would have been better if the house was empty. Still, the Colonel would simply exterminate the two occupants.

It had been far more difficult to figure out how to draw the town's children to one place. Along with Patrin, Fell, and their love interest. And mothers, if possible. The Colonel had decided mothers would make excellent hostages for teenaged boy abominations.

How many ideas had she discarded for being impossible? Finally, she'd recalled the last snowfall and laughing at kids sledding on a garbage can lid. And the perfect plan came together.

Now to put it into motion.

With a sweet smile, Baton accepted money for two child size milks, two donuts, and marked a cup with the mother's coffee order. "One peppermint mocha coming up."

"Thank you." The mother gathered her boys who appeared around five and seven.

Baton looked over to the right. "Hey, Talitha."

Her boss was concocting an elaborate sugar-free, vanilla latte with soy milk. "Yes, Renee?"

"Did you realize the kids here don't have a good sledding spot? Back in my hometown, they'd rope off a steep street after every big snowfall and let us sled on it. We even had a bonfire at the top to warm us up."

"Really." Talitha handed the coffee over the counter to the customer before turning to Baton. "That's a great idea. Just this morning, Mateo was whining at how often snow ruins all their fun. Maybe because they've never sledded."

Perfect, the fish had taken the hook. "There's a street"—Baton waved toward the west—"it's the right steepness and dead ends in the square's parking lot. Um, Paydirt?"

Talitha looked that direction as if she could see. "Paydirt might work. There's no real traffic, and a couple of those houses are empty anyway."

"Cool!" Baton gave her a happy smile. "Our town reserved the sledding hill for the littlest ones in the morning, then the daredevils—you know, the tweens and up—got the hill for the afternoon, like, one o'clock until twilight."

The Colonel said the teens, new to shapeshifting, were the perfect ages for training.

"With how short the daylight hours are, each group would get around three hours—enough time to get properly tired." Talitha winked at the mother with the two little boys. "Keeping our crazy teens away from the littles makes good sense."

"Agreed." The mother smiled at Talitha. "I adore your Mateo and Alvaro, but face it, they'll want to go really fast."

"I'm raising speed demons." Talitha rolled her eyes. "Now I have to find them a sled. Doesn't the ski shop do rentals?"

"There are probably plenty of townsfolk with gear tucked away that they're not using," someone from a table called. "I'll ask around if you tell me where they should drop their stuff off."

Baton managed not to grimace. It was sickening how everyone in the coffee shop listened to everyone else's discussions. Nothing was private in this hick town.

"I'll post a sign if the town council agrees and sets a date." Talitha patted Baton's shoulder. "Thank you for the idea, Renee."

"The council better move fast," said the mother with two boys. "The news forecasters say they're tracking some big snowstorm due in seven or eight days."

"A week is do-able." Talitha bounced once on her toes in happiness. "Watch for a sign going up."

Baton frowned. The sledding day might happen in just a week?

The Colonel needed to know so the Scythe operatives could arrive before the storm. And afterward, they'd need vehicles big enough for transport and suitable for snowy roads.

Excitement rose inside her. This was her chance to shine.

And when the Colonel rose in the organization, he'd take her with him.

## CHAPTER TWENTY-THREE

*New Year's Eve.* It'd never meant much to Patrin before—and meant less now. What kind of a year would he and Fell have without Moya?

Behind the bar at the Bullwhacker, he tried not to snarl as he filled drink orders for the annoyingly festive customers. He shouldn't take his misery out on them.

But *fuck.*

He walked to the end of the bar where Fell had been nursing a beer for the last hour or so. Even without trying, he could feel his brother's unhappiness.

*I fucked up.*

Only he wasn't sure how. An alpha was supposed to keep the pack moving in sync—that's what the bonds were for. How could Moya not understand that? He hadn't singled her out, hadn't used the bonds for his personal desires.

She'd been so angry.

"Yo, Patrin, Fell." Ramón and his brother stood at the bar, shoulder-to-shoulder, both with narrowed eyes. "What'd you do to Moya?"

Fell snorted. "You were there. On the run."

"What? I didn't see anything. Did you do something after we left?" Zorion clenched his fists.

"No." Patrin shook his head. "She's mad because I kept our group of wolves from charging the herd until the deer reached the right spot to drive them to the creek."

"Yeah, sweet timing. You controlled—" Ramón stiffened. "Gods, the pack bonds..."

Zorion's eyes widened. "Frigging fangs."

"Yeah, that," Fell said in a rough voice.

"But you weren't...didn't..." Ramón protested.

"Moya wouldn't care, bro. Just that the bonds were used." Zorion set his drink on the bar and curled both hands around the glass. "Did she bury your relationship under a pile of dirt?"

Like a cat buried its scat? Patrin rubbed the bruise on his jaw that was thankfully concealed by his beard. "After she punched me."

"Gods-dammit. I was cheering for you two. She was so *happy*," Ramón said.

"We don't want it to be over." Patrin held up a finger, went to fill a beer order, and returned. "Got any advice for the clueless?"

Ramón thrummed his fingers on the bar top as he and Zorion considered.

"She's got a hot temper but is reasonable once it cools," Zorion offered.

"I don't know, bro. To her, an alpha using pack bonds is"— Ramón waved a hand in the air—"is like dumping water on a salamander's bonfire."

Patrin winced. A pissed-off fire elemental would scorch a shifter.

Kinda like he'd felt after Moya got through with him.

"Why?" Fell spoke for the first time. "Why does she fear the bonds so much?"

Her brothers exchanged glances.

"Her past isn't ours to tell. Just...ask her what happened before we moved here. Why she moved," Ramón said in a low voice.

"Aye, that," Zorion agreed. "Ask to talk, to understand, to apologize."

Ramón gave them a rueful smile. "Only if you mean it though. She can tell."

Patrin breathed out a sigh. "That won't be a problem."

Yelling started then, around the bar. "Ten. Nine. Eight..."

*Right.* He gave his littermate a half-hearted smile. "Happy Fucking New Year."

---

At her kitchen table, still awake, Moya had heard cheering at midnight. Probably from people partying at the Bullwhacker.

*Good for them.*

A glance at the clock told her it was now past one o'clock.

"Happy New Year to me." Only, face it, right now, it was more like "Miserable New Year." She'd been too depressed for even a pampering session and had simply showered and pulled on her comfy, fluffy robe. Then she spent the evening studying her business records, in-between trying to decide how to talk with Talitha about moving away.

Her friend would be madder than a bee-stung badger. And once she got past being angry, she'd point out how unreasonable Moya was being.

Dammit, she knew she was stupidly jumping off a cliff for something no one else thought was a problem. Yet every time she remembered how Patrin had used the bonds, controlled her, *paralyzed* her, she wanted to throw up. And blindly flee anywhere to get away from him.

Not even Leonard, the alpha in Stanislaus Territory, had been able to steal her will so thoroughly.

Patrin was stronger.

Elbows on the table, she rested her forehead in her hands and tried not to cry. Her heart felt empty, aching with hurt.

He'd *promised*.

That hurt worst of all.

Only...only...Patrin wasn't a liar. How could she reconcile what she knew of him with how he'd acted? She'd considered him and Fell to be two of the most honorable males she'd ever met.

He wouldn't lie—only he had.

Her jaw tightened. *I should talk to him. To them.*

There was a tap at the door. Her stomach clenched.

*I'm not ready to face them yet.*

When the handle turned, she remembered she hadn't locked it when carrying in groceries earlier. Because she'd never bothered to lock up before.

Patrin and Fell walked in, so big and male, and for one second, joy filled her.

Then dark anger—and fear—boiled up inside. "Get out."

Patrin held up a hand, and they both sat on the floor, right in front of the door.

*Didn't I want to talk to them?*

*No, no, I don't.*

She picked up her glass, wanting—needing—to throw it at them. To hurt them. Her hand shook as she forced herself to set it down. "I want you to leave." Her voice shook just as badly.

"One minute," Fell rasped out. "Then we'll leave."

She gritted her teeth—and nodded.

"I'm sorry, Moya. I fucked up." Patrin closed his eyes and pulled in a breath. His usually smooth baritone was as rough as the bricks in the square. "What I promised you... I thought I was promising not to use the pack bonds for personal desires. You thought I was promising to never use them at all. I never meant to break my word to you. I wouldn't do that."

As she stared at him, he just...waited. His eyes, black as the night, met hers. Openly. Pain had tightened the hard lines of his face.

She was just sitting here, so why was her heart beating hard enough to hurt her chest? Unable to tear her gaze away, she could see the unhappiness in his eyes and the darkness beneath that indicated a sleepless night.

Hurting for him and hating herself for it, she turned her gaze to Fell. If anything, he looked even more miserable, more tired. He opened his mouth—and didn't speak.

And that simply tore at her heart.

Patrin scrubbed his hands over his face. "I wouldn't have promised to never use the bonds, Moya. I couldn't. I can't. The ability was given to the alpha for a reason—to keep the pack safe when our animal instincts drive us past reason and into danger."

She pulled in a breath and tried to understand despite the angry, fearful pulse in her head.

"Brett used the bonds in the opposite way," Fell rasped. "To incite our instincts and put the pack in danger."

Brett had done exactly that, pushing anger into the wolves to get them to attack the felines.

On the hunt, Patrin had held the pack back to prevent them from charging forward as their hunting instincts demanded.

Then she remembered how his control had felt. "I couldn't move." Her whisper was hoarse, and her anger rose again. "Not at all." Horror shuddered through her.

Fell's eyes narrowed. "You're cold. Sit by the fire?"

Sit there with them...closer? But the alpha could—

"Just to talk," Patrin said softly. "Nothing more."

He didn't think he'd broken his promise. Had seemed dismayed she thought he'd sworn something different.

A tiny edge of her hurt retreated, letting her take a deeper breath. "Okay."

Before she could stand, Fell was there, offering his hand, as if she had broken legs. Only, her legs were shaking enough she did need his hand.

His warm, warm hand, so strong and steady.

Patrin tossed a chunk of wood onto the fire, then sat at the far edge of her huge floor cushion, as if to avoid crowding her.

Arm around her waist, Fell settled her close to the woodstove, then took a seat also at the edge of the cushion by Patrin where she could watch them both.

After a moment of studying his hands, Fell looked up. "Patrin's order held me back. But it wasn't upsetting. None of the wolves seemed unhappy afterward."

Her jaw tightened. They thought she was just making stuff up or—

"Something happened to you in the past, didn't it?" Patrin asked. "Someone used the pack bonds on you in a bad way—even before Brett."

How would they know that? "What have Ramón and Zorion been telling you?"

Patrin huffed. "They said to ask you about what happened before you moved here."

*Oh, okay.* She wouldn't have to bite her brothers. But to talk about Leonard... She shook her head, emotions raw enough to bleed.

"Moya. I—*we*—don't want to call this quits. We care for you. A lot." Patrin leaned forward and took her hand. "Please, tell us what happened."

Could she? "It was so ugly," she whispered.

"*Cariad*, we've seen ugly." Fell moved closer, leaning against her in the way of wolves. His hard body against hers felt as if he'd wrapped her in a warm blanket.

They...deserved an explanation. She had to try. "I grew up in Stanislaus Territory down in California. Mom's sire ran a construction company and taught Ramón and Zorion. When I was eighteen, Mom moved to Colorado with her new mates."

After that, sometimes she felt all grown-up...and other times like a forlorn cubling. "It was only me and Grandsire then, since Ramón and Zorion went on their year of exploration."

"Sounds as if you had a pretty good childhood." Patrin slid closer until he warmed her other side.

"I did. Until my Grandsire got sick when I was nineteen." She sighed. "Our wolf pack had a good alpha and betas, although they were sad since their mate died a few years before. As I matured, I looked more and more like her."

Moya held out her arm, showing her brown skin. "She was Latina—and us dark-haired, brown-eyes shifters stand out. It seems as if most of the Daonain are descended from Celts and the north of Europe."

"I get it. Darcy and I have Romani blood." Patrin's black eyes glinted. "I'm guessing the alpha wanted you for his mate?"

Fell snorted. "A lookalike replacement."

"He was... It was like he was obsessed. He kept trying to get me interested, only I wasn't at all. I wasn't twenty, hadn't had my first mating heat or anything." She shook her head. "After a while, whenever he talked to me, my feelings got twisted up, and suddenly, I'd like him. Only when he wasn't around, I didn't."

She'd been so confused, unable to understand why her feelings kept switching back and forth. "I thought I was losing my mind." Gods, she hated remembering the dark morass of emotions. How she'd been so alone with no one to turn to and more terrified each day.

"The putrid spawn of a maggot." Patrin's anger was so intense she could feel it radiate from him.

On her other side, Fell growled.

"He wouldn't leave me alone—and no one would help. Grandsire was dying. Mom had left. Zorion and Ramón hadn't returned. I couldn't sleep, couldn't eat. I was a mess."

"All alone." Patrin slung an arm around her waist. "Did you tell anyone?"

"The whole pack adored him, and all my friends were wolves. No one would believe me. I thought I was going crazy—feral or something. Then Grandsire died, and it all got worse."

When Patrin hugged her closer, his silent sympathy made tears well up in her eyes. She swallowed hard.

"Go on, finish the tale," he whispered.

"So, one day, he put his arms around me." *Pulled against his chest, the scent of him too strong. Too... No, she loved his scent. Loved him. Snuggling closer. Stomach twisting with revulsion rising, making her gag. Pulling away.* "I—I..."

Panic ripped through her.

A hand cupped her cheek. "Moya." The voice was raspy, deep. She managed a breath, and Fell's scent brought a sense of warmth and safety.

"S-sorry." Her eyes lifted, meeting his piercing blue gaze.

He studied her for a second and released her. "Finish the story, little wolf."

"We're here." Patrin gave her a squeeze as if to remind her she was safe, then prompted, "The fleabag alpha grabbed you."

"My emotions, they went back and forth. One moment I loved him, and then next, he made me sick. And it felt like something was ripping apart in my chest. Someone called his name, broke his concentration, and I realized what was happening. That he was using the pack bonds."

Patrin and Fell growled again, together in a deadly chorus of support.

And just like that, the tight band around her chest loosened. "The next time, when I started to feel as if I loved him, I punched him as hard as I could. And it worked."

"Ah, our slugger." Fell picked up her hand and kissed her knuckles.

Patrin kissed the top of her head. "No wonder your first instinct is to nail someone in the gut."

"Yes. I hit him anytime he got too close, and he was furious because he was the alpha. The other wolves were angry and would corner me and yell at me for showing such disrespect to the alpha." She'd felt so lost. Nowhere to turn. Unable to figure a way out. "Ramón and Zorion came back and had a fit. I was way underweight and hollow-eyed and frazzled. When I told them, they believed me."

At the relief of their belief, she'd cried like a cubling. "They went to the Cosantir."

"Why didn't you?" Patrin studied her, and his eyes narrowed. "Maybe because the Cosantir has a power over our minds in much the same way?"

"Uh-huh. He was—is—a very pushy Cosantir, and by then, everything was making me panic." She stared down at her knees. How much time had she spent feeling more like a rabbit than a wolf.

Fell gave her hand a squeeze. "What'd the Cosantir say?"

"He didn't believe Ramón and Zorion, but they insisted he watch Leonard with me. When he saw Leonard's face—and mine—and what happened when I punched him, he came down on the alpha like an avalanche."

"Banishment?" Fell asked.

"No, he said the mental assault of abusing the pack bonds wasn't serious enough of a transgression for Leonard to be banished. He sent Leonard away to find a soulweaver and forbade him to return without the soulweaver's permission."

"Huh. Not a bad judgment," Patrin murmured.

After a moment, Fell commented, "Should've bit his tail off first."

"Yeah." Patrin ran his hand up and down her arm comfortingly. "Since you're here and not in Stanislaus Territory, I'm guessing things didn't improve."

"The pack blamed me for him and the betas leaving. Said I was just being all dramatic and casting blame." She sighed and added, "Leonard and his brothers had led the pack for a couple of decades."

Her friends had turned on her with the rest. Their voices still haunted her memories. Screaming at her, *"It's all your fault." "You should've been the one to leave, not our alpha."* Two of them had thrown rocks at her. Called her foul names.

Gods, the sense of betrayal, of loss, had almost broken her.

She pressed her hand over her mouth to hold the sob in. *Don't cry. It's past.*

"Easy there," Fell murmured, wiping the wetness from her cheeks. "S'over."

"It is." She took the tissue Patrin handed her and blew her nose. "I gave up and left. I should have, would have, done it before"—she huffed out a breath—"only when Leonard first started coming after me, and I said I was leaving, going to Mom's, and then somehow, just the thought was too frightening."

"The stinking coyote used the bonds on her to keep her there," Fell gritted out, his voice like gravel.

"He had you going and coming, the bastard," Patrin said.

"After he was gone, the fear went away. I checked out some places and then moved here. Ramón and Zorion were so angry with the pack, they sold out and followed. I helped them start the construction company here, and when I got my part of Grandsire's money, Talitha and I went in together on Espresso Books."

"No wonder you reacted badly when I used the bonds." Moving back a little, Patrin rubbed a finger along his beard-covered jaw.

She nodded.

"To me, using the ties for anything other than pack hunts or keeping our wolves safe is wrong." The muscles in his face tightened for a moment. "When we talked, I thought I was promising to refrain from using the bonds for anything other than for the good of the pack. I'm sorry, Moya."

She realized she was leaning against Fell and tried to straighten.

With an admonishing sound, he stopped her and stroked his hand up and down her back.

He probably had no idea how much comfort she took in his support. After a moment, she looked at Patrin. "I'm sorry too. I wasn't clear and heard what I wanted to hear. Maybe because I didn't know the bonds could be used for something good."

"I should have warned you." Patrin turned his face, staring at the fire. "I knew I'd be using them and trying to learn how they work. There were times with the Scythe…" His voice came out raw as if forced through a tight throat. "With the shifter-soldiers. If I could have made the hotheads stop and listen, kept them from attacking, maybe more would've lived."

By the Mother, what had happened?

"Had a sadist combat instructor." Fell sounded as if he was trying not to growl. "He hit a young werebear too hard. Killed him."

"His littermate lost control and attacked." Patrin's hands were in fists. "He wouldn't listen to me or Fell. The instructors beat him to death."

"Only fifteen." Fell's words held a mournful sound.

"Just a baby," Moya whispered. Barely older than Mateo and Alvaro. Her eyes burned with tears.

"That kind of thing happened too often," Patrin said, his shoulders slumped.

Grief shrouded Fell's eyes.

And Patrin blamed himself. Of course he'd welcome pack bonds to keep others safe.

Her sense of betrayal faded into nothing.

With a sigh, she kissed Fell's cheek. "I'm sorry I was angry with you." He hadn't made any promises to her, just been dragged into this mess.

"Forgiven." He curved an arm around her waist. "Always."

"As for you, Top Dog..." She rubbed her cheek against Patrin's shoulder. "I'm sorry. I should have talked to you before hitting you."

After a second, Patrin straightened. Then his eyes started to gleam with humor. "You should have," he said, oh so seriously. "I have a big, ugly bruise on my face. Don't I, brawd?"

Fell gave him a disgusted stare. "With your hairy muzzle, who'd see it?"

"Damn, Fell, if you'd backed me up, I might've scored frosted cookies." Patrin picked up her hand. "Are we friends again?"

"Yes." Relief and happiness blossomed inside her. "I'm happy to start the new year as friends."

"Maybe more than friends?" Fell said the words for her and wasn't that amazing?

"We want more, you know." Patrin ran his hand down her hair. His scent was changing, to a musky, very male scent. Bending, he caught her lips and kissed her, slow and tender.

"Lots more." Fell pulled her against his rock-hard chest and took his own kiss. Rougher, deeper.

"Not just sex, *cariad*, but for right now, I do want you in our bed." Patrin scooped her into his arms.

Her head spun, and she gripped his shirt.

"*Blodyn,* I wouldn't let you fall," he murmured, and his arms were like iron bars beneath her back and knees.

With Fell handling the doors, he carried her across the hall and laid her down on the wide bed they'd created. "There. I like seeing you there."

The possessive, hungry look in his eyes set up a nervous shimmer inside her.

"Looks right," Fell agreed. Her head was on the pillow, and he bent over her, gathering her loose hair, holding her in place as he took a long kiss. Firm lips, so demanding.

"Oh, I missed you," she whispered.

"Me, too, you." His voice was a harsh rasp, and his blue eyes still held a trace of the misery she had also felt for the last day.

She could feel Patrin's hands undoing her belt and opening her robe. "These pretties are all yours, brawd."

Still kissing her, Fell ran his hand down her shoulder and took possession of one breast, humming in satisfaction.

The sensation of his hard hand on her sent arousal spiraling upward.

Patrin knelt between her knees, pulling her legs up and over his shoulders. Bending, he settled his mouth on her pussy. His hot, wet tongue made a lazy circle around her clit.

Her gasp was muffled against Fell's lips.

Fell sucked on her lower lip, nipped the upper, and moved down to play with her breasts. Capturing one nipple between his lips, he lashed it into hardness.

Then she felt his teeth. The light nipping pushed her to new heights.

She couldn't...think, just feel as both of them touched her, licked her, sucked her in the most intimate of fashions. During the last week, they'd learned just what she liked and used that knowledge now. Ruthlessly.

After sucking lightly on her clit, Patrin ringed it with his tongue, even as his mouth created a hot, torturous suction.

Moment by moment, her clit grew more sensitive.

Fell nibbled on her breasts, his teeth heightening everything she felt.

She went up, so fast and hard, her senses were shocked at how quickly she hovered on the edge of coming.

"That's right, little wolf," Patrin whispered. His teeth closed on each side of her clit, the shock of it freezing her.

He ruthlessly thrust two fingers inside her—and sent her over in a massive explosion of pleasure. Keening in a high voice, she bucked her hips against his mouth.

Chuckling, he released her, then licked her again, sending more jolts of sensation through her.

She swallowed hard. Gods, she'd never come so fast in her life. Didn't even know a female could.

"By the Mother." Her voice sounded as if she'd been running for hours. "Let me up and it's your turn. I can—"

"No, I have apologies to convey—and this is a fine way to do it." Patrin lifted his head long enough to lick his lips and give her a thoroughly pleased smile.

"But..." She stopped, seeing his indomitable expression. The alpha had put his paw down. "Right, right."

Fell laughed.

Turning her gaze his way, she gave him her best pout—the one that worked on her brothers. "I need something to suck on, too, Fell. Please?"

His eyes narrowed, one finger circling her damp nipple, making her squirm at the tantalizing sensation. "Aye, you can have my dick to suck on while Patrin apologizes."

Over the past days, she'd gotten good at the blowjob stuff—and Fell adored it.

"Move her so her head is off the mattress." Patrin's lips tipped up.

Still standing, Fell gripped her shoulders, and they repositioned her so her shoulders lay on the edge of the mattress with her head tipped back and off.

Standing in front of her, Fell fed her his cock. It felt...different. She reached out and grabbed his hips—and realized how vulnerable she was.

Slowly, he moved his shaft in and out, carefully going deeper, and the sense of not having any control uncaged something deep inside her.

And then Patrin pulled her legs apart, settled between them, and took up where he'd left off.

Only she was a lot more sensitive.

*Gods, Gods, Gods.*

Patrin grinned as he drove Moya into another orgasm, then one more. By the God, he wouldn't mind keeping this up all night.

She'd probably bite his throat out for it...once she recovered.

But fuck, she was adorable when she came. Giving her pleasure was perhaps the finest thing he'd ever experienced.

After her third quick climax, Fell obviously worried the little wolf was no longer thinking clearly. Patrin's neck wasn't the only body part at risk. He'd pulled his cock from her mouth, resettled her on the mattress, and was enjoying her breasts instead.

Whenever Fell sucked hard or bit lightly on a nipple, her cunt contracted around Patrin's fingers. And made him harder than a rock.

She was very wet now, her pussy all pink and swollen.

"Brawd." Patrin pointed to a place on the bed beside Moya.

Figuring out what was planned, Fell lay on his back with his lower legs hanging off the mattress. "Come here, *cariad*." He pulled Moya on top, so she straddled him.

She blinked a couple of times, then smiled down at Fell. "Hey. I get to be on top?"

So fucking lovable.

Fell tangled his fingers of both hands in her hair and pulled her down for a kiss.

Patrin smiled at seeing his brother's happiness. Opening the bedside drawer, he pulled out lube and one of those human condoms.

"Aaaah." Moya's breathy sound of pleasure made Patrin's dick throb with urgency. He looked over and saw she was lowering herself onto Fell's cock. He curled his fingers around her hips, half supporting her.

And when she tried to bounce on him quickly, he made a

reproving sound and tightened his grip, imposing a slow rhythm. Up...down. Up...down.

Having rolled on the condom and lubed it, Patrin moved between Fell's knees. Moya's beautiful ass was perfectly positioned. Opening her buttocks, he squirted lube onto the puckered hole—and grinned at her startled squeak. "I'll go slow, little wolf."

As Fell held her motionless, Patrin penetrated her with one finger and worked up to another. They'd done this all week, getting her ready.

But he was bigger than fingers.

Setting his cock against her, he pressed in against the resistance.

*By the Mother's breasts.* Patrin was huge, and Fell was already inside her. "I don't think you'll fit," Moya gasped as the burning in her backhole increased.

"I will." Patrin ran his hands up and down her back, even as Fell reached up to play with her dangling breasts.

Should she be grateful it was Patrin behind her? Although very long, he didn't have Fell's girth.

*Burning, stretching.* Feeling so uncontrollably *taken* as Fell held her breasts—and her top half in place. Patrin's hands on her hips kept her from pulling away. She was pinned between them—and her insides melted with an overwhelming arousal.

Her clit was tingling as she throbbed around Fell's unmoving shaft inside her. She could do nothing except accept the relentless advance of Patrin's cock.

"Almost, *cariad*."

When she whined like a cowed puppy, Fell curved his hand behind her head to pull her down so he could kiss her. But it made Patrin's cock change positions, and she whined again. His penetration felt good and bad and hurt, yet somehow still felt so amazing. Like everything had lit up like the sun and was ready for action.

"All in." Patrin bent down over her back, nuzzling her shoulder. "You're so good. And you feel amazing." Slowly, he pulled back, then pressed in again.

Stretching her. Getting her used to what was happening.

"Good?" Fell asked.

Everything down there throbbed. "Yes?"

They both laughed, and then Patrin lifted her hips up and off his brother. But even as Fell's cock slid almost out, Patrin pushed in. He slowly withdrew then mercilessly slammed her down on Fell's shaft.

Gods, the feeling of being filled and emptied in different places was terrifyingly intense. Shivers ran through her at the sweeping pleasure. Her mind hazed, leaving only the sensation of being controlled and driven to...

To a place where she had no control and was just feeling...everything.

As Patrin increased the speed, the fiery pressure built inside her.

The inescapable climax rolled over her like an avalanche, sweeping everything before it, burying her in pleasure.

Fell grinned and could only watch as the most beautiful female in the world flew to pieces in their arms. Her hips were wiggling—as much as they could with both of them gripping her ass.

Chuckling, Patrin kept up the rhythm, staying in control as they found what worked best. Fuck, nothing felt quite as good as sharing a female in this way. And when the female was Moya, there could be no finer pleasure.

She was magnificent, giving far more than she took, and so open in her response.

Fell tightened his grip on her hips, letting Patrin raise her and set her down—but with Fell determining how far to lift to ensure he stayed sheathed.

The way she throbbed around him tightened his balls to nearly unbearable. Meeting Patrin's gaze, he nodded.

Their pace picked up into quick, short thrusts, and the pressure increased until, with a low growl, Fell let it go. Burning pleasure shot through him in mind-blowing jerks as he gave himself to Moya, filling her.

And he felt his littermate follow.

Again, Fell pulled Moya down for a kiss, and this time, he couldn't keep the words back, "I love you, *cariad*. Our Moya."

Her big brown eyes met his and spilled over with tears. Kissing him, she murmured the finest words in all the world, "I love you. Love you both."

## CHAPTER TWENTY-FOUR

In the Wild Hunt Tavern in Cold Creek, Arthur Wells rubbed his aching shoulder. Earlier, at dawn, finishing his daily PT with a jog, it'd been so damn cold. He had to keep telling himself: *You don't have to like it; you just have to do it.*

Across the table from him, Joe Thorson raised bushy gray eyebrows.

Wells gave the grizzled shifter a sour look. "No denying it; I'm getting older."

And humans aged—and died—much sooner than the Daonain. Although they looked about the same age, Thorson was probably at least three decades older. If they managed to die of old age, they'd go out about the same time.

A tall, leathery-faced man was approaching and laughed. "The alternative is worse. Be grateful you've survived long enough to feel the aches."

Wells tilted his head. "Good point."

"Leland, Happy New Year. It's been a long time." Thorson shoved a chair out. "Plant your tail and tell us what you're doing down from Elder Village."

Wells studied the man who had a few claw marks on his hands

and forearms—nothing like Thorson's set of nearly weblike scars. Leland appeared older than Thorson, which made sense if he lived in Elder Village—an off-the-grid, isolated mountain haven for older shifters.

Leland tilted his head back slightly, his nostrils moving as he scented the air. He shot Thorson a reproving glare.

*Ah*, he realized Wells was human.

Thorson growled a laugh. "Down, dog. Meet Arthur Wells. Your grandchildren might've mentioned him?"

"They did indeed." Leland took a seat and examined Wells with sharp eyes. "You helped free Averi, Kennard, and Fletcher from the Scythe."

*Ah*. He didn't know the girl, but who could forget the two young men? Cat shifters. Wells smiled slightly. They'd thrown a fit when Wells refused to recruit them. "Fletcher and Kennard are fine young men. For their age, they're quite deadly."

"They said the same about you." Leland lifted his beer to Wells. "You'd have made a good Daonain warrior."

Imagining himself with furry ears and a tail, Wells almost laughed. Instead, he said, diplomatically, "With our operation finished, I hope the young men can all move from soldiering to peaceful pursuits."

And he envied the former captives for being young enough to have a chance at a balanced life. It was good the Rainier Territory Cosantir had reminded him of this.

He didn't regret devoting his life to serving his country. He'd been needed, had accomplished what others might not have, and had made it possible for civilians to live without fear.

Yet he could now see—as he hadn't in his youth—he would have enjoyed a bit of peace himself.

"It's good to have them back and safe." Leland had a smile on his weathered face. "In fact, I wouldn't mind seeing a few great-grandchildren before I return to the Mother."

"Return to the Mother. What kind of scat is this? You're not that much older than I am," Thorson's raspy voice was almost a growl.

It took Wells a moment to remember that *return to the Mother* was the shifter's term for dying. The Daonain had a goddess along with a god. Actually, being welcomed home by a Mother Goddess sounded far more comforting than any male God's reception.

"Don't go yowling at me, mouser." Leland grinned at Thorson's glare, then his smile faded. "When Helen died, I would've let the forest take me, but my grandchildren are still working through their past as captives. That's why I'm here—I spent Solstice with Averi. Friday, I'm visiting Kennard and Fletcher in Ailill Ridge. Thankfully, an old friend is lending me his cabin, so I don't have to stay in the ranch bunkhouse."

"Seeing cubs grow, watching the clan increase. Worth a few aches and pains," Thorson said gruffly.

Wells could hear pain in the werecat's rough voice. The last of Thorson's blood had died three years ago, tortured by humans.

"Truth there. I hear you're *caomhnor* to one of the Cosantir's younglings," Leland said.

The deep lines in Thorson's face lessened with his smile. "Toren, best cub ever." He nudged Wells with his shoulder. "This is one of the very few humans chosen to be a *caomhnor*. His Artair is almost as brilliant as Toren."

Leland's laugh was hearty. "Spoken like a true *caomhnor*." He raised his glass. "To our younglings."

Wells clinked his glass against the other two. He'd never thought to be involved with children. But one of his covert operatives, Sergeant Victoria Morgan, had somehow become the daughter he never had. When she called on him to help raise her son, it'd been one of the finest moments of his life.

His one-year-old godson, Artair, was delightful, with the sergeant's big brown eyes and dark hair. He also possessed an excellent command voice when it came to demanding food.

*Is it any wonder I spend so much time in Cold Creek these days?*

Crossing the parking lot to the Wild Hunt Tavern, Patrin was dragging more than a little. He was grateful they'd slept late this morning—and even more so to have woken up with Moya in his arms, all soft and female and welcoming. He and Fell had made love to her again, slow and sweet.

Yeah, *made love* was the right term, because he fucking loved her. So did Fell.

And she'd said she loved them. *By the Gods.* At the time, his heart had felt too full for words.

He rubbed his chest. Still did.

*Okay, okay, focus, wolf.* They hadn't driven all the way to a different territory for Patrin to spend the time daydreaming.

At supper, Darcy had noticed he was distracted although, thankfully, she hadn't figured out why. After the grief he and Fell gave her when she fell in love, she'd be far too delighted to deal some back.

It was good to see her with her two lifemates though. She looked...happy, really fucking happy.

As he walked through the door, he glanced at his brother and almost grinned. *I'm not the only one daydreaming.* And wasn't it great to see how relaxed Fell looked, even in a busy tavern?

Nik had closed the Bullwhacker today, saying the people who liked to drink would be hungover from last night, and few would show up on New Year's Day.

But the Wild Hunt Tavern in Cold Creek, run by the Cosantir of the North Cascades Territory, had a family feel almost like the Shamrock Restaurant in Ailill Ridge. People weren't here to drink as much as to be with friends.

Over the past year, Patrin and Fell had been here a couple of times when visiting Darcy. It was a good place.

He breathed in the scents of beer and wine and roasted nuts. A couple of big guys in thick sweaters were playing pool in the alcove to the right. To the left, a group of females sat in front of the massive fireplace while two salamanders danced in the flames. More people dotted the tables and chairs in the center of the room.

"We should pay our respects to the Cosantir." Patrin headed toward the long, dark oak bar at the back where Calum was manning the bar.

Fell lowered his voice. "Wells is here."

"Yeah?" Patrin followed his gaze. If the Scythe were finished, no need to ignore the spymaster, so he tipped his head slightly.

Wells gave them a chin-lift of acknowledgement but didn't wave them over. Good enough. The spymaster had undoubtedly picked up they were here with a purpose and not to socialize.

The Cosantir was Fell's height with an olive complexion, black hair, and gray eyes. "Congratulations to you, Alpha and Beta. I'm pleased you're moving forward in life."

After checking that no one was within hearing, Patrin bowed his head in respect. "Thank you, Cosantir."

"Cosantir." Fell did the same.

"I believe you're here to see Shay and Zeb?" Calum poured two draft beers, the same he and Fell had enjoyed on their previous visits. The male had an uncanny memory. And with his English accent and aristocratic features, it seemed as if the male should be lording it over some castle rather than tending bar in a rustic mountain tavern.

"We are." Patrin leaned on the bar. "André told you we were coming?"

"Aye. We talk now and then. It's a pleasure to have Rainier Territory in competent and committed hands."

Patrin knew exactly what Calum meant. Rainier's previous Cosantir had apparently been damn lazy before descending into criminal behavior, and then he'd gone feral.

Patrin had been there that day. Had to say, crazy-as-shit bears were damn terrifying.

Calum handed over the tall mugs and glanced at the door. "There the cahirs are now."

Patrin turned.

Shay, the North Cascades alpha, was also a cahir, which meant tall and brawny. Clean-shaven with shaggy brown hair, he had had a battered face much like a human prize-fighter.

His beta, Zeb, was also a cahir and a good six-five. Looking as if he had some Native American blood, he wore his straight black hair past his shoulders. Scars covered his neck and hands.

Spotting them, Shay pointed to an unoccupied table in one corner.

As Patrin nodded, Calum said, "I'll bring their beers over in a minute."

At the table, Patrin bowed his head slightly before sitting. "Thank you for seeing us."

"Our pleasure. We alphas have to stick together." Shay's deep smooth voice had the old-fashioned Gaelic accent Patrin had occasionally heard in Elder Village. "Congratulations on taking the pack. From Brett, we heard?"

"Aye. The minute Roger got hurt and was at a disadvantage, Brett challenged him—and won."

"Brett's a cowardly mutt. Glad he's gone." Zeb gave off a deadly vibe—even worse than Fell's.

"Neither alpha did well by the pack." Fell pulled out a chair and took a seat.

"And that's part of the problem." With a sigh, Patrin ran a hand over his face and realized he hadn't shaved earlier. Because he'd been kissing sweet Moya—and more. He almost smiled at the memory before mentally kicking himself back onto the trail. "As alpha and beta, we're not sure exactly what to do."

"Figured that was it," Zeb muttered to Shay, then rose. "Wait."

Patrin watched him walk over to the females by the fireplace, take one by the hand, and lead her back to the table. The golden-haired, blue-eyed female had curves almost as pretty as Moya's.

"Good idea, Zeb." Shay rose and held a chair for her. "Breanne, do you remember Darcy's brothers, Patrin and Fell?"

"Oh, I do. Before last summer solstice, you gave us lessons on how to fight." She smiled at both of them.

Patrin smiled back. The fighting lessons here had given them the idea of what to offer for reciprocity for Moya's cooking classes.

Shay lifted Breanne's hand, showing the lifemating bracelets. "Our lifemate is the pack's alpha female. They're here for advice, Breanne."

"Rumors are true. They took the Rainier pack," Zeb told her.

Her eyes widened. "Oh, congratulations."

"Leading a pack wasn't even remotely on our wish list." Patrin slugged down some beer. "Especially since we have fuck-all for experience in even being part of a pack. And we might not feel like it, but we're a lot younger than most wolves when they become alphas."

"You—" Shay started to speak and stopped.

Patrin startled.

The Cosantir had managed to walk up to the table without anyone hearing. As he set beers in front of Shay and Zeb, the god's power shimmered around him like heat waves off concrete.

A cold chill ran up Patrin's spine.

The Cosantir's eyes were still gray, but shades darker, as he studied Patrin and Fell with a penetrating gaze. "You are, indeed, young in years. However, adversity has aged you. Although you lack experience with a wolf-only pack, you led and protected your shifters in hazardous conditions for years. In attacks. Even in death. You have been tested in ways far older alphas have not. Leading your pack is quite within your capabilities, Alpha and Beta."

*Leading. Protecting.* Yes, that was what they had done. The knot of worry in Patrin's gut loosened.

Tilting his head slightly, the Cosantir prowled away.

Yeah, he was definitely a cat.

"He's right," Shay said. "Leading is leading. But you were in charge of healthy young males. A pack is more diverse, so let's discuss the older members, the unhealthy ones, the females and cubs. What you should do for them and also what a good alpha female should do."

For the next few hours, they talked about pack dynamics, new members, exiles, discipline. And how to care for *all* the members.

Breanne elaborated on the responsibilities of an alpha female, especially for the females and cubs.

Shay took her hand and added, "The alpha female can unite the pack far more than any male."

Zeb gave a grunt of agreement.

And their blonde wolf blushed a pretty red.

Patrin glanced at Fell. "No question of who we want as our alpha female. Hell, she's already doing a lot of the work, just because that's who she is."

Breanne gave them a quizzical look. "I don't understand. Where did the previous alpha female go? When Shay took over, he basically inherited the alpha female." Her expression hardened. "I had to challenge her. If you're not life-mated, the decision isn't yours."

"Yeah, that was a mess." Zeb's brows drew together, and he asked Patrin, "Who is your alpha female now?"

"Ahhh..." Patrin looked at his brother for help.

Fell shrugged and offered, "Deidre maybe?"

"Who knows? Maybe the one named Cosette, who is just there to flirt her tail."

Breanne snorted then held up her hands when everyone looked at her. "Sorry, but I know exactly the type of female you're talking about."

"I'm afraid you don't get to pick an alpha female," Shay said. "You can throw your weight behind your choice, but it's ultimately up to the females."

Patrin nodded. Made sense, even if the previous Rainier alphas had seemed to pick and choose as they wanted. Then again, perhaps the smarter females hadn't wanted to be in a partnership with Brett or Roger and hadn't bothered to get involved.

Eventually, Patrin got a chance to ask the question that had nagged at him since last night. "What do you know about pack bonds? How do they work? What are the guidelines?"

"Well..." Shay frowned as he considered. "First, both male and female alphas can exert control, although the male has more impact. The effect is immediate and short-lived."

Thank fuck, Patrin thought, or a young Moya would've been stuck with the mangy-tailed alpha in Stanislaus Territory.

Shay added, "How strong the command is depends upon the alpha's strength, how long he's been alpha, and how connected to the pack the receiver is."

Ah, and this was another reason Moya avoided the pack and made up her own group with Heather and Talitha.

"Are some alphas better at using the bonds? Even if they aren't good leaders?" Fell asked, brows drawn together.

"Hmm. We saw that in an Idaho territory." Shay glanced at Zeb and received a confirming nod. "One mediocre alpha had a lot of strength in the order he gave with the bonds."

"And from the other end?" Fell leaned forward. "Are some wolves more receptive—or susceptible?"

Patrin turned to stare at his brother. Was he thinking Moya was especially susceptible to bonds?

"Can't answer you there," Shay said. "Mostly because, like a lot of alphas, I rarely use them."

"I can't *not* use the bonds. If I must stop someone to protect them, I need to be able to do it," Patrin said. A few times with the Scythe he'd managed to keep hotheaded wolves from attacking the teachers, from dying. And when he couldn't, as with Chester and Graham, the cats or bears died. The memory of blood-covered bodies swept over him, suffocating him like a thick smoke.

Fell's shoulder bumped his, jolting him back into the present.

*By the Gods.* "Sorry, bad memories."

"Happens." It was Fell who answered, but Shay and the beautiful blonde female nodded, dark understanding in their eyes.

"Taking a new trail." Fell motioned toward Breanne's bracelets. "We didn't learn about lifemating as cubs. And, last year, I...ah... wasn't always attentive to the Elders."

"Because you'd barely gotten free of the Scythe." Shay picked up his beer and finished it. "It's a wonder you even functioned at that point."

"We...struggled a lot those first few months," Patrin admitted. "All of us did." They'd all dreamed of being free, but their freedom was followed with days of depression, anger, withdrawal. It'd taken months to reach a balance.

But they had.

Pulling in a breath, Patrin picked up the hunt for the answers he and Fell wanted. "So, our sister lifemated Gawain and Owen. We saw them ask her and still don't understand how it works. Or where the bracelets come from. Owen and Gawain didn't have any when they asked her."

"Ah, now." Shay's eyes lit. "Lifemating is special. Many shifters have mates they love and live with. They may or may not stay together. They're still required to attend Gatherings. A lifemating, though, binds your *souls* together for this life, and some say into the next. When a blademage makes the bracelets, if the lifemating is true, the Mother blesses the bracelets."

Breanne added, "Gawain is our blademage. He didn't have the bracelets when they asked because he wanted to make them with Darcy and Owen present."

"Usually the males—or occasionally the female—will get the bracelets before asking." Shay's smile held more than a hint of reminiscence. "It's a test of character in a way. Telling the blademage you've found the female who holds your heart for all time. Even before you ask her."

Breanne's eyes filled with tears, and she kissed Shay and Zeb. "I love you two."

Patrin had to look away, even as his throat tightened.

*By the Mother's grace, this is what I want. Moya with me and Fell for all our lifetimes and into the next.*

Fell's eyes held the same longing. "Visit Darcy...and talk to Gawain, the blademage?"

Patrin nodded, his voice coming out rough. "Let's go test our character."

# CHAPTER TWENTY-FIVE

The scent of coffee and pastries drifted to Moya and mingled with the lovely fragrance of books as she sat at her bookstore desk and made notes on what future releases to preorder. Her toe tapped in time with the rhythm of Lionel Richie's *All Night Long*.

Last night, she had poor sleep—and then no sleep. So, she overruled everyone and chose the music today, hoping the energetic classic rock playlist would keep her awake. Talitha had whined, but seriously, her choice of harp music would've had Moya asleep under the desk.

In the building's center, about half of the tables were full, and the soft sound of conversation filled the air.

A couple of humans browsed the shelves in the bookstore. Corey, one of Talitha's baristas, had finished his shift and come over to find his next read.

Last year, when she asked him what his favorite book was, he said he hadn't read anything since leaving high school—and looked as guilty as if he'd been caught kicking puppies. Since he loved horror movies, she'd loaned him her copy of Stephen King's

*The Shining*. He started it reluctantly, then devoured it and never looked back.

Sometimes, she felt like a drug dealer handing out samples and luring the innocent into a whole new addiction.

Tyrone Farmer, who owned the ski shop, was wandering through the historical novels. His short black beard and long dreadlocks sported some gray even though he was only in his mid-forties. Humans showed their age sooner than Daonain, but being so fit, he'd probably be giving ski lessons into his nineties.

What would Patrin and Fell look like in their nineties?

Smiling at the thought, she tried to imagine Patrin's dark hair turning silver. There'd be more lines at the edges of Fell's eyes, and maybe he'd even acquire some laugh lines.

He should stay with her to make sure that happened. Wouldn't he laugh if she presented such an argument?

*But, yes, stay with me, both of you.*

When the two males left yesterday for Cold Creek, it had been...odd. She rubbed her chest where she'd actually felt ties thin as they got more and more distant.

Pack bonds weren't supposed to work this way...were they?

She'd spent the evening without them, was unable to sleep without them, and was feeling impossibly lonely. Which didn't seem right. She'd been living just fine on her own for *years*.

When he and Patrin returned a little before dawn, they'd joined her in bed and made love to her so thoroughly, she was still tender. Just the memory of what they'd done... Warmth flushed through her from toes to hair.

Unable to help herself, she glanced over and smiled at Fell behind the coffee bar. It still seemed surprising to have such a muscular, deadly male brewing coffee.

He caught her gaze, and his lips curved up in his mesmerizing half-smile. So kissable.

She narrowed her eyes at him.

*Don't even start with me, wolf.*

His smile widened.

Thankfully, Corey walked over and handed her a book: *Demon Seed* by Dean Koontz.

"Fantastic choice"—she pursed her lips—"although I don't know how you can sleep at night after reading this kind of story."

He grinned. "Hey, I know there's really nothing scary out there."

"Right." So young, so innocent, so human. Smiling, Moya rang up the sale, then Tyrone was there with his choices.

On to the next customer and the next.

Eventually, it was three o'clock, closing time. After pulling the gates closed, she locked them and wandered over to the coffee bar.

"Here, *blodyn*, I made you this." Fell set a cup on the counter and added another. "Patrin's on his way in. We wanted to talk."

"Oh, okay." By the time she sat down at her favorite table overlooking the square, Patrin had entered, turned the door sign to CLOSED, and joined her.

He ran his hand over her hair and smiled down at her. "You look beautiful today."

"So do you," she said.

He laughed. But he did, really. His big shoulders filled the sheepskin coat, his face was reddened from the cold, and his black eyes snapped with mirth. Bending, he gave her a long, slow kiss that made her toes curl. His soft beard brushed against her cheeks...making her remember the feel against her inner thighs, and by the Mother, just like that, she wanted him again.

And he could tell, dammit. After a long inhale, he rubbed his cheek against her hair and murmured, "Later, *cariad*. It will be my pleasure to see to *all* your needs."

"So pink, so pretty." Fell sat down beside her. After kissing her hand, he nipped her fingertips.

The tiny pain sent a zing straight to her nether regions. Surely it wasn't healthy to be aroused so often. "I'm not sure I can survive the both of you."

Fell's eyes darkened. "Don't say that."

*Oh, Gods.* "Not like that." She bumped his shoulder with her own and found the courage to be perfectly honest. "I mean you two already have me walking funny, and still, every time I look at you, I want to drag you to bed."

Fell's eyes warmed, and his hand tightened around hers. "Bed sounds good."

"Brawd, no." Patrin backhanded his brother. "Talking, then groceries, remember?"

"Don't be so reasonable." Holding her hand, Fell set her palm against his face.

She could feel the stubble along his jaw and see the small bruise where she bit him during lovemaking. She touched it with her thumb. "Oh, ah, sorry?"

His lips curved. "Come and bite me again, little wolf."

Patrin made an annoyed sound, pulled her hand away, and put a coffee in it. "The Cold Creek alpha, beta, and alpha female gave us plenty of help. One thing came out... Fell and I want you to be the pack's alpha female. *Our* alpha female."

She choked on the sip of coffee. *They want me?* To be their alpha female, to help care for the pack, to run beside them on the trails.

"It'd be a lot of work." Fell's expression was worried.

"Aye," Patrin said. "But you've been caring for the pack anyway. We want to make it official, only...Breanne thought you might have to fight for it."

"Fighting..." Fell gripped the nape of his neck, looking frustrated. "It's not right. Females shouldn't fight."

Moya had to stifle a snort. These warriors were so dangerous, so knowledgeable about the world outside of Daonain territories, yet so endearingly innocent sometimes. Just because females didn't brawl in taverns didn't mean they fought fewer battles.

Females used all their weapons, not only fists, but words and appearance and skills.

If those failed, then fangs worked too.

"I'd be honored to be your alpha female." Moya wanted to hug herself to keep in all the emotions. "And I'll fight for it, if necessary."

Now they both looked worried—and she laughed.

Dammit, the little wolf had no idea of the damage that could happen in a challenge. Fell wanted to grab her, run upstairs, and lock her in their apartment. Keep her where she'd be safe.

But her big brown eyes danced with the anticipation of...of fighting, for fuck's sake. He could smell no fear, no worry. Just confidence.

Sure, they'd been sparring with her. She had skills, true enough, but she was...pint-sized. She was *Moya*.

How could he allow her to get hurt in a fight?

How could he not?

Over the years, he and Patrin had finally learned to step back when a younger shifter-soldier wanted to handle something himself. Toddlers couldn't learn to walk if carried everywhere.

And toddlers became adults.

Fell saw the same resignation in Patrin's gaze. *This isn't our fight or our decision.*

"We also learned a few things about pack bonds." Patrin took a sip of his coffee. "How capably an alpha can use them varies, partly because of his strength. Ones like Brett and your Stanislaus alpha can push an order through the bonds better than others. In addition, there's a difference in how much the wolf feels through the ties."

Moya frowned. "I'm not sure what you mean."

"Fell and I think you're more sensitive to the bonds than other wolves."

Seeing her frown deepen, Fell spoke up. "When Patrin ordered a halt, I could still move. The order stilled my animal enough to feel what the alpha wanted."

She shook her head. "You probably have more resistance since—"

"Your brothers said the same." Fell met her eyes. "Like me, Ramón took a step forward."

Smiling, Patrin ran his hand over his beard. "You gnome-nuts wanted to prove you could but not totally screw up the hunt."

"Ramón could move?" Moya clenched her hands. "I was so paralyzed I almost couldn't breathe."

"See? You're sensitive." Fell rubbed his chin. If he wanted to test it, she'd probably bite him. "Can an alpha female use the bonds?"

"What a dreadful thought." She shuddered, then rose. "I promised to visit with Talitha and Eileen. I need to get going." Her fast walk lacked her usual grace.

*Fuck.* He shouldn't have added that last idea. As Fell was cleaning up their cups, he growled. "That went well. Not."

Frowning, Patrin joined him at the door. "She won't even *think* about using the bonds. What if she needs to?"

"Not all alphas use the bonds." Of course, his brother would want her to have the ability to protect the pack. "Give her time. Where do we start?"

"I was thinking the pack house and neighborhood around it." Patrin's expression stayed tight.

Fell bumped his shoulder. "She'll figure it out."

Because Moya was one of the strongest females he'd even known. Strong, smart, caring.

Soon...soon, they'd ask her to be their lifemate.

Not yet, though. When they'd spoken with Darcy's mate

Gawain about making them lifemating bracelets, he'd started right then. Fuck, they were beautiful.

But the blademage pointed out that the moon was waning and suggested they wait. Asking someone to love them, to start a new life together, was traditionally done when the moon was waxing or full. Crescent moons were the time of new beginnings.

They could wait.

But fuck, it wasn't easy.

## CHAPTER TWENTY-SIX

Since Fell had walked over to talk with Zorion, Patrin tilted his head back to study the two-story house. The construction crew was very competent. The roof was on, windows were in. He nodded at Ramón. "Over the last month, I've enjoyed watching this go up. You don't usually work on Saturdays though."

"We want the place weather-proofed before the storm tomorrow." With obvious pleasure, the male watched his crew working. "We're finishing up now, and I'm sending everyone home."

"Ah, Fell and I have good timing. Any chance I could talk to your wolves before they leave?"

"Sure." Ramón grinned. "I heard what you've been doing and wondered when you'd get to us. Let me round them up."

As he jogged into the house, Zorion and Fell wandered over.

Zorion tipped his head respectfully. "Alpha."

"Zorion."

Before they could talk, wolves in the crew started gathering around Patrin.

Okay then. He spoke just loud enough for the group to hear. "As you know, Fell and I are still putting paws to the trail after being away from the Daonain so long. We're also learning how to be good pack leaders for you."

"At least you're gonna try. That's more effort than we've seen in a long time," Killian said to general agreement, warming Patrin's heart.

"We want to meet everyone, informally, for a couple of reasons. First is..." Patrin sighed. Over the past couple of days, they'd talked to most of the pack—and his speech hadn't gotten easier. "During the last hunt, I used the pack bonds to get the wolves with me to halt until the deer reached the best spot to attack."

All the crew had been in his group.

"Yeah," Jalen snickered. "My mate stopped so fast, I tripped over her. She bit me."

The female beside Jalen punched him in the arm. "You deserved it, bumble-paws."

Everyone grinned.

A knot in Patrin's gut relaxed. "As it happens, Moya got angry at me for using the pack bonds, partly because of how Brett coerced wolves to attack cats."

Faces darkened.

Terence looked particularly pissed off. Brett had influenced him to attack a cat on the crew. "The coward should join a coyote pack. It's where he belongs."

Beside Patrin, Fell snorted a laugh.

Patrin forged on. "After talking with Moya and Fell, I wanted to be honest with our wolves. As alpha, I promise to only use pack bonds as they're intended—to keep the pack safe or to direct the hunt. I will never use the ties for my own selfish interests."

Arms crossed over his chest, Killian made a growling sound of approval. "I like how you nosed the problem right out there for us to sniff. You got my trust, Alpha."

The rumbling sound of agreement vibrated along the pack bonds.

"Part one is handled," Ramón said with a grin. "What's the second part?"

"We'd like to hear if you or any wolf has problems the pack can help with. The pack should be helping our older wolves, cubs, and mothers."

"It's like going into battle—your team has your back," Fell said, his voice low.

The ensuing lively discussion lasted until Patrin realized the sun was low in the west. "All right, wolves. Come to the pack house early for the monthly run, and we'll keep figuring out ways to help."

"A meeting I might finally enjoy," Alana said. "It's gotta be better than being ordered to dump my mate because he's a cat."

Her crewmates grinned.

"We'll keep our cat." Jalen waggled his eyebrows at Alana. "But your wolf mate is far, far better in bed."

Alana thumped him. "The cat wasn't the one who ate chili, then farted so bad during sex we had to sleep in the living room."

As the entire crew busted up laughing, Patrin grinned and headed away with Fell. "That ran long. I need to shower and get my tail to the Bullwhacker for work."

"Poor pitiful Top Dog." Fell easily dodged Patrin's backhand. "Moya and I are grocery shopping. She wants to stock up for the storm tomorrow and do some baking tonight in case the power goes out."

Baking? Even in human form, Patrin could almost feel his ears perk up. "Can you talk her into making that chocolate cake with frosting in the middle and top?"

*All the frosting. So good.*

"Do my best, oh beloved littermate..."—Fell smirked—"if she's not too tired after making me cherry pies."

*Beloved littermate, my tail.* A shove rammed his beloved littermate into an apple tree hard enough a pixie woke and scolded them both.

---

A little before sunset, Moya crossed the square with Fell beside her. The male had insisted on adding several items to her grocery list—all of them for making cakes and pies. "You two are going to end up so portly your bellies'll drag on the ground during pack runs."

"You think?" Fell took her hand and ran it down the hard ridges of his abdomen.

When her cheeks turned hot, he gave her a slow, very warm, smile. Because she'd totally licked each one of those ridges last night.

"Hey, Fell!" A couple of tall, lanky young men—no, she caught their scent, young *shifters,* approached. Brown eyes, brown hair, and obviously siblings. "Did you and Patrin know Wells is in town?"

"Is he?" Fell smiled down at Moya and pointed at the male on the left. "Fletcher." The one on the right. "Kennard. Shifter-soldiers."

The two couldn't be much older than eighteen, although Kennard's face was scarred enough to have been in a war. "It's good to meet you both. Are you living in Ailill Ridge now?"

"Yes, ma'am," Kennard said, bobbing his head.

"Ma'am?" Moya raised her eyebrows.

Fletcher grinned. "We work out at the Summerland Ranch, and our boss, Daniel, fostered in Texas. And talks like it too. Guess we've picked up some country."

"Oh, Daniel, right. I understand." Moya laughed and glanced at Fell. "He and Tanner are Heather's littermates, if you haven't met them yet."

"Not wolves?"

"Bears, both of them." Fletcher grinned. "Kinda laid-back and fun. Good bosses."

Moya smiled at the two former captives bursting with health and enthusiasm. Daniel and Tanner would be amazing mentors, and their ranch would be the perfect place for these young males to finish growing into their paws.

Fell's eyes narrowed, and his question, "What drew Wells here?" made Moya stiffen. Was that spymaster going to pull Patrin and Fell back into his clutches?

Kennard caught on to the tone in Fell's voice. "Nothing for, uh...*business*. Grandsire's visiting until Tuesday and brought an old friend from Cold Creek."

"Thorson's his name. He's one scary werecat, and he brought Wells with him." Fletcher grinned. "I bet Wells will swing into town and look you two up on Monday."

Moya checked Fell's expression and was surprised at the slight smile. "You *want* to see that human?"

"Sure." Fell looked down then, as if he understood how appalled she was, kissed the top of her head. "He was as dedicated to eliminating the Scythe as we were. And he was careful with us. I think he forgot we're not his regular human soldiers who'd signed up."

"Oh." She crossed her arms over her chest, not sure she'd be so quick to forgive the spymaster.

"He's why we have money and IDs," Kennard added.

"Hey, brawd, we need to get going." Fletcher poked Kennard in the ribs. "Tanner'll skin us if we don't get the truck loaded up and back on time."

"Right, right." Kennard half-smiled at Moya and lifted his chin at Fell.

Fell did a chin-lift in return.

"Good to see you, Fell, and meet you, Moya." Fletcher grinned at them and chased after his brother toward the ranch and farm supply store.

"They seem to be bouncing back from the Scythe." In fact, she'd seen the two at Gatherings, but hadn't paid them any attention. Too young. Actually, most males seemed too young even when they were her age.

Patrin and Fell, though, sometimes seemed as if they were already in their forties.

A sound caught her ears, and she paused.

"A baby crying?" Fell looked around.

"Oh, over there." Moya pointed to a bench outside the grocery where one of the pack's new mothers appeared close to tears herself.

With Fell following, Moya hurried over. "Glenys, what's wrong?"

Glenys was in her mid-thirties with dark auburn hair cut short and pale skin. She visibly tried to stifle her tears as she cuddled her two infants on her lap. "It's just... I need to get groceries before the storm tomorrow, and I don't have enough hands."

"We have plenty. Give me one." Moya looked down at the tiny cubling, still so new as to have only wispy blond fuzz on his head. "Aren't you precious? This is Cadfan, right?"

Glenys' blue eyes lightened with a mama's pride. "Yes."

"Here, you hold him, Fell." She allowed no trace of inner laughter to show as she arranged the big warrior's arms to hold the infant properly. "Support his head like this. With all those muscles, you won't even notice his weight."

Glenys tensed as if she thought Fell would bury his fangs in Moya's neck.

Giving Fell a pat, Moya took Gruffudd, the dark-haired baby. "Don't worry, Glenys. Our beta might look mean, but he has a soft heart for females and cubs."

He was staring down at Cadfan with the most enchantingly worried, tender expression on his hard face.

After a moment, Glenys whispered, "Awww, who would have known."

"*Right?* Go on and do your shopping. We'll wait out here and have some quality cub time." Moya snuggled the infant closer, knowing Glenys could hear the happiness in her voice. "Thanks to the Scythe, our alpha and beta know *everything* about the needs of teenaged males, but nothing about younger cubs and females and seniors—and they want to learn."

Receiving a disbelieving look, Fell murmured, "Moya's right. We do."

"Oh." Glenys stared at Fell, simply shocked. And wasn't that an indication of how intolerable the last couple of alphas had been.

A crease appeared in Fell's cheek. "Go shop. We'll be here."

Glenys' relief changed her whole face. "Wow. Okay, thank you!" She disappeared into the store on light feet.

Fell frowned after her. "She doesn't have help?"

"The cubs are Gatherbred, and she doesn't have mates. I think a couple of her friends are helping her, but... It can be embarrassing to always need help." Moya kissed the infant's tiny dark head, enjoying the milky baby fragrance. "The pack in my town..."

When her voice died, Fell tilted his head and prompted, "The pack under the alpha who messed up your life?"

She stilled and had to remind herself it was in the past. "Yes. He was a good alpha except for his obsession with me. Mothers with cubs got some financial aid and cub-sitting help from the pack. Stuff like that. André's trying to get the whole clan organized to support the shifters who need help. Nonetheless, a wolf pack should do better."

"Yeah." Fell smiled at her. "Breanne said alpha females coordinate help for females and cubs. Like you already do."

"I do some, yes." She couldn't order other wolves around. Those were alpha female responsibilities. She mostly volunteered herself and her friends.

If she was the alpha, she'd have the power to set up a support system for pack members needing help. "I might have to call Breanne," she muttered.

"There you go." As Cadfan waved an arm in the air, Fell touched it. His thumb was almost as big as the tiny fist. "So fucking little."

Watching him with the infant was melting her ovaries. And more... Even though almost dark of the moon, her desire for him was reaching full moon levels.

Fell rubbed his knuckles over Moya's cheek with the same tenderness as he'd touched the cub's hand. "I like seeing you with a baby."

After kissing Gruffudd's little head, she rubbed her cheek against Fell's callused fingers. How could he be so deadly...and so sweet? "I feel the same way about you."

When she met his gaze, the love in his eyes filled her world.

---

After Glenys finished shopping, they helped her carry her groceries home and returned to do their own grocery shopping.

Leaving the store, Moya frowned at Fell and the three canvas market bags on his arm. He'd let her carry only one.

*Males.* His over-protectiveness was annoying...yet she also felt all warm and loved. How confusing.

In the darkening town square, the streetlights flickered on, one by one. Fell scowled up at them. "Short days suck."

He was so cute. "Tomorrow will be worse, what with a blizzard and at least a foot of snow." Moya switched the bag to her other arm. "I was enjoying snow-free days."

"Easier on paws. Mateo talked about a sledding day?"

"Oh, right. The town's cordoning off a street for the younglings to sled on." She grinned. "Poor Talitha and Eileen. The cubs are going to come home cold and drenched."

When Fell made a rather disgusted sound, Moya was startled.

He didn't like sledding? Oh, he was looking off to the left, and she followed his gaze.

A fair number of people were around the square, especially near the bar and Shamrock. More at the grocery.

And uh-oh, there were three females heading straight for them. Tall Deidre, the latest of Brett's short-lived alpha females, was accompanied by short, chronically pouting Cosette, who'd briefly been one of Roger's alpha females. Gretchen's sister, Sarah, walked beside them.

"Moya!" Deidre shouted. "You effing *slut*."

Ignoring Fell's low growl, Moya asked politely in her professional storekeeper's tone, "What seems to be the problem?"

Deidre didn't lower her voice. "You're the problem. Acting like you're the alpha female."

Fell's growl grew louder. "This is a public place. Keep it down."

Deidre flinched, obviously not having realized Moya's companion was their beta. But, as typical with self-absorbed individuals, she barreled ahead anyway. "You're not the alpha female, Moya. I am."

Moya blamed Roger and Brett for this idiocy. They'd told each mate-of-the-month she was the alpha female. As if a male could bestow the title. "Did you challenge the previous alpha female?"

Surprised, Deidre glanced at Cosette. "No. When Brett took over, Cosette, uh…"

Cosette wrinkled her nose. "Brett's a real maggot, so I quit."

"So, Deidre, you think you got the title simply for fucking Brett at the time?" Moya deliberately used the unattractive human term for mating. "Are you performing the responsibilities of the alpha female—setting up cubsitting, arranging help for our older pack members, checking on all our females to—"

"Whyever would I do that?" Deidre was wide-eyed.

"Alpha is more than a title," Fell snapped.

"Alas, this is true." Moya gave her a sympathetic smile. "You have to protect and care for all the members of the pack."

Exchanging an appalled look with Cosette, Deidre shook her head. "I don't... I don't want to."

"Of course you don't." Moya smiled at the young female who was just twenty-two. Despite being only twenty-four, between the trauma in Stanislaus Territory and running a business, Moya felt much, much older. "This is your time to have fun. Someday maybe, you'll want those responsibilities. For now, I'm taking them on."

Deidre nodded, then frowned at losing the respected title.

"Do I need to challenge you?" Moya looked her straight in the eyes, showing she'd flatten the female if needed. Even if Deidre was half a foot taller.

"No, uh-uh, no way. I'm good." Deidre bowed her head slightly. "Alpha." She did the same with Fell. "Beta."

She dragged her companions away fast, as if a gnome had fastened its teeth in her tail.

As Moya and Fell headed toward the walkway beside Espresso Books, Fell was quoting under his breath, "'*No, uh-uh, no way*'."

"Shut up." With a growl, she pinched his very tight butt.

The gnome-brain chuckled.

Although she scowled at him, inside she was filled with happiness. Because when he first arrived, he'd been almost completely silent and never even smiled.

She moved the grocery bag to her other arm. Honestly, the damn thing was growing heavier. "I can't believe you talked me into making cherry pie. You're going to learn to bake this week."

"Sure," he said agreeably. His eyes crinkled with his smile. "Cooking means eating. I'm in." Glancing down, he stopped.

"What?"

A gnome's beady black eyes stared at them from behind the storm drain grating.

Taking a piece of pastry from his pocket, Fell set it on the grate.

A second later, a small hand swiped the pastry.

"*You* feed them too?"

He shrugged. "Patrin couldn't today. And it's cold out."

*Awww.*

"You and Patrin, the toughest of the tough. So deadly you can take on entire legions of humans and win." She snorted. "Complete tenderhearted softies."

Fell glowered at her—and she busted out laughing.

As they moved past the gnome, she noticed the three females had joined Gretchen in front of the diner.

"Gretchen!" Invading her sister's space, Sarah shouted, "You are a total *loser*."

"I'm not." Gretchen retreated a step, her fair face growing even whiter.

Around the square, people were turning to look.

"You're worthless at running the B&B. And Brett says Cosette was his alpha female. Not you. And now it's Moya. Not *you*." Sarah's voice grew sharp enough to flay skin. "If Mother were alive, she would be ashamed of you."

Gretchen's shoulders hunched as if being physically whipped.

*"If Mother were alive..." Oh, no.* Had Gretchen lost her mother? Moya couldn't imagine. And that left the poor female with only the insufferable Sarah for family.

Gretchen's chin rose. "I won't let Mother down." Turning, she headed straight for Moya.

"Oh Gods, this isn't going to go well." Moya put out an arm to stop Fell from confronting the blonde wolf. "I got this, Fell."

"You don't need to."

*Awww, he is worried for me.*

"This kind of problem comes with the title, right?" She glanced quickly at the ground, checking the footing. Just in case. "Hi, Gretchen. How are you today?"

"Being alpha female is earned, not given." Gretchen tossed her blonde hair back. "You haven't earned it. No one wants you as our alpha female."

The offensive statement raised Moya's hackles. No, this was just Gretchen being rude. Moya knew only a few females wouldn't want her as alpha. Very few. "All right, I hear your objection although I'm not sure where it's coming from. How did you earn the title when Roger was alpha and you were alpha female?"

After a second, Gretchen's fair skin flushed. Because she hadn't earned it—Roger had simply informed the pack she was alpha female, and since being alpha female meant getting ties to the alpha, no one else wanted it. "You...you're a stinking mongrel."

Moya stepped forward to go face-to-face. Unfortunately, she was quite a few inches shorter. *Why are there so many tall shifters in the world?* "Are you challenging me?" She hesitated, then added, "I feel it's only fair to tell you—I've been taught how to fight, and I'm good at it."

Gretchen froze, glanced at Sarah, and her mouth tightened. "Yes. I challenge."

"Okay then. I'll let the wolves know there's a formal challenge, say, in an hour. Anyone who's free can follow us into the forest to witness." Moya pulled out her phone.

"No." Gretchen crossed her arms over her chest. "Right here, right now."

*I am trying to be reasonable. Can't she see that?* Resigned to a fight, Moya glanced around. "All right. We have Deirdre, Cosette, and Fell. We'll grab Riona and Ena from the shops for added witnesses. We can fight out of sight behind the grocery."

"Do it now, you cowardly bitch," Sarah called.

Moya wrinkled her nose. "I don't know if she's yelling at me or you, but I'm sorry you have such a mean sister."

Gretchen's eyes dampened for a second, before she shook her head. "Don't talk about my sister. Ever. We fight here. Right here."

Even as Moya turned her head to ensure no humans were around, Gretchen swung her fist at Moya's head.

The attempted punch was slow, clumsy, ineffective, and Moya blocked it without thinking. "Gretch, seriously, I don't want to hurt you."

Gretchen growled. "Fight me or submit." She swung again, harder.

*Gods, the influence of peers and families.* With an unexpected sense of pity, Moya punched Gretchen in her flat abdomen and followed with an uppercut to her chin.

*Ow!*

That perfect chin was really hard. She shook her stinging hand and ignored the *huff-huff-huff* of Fell's almost silent laughter.

On her butt, Gretchen rubbed her jaw and stiffened. Because, aside from Sarah and her companions, every shifter in the square was laughing and cheering. Humiliation showed in her face. "They prefer you? But I'm...I'm way more beautiful."

"Beautiful face; ugly character," Fell said under his breath.

From the way Gretchen stiffened, she heard him.

Moya held out her hand. "Let's get you up and on your feet."

Mouth tight, Gretchen glanced around, then took the assistance and even let Moya steady her for a second.

"All right, what's going on here?" Bron strode across the square. The Chief of Police badge on her leather coat glinted under the streetlights.

*Oh, won't this be a fine day. Ramón, Zorion, can you bail me out of jail?* "Um, hi, Chief."

"Evening, Chief." Fell pointed to Gretchen whose face had gone pale. "She challenged and lost." He pointed to Moya. "She won."

Bron's mouth twitched upward before she regained control. Her hardass attitude was becoming legendary in the territory. "Wolves, settle your pack business outside of town."

Gretchen nodded.

Exhaling in relief, Moya nodded. "Yes, Chief. Sorry."

With a huff of annoyance, Bron stalked away, past the other three females.

Tears in her eyes, Gretchen walked slowly toward her B&B. Not toward her sister, Moya noticed.

"Loser." With a sneer, Sarah followed after Gretchen.

*Great family there.* Moya felt another moment of pity for Gretchen. The female had done a lot of spiteful things, but no one should be tormented like that.

Was there a way to help?

"C'mon, Alpha." Fell grabbed all the grocery sacks in one hand.

*Oh, wow, I'm officially the alpha female of the pack.* The reality bubbled up inside her, making her want to laugh...or flee.

He slung an arm around Moya's shoulders. "We'll ice your knuckles. Didn't we teach you to aim for soft spots?"

Moya snorted. "Fell, you taught me to aim for the *fatal* spots. I'm not going to kill members of the pack."

"Oh. Right." They walked a few steps. "In that case, good aim."

"Thank you." A couple of steps later, she caught the scent of pure lust.

"Fell?" Looking up, she met his gaze.

There was so much heat in his eyes that fire licked through her body. She looked down and saw a thick bulge in his jeans. "Bad wolf. Bad, bad wolf."

"Not my fault." With an almost silent laugh, he pulled her closer. "You're fucking sexy when you fight. Supper will be late tonight."

## CHAPTER TWENTY-SEVEN

With Moya and Fell talking quietly at the table, Patrin settled into his chair, sipped his coffee, and soaked up the warmth of the coffee shop. Behind the counter, Talitha and Renee were discussing various kinds of sleds with a couple of humans waiting for their drinks.

Quiet Celtic music came through the speakers. Hanging foliage plants and small corner bushes provided a reminder of summer in contrast to the snow-covered world outside. Moya had told him they'd been trying for the feel of a cozy wolf den.

Yesterday, a blizzard had dumped a scat-load of snow on the area...on dark of the moon, no less. Even hellhounds stayed home in this kind of weather.

This morning, the coffee shop bustled with people seeking contact. And caffeine, one of nature's best gifts.

Biting laughter drew his attention to a nearby table where Sarah was making fun of the bruise on Gretchen's fair-skinned face. They certainly didn't look alike, one tall and blonde, the other short and curvy.

Neither could compare to Moya.

Smiling, Patrin rested his arm on the back of her chair so he could play with the little wolf's hair. Damned if it wasn't difficult not to touch her. Everything inside him wanted to stay close enough to breathe her in.

And when they were apart, his chest felt as if he had a hole in it.

As if she could hear him, Moya leaned closer and rubbed her cheek on his biceps. "Okay, I sent out your request. Jens, Riona, and Lucius agreed to check on our senior pack members who live on the north half of town."

"No problem with them getting off work?"

"With the snow everywhere, neither the diner nor the ranch store will be busy today." The way her pretty lips tilted up couldn't be ignored.

He indulged himself with a quick kiss. "And the south?"

"The construction crew has the day off. Jalen and Alana will go. And even though he's a cat, Jarlath wanted to go with his mates."

All three were sturdy shifters and could handle anything the snowbound seniors might need. "Perfect. What did you plan for the three of us?" Patrin asked.

Fell answered, "The ones farther out of town."

"We're visiting two seniors down Argonaut to the south. They're just too stubborn to come in for storms." Moya half-grinned. "I'll probably be just like that when I'm nearing a hundred."

Patrin exchanged smiles with his brother. "Yeah, you will be." The vision of Moya at a hundred, tiny and wizened, filled his heart with tenderness and love.

"You're not supposed to agree, rude alpha." She jabbed an elbow into his thankfully healed-up side, making him grin. "*Anyway*... In case they didn't stock up, we'll take food and a couple of cans of gasoline. We can cut up and bring in firewood. Clear snow if needed. Ethel will need to reach her hen house."

Patrin grinned. "Sounds like fun." And fucking rewarding.

Caring for the pack—*their* pack—satisfied something deep inside him. "How long will it take?"

"A while, I'm afraid. Although Argonaut's been plowed, they're on private roads and drives." Moya bit her lip as she calculated. "If we leave soon, we should get to the first place around ten, the second around noon, and be headed back to town around one-thirty."

"And be back around two-thirty? Sounds great. Leaves us time to join the older cubs on the sledding hill." Anticipation rose inside Patrin. Cubs shrieking with laughter and excitement—could anything be more fun? "I promised Mateo and Alvaro we'd be there."

A corner of Fell's mouth tipped upward, showing he was looking forward to the sledding day. They both missed being with young shifters.

Even better, the Rainier Territory younglings hadn't been tormented or groomed to be soldiers. They laughed freely and often—as cublings should.

With the bullying stopped, the wolfpack pups were happier too.

He picked up Moya's hand and kissed it. Life was good—and she made it better.

Smiling back, she ran her hand through his hair.

"Ugh, how nauseating. I'm not going to visit the sledding street if those smelly mongrels are there." Sarah rose. Ignoring Gretchen's hissed "Sarah, that's the *alpha*," she stalked out of the coffee shop.

Gretchen followed.

A growl sounded in the room, and Patrin realized it came from Terence, one of the wolves sitting with Ramón, Zorion, and a few others from their construction crew. The young wolf looked furious.

Rather than angry, Zorion was grinning. He clutched Ramón's

arm and said in a high falsetto, "Mongrels? *Ewww*, I can't stand stinky, howling mongrels."

"Bro, I hate to share this with you but"—Ramón patted Zorion's hand—"if our sister is a mongrel, what does that make us?"

Zorion's eyes widened. "*Nooo*." He sniffed his armpits and wailed, "I, too, am a stinky mongrel. Just let me die." He pressed the back of his hand to his forehead and swooned.

The customers in the coffee shop all roared with laughter, even young Terence. The humans had no clue as to the underlying meaning of the banter—but were laughing too.

"Fuck." Fell actually grinned as he eyed Zorion and Ramón. "You grew up with those two?"

"Uh-huh. You should pity me."

"No wonder you can deal with just about anything," Patrin said and set her to giggling.

He could listen to her laugh all day long.

As he finished off his coffee, his phone dinged. The display showed it was his boss at the Bullwhacker. "Hey, Nik, what's up?"

"I could use your help in the back room today. A delivery came in before the snowstorm. The drivers were in a hurry and piled everything just inside the door. With my back acting up, I can't get the boxes moved."

Ah, the ugly part of being human. Daonain not only lived longer, but usually stayed healthier until the final year's rapid deterioration. Patrin glanced at Moya and Fell, who would have heard Nik's loud voice.

Fell shrugged. "We can check on the seniors without you. Go help him."

Moya nodded her agreement.

*Okay then.* "Sure, Nik. I'll be over in a little while." Extra money wouldn't hurt, even if he, Fell, and the other shifter-soldiers had a decent cushion from raiding Scythe accounts.

As he pocketed his phone, a frisson of worry ran up his spine.

Forests and mountains after a fresh snowfall could be risky. Two people seemed inadequate.

He eyed Fell. "Considering the amount of work Moya has planned, you should take someone to replace me."

Before Fell could answer, Ramón called, "Yo, sis. We gave the crew the day off. Zorion and I can go with you."

Patrin nodded. "That'll work. I want you safe."

"You, Top Dog, are as bad as my brothers." She thumped her head on his shoulder in pretend annoyance...and he could hear the love in her voice.

---

"Thanks for stopping, guys." In the back seat, Moya leaned over to give Fell a quick kiss, jumped out of Ramon's big SUV and headed for the nearest bush.

Climbing out to stretch his legs as he waited, Fell could still feel the light, soft press of her lips on his. She loved him—and had no trouble showing it.

Would he ever accept the glory of that?

Smiling, he looked around. The green and black branches of the surrounding forest had bowed beneath the new snow. Pristine white covered the steep slopes of the mountains on each side of the valley they were driving through, and the air was so crisp and clear, it almost snapped.

This territory was fucking beautiful.

"Hey, Fell." Ramón got out and leaned against the SUV. "Be warned. Our sister has a bladder the size of a pin cushion."

"Or smaller." Zorion joined them. "We shouldn't have let her drink any of the coffee we brought."

Fell huffed a laugh. Moya's littermates probably drove her crazy. Living with Patrin, he knew the feeling. "If we need to stop every five minutes, then that's what we'll do." His tone was light, but he meant every word. Having her along was worth any inconvenience.

"I...see." Laughter gone, Ramón narrowed his eyes. "As long as we have you here, what exactly are your intentions toward our littermate?"

Beside Ramón, Zorion had an unreadable expression.

*Interesting.* The Moreno brothers sounded like Fell and Patrin had when Darcy was falling in love. Now he knew how annoyed Gawain and Owen must have felt.

It was good the little wolf had littermates to guard her.

"Our intentions are..." Anxiety traced a cold path up his spine. "We went to a blademage."

Zorion drew in an audible breath. "For lifemating bracelets?"

Fell nodded, unable to speak. All their hopes were bound up in those thin bands that held the very essence of the Mother.

*What if Moya says no?*

*What if her brothers say no?*

Fell tensed, preparing for a battle he couldn't win.

"Well..." After a second of looking as if he'd been clubbed in the head, Ramón straightened. "Okay then."

Fell stared at him. *What?*

"Yeah." Zorion's mouth curved into a wide smile. "Welcome to the family."

And now, Fell felt as if he was the one who'd been clubbed.

---

Standing near the sledding hill, Gretchen watched the younglings climb on bright-colored sleds and tubes and fly down the snowy slope, screaming and laughing.

Since the closed off street was just outside the parking lot on the other side of the square, she'd been able to hear all the shrieking and laughter. How could she resist taking a look for herself?

She wasn't the only one. It seemed as if a lot of the town shifters were here.

The Cosantir had just arrived with Sky and Talam, the two cubs he and his mates had taken in. His *lifemates*.

Her mood soured. At one time, she'd taken it for granted *she* would be the lifemate of one of the Gods-called. Mother had said it was the destiny of her daughters.

But none of the Cosantirs, cahirs, or even the healers had pursued Gretchen.

She was beautiful and behaved just as her mother ordered, yet nothing had worked. Even here, in Gretchen's own town, when André, Niall, and Madoc arrived, they'd chosen Heather.

*Not me. Why didn't they choose me?*

Thankfully, Heather hadn't come to the sledding hill. There was no fondness between them.

*No, be honest—she hates me.*

Gretchen shook her head. She'd never cared before what anyone thought of her. Especially other females. They were just...competition.

But more and more, she noticed how no one...liked her.

She watched Eileen arrive and get cheerfully greeted and hugged. And then Noreen, who ran the wilderness tour store, got the same kind of welcome. They were all chatting together near the big bonfire.

No one even spoke to Gretchen.

Turning her back on the adults, she watched the cubs sled down the hill. An aching tightness closed around her ribs.

Years ago, she'd been the cub laughing in joy at new-fallen snow. Squished in a laundry basket, she flown down the hill behind their house, screaming at the thrill. The cold wind had stung her face and blown her hair around, and at the bottom of the slope, she'd rolled out of the basket, giggling her head off. She'd been free and happy and alive.

But Sarah had seen. Sarah had told their mother.

Remembering what came after...Gretch shivered, not from the cold but from a place deep in her bones. *"My girls are the prettiest of all the female cubs. They don't get dirty or wet or act like...like disgusting males."* The white of the snow had turned to blackest darkness—as the basement root cellar door closed. Sobbing, Gretchen had fallen onto the cold concrete, begging to get out. But the root cellar was fully insulated and at the back of the house, so no one could hear her screams and pleas. Or her whimpering as the hours passed.

A whooping laugh snapped her back into the present, and she shuddered. Arms around her waist, she headed back to the B&B. Away from the memories.

She was beautiful now—the most beautiful in the territory. Surely, Mother would be pleased.

*I'm happy now...right? Right?*

She didn't feel happy.

And Mother had gone on to whatever next life there was.

Entering the B&B, she removed her boots, hung up her coat, and smiled at the light scent of cinnamon in the air. She'd noticed how wonderful Rebecca's B&B in Cold Creek always smelled, so she'd done the same here.

She ran a finger over the top of the dining room buffet. No dust. Good.

But in the kitchen, her sister had left dirty dishes and food strewn over the table and counters. Nothing new there. All their lives, Sarah had the manners of a gnome, digging through garbage. Wherever she went, disorder followed.

If anyone complained about the mess, Sarah blamed Gretchen.

With a sigh, Gretchen did a quick clean-up.

When Mother sold her house and moved to Elder Village, she asked her daughters what they wanted. Sarah wanted money. Gretchen requested the B&B, and Mother had signed it over with the proviso that Gretchen would use some of the profits to bring her food every six months.

Grethen had faithfully done so. Although...it had been difficult. When tourist season ended, the B&B was often empty, and Gretchen had to skimp on her own food to provide Mother's provisions.

And then Mother would scold her for getting skinny and ugly. Because beauty was all that mattered.

She found Sarah in the living room, and thank the Gods, the B&B was empty, because the mess she'd made would drive guests right out of the place.

"Where have you been?" Sarah scowled. "There's nothing good to eat."

"I went to watch the cubs sledding on the hill."

"Cubs, ew." Sarah wrinkled her nose. "What kind of idiot are you to want to look at stupid younglings?"

Gretchen could feel her shoulders hunching against the words.

During winter, Ina Donnelly hung homemade suet-seed balls behind the grocery. Birds would peck, peck, peck away at the ball, slowly reducing it to a formless lump. How much of Sarah's constant criticism could Gretchen take before her spirit was eroded to nothing?

She straightened her spine. "As it happens, I like watching cubs and being outside. It's a pretty day."

"Gods, you sound stupid. Like a menial."

Gretchen flinched. Mother had taught them to use a high, breathy voice, a haughty one so everyone understood they were special. With a naturally low voice, she felt like a squeaky chipmunk when she talked the way Mother wanted.

Taking a breath, she used the correct voice. "Sarah, I asked you not to make a mess in the areas guests will use."

"Eh, go chase your tail." Sarah's upper lip rose into a sneer. "I'm leaving soon enough—to live in the biggest house in town."

"You mean the house Brett and Caleb were renting?" Back when Pete was Cosantir, he and Roger lived there. It had stood empty for a while, but Brett and Caleb moved in right after Brett became alpha. The mutt had probably used pack funds to pay the rent.

"Yes, Brett's house." Sarah finger-combed her long brunette hair. "He and Caleb like me. A lot. I'll make a great alpha female."

"What? If you want to be alpha, why did you push me to challenge Moya?"

Sarah smirked. "Because you'd give me the title without me having to fight for it."

It was probably true. Frustrated anger made Gretchen's eyes burn, and she spat out the words, "You're behind on the news. Brett doesn't have a house here. He isn't alpha any longer. Patrin is—and he kicked Brett and Caleb out of the territory."

Sarah snorted. "My sweet Brett and Caleb will remove the two wanna-be-top-dogs today."

"They'll challenge Patrin and Fell? That's suicide. Patrin wiped the ground with Brett." And no one in their right mind would take on Fell. Caleb sure wasn't that brave.

"Oh, they won't challenge."

"Then...what?"

"Didn't you hear the alpha and beta talking in the coffee shop? They're going to visit some old shifters down toward Mt. Rainier." Sarah patted her hair and smirked. "I called Brett to tell him and give him their schedule. On their drive back... Brett said it'll be like what humans call *shooting a sitting goose* or something."

Gretchen stared at her sister in disbelief—and horror. Of course, Brett would murder the alpha in such a foul way; he'd already tried once. But her sister was helping?

"You set Patrin and Fell up to die. *Why?*"

Sarah face twisted into a malicious expression. "I offered the alpha and beta my favor at the Gathering, and they turned me down. *Me.*"

Her words were so familiar. Gretchen had felt that way, said such things when *she'd* been turned down. After all, Mother said, over and over, they were entitled to anything they wanted. Because they were special. Beautiful.

Is a person beautiful or special when she helps in a murder?

*This...this isn't right.*

Gretchen stood for a moment. What could she do? Turning, she almost ran out of the B&B. On the porch, she pulled out her phone and...

*I don't have anyone's numbers.*

What could she do?

Looking around frantically, she saw the Cosantir strolling toward the Shamrock Restaurant.

"André!"

---

*By Herne's hide and hooves, this day sucks.*

In the back of the SUV beside Moya, Fell stared out at the surrounding forest until his eyes burned. His shoulders were taut with anticipation as he held the rifle across his lap. Streaming through the open window, the air chilled his fingers on the cold metal.

The others in the vehicle were silent.

At least they'd had a warning about the potential ambush.

They'd been leaving Ethel's house when the Cosantir called to say Brett and Caleb planned to attack—and, once again, from a distance.

*The cowardly spawn of cockroaches.* No Daonain worthy of the name would shoot at another shifter. Even ferals were killed face to face.

But apparently, an ambush it was.

There were several options, even staying with Ethel for another day. But today, they knew approximately where Brett and Caleb would be. Personally, Fell would rather deal with them now rather than have the boggarts attack when no one was ready.

Supposedly, the targets were him and Patrin. What if the pond scum went after Moya? What if she was alone then? Fell growled under his breath at the thought. Yes, they needed to eliminate the mongrels now.

Fell had told André not to send anyone. Why risk Brett and Caleb shooting at someone else? Despite being furious, the Cosantir had eventually agreed to let them handle this without putting others at risk.

Up ahead, the light brightened as the road left the forest for an open valley. "Stop."

He wished the little wolf had agreed to remain at Ethel's.

So fucking stubborn.

Ramón braked the SUV to a halt. "See something?"

"No." Fell's voice came out a harsh rasp. "But out there is where *I'd* set up an ambush."

They were about halfway back to town. On the left rose a steep treeless mountainside, scattered rock outcroppings breaking the expanse of white. On the right was probably a creek bed since there were clusters of firs alongside the road.

"You think they'll set up behind one of the trees?" Zorion asked. "Or in the rocks?"

Ramón narrowed his eyes at the fir trees. "The rocks."

"Bro, neither Brett nor Caleb can shoot worth shit. It's a joke in the pack." Zorion waved at the fir trees. "With poor aim, they'll want to be close."

"You'd think, but Brett's a chicken-livered soul." Ramón tapped his fingers on the steering wheel. "He'd worry about not being able to shoot us all before one of us reaches him."

"Good point," Moya said. "Patrin and Fell terrify him."

Zorion made a disparaging sound in his throat. "So to stay safe, they'll shoot a whole lot of bullets from a long way off. Yeah, bet you're right."

Fell glanced at the two in front with respect. Ramón had

almost as good a talent at reading people as Moya did. Zorion looked as steady as an old oak tree.

He studied the open area and the trees. No sign of anyone in the vast whiteness. If it'd been him and he intended to use the mountainside, he'd flatten out behind one of the stone outcroppings—and not be visible until he took a shot. "No help for it. Go on."

As the SUV moved forward, Fell took Moya's mittened hand and felt the fine tremble of her fingers.

She squeezed his hand and—like a trooper—continued to scan her half of the landscape.

Ramón kept the car at a speed slow enough they could dive out if needed. "You know what? They won't expect return fire. This might be fun."

Actually, Fell almost agreed...if Moya hadn't been there. Risking her...not acceptable.

From the tightness of Ramón's jaw, he knew fun wasn't the right word. The chances were high one or all of them would die. But much like Patrin, the male made jokes before battle to dispel tension and keep muscles loose enough to move.

*Good male.*

And he had a point. Fell had a rifle.

Shifters rarely owned weapons. However, Ethel had grown old enough she couldn't chase after the predators eating her chickens as most shifters would. When André warned them of the ambush, she had this old Winchester 1873 to loan them.

The SUV traveled on.

They were exposed on the left now.

The hair rose on the nape of Fell's neck. They were being watched.

Something struck the side of the car even as the crack of a rifle sounded.

"Out!" Fell yelled. Aiming at a puff of smoke upslope, he

snapped off a shot to force the shooter to duck. To give the Morenos time to escape.

With her brothers, Moya bailed out and sprinted for the trees. Lunging across the back seat, Fell followed out the same door.

The shooting started again. *Crack, crack.* Out in the open, he could only run. He zigzagged one way, another. Almost there. *Crack, crack, crack.*

His right leg buckled, and he staggered and dropped to one knee. His thigh burned with pain.

"Fell!" Moya dashed back out from the trees.

*No. She mustn't.* "Stay under cover."

Ramón was right behind her. They grabbed him and ran for cover, dodging behind two giant fir trees.

A bullet *thunked* into the tree, spraying bark everywhere.

*By the God, I'm still alive.* That was unexpected. Because of Moya. And Ramón.

Half in shock, he rolled onto his belly and checked the others. All safe and hunkered down behind the trees.

Despite being shot, the pain, the run, he still held the rifle— that'd been a painful, hard-won lesson of the Scythe. *Never drop your weapon, no matter what.*

Working the action, he ejected the used round and chambered a fresh cartridge. *Ready.*

"Fell." Zorion's gaze was on the mountain. "They ran to the rocks on the right."

Gritting his teeth against the searing pain, Fell went up onto a knee, easing out to look toward the right. More bullets peppered the trees.

And there... Grayish-white smoke, almost invisible against the snow, drifted upward over a stand of rocks.

Fell glanced at Zorion and nodded. *Well-played, Moreno brothers.* Ramón had come for him while Zorion had served as spotter. "Got them."

Easing out just far enough, Fell shot, worked the lever, shot.

Over and over. His bullets sparked against the exposed rock formation.

"I don't see them," Moya said in a low voice. "How can you hit them?"

"Don't have to," Fell answered and started reloading the rifle.

Ramón's laugh held a dark satisfaction. "He's peppering them with rock splinters. They're not brave enough to hold up under that kind of barrage."

No, they weren't.

Far up the steep mountainside, two figures darted out from behind the outcropping. Running as hard as they could, Brett and Caleb moved horizontally across the long expanse of white.

Zorion had a vicious grin as he commented, "No cover. Think you can hit them, Fell?"

"Oh yeah." Fell straightened, lifting the rifle to his shoulder.

Before he could fire, the air filled with a cracking sound. One different from the ear-splitting noise of rifles—the *whoomph* made every cell in his body tense.

A few times in their lives, he and Patrin had heard the sound of a snowpack collapsing, marking the start of an avalanche.

"Oh fuck." There was a heavy load of fresh snow on the mountain. The two big males were running on top of it, impacting it hard with each step.

"Herne help them, they triggered an avalanche," Zorion whispered.

Using the tree for balance, Fell could only stare at the surreal picture. Everything was white—and was moving. With an ear-splitting rumble, the mountainside poured downward—and swallowed the two dark figures like quicksand.

With a choked sound, Moya wrapped her arms around him and buried her head against his shoulder.

Holding her, knowing she was safe, his own world felt as if it steadied.

Still hugging him, she called, "Ramón, get the first aid kit, please."

"Will do." Footfalls crunched in the snow.

"Hey, Ramón." Zorion came from near the SUV. "Do you think your SUV will even start again?"

"Bro, it better start. It's a long way back."

Fell considered the pain in his thigh. The miles back to town. About the same distance to Ethel's.

*Oh. Fuck.*

---

Patrin had always loved the day after a blizzard when the entire world turned white. When snow covered tree branches and roofs. When every sound seemed clearer.

Like the yelling of the cubs on the sledding hill past the west parking lot.

Reaching the top of Paydirt Avenue, he paused to appreciate how the townsfolk had set up the area for their younglings. A bonfire blazed in an empty lot next to the sawhorses blocking the street. A couple of older men fed the fire from a tall stack of firewood.

In the hottest flames, three salamanders spiraled upward in an exuberant dance. He grinned. A huge fire outside in freezing weather—of course, the elementals were pleased.

A few cubs and adults sat on wooden benches and warmed their hands. A big metal kettle near the coals was probably heating water for hot chocolate.

Spotting a table with food, Patrin made an immediate detour and snagged a cookie covered in red frosting. It was gone in three bites. So damn tasty. Could life get any better?

And then he found out it could.

"Patrin, you came!" Mateo halted a few feet away, obviously

striving to look grown-up. Probably influenced by human idiocy of looking cool. "It's, ah, good to see you."

Alvaro, though, ran right up and thumped into Patrin.

Grinning, Patrin gave him a hearty hug.

When he stepped away, Patrin moved closer to Mateo and kept his voice low. "Shifters, especially wolves, enjoy affection. We're not human and don't want to be. So...want a hug?" He opened his arms.

Mateo lunged forward, wrapped his arms tightly around Patrin's waist—and clung.

Oh yeah, the cub had wanted a cuddle. Patrin gave the youngling a good hug.

The world was changing, and the Daonain were no longer isolated. Cubs were attending human schools to learn to fit in and master technology. But learning the human ways didn't mean shifters had to embrace them.

"So, lads, let's see you fly down a hill. Have you got sleds?" Patrin eyed the two...things...the cubs had abandoned nearby.

The ski shop's owner, Tyrone, was delighted when the town wanted to rent sledding equipment for the day and had apparently provided a huge variety.

"Mine's a snow tube." Mateo picked up the tow line of an inflatable PVC tube the size and shape of a tractor tire. Handles were embedded in the sides.

"I got a sled." Alvaro grabbed the pull rope for a bright yellow, plastic sled reminiscent of an old-fashioned wooden toboggan.

He followed them to the top and studied the various runs. The middle tracks went straight down. But on each outside edge, the compacted snow showed the course had twists and turns.

Several cubs, from ten years old to mid-teens, waited their turn.

"Patrin, good to see you here," Niall called. On one side, the cahir and his mate Heather were helping younglings as needed.

On the other side, Eileen worked with Noreen from the

wilderness tour store. More adults, including a few humans, were scattered here and there. The cubs were adequately supervised.

With a frown, Patrin realized some of the cubs hadn't joined in but were clustered off to one side. Too nervous to try sledding?

"Our turn, brawd. Let's go!" Mateo jumped on his tube, Alvaro on his sled, and the two pushed off together, screaming their way down the slope.

To Patrin's surprise, Niall sat down on an unused toboggan and then frowned. "I think I need an extra rider. C'mere, you." He beckoned over one of the timid cubs and settled the lad between his long legs. "Give us a shove, Patrin."

Patrin pushed—and by the Gods, the cahir was heavy. "You need to get on a diet, Niall."

The cahir's hearty laughter broke out and turned to a whoop as they picked up speed. The cub with him was giggling in between shrill shrieks.

Laughing, Patrin joined Heather. "Your mate has a hefty dose of craziness."

"He does." She grinned, then tilted her head at another stray cub who looked longingly at a bright yellow tube. Her voice dropped to a murmur. "Go help, Alpha. She's one of yours."

He still hadn't met all the pups in his pack.

Whether this girl was his or not, he'd never refuse the plea in the youngling's blue eyes. He walked over to the tube and smiled at her. "Hey, lass. I haven't been on a sled since I was younger than you. Want to ride one down with me so I'm not alone?"

Her eyes widened. "Alph—um, me?" When he pointed his finger at her in confirmation, her face lit up. "Yes!"

Patrin pushed the tube to the edge of the downward slope and sat at the back, his boots hanging over the rim.

With no hesitation, she plopped down in front of him.

A burly, grizzled male bent over to give them a push and murmured, "Gotta say, us cats are happy with the new pack leadership. Welcome, Alpha."

Before Patrin could respond, the old guy shoved hard.

They went shooting down the slope. The little mite in front of him screamed happily as they shot past a couple of slower sleds. The tube was incredibly fast—and bounced with every divot in the snow.

Thank fuck there was a long flat area at the bottom that allowed them to stop before reaching the parking lot.

The cub jumped off, grinning so wide every tooth showed. "That was so cool! Thank you, al—um."

"Call me Patrin, and what's your name?"

"Grainne."

"Ah, a good Celtic name." He grabbed the pull rope and started the long haul up the slope, listening as she chattered away beside him, all shyness wiped out by adrenaline. At the top, he smiled at her, then pointed to Mateo and Alvaro. "You two—put her between you on a toboggan. With the weight of three, you'll be the fastest out there."

"Ooooh, we will!" Mateo grinned and grabbed her hand. "C'mon, Grainne, Alvaro. Let's fly!"

There, one shy pup launched.

Before he could find another, Jens walked over with Riona, an energetic wolf in her twenties. They both bowed their heads slightly. Jens kept his voice low. "Alpha, our three finished checking on our older pack members. We handed out food to a couple of them and shoveled sidewalks and drives."

"No problems?" Patrin asked, with a touch of guilt. He'd essentially ordered the pack members to work.

"None." Riona shook her head. "I'm so glad you sent us. Clarence didn't have nearly enough food. And Ruby would've been stuck inside. The snow had drifted halfway up her front door."

Jen's expression was rueful. "They were so damned grateful, and we should've been looking out for all of them, before this. They're pack and part of us."

Warmth filled Patrin's chest. They got it. "Yes. We're *all* needed if we're to be strong."

Their faces grew more serious as they took in his words, but... the light in their eyes didn't dim. "Yes, Alpha," Jens murmured, and they took themselves off.

Leaving space for Jalen and Alana, who were also waiting to give their report.

After they finished, Patrin was free—and feeling incredible. He'd missed leading, looking after everyone, protecting them all. There was nothing as fulfilling.

His pack was coming together, faster and better than he'd expected. They were good wolves.

And this town... He smiled at the humans and shifters who were watching to ensure the younglings had a safe, fun time.

*This is a good town. A good territory.*

Still smiling, he walked back to Heather. "Any more cubs who need a paw held?"

---

Moya shook her head as she crouched to help Fell remove his pants.

As Zorion had feared, after being shot full of holes, the SUV refused to start. Ramón had filled the air with impressively inventive swearing. They'd be running back to town.

But how could Fell run?

"Oh, your leg doesn't look good." At the sight of the blood, she felt her stomach clench. Regaining her feet, she rested her hand on his shoulder, just needing to...touch him. To feel the warmth of his skin, to know he was alive. Gods, she'd been scared for him.

The bullet had struck mid-thigh, along the side. Nothing essential, except he had no fat on his body, which meant the gouge went through muscle. It must hurt every time he put weight on that leg. "Why don't you stay here, and we'll send a—"

"No, little wolf." His jaw turned so hard she could see the line of muscle. "Where you go, I go." He tossed his pants into the SUV. Pulling her against his powerful frame, he kissed her long and slow. "You scared the scat out of me when you left the trees and came back for me."

"Sounds fair. I had a heart attack when you got shot." And now her heart was so full of love and worry, it might burst all on its own. She rose on tiptoes to kiss him again. "I love you, you impossible wolf."

His eyes blazed, and his arms tightened around her to the point of pain.

"Yo, you two, trawsfur and let's move," Ramón called. "If we don't hurry, we'll be running in the dark."

Her brother had a point. "Aye. I wish we could call Patrin." Unfortunately, they were outside cell phone service area.

"Time to run." Fell eyed his leg and then trawsfurred. The sight of blood on his pale fur made her want to cry.

*No. Focus, girl.*

Moya stripped fast—*oh, so cold!*—and put her shirt and pants in the SUV.

After locking the doors, Ramón buried the keys behind the front wheel.

Moya shifted and joined Fell. He was gorgeous, all silvery wolf. Unable to help herself, she gave his muzzle a little lick.

With a rumbling, sexy whine, he nibbled her cheek ruff, then mouthed her muzzle.

"Please, no wolfy smooching in front of your brothers." Ramón pointed toward town. "Let's get moving."

Her brothers shifted and headed down the road.

She glanced up the mountain and shook her head. After this long, there was no chance of survival for Brett and Caleb. Perhaps they would learn and do better in their next life.

Turning, she joined Fell, and they followed her brothers.

Worry niggled inside her. Patrin was going to worry when they didn't show up on time. Fell wasn't limping—quite—but was being careful with his injured leg. She'd damned well make sure he didn't push so hard he'd make the injury worse.

Farther down the road, they could cut the distance by taking some trails. But it was still going to be a long run.

*Sorry, Patrin. We're gonna be late.*

---

The Colonel sat at the dining room table in the house Baton had chosen for this operation. Not a bad location. On Sunday, the two residents had been easily eliminated prior to the blizzard, and everyone had settled in to wait the storm out.

Finally, Monday came. He glanced at his watch. 15:45. The operation was starting right on time.

The snipers were getting their weapons loaded with tranquilizers, then would get set up on the ground and second floors.

His phone vibrated. The display showed it was the operative leading the diversion team. "Go."

"We're in place. As planned, the vehicles are behind the B&B near the riverside park and the diner on the south alley."

"Very good. Wait for my signal." Disconnecting, the Colonel considered again the downtown part of the multi-stage operation.

He'd originally planned to blow up the square itself. But, as far as he could tell, the abominations made up only about half of the Ailill Ridge population. Killing a large number of humans to acquire mutants would be frowned upon by the Committee.

A small amount of...breakage...was acceptable.

The next call came from Baton. "We're set up around the sledding area. I'll notify you if they start to leave early."

"Good. Remember, along with our three targets, I want only mothers and children." He could almost hear the question in her silence. And being an excellent leader, if he said so himself, he indulged her curiosity.

"Being heavy, the men would take too much time to load. And once here, we'll need to separate the mutants from the human women and children. No need to add more work by having to secure the men too."

"But..." There was a moment as she obviously thought about what he'd said. "Ohhh, only shapeshifters will attack the house. That's how you'll get the men."

Yes, Baton showed some potential. "Exactly." He disconnected.

Now, to wait for darkness.

---

At the hill, Patrin had sledded more with various timid cubs. Since Riona had stayed after her time checking the seniors, he recruited her to help with the shyer girls. Before First Shift, a cub wouldn't carry the scent of a shifter, and oftentimes today, neither of them knew if the younglings were human or not. It didn't matter.

He'd taken time to indulge in cookies and hot chocolate while talking with the adults, especially the mother wolves in his pack.

He had a *fine* pack.

The adults were starting to talk about ending the activities. Niall had herded pregnant Heather home a while back, leaving Eileen to keep an eye on her cubs along with Sky and Talam.

After hauling another sled—and an exhausted cub—uphill, he handed the youngling over to his mother and waved away her thanks.

If nothing else, the exercise had warmed him up again, and he unzipped his coat. Tipping his head back, he frowned at the darkening sky. Where were Moya and Fell? They should have been back by now.

They didn't answer their cell phones. Could they have had a breakdown? Slid off the road?

He checked his phone and frowned, seeing he had a text from the Cosantir. The noise here must have drowned out the notification sound. What did André need from him? He displayed the text. "*Call me, please.*"

All right. He started to hit the call icon—then a piercing shriek changed his mind. There was no way he'd be able to hear the soft-spoken Cosantir. He pocketed his phone.

Meantime, the cubs shouldn't be sledding in the dark. "Time to put the fire out," he called to the adults tending the bonfire.

"Yes sir," one of the humans said.

Patrin winced. He hadn't intended to sound like he was giving orders.

Seeing him wince, Kane, the wolf next to him, clapped him on the back. "Relax. You can't help being alpha any more than I can help being tall."

Patrin made a rueful face, got a laugh, and they both walked down the hill to begin the clean-up.

In the parking lot, several adults worked on deflating the snow tubes. Regaling each other with their exploits, younglings lined up with toboggans and sleds to get checked off a list before returning them to the shop.

Several mothers had shown up to collect their offspring.

Naturally, a half-dozen cubs were trying to get in one more run.

Patrin raised his voice. "The slope is closed. Equipment gets returned...now."

The miscreants jumped and trudged down to join the line.

Patrin nodded in satisfaction and pulled his cell out. Now to call André

*Boom.* The sound almost shattered his ears, and Patrin instinctively dove to the ground, then looked for cover.

*Boom.*

*What the fuck.* Had something exploded?

The blasts came from the square—and there was shouting. As flames flickered into existence, smoke rose into the gray sky.

---

*Mother of All, my head!* Gretchen groaned and realized she was on the ground. There were cold bricks beneath her hand. *Bricks?*

Oh, she was in the town square. Memories drifted into her mind as if through a heavy fog.

Sarah had planned the alpha's murder.

Gretchen told the Cosantir. He'd been so angry. His eyes had turned dark, almost black.

She'd fled. Had gone to the pack house, used the portal into the forest, and shifted to wolf. And just run.

*Hating her sister. Hating her life. Hating herself.*

When it started getting darker, she'd returned to town. André had been working in his gift shop. He said he hadn't heard back from Fell and the others, but they were alive, and the ambush had failed.

She'd forgotten a Cosantir could find anyone in the territory. Of course, he knew. From the darkness in his gaze and the lack of worry in his expression, she'd realized Brett and Caleb were no longer alive.

*Gods.*

And then...then...what happened then? *And why does my head hurt so badly?* Oh, he had wanted to speak to Sarah. She'd been walking with him across the square to the B&B.

Then those deafening booms.

Her ears were still ringing, she realized. Groaning, she rolled onto her side and saw André. Shaking his head, he was propped up on one arm. The Cosantir was all right, thank the Mother.

*Oh, Gods, I hurt.* She rubbed at her ears, at her head. Her fingers came away covered in blood. Blinking, she realized acrid smoke filled the air.

Nearby, something flickered with a bright light against the dimness. A fire? Coat hampering her efforts, she struggled to sit up. The square looked different, wrong.

Off to her right, the diner was burning.

She turned her head and winced at the stabbing pain. Espresso Books was fine, so was the bank, and the realty office. Her B&B was at the end...

Horror stabbed into her heart like an icy blade. "*Noooo.*" Part of the front had been blown out, leaving rubble strewn into the square. The roof sagged. Flames showed in the wide-open building.

No one was there. She had no guests, thank the Gods.

But...she did.

"*Sarah.*" She struggled to her feet. Stumbling, running, falling. Tripping over wreckage. She clambered up over the shattered porch. There was no longer a door, no wall. "Sarah!"

Smoke blinded her, burning her lungs, choking her. Flames snapped at her, scorched her face as she tried to get past the burning walls. In her ringing ears, she heard the building groan as it died. Felt the rush of air as the timbers above collapsed.

"Sarah!"

Something struck her shoulder, her head. The ceiling was falling. She raised her arms to protect her head.

"Sarah!" Everything went black.

---

Something had blown up in downtown? Patrin would've thought maybe an explosion in a restaurant kitchen, only the smoke came from two different places.

Along with the rest of the adults, Patrin ran across the parking lot toward the square.

Unlike everyone else, a man jogged away from the square. Clad all in black, he ran directly toward Patrin—as if to attack for fuck's sake.

Catching the stink of human and gunpowder, Patrin knew—he *knew*.

*Scythe*.

Dodging to the right, Patrin punched the human in the temple hard enough to feel bone break. Using every ounce of alpha command, he shouted at his fellow shifters, "It's the *Scythe*. Scatter and run."

After a stunned second, the Daonain fled, dodging through the parking lot, in and out of the vehicles, trying to reach the shelter of the buildings on each side.

Patrin sprinted to guard the cubs.

Something bit into his neck. His leg. Darts. Tranquilizers. *Fuck*. "Run!" he yelled at the pups.

But even as his thoughts slowed, as numbness crept up his limbs, younglings fell. Mateo, Alvaro, Sky. Trying to reach them, Riona, one of his wolves, went down.

Patrin's knees buckled.

Two black trucks entered the parking lot, and a wave of human monsters stepped out from among the cars.

*No.*

# CHAPTER TWENTY-EIGHT

Moya got out of Zorion's Jeep and stared in horror across the parking lot toward the square.

*What in the Mother's love happened while we were gone?*

When she, Fell, and her brothers finally—finally!—reached the town limits in wolf form, they'd detoured to her brothers' house to clean up, get dressed, and tend Fell's leg. And she'd called Patrin. Several times.

*No answer.*

So they'd piled into Zorion's Jeep and driven here to the sledding hill. Down one alley, emergency vehicle lights strobed into the night sky. People were crying, others were shouting frantic commands.

Dread iced her spine as she turned in a circle, squinting through the thick smoke in the air.

*Patrin, are you hurt? Where are you?* Her hands clenched as panic rose inside her. She moved closer to Fell.

He protectively pulled her against his side. "Are those bodies?" He headed toward the sleds and snow tubes at the bottom of the sledding hill.

"What do you mean bodies?" Her mouth dropped open as she

realized people lay on the ground, wrapped in blankets. Unmoving. Others were bending over them.

"What the fuck is wrong with them?" Ramón jogged toward the line of blanket-wrapped people.

Fear stabbed Moya's heart. Patrin had wanted to watch the sledding. Was he one of those lying so still? She ran after Ramón.

Orla, a cat carpenter, was turning a body onto its side. She looked up at Ramón. "Gods, I'm glad you're here, boss. The diner and B&B got blown up."

"Blown up?" Ramón stared at her.

Orla lowered her voice. "Then men—humans—attacked the cubs and adults at the sledding hill. We found darts on the people here. Like tranquilizers. They're still out cold."

Moya forced out the question through a dry mouth. "Is Patrin...?"

"I haven't seen him, Moya." Orla jerked her head toward the square. "I don't know what's going on over there. Maybe talk to the Cosantir or Bron? If you have a first aid kit, take it with you."

"I'll get it." Zorion ran for his Jeep.

Fell was studying the unconscious people on the ground. "Orla, where are the cubs?"

"None of them are here." Orla's expression was grim.

*Mateo, Alvaro? No!* Fear weighted Moya's chest, pressing down so hard her lungs didn't want to work. "We—we need to learn what happened."

*Find Patrin. Find the cubs.*

"Aye, that's first." Fell laced his fingers with hers. Tugging her forward, he broke into a limping jog toward the arched opening into the downtown.

The pedestrian square was...a *nightmare*. More shouting, cries of pain, people running. Glass from broken out store windows. Black smoke poured from the bombed diner. Flames rose from the B&B, where the fire chief yelled orders at his men and volunteers.

*What can I do to help?* Feeling frantic, she looked right and left. *Where can I even start?*

Blood streaking his white hair and beard, Murtagh was helping an older person into the Shamrock. The restaurant's tables had been shoved to one side to make room for the injured.

"There's the beta!" someone shouted. A group—almost all pack—along with the police chief headed straight for Fell.

"They took Patrin!" Jens shouted.

Moya froze at the fear in the wolf's voice.

"Moya, they have our *cubs*." Talitha grabbed her around her waist. "And Eileen. They have my heart."

"Who?" Moya froze. Air came in little more than gasps as she struggled to understand what had happened. "*Who* has them?"

When Fell growled, she felt sheer terror at the fury in his expression.

"The Scythe." Every muscle in Fell's body tightened as it all came together. "The Scythe made their move." He pointed to the burning B&B and diner. "Those were diversions for the kidnapping."

He paused, opening his senses to the bonds inside him. "Patrin's alive." He had no sense of direction or health. Very few littermate bonds gave any information other than knowing a sibling was alive.

He turned his attention to Jens, a skinny, young male. "What happened at the sledding slope?"

"Vigulf was there." Jens yanked an older cub forward. "Tell the beta."

Fell pulled in a breath, knowing how Patrin felt. Being responsible for others was an almost unbearable weight.

Vigulf was one of the cubs who'd been a bully. Now, his face was tear-stained, and he shook like a leaf in a winter wind. The cub swallowed and managed to speak. "There were big booms in the square, and we ran that way. Only the alpha, he shouts, '*It's the Scythe. Scatter and run.*' I did. I ran. A male—no, a human all in black, he tried to grab me, but I got around a truck and rolled under it. An' he tried to grab me, but the trucks were leaving so he left."

Joining him, Bron motioned for him to keep going.

"Trucks?" Fell asked.

"Yeah. More humans in black were throwing cubs 'n' females into two big black trucks." The youngling's voice hitched, and his chin wobbled. "They took Torkil."

*His littermate. Fuck.* Fell put a hand on the youngling's shoulder. "We'll do our best to get him." He knew better than any of them not to promise the cub or anyone else would be recovered. Or alive.

Anger turned his voice rough. "Go on, cub."

"Uh, most of the ones they took—they were, like, asleep or something. Those Scythe men left the males 'n' seniors laying on the ground. And then they drove away."

"What happened to Patrin—the alpha?" Although Moya's words were calm and quiet, she'd wrapped her arms around her waist and was shivering.

"Right after the alpha shouted, he fell. Like the others and they took him too." The cub had tears on his face. "I should've fought. Should've—"

"No, you did right." Fell slung an arm over his shoulder for a reassuring squeeze. "The alpha would've made it a command for his wolves. You didn't have a choice."

"*Oh.*" The sound Moya made showed she'd figured out why an alpha had the power of command over his wolves. She managed to smile at the youngling. "You did good, Vigulf. If they'd caught you, we wouldn't know what happened."

"But we don't know where they took our people," Jens almost wailed. "We don't *know.*"

This was one massive goatfuck.

And they had two leaders. He turned to Bron. "Do you—"

"No. I'm not a soldier." Her voice was harsher than normal from the smoke. "You've dealt with the Scythe You lead; I'll back you up."

Fell nodded. As he eyed the burning buildings and considered the timing, a chill ran up his spine.

In the Scythe, every commanding officer had his favorite go-to tactics. The Colonel often employed double explosions to divert attention from an assassination. This held all the characteristics of one of the Colonel's operations. His gut said...*the Colonel is alive*.

Patrin and the others had been tranqed. The Scythe wouldn't have carried away the dead.

Moving away from the group, Fell tried to think.

First, find where Patrin and the rest were taken.

Then...get them back, which wouldn't be easy. The Colonel's operatives would be well armed and prepared for how deadly an animal shifter could be.

How could he organize a rescue without getting everyone killed? They'd need firearms of their own—and shifters who could shoot. He should pull in Fletcher and Kennard. They had experience and...

*Wait*. There was someone in town who'd actually run operations. And knew how to shoot. He pulled out his phone and swiped on the contact labeled "W."

"Wells."

"You in Ailill Ridge?" Fell held his breath.

"I am."

Fell exhaled in relief. The spymaster was still here. "The Scythe kidnapped Patrin and a group of Daonain. Carried them off in two black vans."

There was a moment of silence. "Lay it out for me, soldier."

In terse words, Fell explained, piece by piece. Finally, he summed it up. "The operation stinks of the Colonel."

Sitting at a kitchen table in the home of Leland's friend, Wells tightened his fingers on the phone. Fell's report had been clear and concise. He and Patrin were the best of the shifter-soldiers.

Explosions as a diversion, tranquilizers, kidnapping. "Yes, it stinks of the Colonel." Impatience lit up Wells' nerves like an artillery barrage.

The Colonel was alive. And he'd made his move. *About fucking time*.

But bombing a town square was extraordinarily public. Add in the unprecedented collateral damage? "A very *desperate* Colonel."

And desperate kidnappers often cut their losses when it came to captives.

There was silence for a moment. "Fuck." After a beat, Fell added, "Could use your help."

"I've got your back, soldier." As if Wells would say no to any of the men who worked for him.

Even more... The Colonel had taken the most vulnerable. *Damn the bastard*. Protecting women and children—that was what Wells had vowed to do, so many years before. "I can be at the Shamrock in a few minutes. I have my sniper rifle and other weaponry."

Tucking the phone into a pocket, he rose.

Across the table, the snoopy werecat had been openly listening. Thorson gave Wells an implacable stare. "I'm coming."

Leland was on his own phone. Shoving it in his pocket, he nodded. "My grandchildren are already there and will be fighting. I'm joining you."

*Damn civilians*.

Then again, he'd seen Thorson in action. In cougar form, the shifter was lethal. He eyed Leland. "I don't suppose you're a cat too?"

In the days they'd spent here, the old rancher had come to be a friend of sorts. As much as Wells ever allowed.

"You betcha." Leland's smile was smug. "Don't worry, human. I'll keep up."

"Stubborn werecats. Fuck me." Wells jerked his head toward the door. "Gear up and let's move."

---

Taking shallow breaths against the smoke, Moya half-listened to Fell speak on the phone while she tried to comprehend what had happened. Black vans, multiple attackers in black. The Scythe had obviously planned for this night operation.

The pack had grouped around her and Fell, waiting for instructions. Pride swept through her, seeing how those who could shoot had armed themselves with pistols and rifles. A couple carried first-aid kits. Everyone was in dark attire.

*We're coming for you, Patrin. Cubs. Hold on.*

Fell shoved his phone into his pocket and said to everyone, "The spymaster is coming in to help. He'll have more weapons for us."

"We don't know where the Scythe have taken our shifters. They're probably fleeing the area as fast as they can." Moya's spirits spiraled downward—and then she gripped Fell's arm. "Hey, André could locate Patrin and the others." Cosantirs could locate any shifter in their territory.

"He could if he was conscious." The Chief of Police joined Moya and Fell. "As he was pulling Gretchen out of the B&B, the building collapsed. He got hit hard."

"Our Cosantir is hurt?" Everything—everything was falling apart. Her voice came out almost tiny. "W-will he be all right?"

Bron patted her shoulder. "We think so. He's opened his eyes a couple of times. But...he can't help find our captured shifters."

"I saw them go that direction." Young Vigulf pointed to the west.

*West. All of the west.* Moya managed to smile at the lad and give him a nod for his help.

Automatically, she turned to face that direction...and felt her tie to Patrin warm slightly. The same way it had cooled when he and Fell drove to the North Cascades Territory. She turned to the south, then back to the west, and felt the faint response.

Moya pulled in a breath, cleared her mind, and...opened her heart. Because Patrin and Fell were right there, in her heart.

Without her instinctive resistance, she could feel her bond with Fell—thick and strong because he stood right beside her.

The one to Patrin was thinner, but... "Our alpha is alive."

Whispers ran through her pack followed by silence.

She pressed her hands over her heart, over the warmth of the ties. "He's not moving, the distance isn't increasing. He...he isn't too far away. Still in town, I think."

Fell bent and kissed her. "Bless the Mother for making you so sensitive to the bonds."

She had despised how the sensitivity made her easy to coerce. But now—if it saved her clan—her Patrin—she'd be grateful. "I need to follow the pull and find him. Find them all."

Fell's eyes darkened, and she could feel his worry. His fear for her. His jaw tightened, creating hollow shadows under his cheekbones. He nodded. "Aye, dammit. You're our best bet for locating them. Got your phone?"

"I do." She could see his inner struggle, his need to come with her. And oh, she was scared to do this without him. But there wasn't any choice. She firmed her voice. "Fell. You have to stay and direct our pack and the rest of the rescuers."

After a moment, he inclined his head in acknowledgment. "*Cariad.*" He looked past her and called, "Ramón, Zorion."

Her brothers jogged over.

"Moya has a tie to Patrin. Help her hunt. When she says

you're close, switch to foot and be cautious. The Colonel's operatives know what we can do. Call me with the location." His voice dropped. "And keep her safe."

Zorion clapped him on the shoulder.

"We will, Beta," Ramón said.

Fell caught her in a hard hug. "Please careful out there, little wolf." The tightness of his voice, the look in his eyes, all showed his fear for her.

And his love.

---

Headlights came out of the blackness, and the Colonel's two cargo vans pulled up in front of the house. He waited on the porch.

His operative, Baton, jumped out of the first van and stopped on the porch steps. "Sir."

"You're late, Baton."

This operation had been planned down to the minute.

In the dim light from the house, her face paled. "Sorry, sir. There were more children and adults than planned. Shooting and collecting them took longer." She drew herself up as if expecting a blow. "And then a big Chevy Suburban slid through a stop sign and rammed into one of our vans. We had to deal with the driver of the Suburban and get his vehicle out of sight."

Which meant the driver was dead. The Colonel grunted approval, although the collateral damage and loss of time was unfortunate. "Did you obtain our primary targets?"

The way Baton's muscles tensed wasn't a good sign. "We have Patrin, but Fell wasn't there, and neither was Moya, the woman shapeshifter he's been fucking."

"Only one of the three?" The Colonel barely kept from backhanding the incompetent agent.

"We did get the cubs Patrin plays with," Baton said in a rush. "He obviously cares for them."

The cubs might work to leash the best assassin the Colonel had ever seen. "All right." He swept his gaze over the front lawn. "The trap should draw Fell in, even if we've lost our chance for the female mutant."

---

Patrin woke—and thanks to training—didn't move a muscle. His mind kept blurring, and his limbs felt disconnected from the rest of him.

*I've been drugged.*

Around him, the air was cold, carrying the fragrance of evergreens polluted with the stink of gun oil and of humans with their myriad of nose-wrinkling chemicals—deodorant, cologne, mouthwash.

*Where the fuck am I?*

His brain felt as if it had been hibernating for the winter.

There'd been a blizzard. *Yes.* He'd moved crates for Nik at the bar. *Yes.* He remembered cubs laughing. The taste of hot chocolate. *Right, sledding.*

Then... *Explosions. Running. Yelling about a Scythe attack.*

*The Scythe.* He'd been caught. And not just him. Cubs had been falling, dropping like leaves in an icy autumn. Sickness surged up in him so quickly he almost vomited.

*Don't move, wolf. Stay quiet.*

He could hear people talking nearby, and one voice was familiar. The *Colonel*. Fury seared along every nerve pathway in his body—and cleared the last of the drug.

The Colonel was talking to a woman.

*I know that woman.*

"Should I leave for town now?" The voice belonged to the

human female who worked in the coffee shop with Fell. Her name was...was Renee.

"Not yet," the Colonel said. "I want the mutant adults restrained. Put the children into the cages in the dining area. Except for the two needed as bait. Choose one of the boys Fell likes and another whose death will set the mutants off. Fair-skinned if possible. Shows the blood better."

"Oh, I know just which ones to pick."

Patrin's hands closed into fists. *I'll kill her. Kill her and him.* This time, he couldn't smother a growl.

The Colonel laughed harshly and then a boot slammed into Patrin's stomach.

Pain exploded in his gut, and he curled into a ball.

"Welcome back, you stinking mutant. You've cost me more than you know." The Colonel kicked him savagely in the chest and shoulder.

Hands restrained behind his back, Patrin couldn't block anything.

"You're going back to work for me, mutant. Or everyone you love will die screaming in pain."

Wind kicked out of him, Patrin could only gasp for air.

"Baton, after the abominations are secured, you can leave for the next step. I assume you can find one of the mutants you've identified?"

"Yes, sir. They're probably all at the square now."

"Good. Give them your sad story and the address here." The Colonel chuckled. "When they come to rescue their children, I'll acquire my first abomination army."

Dread rose in Patrin until his mouth tasted like bile.

*A trap. This was all a trap.*

Eyes half-closed, Moya listened to the crunch and hiss of tires on the barely plowed street. In the dark night, the engine of Zorion's SUV purred quietly, like a big cat.

"*Gods-dammit.*" Zorion swerved the vehicle to avoid a tree branch.

In the back seat, Ramón stayed silent.

Closing her eyes, Moya felt for the bonds within her. Her sense of Fell had lessened as the SUV moved southwest and away from downtown. But her tie to Patrin was strengthening.

"Go right." Minute by minute, she directed Zorion. And the only way she could tell where to go was when the bond connecting her to Patrin grew slightly stronger. It was so awkward and inefficient and *slow*. "More to the right still. Angle that way."

She opened her eyes to see where they were.

Ah, this was High Rigger Street, out near the edge of Ailill Ridge at the bottom of a steep mountainside. The neighborhood was popular with Daonain since the isolated houses were on several acres of land. Most had long private drives swathed in forest with wide front lawns.

Another two blocks went by, and she sat up straight. "We're close. Don't go farther."

Zorion reacted instantly and tapped the brakes. "Let's back up and leave the car two houses back. The driveway on one of them wasn't plowed. I doubt anyone will be leaving tonight."

"Good plan," Ramón said from the backseat. "We'll trawsfur and cut through the forest."

A few minutes later, in wolf form, Moya jumped a low fence and led her brothers through a forested area until she reached the tree line marking the edge of the next house's property. She stopped there despite the way her heart urged her forward.

*My Patrin is close. So very close.*

Her sensitivity to bonds had brought her here. Had found him. For one brief second, she closed her eyes and thanked the Mother for the gift.

# BONDS OF THE WOLF

Her ears swiveled to take in the nearby sounds. No wind, just the occasional plop of snow from overhead branches and the tiny patter of a rodent.

She lifted her nose and found only the clean scent of snow and the musky wildness of her brothers.

However, there were humans farther away. *Oh yes, there were.*

She shifted to human form and kept her voice to a bare whisper. "Patrin is there—in that house."

Ramón also trawsfurred to human, leaving Zorion on guard as a wolf.

Staying under cover of the trees, she looked out over a wide, snow-covered lawn that ended at a two-story house. The porch light spilled onto two black cargo vans. On the porch, a tall man with military straight posture talked with someone standing on the steps.

Humans were carrying limp cubs from the vans into the house.

Moya growled, fighting the urge to trawsfur and attack. To save the cubs. To find Patrin.

*No, concentrate. What does Fell need to know?* "The forest is close to the house on the sides and in the rear. We might get in that way."

"A front approach is sure impossible." Ramón's gaze was on the bare expanse. "If they have weapons, it would be a slaughter."

Shivering in the cold, Moya bit her lip. "Ramón, why did the kidnappers hole up here? Why not keep going?"

"Doesn't make sense, does it." Ramón narrowed his eyes as he studied the activity.

A light flickered in a dark upstairs window, as if a door to a lighted hallway had opened. Silhouetted by the light was a dark figure inside the window—and the distinctive outline of a rifle. "By the Goddess, they're here because it's a trap. There are people with rifles in the upstairs windows."

Zorion laid his ears back, silently snarling.

She felt like snarling too. "They want to capture more of us."

"If they're expecting us to show up, we're in trouble." Ramón shook his head. "But...none of them would know about the Cosantir's or your ability, sis."

Huh. They hadn't left clues for the Daonain to find them. Wouldn't know she could track Patrin. However, if they made a trap, they wanted to be found, right? "They must plan to show or tell us where the cubs and captives are. But not until they're all set up for us."

Ramón nodded agreement. "That's my take on it."

"Time to report in. We need to tell Fell to attack before they're completely set up."

---

Sitting at a table in the Shamrock, Fell couldn't stop growling. The little wolf had found Patrin—and the whole thing was a Scythe trap.

They needed a plan.

He glanced around the restaurant. The wounded who still needed care were lying or sitting over on one side. Murtagh sat slumped against the wall while his wife bandaged his head wound.

Daonain who'd volunteered to fight clustered near the back.

The families of the kidnapped shifters were at tables near them.

The ones planning the assault were sitting around the oversized table with Fell.

After leaving his two companions with the fighters, Wells had taken a seat beside Fell. Across from them were the town's two cahirs, Bron and Niall, along with Heather, her mate Madoc, and the Elder Ina, who knew everything about the area.

Pale and obviously hurting, the Cosantir had insisted on joining them. Sky and Talam were among those captured, and he and his lifemates looked drawn with worry.

At the thought of all the cubs, Fell closed his eyes for a moment. Gods, Mateo and Alvaro must be terrified.

*No, thinking of them doesn't help.* There was no time for anything but action. They needed to move quickly—yet carefully or they'd be walking into a deathtrap.

Niall had printed off a satellite photo of the house and neighboring forest, and Fell used it to illustrate the plan. Despite Moya's help with his speech, he still had to concentrate to ensure he laid everything out clearly.

"Wells brought his sniper rifle and will eliminate the Scythe in the second-story windows overlooking the lawn. Those will be the most difficult shots, from the farthest away. Other sharpshooters will target the ground-floor windows, aiming high in case our cubs are on the floor. This initial barrage is only to remove the Scythe snipers and will last only a few seconds."

When he got nods of agreement, he continued, "After the shooting stops, our fighters go through the windows and door to free the hostages." The Daonain sniping needed to stop once their own shifters were moving through the building.

After an exchange of glances and nods with the others, André said, "Good plan. *Oui.*"

"For the internal attack"—Fell looked across the table—"Bron, can you and Niall get into the second floor and kill any Scythe left up there?" The cougars were highly suited to that sort of forced entry.

The Chief of Police and Niall nodded.

"We're forced into a basic assault at this point. Even attacking through doors and windows, if they're set for us, is a risk. To the captives—and us." Fell's chest was so tight it was a wonder he could breathe. Far too many shifters would die today. The cubs might die—it would only take one Scythe with an automatic weapon.

Heather frowned at the map. "You know, that area looks familiar."

"Don't think you were here when Fell told us the address." Niall handed her the paper with the house address. A place on High Rigger.

"I do know this house." Heather waved the paper. "I rented it last month to a couple of older littermates."

"It's clan property?" André asked slowly. "*Mon amour*, does it have a shifter portal?"

Fell looked at Heather as hope bloomed in his chest. The shifter portals were ways to get into the forest without being seen—like the tunnel he and Patrin used when killing the Director.

Someone could use it to get *into* a house as well.

"Yes, it's a tunnel portal." She thought for a moment. "The entry is inside the garage. The tunnel exits southeast of the house in a thicket of trees and huckleberries. Let me get the keys from the realty office."

By the time Heather returned, they had a revised plan and a timeline.

"Wolves," Fell called to the pack who were waiting off to one side of the Shamrock. "You will be infiltrating the forest on each side." Who would be best to keep them steady?

His gaze fell on one of the males who owned the ranch supply store. In his fifties. Yes. "Lucius, park where Ramón did, take them through the forest, and meet up with Moya and her brothers."

"You're not going to be with us?" Lucius asked.

Fell took the keys from Heather. "No, I'm sneaking in through a portal. Be cautious and take Moya's orders."

Lucius inclined his head. "Aye, Beta."

With Madoc beside him, Fell headed out, glancing at Bron on the way. "Any chance you have a flashbang?"

"Oh, what a lovely, clever shifter. Yes, I do." Eyes alight, she grinned. "Niall, we're going to have *fun*."

Her cahir nephew eyed her, heaved a sigh, and scowled at Fell. "Did you have to encourage her, Beta?"

With his littermate beside him, Daniel jogged across the town square. They'd just finished the ranch chores when Heather had called, asking them to come and help.

They'd driven in as fast as the snowy roads permitted—but the Summerlands Ranch was miles outside of town.

"By the Gods." Daniel stared at the destruction. The diner and the B&B were almost unrecognizable. Windows had been blown out on other stores. Blood stained the snow here and there.

"And they call *us* animals," Tanner muttered as they approached the Shamrock.

Seeing them through the window, Heather rushed outside. "Gods, thank you for coming." She was shaking, his sister who could handle almost anything life threw at her.

"We'll get through this, sis." Tanner pulled her into his arms for a moment, then handed her over.

"We will." Daniel hugged her, holding her tight. "We'll get Sky and Talam back—and the rest too." He glanced into the restaurant, seeing the worried faces. "All the families of the captives are here?"

"All the injured and those who can't fight. There's comfort in numbers."

*Herne help us.* Dread made an ugly hole in his gut. "Talitha's here. The cubs...?"

"The Scythe got Mateo and Alvaro—and Eileen too."

"Fuck," Tanner spat out. "Fuck the bastards. Where are the fighters? We'll join—"

"No." Heather's voice lowered. "The ones doing the assault have left."

*Dammit all.* "So quickly?" Daniel scowled at being denied an outlet for his rage, at not getting to *help*.

"We figured out the whole thing was set up to be a trap to catch us all. We're hoping to attack before the Scythe are ready."

Tanner frowned. "Why wouldn't they be ready?"

"They wouldn't expect us to have found them. And since a trap won't work if the prey doesn't show up, we expect a call or some way for them to *reveal* the location." She put air quotes around the *reveal*.

"Logical," Tanner said.

Her face fell. "Only no one has—"

"Oh, help!" A young woman ran across the square, straight toward them. She was average in build and looks with long black hair. Her gaze was on Heather. "I need help, please."

Heather stepped forward. "What's wrong?"

"There are black vans—and men. And I think they kidnapped people." The woman looked frantic.

"I see." Anger flashed over Heather's face before she took the woman's arm. "Let's go inside and get some help."

"Oh, yes, yes. That's a good idea." The woman accompanied Heather through the door.

Daniel exchanged a cynical look with his brother and followed.

"André," Heather called. "This woman says the black vans—the ones involved in the kidnapping—have parked at her house."

Daniel saw the Cosantir sitting at a table. He looked like roadkill with smears of blood and dark ash on his face.

"In that case"—André's jaw tightened—"come here, please, miss."

Giving the woman a light push, Heather stayed back beside Daniel.

Tanner eyed the woman. "Isn't that the human who works for Talitha?"

"It is." Heather's voice came out a low growl. "Her name's Renee. And I'm going to kill her."

A chill ran through Daniel as he realized a barista was the perfect occupation for a spy. In fact, seeing Heather, Renee had run straight for her. How many of the Daonain had she identified for the Scythe?

Putting his rage on hold, Daniel wrapped an arm around his sister's shoulders and pulled her close. "Let this play out, sis."

Then he'd deal with the spy.

Silver-haired Ina was at the table with André. She smiled at Renee. "Hello, dear. I'm afraid the Chief of Police isn't here right now, but I'm on the town council. If you tell me the problem, I'll give her a call. What's happened?"

"Oh, oh, it was awful." Renee wrung her hands. "Two black vans pulled into my driveway, and when I told them to leave, they hit me. And then they started pulling people out of the vans. Little kids and women, unconscious and all tied up."

Daniel barely managed to smother a growl.

"Did they simply let you leave?" André asked, his French accent somehow making his words sympathetic.

"They shoved me into the house, but I snuck out and got in my car and skidded right out of there. They shot at me." She pressed her hand to her heart, and her voice rose. "I could have *died*."

"Where is your house?" At the table, Ina picked up a pen.

The human rattled off the address. "I would have called, but my phone and purse are still in the house."

Daniel would bet his claws that her phone was in her pocket, so she could report back.

Abandoning Daniel and Tanner, Heather moved to stand behind André. "You know, I rented that house to a couple of older men."

Renee stiffened almost imperceptibly.

Quietly, Daniel edged closer to the door. Just in case.

Heather crossed her arms over her chest. "A part-time barista sure couldn't afford the rent."

Fear soured the young woman's scent although her expression didn't change at all. "Of course I can't. I was visiting them," Renee said so assuredly Daniel was impressed. "They're friends. And I'm worried about them, with those horrible people. Can't you—"

"What are their names then?" Heather's tone had gone grim.

Daniel knew his sister had just realized the shifter males were probably dead.

"Why are you being so dense?" Renee's voice rose, and she waved her hands in the air. "Don't you realize my friends are probably being hurt right now?"

Was Daniel the only one who noticed she'd smoothly moved a couple of steps away from the table?

"*You* did this. *You* suggested the sledding day." If Talitha had been in wolf form, her ears would have been pinned back, her fangs exposed. "You wanted our little ones all in one place."

Easily dodging Talitha's fist, the human spun and sprinted for the door. An older shifter moved to stop her, and she hit him hard in the sternum, clearing her way without slowing.

Daniel's growl was a low rumble in his throat as he stepped directly in front of the door. Being bear-sized, he blocked it completely.

"Move!" She yanked a pistol from her coat.

As she brought it up, he slapped her hand to one side and swatted her to the floor.

"Never fuck with bears." Chuffing a little, Tanner bent and relieved her of the pistol.

With a moan, she sat up, rubbing the side of her head.

André asked quietly, "Daniel, Tanner, does she have a mobile phone?"

Daniel pulled her arms behind her back while Tanner searched her pockets. He found a cell.

"Very good." André rose, staggered slightly, and had to brace one hand on the tabletop.

"André, you're not up to this." Heather put a hand under the Cosantir's arm.

Daniel had to agree. Corpses looked healthier. "What're you planning, André? Maybe Tanner or I could handle it for you?"

"I believe this task is mine alone. Being who I am."

That didn't explain much. Who he was—was the Cosantir, called by the God to...

*Oh.*

The Cosantir's smile was fleeting but there. "I think our young spy might want to report in and perhaps tell her boss she was delayed. So much snow, *oui?*"

Daniel almost felt sorry for the human.

Herne gave His guardians an impossible job but provided them with equally impossible talents. Like removing memories... or planting an order right inside a mind.

The Cosantir was one tricky werecat.

---

Patrin lay on his side, arms aching from being restrained behind his back. The steel handcuffs itched and burned against his skin. A rope attached to his cuffs tethered him to an eyebolt in the baseboard.

If he could shift, he'd be able to step right out of the handcuffs. But the Scythe had fastened a steel collar with inward-facing spikes around his neck. He could move around with it on; however, since a wolf's neck was larger than a human's, trawsfurring would drive the spikes into his throat and carotid arteries. He'd die. Messily.

He still had nightmares from watching it happen when the Scythe first figured out how to restrain shifters. Chester and Graham's father, enraged at the loss of his mate, had lost control and shifted...and died, choking on his own blood.

*Stay in control, wolf.*

The ring with the keys to his cuffs and collar dangled from a hook near the front door. Frustratingly out of reach, considering his hands were secured behind his back.

The shifters captured at the sledding hill were restrained in the living room. He could hear them as they woke. In cages, cubs were whimpering, sobbing.

"Where are we? Why are you doing this?" The slurred voice was young Riona's, still drugged and confused.

"Shut the fuck up, mutant." The harsh sound of a slap and a pained cry left Patrin fighting against his instincts. The need to trawsfur and start killing was unbearable.

The Colonel strode into the foyer, a cell phone to his ear. "I don't give a fuck how slick the roads are, Baton. You get that car to town and give the abominations this address. We need those mutants here now—and in a frenzy. I don't want them to have time to get organized. Move it."

Turning, the Colonel yelled to his operatives, "Stand down for now."

Patrin frowned. The woman operative should have had plenty of time to reach town. Then again, the longer she took, the better.

Coming closer, the Colonel nudged a boot into his ribs. "Feeling frustrated, freak? Won't be long before I have all of you —and more—back under control." He kicked Patrin harder. "A year ago, I was set to show my colleagues what I'd accomplished using your mutant skills. And you destroyed the compound and all my plans."

Another kick. Tethered to the wall, Patrin couldn't even move out of the way.

"Once I demonstrate the uses of my abomination army, the Council will overlook the loss of the Seattle compound—because of the Director's incompetence, of course. I'll get my place at the top, running the world. Power and riches." He smiled slowly. "And you will, once again, be my masterpiece."

Patrin ground his teeth together to keep from responding.

There was no point. And he needed to be conscious to help whatever rescue occurred because the Daonain wouldn't leave the cubs and females in the Scythe's grip.

"Always thinking, aren't you, Patrin." The Colonel rested his boot on Patrin's shoulder. "You're counting on your fellow abominations to come for you. So am I. I'm going to get the rest of them, then I can keep the ones who'll be useful and kill the rest."

"They won't walk into a trap," Patrin gritted out. The spikes dug in painfully against his throat.

"Of course they will. I know how you animals react when one of your mutant children gets cut to pieces."

Patrin felt as if he'd been sucker punched. Because, even knowing it was a trap, a Daonain would attack if a cub was being hurt.

*What can I do? How can I prevent this?* Patrin pulled in a breath and tried to think. If he shouted—used his command voice to keep them in place—

"Shut this one up," the Colonel said to the human next to him.

The operative slapped duct tape over Patrin's mouth and rubbed it firmly over his beard and mustache.

A growl rolled out of Patrin. He'd be unable to warn his clan. The Scythe would capture his new friends, his pack. His brother. Moya.

*God of the Hunt, just give me one chance to kill them all. Just a chance.*

---

*By Herne's hide and hooves, where is the fucking door?*

In wolf form, Fell searched the steep, forested slope behind the target house, growing increasingly frustrated.

Movement at the back of the house caught his attention. A

cougar silently leaped from the mountainside into one of the roof-high shade trees. Niall and Bron had arrived.

Off to his right was the Cosantir's littermate. A damn big bear, Madoc nosed around, also trying to pick up the scent of the portal.

Spotting a thick clump of underbrush, Fell squirmed through the huckleberries, wincing as the branches dragged against the bullet gouge in his rear leg. In the center of the space was a wooden trapdoor. *Yes!* He gave a barely audible woof.

Madoc had more trouble in the undergrowth, as the oversize shifter-pack strapped to his neck and belly caught on the bushes.

Shifting to human, Fell removed Madoc's pack, which was full of his own gear. Once dressed, he clipped his pistol to the cloth belt and shoved Bron's gifts into his cargo pants pockets.

Silently, he lifted the trapdoor, pleased when tiny LED motion-detector lights lit the way.

Staying in bear form, Madoc padded down into the tunnel. Fell followed and closed the door behind him. The cool, damp air smelled of clean dirt and rock.

A human-sized door blocked the end of the tunnel. Fell pulled the key from his pocket and unlocked the door. Opening it a crack, he listened.

Distant voices. Nothing close.

Opening the door farther, he scanned the area and then sniffed. Only the scents of metal, gasoline, rubber. No one was in the garage. He stepped out with Madoc behind him.

A pegboard used to hang tools concealed the portal. Nice. He closed the door, leaving it unlocked. Just in case.

"Here goes," he said under his breath, and Madoc huffed in agreement.

As they crossed the garage to the kitchen door, urgency hummed in Fell's bones. Theirs was the most critical part of the plan—and they were out of time.

Baton hadn't called again. The Colonel tapped his fingers on the pistol holstered on his belt. It'd been too long.

Possibly she'd had a car accident. But he hadn't heard sirens—and he would have. After the explosions, he'd been able to hear the fire engine screaming toward downtown.

Next possibility: she might not have been able to find any of the abominations she'd identified. Also unlikely. She'd had a fair-sized list. What with the disaster downtown, some of them would be there.

Finally, the most unpalatable possibility. She'd been forced to call him with false information, then removed from action.

Had she sounded different when she phoned?

His mouth compressed...because she had. She was always tense when talking to him, and her speech was usually fast and staccato. This time, her words had been slow, almost halting.

Dammit. How much time had he lost waiting for her call?

His men, upstairs and downstairs, were sprawled out comfortably on floors and chairs.

Damn the mutants. He lifted his voice. "Set up for action. *Now.*"

---

Phone gripped tightly in one hand, Moya held the neck of the tunic closed against the cold wind. Shivering, she stared out across the stretch of white snow.

When her pack had arrived—thankfully, bringing her the quilted tunic and soft boots—she'd moved closer to the house, staying just inside the forest. As soon as Fell and Madoc called to say they were inside to defend the captives, the attack could start.

*What is taking you so long, Fell?*

Everyone else was ready.

The pack and other shifters were in the surrounding forest. Some in human form with weapons, some in animal form. Mostly male, but with a fair number of females. Many were mothers of the captives.

Bron and Niall were in a tree behind the house.

Wells had texted to say he was ready—and sent a man's photo labeled: *The Colonel, don't let him escape.*

The Colonel's skin was drawn tight over sharp features. His head was shaved, his lips thin. He looked terrifyingly cold and cruel.

Fell and Patrin had told her about this human monster. Their nightmares had told her more.

If she had the chance, he would die.

Suddenly, floodlights blazed across the wide lawn.

As if her thoughts had brought him forth, the monster walked out of the house, leaving the door open behind him. He had Sky and Mateo, both tied up.

*Oh no.*

He'd shielded his face and chest by holding Sky high against him with an arm around the cub's waist. With his free hand, he dragged Mateo by one ankle across the porch.

Fear paralyzed Moya. The younglings were shirtless, their skin pale in the harsh porch light.

Dropping Mateo's ankle, the Colonel set a foot on his back—and pulled a knife. With Sky still held high in front of him, he yelled, "Shifters, I know you're out there."

Her heart sank.

"Walk forward and kneel on the lawn. Right now—or I'll slaughter these boys."

The desperate compulsion to attack surged through her. She'd kill this monster who would hurt cubs. Bury her fangs in his throat.

*No, no. I can't.* There were other younglings inside. Why weren't Fell and Madoc inside by now? They needed to kill the

Scythe guarding the hostages before any attack out here could happen.

*Hurry, Fell.*

Feeling the instinctive movement from the shifters all through the forest, she growled loudly in an order to hold. As the sound rolled through the quiet night air, the movement stopped.

"No?" The Colonel laughed, harsh and cold. "You want to see this boy die?"

*Do something, someone.* But what could anyone do? All options were...wrong. They needed more time for Fell and Madoc.

*I'm the alpha female. And Mateo is pack.* From what Patrin and Fell had said, this human wouldn't see a female as a threat.

She stepped forward, out into the open, and raised her voice. "Are you the Colonel who I've heard so much about?" *Stall, wolf. Stall for all you're worth.* "No one has heard from you for a while. We thought you were dead."

With Sky in front of him, only a small part of the Colonel's face could be seen—and it darkened. "You fucking abomination. You have no idea of the damage you beasts have done. Not that you care."

His eyes narrowed. "You're stalling." He sliced his knife down Sky's chest.

As blood spilled down his front, Sky clamped his mouth shut. Only the tiniest of whimpers escaped him.

And fired rage in her soul. She took a step forward, feeling the shifters all around start to move, even as she knew it was a trap.

*Stop!* Her pack bonds burned with the alpha's harsh order. Her feet froze.

Patrin—it was Patrin, and he was alive.

But the other shifters were still moving. With her sensitivity, she'd received and responded to the coercive order far stronger than anyone else.

This time, rather than fighting Patrin's command, she *ampli-*

*fied* it. Yelling as loud as she could, "*Hold*," she put the full force of her own alpha authority behind it.

No one moved, not even the cats or bears.

The Colonel raised the knife again, and she shook with the dread of what he'd do. She ran farther out onto the lawn. "Colonel, I'll—"

A furious growl came from inside the house—and the screech of something metallic. Hands behind his back, Patrin charged through the doorway. Head down, he barreled into the Colonel and knocked him away from Sky.

"Fucking mutant!" On his back, the Colonel twisted and kicked Patrin's legs out from under him—then booted him in the head.

From the forest, a man's voice boomed into the night. "Shoot now!"

Like a fireworks finale, the dark woods lit with a myriad of lights. From muzzle blasts.

The world exploded in gunfire, shattering glass, screams, and shouts.

*Oh Gods.*

Ripping off her tunic, Moya shifted and leaped forward.

# CHAPTER TWENTY-NINE

At the inside door to the house to the kitchen, Fell started to text Moya to begin the attack.

Guns outside the house began to crack and boom.

*Herne help us, the attack has started.*

Stowing his phone, he quickly crawled across the kitchen, hidden by the island dividing the room from the dining area. Madoc followed. A glance around the edge of the island showed the dining area where two Scythe guarded the caged cubs and tied adults.

On the far side, a doorway into the living room revealed a scatload of black-clad humans.

"Cover," he snapped to warn Madoc and unclipped the stun grenade from his belt. Under his fingertip was cold metal with small surface holes—and the safety pin.

*Sorry, cubs.* He pulled the pin and popped up long enough to throw the grenade through the living room door.

Dropping behind the island, he curled up and covered his eyes and ears, seeing the bear doing the same with giant paws. Only one Scythe reacted fast enough to get a shot off before—

*Crack!*

Despite exploding in another room, the light was blinding, the bang ear-splitting. Through the ringing in his ears, he heard cubs and females screaming in pain. His heart hurt for them. Flashbangs and shifter hearing didn't mix, and they had no idea what was going on.

Drawing his pistol, he rose. Two shots took out the disoriented Scythe in the dining area.

Madoc charged past and into the living room. Harrowing screams from the humans filled the air.

Shrieks and snarling sounded from upstairs. Bron and Niall must have successfully jumped in from the trees.

*Where is Patrin? No, can't search. Must clear the area to be sure the cubs and females are safe.*

Next room. Fell turned a knob, then kicked open the door. Shot the Scythe inside.

Turned and the bullet meant for his heart seared across his back. He shot back, a double-tap, and sent another human back to his god.

A wolf crashed through the window, followed by a bear. Ah, reinforcements had arrived.

Fell nodded and limped to the next room. Next time, he'd remember not to kick the damn door...

---

On his side, Patrin blinked dizzily, and pain ripped through his skull. *Fuck, that hurts.*

*What is happening?*

The noise—that was gunfire, coming from...everywhere. Screaming, snarling.

*I'm on the porch.* The Colonel was here, somewhere, with the cubs.

*Cubs—Gods, I have to move.* He blinked hard, trying to get his eyes to focus.

The flood lights on the snow-covered lawn went dark, one by one. Shot out. As he stared through the railings out at the darkness, the open area was rippling, moving. He shook his head, winced. Not his eyes—those were wolves and cougars flowing through the darkness.

He turned his head and spotted Mateo and Sky. Still bound, the cubs had scooted back against the wall of the house. Smart cubs.

Where was the Colonel? *There*. Crouching behind a stack of firewood, the Colonel had a pistol in one hand, knife in the other. He took aim, fired—and a wolf yelped.

*My pack.* Rage drove Patrin to his feet. Hands still secured behind his back, he gathered his legs under him and dove at the Colonel. His head and left shoulder hit the human's ribs and smashed him into the porch railing.

"Give up, mutant." The Colonel kicked him in the chest, and Patrin landed on his knees. "If nothing else, I'll take you with me."

Head spinning, Patrin stared into the barrel of the firearm pointed at his head.

A wolf soared over the railing. Its paws hit the Colonel's outstretched arm, knocking the pistol from his hand—even as he pulled the trigger.

The bullet sliced the outside of Patrin's arm like a red-hot knife.

"Goddamned creatures!" Pistol gone, the Colonel swung his knife at the wolf.

The small, dark gray female wolf. Her scent filled the air. *Moya.*

She yelped in pain.

*Fuck no.* Frantically, Patrin struggled to get a foot under himself, to—

A man stepped in front of him, blocking him from the Colonel.

*Bang, bang, bang.*

Heart already wailing in grief, Patrin rammed into the legs. Snarling, trying again. He'd kill the Colonel, just as he'd killed Moya.

"Brawd. Brawd, ease down. It's all good." Fell's voice and scent broke through Patrin's fury.

"Mmmph, mmmph." The duct tape removed his ability to tell his brother to help Moya.

Smaller arms wrapped around him. "Gods, Patrin, he almost shot you. Are you crazy?" Moya grabbed his shoulders, shook him, and hugged him again so hard his bruised ribs sent up an ache.

*Alive. She is alive.* Two cubs landed on him—Sky and Mateo, both crying. They all were. Moya and Fell eased back slightly and squished the cubs between them all in another hug. He closed his eyes against the overwhelming joy and relief, then opened them to reassure himself it really was true.

"C'mere, pups." Fell drew a knife and cut through the ropes around their wrists. Ripping off a sleeve, he folded it and pressed it against Sky's chest. "Hold that till we find the real bandages."

Moya kissed the top of Sky's head. "You were so brave. You both were."

Then she turned to Patrin. "I suppose we better fix it so our alpha can talk."

The younglings giggled a bit hysterically. At least they were alive.

And the pain in his beard as she carefully pulled off the fucking sticky tape served as a confirmation *he* was alive. "Thank you, *cariad*. Fell, the keys to the collar and cuffs are just inside the door."

A minute later, Fell unlocked the handcuffs, tossing them to one side. The rope, eyebolt, and part of the baseboard were still attached. It'd taken several lunges with all his weight to break the tether free.

"This is gonna hurt, brawd." Fell unlocked and carefully eased the spiked collar off.

Blood from the gouged areas made warm trails down Patrin's neck and chest. "Thank you." With Moya's hand under his arm and Fell's help, he managed to stand.

The Colonel lay nearby. Three headshots had erased most of his face. Patrin eyed his brother. "You?"

"Seemed like a good idea at the time. He was trying to slice up our little wolf."

Patrin scowled and turned to Moya.

"Not so bad." She showed a long, shallow slice across her upper thigh.

Yes, she was all right, thanks to Fell. Patrin grinned. "You're my favorite brother."

"I'm your only brother, you maggot." Fell ripped off his other sleeve and wrapped it around Moya's leg. "Looks like there's only cleaning up to be done."

Tears burned Patrin's eyes, and he hugged them all again—cubs and brother and Moya. His gaze met Fell's. "It's over, brawd."

Their past was done, finally done. Now, as he rubbed his cheek against Moya's hair and felt his brother's arms around him, he could look forward to the future with a clear heart.

---

Followed by Zorion, Ramón leaped over the porch railing and shifted to human. Ears still ringing from the gunfire, heart still pounding, he used his arm to wipe the blood from his mouth and chin. Maybe it was psychological or something, but humans didn't taste good at all.

On the porch, Moya was squished with Mateo and Sky between Patrin and Fell. Like a shifter sandwich. They looked so good together it made his heart happy.

*Nonetheless.*

He scowled at her. "By the Gods, sis, you were supposed to stay with us."

"That was the plan," Fell agreed and also frowned at Moya.

"Hard to guard her when she takes off like her tail's on fire." Zorion crossed his arms over his chest.

She rubbed her cheek on Patrin's shoulder. "It's not my fault if you two can't keep up."

"Yeah, as it happens we were right behind you until four Scythe ran out a side door. They'd've flanked you."

Patrin's gaze met his. "You got them all?"

"Aye, we did." Ramón's gut clenched. Four humans with weapons against him and Zorion—it'd been far too close. They weren't small wolves, and construction work kept them strong. Still... He wanted to be tougher. Faster. Bigger.

What with ferals, hellhounds, Scythe, even shifters like Brett and Caleb, sometimes it felt as if the clan was up against far too many dangers.

*We need more fighters.*

Zorion met his gaze. His side and thigh were still bleeding.

Ramón's chest tightened at the memory of a human shooting at his brother. Thank the Mother that Zorion was almost as fast as Moya and good at dodging.

They'd both done some fancy paw-work before getting within teeth range of the humans.

Ramón had killed the one who'd shot Zorion. And collected a knife slice across the top of his shoulder from the next human. Since the bastard had tried to shove the blade through his throat, a shoulder wound wasn't a bad outcome.

"You're bleeding! Both of you." Moya started to rise.

"Nah, nah, nothing critical." Zorion motioned for her to stay put. "We're going inside to get bandaged up."

"In fact"—Ramón eyed the two cubs—"come with us, lads, so we can get Sky taken care of and then find your brothers."

In dangerous times, brothers did better when side-by-side.

The younglings ran over, and Ramón grinned at Zorion as Patrin and Fell hugged Moya again.

Looked like their sister had truly found her mates.

---

Sniper rifle slung over his shoulder, pistol in hand, Wells crossed the snowy expanse to the house. The chill from the long wait in the cold was gone, chased away by the adrenaline still coursing through his blood.

He'd come through the firefight with only a few nicks here and there, mostly from trees splintering under the Scythe's answering barrage. He and the other snipers had eliminated the men who'd been using tranquilizer guns, but there'd been a houseful of operatives armed with real bullets.

A bleeding gash on his forehead was streaming blood into his eyes. Damn thing. After slicing a strip off his shirt, he tied the makeshift bandage around his head. Made him think of the old *Rambo* movies from way back when.

The body count seemed similar too.

Looking around, he felt heartsick at the waste of lives. Garish blood-splatter marred the white snow. Black-clad Scythe still lay here and there.

Two Daonain from the rescuers also lay dead.

They hadn't been with his team—the snipers in the forest with him were all up and walking.

Thorson with Leland and a few other cat shifters had orders to enter the house through the side windows. They should already be inside.

Reaching the porch, he spotted Patrin and Fell with a naked, lovely little brunette snuggled between them. Now that was worth a smile. He couldn't think of a pair of soldiers more deserving.

He gave them a quick once-over. Nothing pouring blood, but

they were dinged up good.

A couple more steps away was the Colonel's body. He'd been killed by expertly placed head shots.

*Very nice.*

Wells never had any need to be the one pulling the trigger. Getting the job done was all he needed to be satisfied. This death, though, brought a huge amount of relief. Finally, he could release all the shifter-soldiers with an easy mind.

He glanced at the body again. In the cold world of spy versus spy, some opponents were worthy of respect.

The Colonel wasn't worth spitting on.

Wells walked past and entered the house. One of the Daonain snipers gave him a respectful chin-lift.

Nodding back, Wells turned his gaze away. As much as he'd been around the shifters, he still wasn't accustomed to seeing more naked bodies than at a nude beach.

Unable to face the hostages—not yet—he climbed the stairs to begin his evaluation of the action and what the Scythe might have left behind.

In the front bedroom, he checked the dead Scythe snipers, one under each of the three windows. The head shots proved he hadn't lost his touch.

Many more Scythe had died in the upstairs rooms. A few from bullets, the rest from claws and teeth.

The ground floor was littered with black-clad bodies.

In the dining area, shifters were freeing the caged children. Others were unlocking the savage spiked collars and cuffs that'd been used on the women.

*Fucking Scythe.*

His gut tightened. Were all the captives alive?

He moved farther into the room.

There was the skinny blond boy the Colonel had used a knife on. The kid had a shirt on with a lump under it; someone had dressed his wound. The boy was glued to Madoc's side.

Niall was opening cages, despite being handicapped by the brown-haired boy tucked under his arm.

"Madoc." Wells' voice came out harsh when he asked, "Did you and Fell get inside in time to keep the children from being hurt?"

"We did." Madoc tilted his head. "Was it you who started the shooting?"

"It was." It'd been the best decision at the time, but he still felt damned guilty. "I started the action early. The Colonel had already cut that child there"—he motioned to the blond boy—"and when Patrin knocked the Colonel away, it seemed the best time to attack. It's my fault if anyone in here got hurt."

His gaze swept over the room. All the hostages seemed to be alive. Most were crying and terrified.

"No one got shot, Wells." Madoc reached out a big arm and thumped Wells on the shoulder.

Relief filled Wells, the guilt lightened...even as his arm went numb. He took a quick step sideways to maintain his balance. *Ah, right, the big shifter is a bear.*

"You timed it nicely. Fell was starting to text you when the shooting started. The crying is because of that gods-be-damned device." Madoc pointed to the few bits and pieces of the stun grenade lying in the living room. "My ears are still ringing."

"If it isn't our spymaster sniper." At the sound of a woman's deep, slightly harsh voice, Wells turned. "Good to see you survived."

Although the town's Chief of Police had annoyed him when she killed the Director during the fucked-up operation last month, she was still quite a woman. Damned tall—his height—with a muscular build, short black hair, and an attitude that just didn't quit. If she'd been male, he'd have pegged her as a Navy SEAL. She had a Daonain designed pack clipped to a cloth belt and had already donned a long-sleeved hiking shirt and trail pants snug enough to show off her sleek form.

Hey, he was male, and admittedly, violence got his blood moving. And being well-taught, after a quick glance, he kept his eyes on her face—which was spattered with blood. "Nice work upstairs, Chief."

She inclined her head in acknowledgment. "Thank you. When you killed off the snipers at the front of the building, everyone rushed forward to shoot at you. You make an excellent diversion."

He snorted. "Happy to be of service."

Leaving the intriguing Chief, he continued checking the house while looking for Thorson and Leland with growing worry.

He found some Daonain in the kitchen, fetching bottled water for the wounded. One was the black-bearded shooter named Lorcan.

Wells pointed to the sodas in the fridge. "Give those to the children," he suggested. "Works great for shock."

"Aye, good idea." Lorcan picked up a six-pack of Coke and headed for the dining room.

Two more dead Scythe lay in a downstairs hallway with another in a doorway to a bedroom.

And there was Thorson.

Inside the bedroom, Thorson was bent over someone lying on the floor. A couple of Daonain, wearing only shorts, knelt beside him.

Wells halted, recognizing Kennard and Fletcher, the eighteen-year-old shifter-soldiers. Whose grandfather was...

*Oh fuck.*

"Leland." Wells went down on one knee beside Thorson.

"Ah, the human." Beneath a dark tan, Leland's face was gray. A light blue blanket covered his body except for his shoulders and arms. Blood soaked the blanket over his chest and stomach.

Wells glanced at Thorson. "How bad? Has someone called an ambulance?"

"I won't be with you long." Leland's huff of a laugh ended in a groan. "By the Gods, couldn't the gnome-brain have shot cleaner?"

"Grandsire." Kennard's eyes were filled with tears. "Don't leave us."

"Cub, when the Goddess calls us home, we answer." He lifted a shaking hand to the young man. "Say goodbye, youngling. I'll give your mum your love if she's still there." He smiled slightly. "Maybe I'll see Helen again."

Choking on a sob, Fletcher leaned forward to kiss his grandfather's forehead.

*Dammit.* Thorson's eyes blurred with tears. This was why civilians shouldn't be allowed anywhere near—

"I sent two of them off to their human hell," Leland said smugly. "Would've been fine but..." His voice failed as he grimaced in pain.

Fletcher motioned toward a Scythe lying on top of a... Damn, was that an AK-47?

"The man was at the top of the stairs with the machine gun," Fletcher said. "He was gonna spray the room with the cubs to kill them all. Grandsire was below and jumped in the way. Gave us a chance to kill him."

If the AK-47 had been on full auto, it was a wonder Leland was alive at all. Wells bent his head in respect. "It was an honor to fight with you."

Leland's smile took an obvious effort. "You're a good male, human." Then his eyes narrowed. "And *caomhnor* to one of our cubs. Yes...yes, why not?"

"Grandsire?" Fletcher leaned forward, tears spilling over.

Leland ran his hand over the boy's wet face. "Water, the shapeshifting source of all life." He plucked a leaf from his other grandson's hair. "Earth, the green of the mother."

Beside Wells, Thorson stiffened.

*What the fuck is going on?*

Leland rested his hand in the blood pooling in his stomach.

"Fire and passion in blood." He puffed on his fingers. "Air to lift us up."

"Leland..." Thorson gritted out.

Leland tilted his chin up a fraction. His voice had faded to just over a whisper. "Joe, you got a gift from Lachlan. Here's one from me. You need a brother, my friend."

The old werecat's eyes filled with tears.

Leland's gaze turned to Wells. "Human." The word was barely audible.

Chest tight, Wells leaned forward. "Whatever you need, just tell—"

With a grunt of effort, the shifter lifted his hand. He pushed up the wrap around Wells' forehead, and his fingers dug painfully into the bloody gash. "My spirit to bind the gift together. You're ours now, warrior."

His hand fell, and Wells caught it.

But the werecat was gone. If there was any fairness in the world, he'd returned to the Mother Goddess they all seemed to revere.

Gently, carefully, Wells closed Leland's open eyes and held his hand there, feeling the emptiness of the body under his palm. With a resigned sigh, he sat back, then looked up.

The young men cried silently. Thorson's expression was tight. And all three were staring at Wells.

He frowned. Lifted his chin slightly.

And Thorson barked a laugh. "You are so fucked, Wells. Welcome to the Daonain side."

"Yeah"—through his tears, Fletcher almost smiled—"we got the best cookies."

---

André's head hammered as if a dwarf was using it for an anvil. Dizziness came and went, and he was grateful Heather had an arm around him as he climbed out of the Jeep. She wasn't happy he'd insisted on coming here.

But as Cosantir, he needed to see to his clan. To witness what had happened. And to find his loved ones.

Heartsick, he looked over the white lawn with dark splotches of blood and long drag marks showing the removal of the slain. He could only hope the human god had mercy on the Scythe, for he couldn't find any in his soul. Because, tied to the territory, he'd felt the loss of each Daonain whose spirit returned to the Mother.

"André." Niall jogged out the front door and down the steps. Seeing him relieved one worry in his heart.

From the littermate bonds, he knew his brothers were alive—but not whether they'd been injured. "How badly are you hurt?" Since Niall wore only a pair of shorts, André scanned him for damage. Blood-covered, *oui*, but the scent was mostly human blood.

"I'm good. The plan went like clockwork." Niall gave Heather a long, hard hug before putting a steadying hand under André's arm. "Madoc and the cubs are inside—all are fine. Sky was hurt—"

A high yell interrupted him. "Heather!" "André!" Their cubs jumped off the porch. Sky hugged Heather.

And Talam tackled André. At the bodily contact and the scent of the youngling he'd come to love, André felt his spirit begin to mend. Turning, he wrapped another arm around Sky, pulling him away from Heather long enough to know in his innermost heart that the youngling was alive.

He scented blood on the cub and could feel a bulky dressing beneath his shirt, but nothing worse. "Thank the Mother you're both safe." Managing a smile, he passed them to his mate.

Heather sobbed once as she hugged them tight, and André exchanged smiles with Niall. Carrying their unborn made their tough female adorably emotional.

He himself was blinking against tears.

"Cat." Madoc had followed the boys.

"Bear." Like Niall, blood smears covered Madoc. At the visible reminders of the danger his brother had been in, André gave him a hard hug. "How is our aunt?"

Niall snorted. "The Chief is fucking terrifying when she gets going. I think she made more kills in that master bedroom than I did."

At the sound of a vehicle coming up the long drive, André turned his head and winced at the pain.

An extended cab pickup pulled to a stop behind the Jeep. Daniel climbed out, walked around, and lowered the tailgate. Tanner jumped out of the passenger side.

Hearing his mate huff, André took their cubs back, one under each arm.

"Now you show up." Crossing her arms over her chest, Heather frowned at her brothers. "You left with that spy and never came back."

"S'okay, sis. Your lady spy is in the back passenger area, all trussed up." Daniel smirked. "You know how much Tanner likes to play with rope. Don't think Renee appreciated his skill though."

"Where have you *been*, gnome-brain?" she asked again.

The cubs huffed little laughs, and André grinned. Her interactions with her brothers made him wish he and his littermates had been blessed with a sister.

Then Daniel motioned toward the open pickup bed—and the bodies in it. "See, sis? We were being productive."

"Productive," Heather said in a faint voice.

"Where did those come from?" André asked.

Tanner shrugged. "We were too late to help with the round-up here. But on trail drives, we used to ride drag and round up stragglers. So we did that."

"Bears have good noses," Daniel said. "We caught a couple of Scythe observers west on High Rigger, and then dealt with the ones who ran after realizing they'd lost."

*More deaths. But necessary ones.* "You did very well. *Merci.*"

"Where should we put them?" Tanner asked.

André glanced at Niall.

"We're dumping them in this cargo van for convenient disposal." Niall pointed to the vehicle closest to the house.

"We'll get them moved," Daniel said.

"Merci, Daniel, Tanner." André sighed. Erasing years of memories would not be pleasant. "Bring the woman spy in when you're finished."

As Heather's brothers began, André moved away with the cubs. No need to see more death. "Does your chest hurt, Sky?"

"I'm fine," the pup said, chin up.

André could only smile—and turn to Niall. "How was Sky hurt?"

The muscles in Niall's cheek went rigid. "The Colonel sliced his chest to get the shifters to attack."

"What?" Heather pulled up Sky's shirt.

The cub's blue eyes fastened on her face. "I'm okay. Really." The bandage showed drying blood, but nothing fresh.

André's stomach unclenched. "And?"

"Somehow, Moya and Patrin kept the shifters from attacking. One of the wolves said something about pack bonds along with an impressive command voice." Niall looked impressed.

"Patrin had handcuffs on." Sky put his hands behind his back —and winced as it obviously pulled on the wound. "An' he knocked the Scythe man—the Colonel—away from me."

Still tucked under André's arm, Talam shivered. *Oui*, the lad had come close to losing his littermate. Having experienced the gut-wrenching fear before, André pulled him closer.

"Wells yelled for the shooting to start then," Niall added. "He took out the snipers upstairs. Bron and I saw them fall. He's terrifyingly accurate."

"Moya jumped on the Colonel," Sky added, "and then Fell shot him."

"Fell has skills," Madoc agreed. "He flashbanged the room and shot the Scythe guarding the cubs before they could move."

"We owe him and Patrin a debt," André said slowly.

"No, Cosantir," Heather said formally. "The alpha and beta were protecting their pack—and their clan."

André inclined his head in acknowledgment of the truth.

"Actually, for the Colonel, they very much needed him dead." Heather sighed. "When they were shifter-soldiers, the Colonel tortured and murdered some of their fellows."

"Fuck." Niall rubbed his face, his expression hard. "Yeah, I get it."

Giving his brother a pat on the shoulder, André stayed silent. The cahir had lost a couple of younglings in Canada—and had slaughtered their murderers. Niall understood how the shifter-soldiers felt.

Moving inside the house, André checked on the Daonain who'd been captured. Thank the Mother, most had only bruises. While he talked with them, Heather was calling shifters for transport for them.

Within a few minutes, the first frantic family member arrived.

"Eileen!" Talitha rushed inside, looking around. "Mateo, Alvaro!"

"Over there," Heather grabbed her friend and redirected her toward the other side of the room.

"Here!" Mateo jumped up, and a second later, the slender wolf had two cubs in her arms. They were all crying...and André had to blink tears from his own eyes as the three settled down next to a still groggy Eileen.

If the lads had been a few inches smaller, they'd've been in the two females' laps. Still, an almost palpable sense of contentment came from the group as they cuddled together as closely as possible.

There was no doubt at all in the lads' hearts that they were loved.

## BONDS OF THE WOLF

Smiling, André watched a few more of his clan arrive and be reunited. Then he had to turn to less enjoyable activities.

Because, the Scythe had also captured humans...

Thankfully, their minds were still shaken from the stun grenade. Despite his throbbing head, he managed to remove their memories of waking in cages or handcuffs and the subsequent battle.

Drafting more help, he had them taken to the Shamrock where the volunteers would explain they'd been knocked out by the explosions and get them home. Simple explanations were best.

The Daonain had lost only three in the battle. Surprising, yet still tragic. One older wolf. A young male bear. The third wasn't part of André's clan, but an older cat visiting his shift-soldier grandsons.

When André talked to the grandsons, they said they'd take their grandsire's body home to Cold Creek for the Return to the Mother Rite of Passage. And then they said their Grandsire had performed the Death Gift...on the spymaster Wells.

*Merde.*

Still trying to wrap his aching brain around *that* surprise, André tracked down the spymaster who was in the company of a tough-looking older shifter. "Wells. This is rather unexpected."

Wells gave him a sardonic look. "Isn't it, though."

"I fear you will not be allowed to resume your previous occupation—at least, not for several months. Not until you have shown acceptable control in trawsfurring." André studied the male. Was he going to cooperate?

"Cosantir." The grizzled male with him nodded in respect. "I'm Joe Thorson. With your permission, I'll take him back to Cold Creek. He already has ties there."

When André lifted an eyebrow, Thorson added, "He's *caomhnor* to one of Calum's cubs."

Ah, Calum had mentioned his mate was fond of her old

employer. André remembered Vicki from the summer solstice battle. A most formidable female. Naturally, she appreciated a warrior like the spymaster.

Wells had more than one bond with the Daonain, actually. As Cosantir, if he wanted, André saw more than most realized...like a faint bond between the two males. Bonds made for healthy shifters. All right then. "Because of your...friendship, and since Calum has experience with orienting a new Death Gift recipient, I will permit this."

He'd call the North Cascades Cosantir to ensure he'd monitor the spymaster.

"Thank you, Cosantir." Thorson bumped a shoulder against Wells in an obvious prompt.

The spymaster shot Thorson an irritated look before echoing, "Thank you, Cosantir." After a moment, he added, "I have resources that can handle the bodies. Admittedly, questions might be asked. And it might take a few days to get them—"

"We will deal with the mess." André smiled slightly. Over the last months, he'd learned Rainier Territory had extensive caves. Several of the seemingly bottomless holes were quite suitable for unwanted bodies. "We'll clean out the cargo vans and leave them in the more crime-ridden sections of different cities...along with the young female operative."

"You can't let her tell—"

"Although a distasteful solution, her memory of the last few years will be removed."

Wells' eyes widened, then narrowed. "Can't believe I forgot your people could do that."

"Your people now, I believe." André half smiled, then turned to watch the two shifters he'd stolen from the spymaster.

With Patrin between them, Moya and Fell were following Zorion to a car.

The shifter-soldiers had done very, very well. Off to one side, he saw Bron watching. When she glanced at him, he knew she was making plans for the two, and he nodded. *I approve.*

His gaze turned back to Wells. The spymaster was a headache he was happy to hand to Calum.

*However, the new pack alpha and beta are all mine.* He smiled, seeing the glow of a Mother-blessed bond running between the brothers and the courageous petite wolf he'd grown fond of.

And he could feel the God's satisfaction.

*The clan increases.*

---

Feeling like something a coyote had puked up, Patrin tried to walk in a straight line. Moya and Fell had him bracketed between them. And he had a feeling Ramón was walking behind just in case someone had to catch him.

Fuck, he hated being weak… Yet the concern and care almost offset all his aches.

Up ahead, Zorion stopped next to his red SUV.

Behind Zorion's vehicle, Heather's brothers were pulling a tied-up woman out of the passenger seat of their pickup.

Fell stiffened. "What's Renee doing here?" Ah, right, Renee worked with Fell in the coffee shop.

Daniel heard him and glanced over. "She's a Scythe spy."

Face set in stone, Tanner cut through the ropes securing her ankles. "Now, she can walk her ass inside."

The woman stared around her at a few bears and cats and the barely dressed shifters in human form. "You…you're *animals.*"

"Well, duh," Moya muttered, making Patrin choke on a laugh.

"Here, Jens, can you take her to the Cosantir?" Tanner said.

The young wolf took a step back and held his hands up in protest. "Tanner, that's Renee, one of Talitha's baristas."

"Yep, and Renee is a Scythe spy." Daniel's jaw tightened. "She suggested the sledding day just to make it easier to kidnap the cubs."

Patrin realized he still wanted to kill the female. "She selected Sky and Mateo for the Colonel to torture."

Oh, that did it. None of the shifters within hearing had any sympathy for her.

A rumbling growl came from Bridget, the clerk from the fishing shop. The bear had insisted on joining the fighting... because her cubs had been kidnapped.

Tanner gripped her arm. "Into the house with you." He paused as two shifters carried the Colonel's body down the porch steps.

Renee saw them, and her expression turned to violent rage. "You killed him. You stinking mutants, you killed him."

The ugly slur, so often used by the Colonel while he was growing up, rubbed against Patrin's nerves like sandpaper. His feet came to a halt.

"Did I remember to thank you, Fell?" Moya's voice and his brother's answering snort broke through Patrin's memories. When Moya rubbed her silky head against his bare upper arm in a gesture of sympathy, the grating sensation in his chest dissolved.

"Animals!" Renee rammed a shoulder into Tanner's chest, knocking him back a step, even as the ropes dropped from her wrists. A short knife gleamed in her right hand.

She stabbed it toward Jens' throat. He yelped and jumped back, barely in time.

The way clear, Renee sprinted for the forest.

Still in bear form, Bridget broke into a run, her big paws moving fast. Patrin almost smiled. If pushed, bears could reach wolf speed.

A tawny cougar sprang over Zorion's SUV and chased after. Maura from the diner, mother of Riona.

Together, the black bear and cougar took Renee down. The human was screaming as she disappeared under the two animals. The abrupt silence marked her end.

Ears flat, tail twitching, Maura expressed her opinion of the spy by scraping a pawful of snow over the body. Then the two mamas bounded back to the house...and their offspring.

Daniel leaned against his pickup, arms crossed over his chest. "It appears the Cosantir won't be forced to erase her memory after all. He'll be relieved."

Patrin exchanged wry smiles with Fell. Protecting females—even human ones—was a deep-seated Daonain instinct.

But when justice was dispensed by an angry mama bear?

Even Herne would approve.

"Patrin, Fell." Moya smiled up at them. "Come on, let's go home."

*Home.*

*Yes.*

# CHAPTER THIRTY

*Not that one.* Moya pushed aside the yellow top. *No, I'm not in a white mood—not with all this snow.*

Black was too much like mourning.

*Honestly.* She thumped her forehead against the closet wall.

It had been a week since the battle with the Scythe, and like many Daonain in town, she'd been unsettled and grumpy.

But the Cosantir declared it was time to move forward and was hosting a party for the shifter captives and the ones who'd fought that night.

All the previous shifter-soldiers—the ones who were adults now—were invited too. André said they needed a way to celebrate the end of hunting down the Scythe. Many of them had already been in Cold Creek and Ailill Ridge, finishing up what they'd gotten from the Colonel's belongings. Patrin and Fell had spent the day up there with Wells.

She pulled in a breath. They were back now. Everything felt better when they were near.

*So I need to find a top.* She rummaged through two more shirts—and *yes, this one.* Moya squirmed into the form-fitting, hot pink, ribbed sweater. The pronounced V-neck made her smile in satisfaction. *Ah, cleavage, there you are.*

"Hey, is there a feisty female in here?" Patrin called and, not waiting for an invite, walked into her apartment.

One of these days, she'd lock the door, just to hear him thump into it. "In the bedroom."

He entered and stopped, color rising in his face, his scent changing to a musky *let's-mate-right-now* scent that made her laugh. Males were so predictable.

Shaking her head, she turned to check her appearance in the tall mirror.

Patrin stepped up behind her, his chest against her back, and reached around to cup her breasts. "How about we stay in tonight, *blodyn?*"

Heat sizzled through her blood. "No, Top Dog, your pack and shifter-soldiers expect you."

"Maybe we could arrive at the party late?" His voice was husky. Bending down, he nibbled on the skin exposed between her neck and shoulder. His breath teased her skin.

She huffed out a breath...because he wasn't the only one aroused. "You are a mangy mongrel." Spinning in his arms, she went up on tiptoes to press a kiss to his lips.

His arms tightened around her. "Yeah, we're gonna be late."

She ran her hands up his shoulders and around his neck. Under her fingers, she could feel the almost healed wounds from the spiked collar—and a pang ran through her.

*I almost lost him.*

But he was fine...and being a *bad* wolf. She nipped his chin sharp enough to make him jump and allow her to break free and retreat.

A barked laugh came from the bedroom doorway. "Nice escape." Fell sauntered in, dressed in his favorite black, long-sleeved T-shirt and black cargo pants. Pulling her close, he kissed her long and deep, curling his hands under her ass to pull her against him tighter.

Desire hummed through her.

It increased when he ran a finger over the edge of her top, dipping down between her breasts. "*Fy nghariad*, you'll have me half-hard all night."

Warmed by his calling her sweetheart...and amused, because he was already past half-hard, she nibbled on his jaw. "That's the idea.

"Let's go before we don't get to the party at all." Patrin growled under his breath as he adjusted himself in his jeans. "When we get back, brawd, you pin her down while I feast on her."

"Good plan."

Moya bit her lip to suppress a moan. Great, now she'd be smelling of arousal all damned evening.

---

After studying the selections, Patrin handed Moya a cabernet, then availed himself of an excellent IPA. One sip and he fell in love with the tangy, hoppy flavor.

Fell, of course, found an almost black porter. No accounting for tastes.

Closed on Mondays, the Shamrock was the perfect place for a private party. Especially since the Cosantir's brother made drool-worthy finger foods to go with an excellent selection of beers. Wines too.

"Moya, over here." Across the room, Eileen was with a group of females. "Join us."

"Coming." Moya turned and smiled at Patrin and Fell. "Are you two going to behave?"

"Hey, we're the most peaceful males in the territory." Patrin tucked his bruised hand behind his back. His knuckles still stung from his...chastisement...of Pavel and Ilya this morning. They now sincerely regretted harassing the werecat.

"Aye, very peaceful." Fell tried to look innocent—and failed completely. The bruise on his jaw might have something to do with it.

Although Moya hadn't seemed to notice.

"Riiight." Moya glanced over at a group of wolves, her gaze lingering on Pavel and Ilya. "Just remember the Cosantir frowns on fighting, okay?" Going up on tiptoe, she kissed him and Fell before crossing the room to the group of females.

"She knows about the fight." Fell's gaze followed her.

"So it seems. I swear she manages to hear about everything going on in town." Because everyone adored the little wolf. How could they not?

"Just the two I wanted to talk with." Holding a bottle of beer, Bron joined them.

Patrin tensed slightly. The Chief of Police had maintained a chilly reserve ever since the trap where she'd killed the Director. "Chief, what can we do for you?"

He'd heard the female was a Canadian Mountie before André talked her into moving here, but unlike other Canadians he'd met, she rarely bothered to be polite, let alone charming. She was at that unidentifiable age between past-childbearing and before death, and the look in her eyes held bitter, hard-won experience.

To his surprise, she smiled. "Now that you're free of the Scythe, I'd like to hire you as police officers."

Standing close enough their shoulders touched, Fell gave Patrin a *you-talk-for-us* nudge.

All right then. "Of course, we're interested, but honestly, I'm surprised you want us."

"Because you mongrels conducted an operation without telling me? Not your fault. When I asked him about it, Wells admitted it was his decision, and you hadn't agreed."

Patrin wasn't surprised. For being in covert ops and making a living lying, Wells was unflinchingly honest with his team.

"I might run up to Cold Creek to slap some sense into him when he gets comfortable on his paws." Bron's smile held evil amusement. "He's going to be a cat when he shifts."

*Fuck*. Wells had better watch his whiskers. This female was a cahir—and lethal.

As to the job offer, she needed to know… How could he phrase this? "Were you informed that our activities for the Scythe—and later, the spymaster—didn't always remain within the scope of the law?"

In other words, much of what they'd done was completely illegal.

His brother half-sighed, tipped up a corner of his mouth, and nodded agreement with the admission. Even knowing it ended any chance of a job.

They were both done with lying.

"I'm aware. I'm pleased you aren't trying to cover it up." Bron tilted her head. "I've talked with your fellow shifter-soldiers. They still look to you as their leaders. I hear you took on their punishments, got beaten for trying to intercede, and kept them out of trouble. The Rainier pack is delighted to have you. I like the changes you're making with them, by the way."

Unsure if he was embarrassed or proud, Patrin had to look away.

Fell cleared his throat. "Aren't you already fully staffed?"

"Actually no." She ran her hand through her short black hair in exasperation. "The previous Chief of Police was a verminous weasel, and the human officers were infected with his corrupt attitude. I'm removing them and only keeping Duffy."

Hope rising, Patrin made an interested sound. "I see."

She continued, "During the winter, you'll work fewer hours. Summers, we'll hire part-time, but your hours will be long." She met his gaze straightforwardly and did the same with Fell. "Lads, you risked your lives for Sky. For the clan. I think we can run the trail together."

*Gods yes.* After getting a nod from Fell, Patrin grinned. "We'd be delighted to work for you."

Her smile transformed her hard face. "Good. Check with your current employers and let me know when you can start."

As she moved away, Patrin looked at Fell. His shocked brother looked as if a pixie had dropped a bush load of flowers over his head. Patrin's expression was probably much the same.

Fell opened his mouth to speak—and then shrugged and bumped Patrin's shoulder.

"Yeah, I know." Patrin couldn't stop smiling. "We'll get to protect rather than kill." Thank the Mother, it was what they'd always wanted.

Movement near the fireplace on the right wall caught his attention.

"Shifters." André stepped up onto the coffee table. "It's good to see you all here. Some of you were captured by the Scythe—and I can think of nothing more terrifying." He looked around, his smile filled with understanding.

Beside Patrin, a young female pulled in a shaky breath. Another one appeared close to tears.

André continued. "We want to thank those of you who fought the Scythe for the last year as well as the ones who fought in Ailill Ridge last week. You risked your lives to save our clan, and it won't be forgotten.

"Tonight, Rainier Territory wants you to have a chance to... decompress." He glanced at Patrin and Fell. Once, when talking to him about living in a barracks, they'd mentioned how it helped the shifter-soldiers to simply talk with others who'd had similar experiences. Killing—and captivity—were impossible to explain to a civilian.

As a result, André got Madoc to host this event and invite only those who'd been through the fires.

André smiled at the shifters. "Tonight you can discuss the battle—or being trapped. This is where you can be open with others who understand. Elsewhere, you'll have to be discreet, especially around humans who were kidnapped with our cubs. They won't remember more than the explosions and blacking out."

The shifters exchanged smiles. A Cosantir's ability to erase memories was one of the Daonain's most protective weapons. And this Cosantir was strong in the ability.

"There are no more Scythe who know about the Daonain. The hunt for them is over." André's smile widened. "Shifter-soldiers, you have our clan's gratitude as you move on with your lives. Come to me—or any Cosantir—if you need help finding your way."

Patrin could tell his fellow shifter-soldiers heard the sincerity in André's voice. A knot in his gut relaxed. His lads would have help if they needed it.

"Along with the ugliness, remember you have already overcome many trials and gained useful skills." André motioned to Patrin and Fell. "As an example—Ailill Ridge is delighted to welcome our two new police officers, Patrin and Fell MacCormac."

The enthusiastic cheers had Fell taking a step back—and surprised Patrin, even as it warmed his heart.

He saw dawning hope on the faces around him. André had known just what he was doing when he said the shifter-soldiers did have valuable skills and used Patrin and Fell as examples.

Madoc stepped up beside his brother, and the coffee table groaned under the bear's hefty weight. "People, the buffet is open." He pointed to the long table. "Let's eat and celebrate!"

A roar from the audience greeted his words.

. . .

To find the other shifter-soldiers, Fell followed his littermate to the food. Since years of near starvation taught the captives to eat whenever given a chance, it was the easiest way to find them.

And there they were.

"Yo, Top Dog. Fell."

"Congratulations."

As their comrades gathered around, Fell smiled at them. "Got news for you." He glanced at his littermate.

Patrin took over. "If you haven't checked your bank accounts recently"—which few of them did—"more money came in. With the help of Niall here and Ryder up in the North Cascades, we cleaned out the Colonel's accounts. You should have enough money to give you time to explore where you want to live. To find the right jobs. Even to learn new skills."

The relief on their faces was heartbreaking.

"We even gave Wells a share of this last haul since the North Cascades Cosantir won't allow our spymaster to return to his old job soon, if ever." Patrin grinned. "The spymaster and the Cosantir have already butted heads."

The shifters began laughing, and the comments flew:

"Ha, no one can win against the God's guardian, not even Wells."

"Good to know Wells will have funds. Can you imagine learning to shift at his age?"

"Heard he'll be a werecat—talk about fucking appropriate."

"He deserves the money. Worked harder than we did."

"Tough old buzzard. Glad he's Daonain now."

"Wells took on a Cosantir." Fletcher punched his brother Kennard in the arm. "Grandsire would be laughing his tail off about now."

Kennard's eyes reddened even as he snorted. "Yeah, he would."

After talking for a while, Fell spotted Moya surrounded by pack wolves. Tiny females were sure difficult to spot sometimes.

But there she was. Damned if he could resist the pull. "Brawd, let's go harass a pretty wolf."

"I was looking for her." Patrin followed his gaze. "Ah. Yes, let's go."

The pack members were listening to Ramón who stood beside his quieter brother.

Fell eyed Moya's brothers. As with the hellhound, the two had jumped into the battle when needed. Good males, there. Reliable, courageous.

"And then, since the diner's closed, Maura wanted us to install bigger stoves. After that, she went for a new sink—which meant tearing out another wall." Ramón and his crew were rebuilding the diner.

"Sounds like a fucking mess," Fell said.

"Bron said the SUV outside the diner was filled with explosives." Terence, one of the construction crew, shook his head. "Set off by remote."

"Car bombs." Kane, from the ranch and farm supply store, curled his lip up in a snarl. "Fucking humans."

Moving next to Moya, Fell put an arm around her. Her welcoming smile turned his heart into mush.

Trying not to haul her up and kiss her, he asked her brothers, "You fixing the B&B too?"

"Nope." Zorion's expression was hard. "The damage was more extensive. I doubt Gretchen can afford to rebuild."

"She may not even want to," Ramón said. "Not after her sister died in there."

"She's lost to grief and not thinking too clearly." Kane smoothed down his beard. "She got a concussion and a busted arm. And burns—even lost her hair. Too much pain, she's pretty much out of it still."

"By the Mother," Riona from the diner murmured. "I suppose with the snow, no one could get her to Cold Creek and the healer there?"

"North Cascades roads were closed until yesterday." Fell said. Their trip up had taken a fucking lot longer than normal.

Patrin grinned. "Thorson—his bookstore friend—rented snowmobiles to get the spymaster the last few miles into Cold Creek."

"That's smart. Get Wells into the proper territory before he goes through First Shift." The middle-aged wolf from the ranch and farm supply store laughed. "Or maybe he figured André might keep a new shifter. Cosantirs like nothing more than to see their clan grow."

"Wells and Thorson on a snowmobile. I'd've given money to see that," Patrin said.

"A shame Gretchen is too damaged to take one," Kane said. "Although we asked if she wanted us to try to get her to the North Cascades. She refused."

Moya looked at Kane. "Well, the North Cascades Cosantir did exile her from his territory."

"You mean he cast her out?" Ramón asked. "But she doesn't have the scars..."

"It wasn't a casting out." A glass of juice in her hand, Heather joined them. "Calum wouldn't inflict such a harsh punishment for her lies. However, if someone's behavior is too—I think the humans call it toxic—a Cosantir can bar them from his territory, much like our alpha wolves do. I doubt Calum would kill her in a case like this, but...as it happens, it was the healer she lied to."

"Gods, now that's a harsh lesson in consequences," Kane said.

Moya leaned her head against Fell's shoulder. "She hasn't been a nice person, but it's still sad. With the burns and cuts, she's going to have scars."

As Patrin leaned on her from her other side, Fell kissed the top of her head. Their little wolf had a soft heart.

And she felt just right cuddled between them. He savored her warmth as he looked out the windows to the night.

Smiling up, she kissed him, then Patrin.

Grinning, Patrin pulled her closer. "We should go—have our party back at the apartment."

"Absolutely not." She rolled her eyes.

Yet, Fell could scent her interest.

Patrin wagged his eyebrows. "I know how to use coercion."

Rather than the threat making her flee, she snorted and punched him in the belly. From the sound, she'd lightened the impact to ensure he wasn't hurt.

However, groaning loudly, Patrin folded, holding his gut. Hamming it up for all he was worth.

"What? I didn't hit you that..." Moya scowled as she saw the laughter in his eyes, then her gaze caught on something farther away. "Oh, noooo."

Fell followed her gaze—and saw the Cosantir was watching.

Turning red, Moya hid her fist behind her back like a cubling caught with a stolen cookie.

Expression hard, André studied her and, after a long moment, turned away. If Moya had been listening instead of cursing under her breath, she'd have heard him laughing.

"Look what you made me do." Moya glared at Patrin and stalked away to join Heather.

Grinning, Fell backhanded Patrin in the same spot Moya had punched. "Bad wolf."

"Moya, sweetie, I can't believe you're in trouble again." Laughing, Heather was teasing Moya about getting caught hitting people again. The redhead rested a hand on her pregnant belly as she talked.

Watching, Fell pulled in a breath as his mind provided an image of what Moya would look like if she was with young.

His next breath didn't want to arrive. He and Patrin might someday have cubs of their own. What a glorious thought. A terrifying thought.

But Moya would be the mother, and with the three of them, they could handle *anything*.

Somehow, the Gods had shown him a future he'd chase with all his heart.

*In fact...*

The moon was now waxing in a perfect quarter curve—the time of new beginnings. He and Patrin had put their plans on hold, wanting to wait for the memories of the violence to pass. For a time when they could look forward instead of back.

The bracelets in his pocket seemed to grow heavier. As if to nudge him into action.

*Courage, wolf.* He gripped his brother's shoulder. "We ask her now. Here."

Patrin looked at him as if Fell had gone moon crazed. "Here... in front of everyone?"

"Here. Now." Fell put his hand in his pocket and smiled at the faint sense of the Mother in the bracelets. "Our Moya doesn't hide her joys. This is what she'd want—to create our new bond in the midst of the clan."

"*Fuck.*" Patrin stared through the window where the moon shone in the dark night. "You're right, you fucking, flea-bitten mutt."

Fell snorted, knowing the insult originated from the fear they shared—that she might say no.

After closing his eyes for a second, Patrin inhaled slowly. "Give me mine."

Silently, Fell handed over a bracelet.

---

Moya and Heather had taken up a station near their favorite finger foods. Moya was explaining why she'd been so annoyed with a recent book club read. "...And the human in the book was constantly whining about how much work her child was."

Heather snorted. "Only one child?"

"Right?" Moya grinned. "So me and Riona and Claire started

boasting about the most idiotic things we'd done with our littermates as pups."

"Knowing Ramón, Zorion, and you—I cringe," Heather said in a dry voice.

"Oh thanks. Claire came in third. At five, she figured out how her mother started the car. Her poor mom was in the bathroom, and they grabbed the car keys. Her brothers stood on the seat to steer, while Claire pushed the gas pedal down. They almost reached a major road"—Moya heard Heather's moan—"and her brothers started fighting over which way to go." Moya pantomimed the steering wheel getting jerked back and forth. "They ended up in a ditch."

"Thank the Mother," Heather murmured. "Wait, Claire's was the *third* worst story?"

Moya giggled and told the next terrifying tale. She wasn't smirking at the way Heather's eyes widened at the near disaster. Of course not. She was just being an awesome friend and helping prepare her friend for her own litter. *Really.*

"I'm going to live in terror, you boggart butt." Heather growled. "When it's your turn to carry a litter, just you wait."

Moya gave her a smug look. "I think I'm safe."

She looked up as Patrin and Fell stopped in front of her. Their expressions were hard, their muscles tensed.

Had a Scythe shown up?

"What's wrong?" They even carried the scent of danger. Moya felt her heart rate pick up. "Fell?"

As the entire room went silent, they knelt, together, shoulder-to-shoulder.

Patrin opened his hand to show a lifemating bracelet glowing in the light. The silvery, moon-shaped discs graduated through all the stages of the moon. "Moya, I love you; we love you. We want you as our lifemate, to carry in our hearts and souls."

The traditional words. Wherever had they learned them?

Speaking slowly, clearly, Fell finished the sentence, "...throughout this life and into the next."

"Let us run together on the trails, hunt and play and sing to the Mother," Patrin said.

Fell's gaze held hers, his blue eyes burning with passion. "Our strength and skills are yours, and we'll gladly give our lives to keep you safe."

She already knew they would.

And then, Fell added something so much harder for him. "I'll talk and share my worries—and be there when you need someone to listen."

"I'll never push you through the bonds—although coaxing with words, oh yeah." Patrin's grin flashed before his voice turned rough with emotion. "You're already in our hearts. Your hands carry all our hopes."

They waited, her patient, experienced hunters, as she struggled to find her breath.

"Yes." The word came out sounding like a strangled werecat, and she tried again. "Yes, yes, I will be your lifemate. I love you both, so, so much."

The room exploded with cheering and whistles, Ramón's and Zorion's yells louder than the rest.

But her whole world narrowed to the two most wonderful males in all the world.

She dropped to her knees between them, one arm around each neck, almost choking them until they squashed her between them.

Patrin's hard fingers curled around her chin, holding her as he firmly kissed her, sending her off into a world of emotion. After sliding the lifemating bracelet onto her wrist, he turned her into Fell's arms.

"*Cariad aur*," Fell whispered. "I love you." He kissed her, his lips and tongue heating her to the core, sending desire to accompany the love. Gripping her wrist gently, he added his lifemating bracelet to Patrin's, showing to all the world that she was theirs.

Her fears of being trapped, of being forced to be with someone were gone. These two amazing males were her choice—the right choice. The bonds between them were strengthening, growing thicker and warmer. Lifemating bonds—and she welcomed them with all her heart.

With hope in his gaze, Fell handed her two male-sized bracelets.

"Yes." Perfect—because the wolf in her was feeling extremely territorial.

"Mine," she said to Patrin, putting the bracelet on his wrist. Setting her hands on each side of his face, she kissed him and repeated, "Mine."

"Yours," he agreed in a purring growl.

Turning to Fell, she leaned into him, letting him wrap his arms around her as she worked the bracelet over his hand to his thickly muscled wrist. Tilting her head up, she met his gaze. "For as long as life shall last and long beyond, I'll be your lifemate. You are mine. All mine."

Fell's smile was almost blinding. "And you are ours, little wolf. For this life and into the next."

# DAONAIN GLOSSARY

The Daonain use a conglomeration of handed-down languages from the British Isles. Some of the older villages still speak the Gaelic (Scots) or Irish Gaelic. Many of the more common (and mangled) shifter terms have descended from Welsh.

Errors and simplification of spelling and pronunciation can be attributed to being passed down through generations...or the author messing up. Below are a few of the more common words and terms used by the shifters. And, just for fun, I added pronunciations (good luck with those).

- *banfasa*: wise woman/nurse (Irish Gaelic from bean feasa) [ban-FAH-sa]
- *blodyn*: flower, esp for someone who is cute & lovely; my lovely (Welsh) [ BLAH-din ]
- *blodyn tatws:* sweet flower, literally, potato flower; (Welsh) [BLAH-din TAT-toes]
- *brawd*: brother [br-ow-d. Don't need to roll the "r"]
- *cahir*: warrior (Irish/Gaelic from Cathaoir) [ka-HEER]
- *caomhnor*: protector/guardian of children (from Caomhnóir) [kuheeoo-NOR]
- *cariad*: lover, darling, sweetheart (Welsh) [core-ee-awt]
- *cariad aur:* precious love / darling (Welsh) [core-ee-awt EYE-er (roll the "r")]
- *cosantir*: guardian or protector (Irish Gaelic from An Cosantóir) [KOSS-un-tore]
- *Daonain*: the shifter race [DAY-ah-nan]

- *trawsfur*: transform or shift (Welsh from trawsffurfio) [traws (rhyme with laws)-fur]

# ALSO BY CHERISE SINCLAIR

## **Masters of the Shadowlands Series**

*Club Shadowlands*

*Dark Citadel*

*Breaking Free*

*Lean on Me*

*Make Me, Sir*

*To Command and Collar*

*This Is Who I Am*

*If Only*

*Show Me, Baby*

*Servicing the Target*

*Protecting His Own*

*Mischief and the Masters*

*Beneath the Scars*

*Defiance*

*The Effing List*

*It'll Be An Adventure*

## **Mountain Masters & Dark Haven Series**

*Master of the Mountain*

*Simon Says: Mine*

*Master of the Abyss*

*Master of the Dark Side*

*My Liege of Dark Haven*

*Edge of the Enforcer*

*Master of Freedom*

*Master of Solitude*

*I Will Not Beg*

*Master of the Wilderness*

## **The Wild Hunt Legacy**

*Hour of the Lion*

*Winter of the Wolf*

*Eventide of the Bear*

*Leap of the Lion*

*Healing of the Wolf*

*Heart of the Wolf*

*Bonds of the Wolf*

## **Sons of the Survivalist Series**

*Not a Hero*

*Lethal Balance*

*What You See*

*Soar High*

## **Standalone Books**

*The Dom's Dungeon*

*The Starlight Rite*

# ABOUT THE AUTHOR

Cherise Sinclair is a *New York Times* and *USA Today* bestselling author of emotional, suspenseful romance. She loves to match up devastatingly powerful males with heroines who can hold their own against the subtle—and not-so-subtle—alpha male pressure.

Fledglings having flown the nest, Cherise, her beloved husband, an eighty-pound lap-puppy, and one fussy feline live in the Pacific Northwest where nothing is cozier than a rainy day spent writing.